QU

BITTER

THORN

ALSO BY KAY L MOODY

Fae and Crystal Thorns
Flame and Crystal Thorns

The Fae of Bitter Thorn
Heir of Bitter Thorn
Court of Bitter Thorn
Castle of Bitter Thorn
Crown of Bitter Thorn
Queen of Bitter Thorn

The Elements of Kamdaria
The Elements of the Crown
The Elements of the Gate
The Elements of the Storm

Truth Seer Trilogy
Truth Seer
Healer
Truth Changer

Visit kaylmoody.com/bitter to read the prequel novella,
***Heir of Bitter Thorn*, for free**

QUEEN

OF

BITTER

THORN

KAY L MOODY

THE FAE OF BITTER THORN

4

Queen of Bitter Thorn
The Fae of Bitter Thorn 4
By Kay L Moody

Published by Marten Press
3731 W 10400 S Ste 102, #205
South Jordan, UT 84009

www.MartenPress.com

Cover by Angel Leya
Edited by Justin Greer

ISBN: 978-1-954335-03-5

CHAPTER 1

Sleep often made the worst problems seem more approachable. But not always. When Elora woke from her spot at the bottom of a hill, a thin layer of ice had formed over her boots. That alone meant her problems had only compounded overnight.

Frost curled around every surface in Noble Rose. It stretched over cobblestones and encased grass blades. Elora had only her leather pants and fitted leather shirt to stave off the chill. While traveling the night before, those had been sufficient. But then she had to stop and rest.

Bumps rose on the skin of her arms as she lifted her head from the frosty grass beneath her. Two braids still hung over her shoulders, but thick sections of hair had come loose from them. Untying the leather strings at the end of each braid, she used her fingers to comb through the mess her hair had become.

Her shoulders ached every time she lifted her hands higher than her heart. She had flown as far as she could the night before. She had flown faster and farther than she even thought possible.

It still wasn't enough.

Even after her beloved got kidnapped by the fearsome High Queen Alessandra, Elora couldn't fly indefinitely.

She had found a cozy-looking spot at the bottom of a hill in Noble Rose to rest her head for the night. Manicured rose bushes and a quaint cluster of daisies made the space look inviting, warm even.

Unfortunately, the looks had been deceiving. The spot grew colder throughout the night. Before day dawned, she woke from the cold attempting to burrow into her bones. Her muscles ached, but moving was the only tool she had to stave off the chill.

After rubbing the sleep from her eyes, she brushed ice crystals off her leather shirt and pants. Even her braided belt that contained purple ribbons from her mother's old skirt sparkled with a thin layer of ice.

High Queen Alessandra's influence over the court of Noble Rose continued to spread. Soon, the court would probably look exactly like Fairfrost. That gnarled thought felt as icy as the air.

At least Elora's sword still worked, no matter the temperature.

She gripped its leather hilt and pushed out the wings from her back. A shudder rocked through her entire body, nearly dropping her to her knees. Gasping, she pulled the wings back.

There would be no flying today. Even with her fae strength and healing, she had pushed herself too hard. Her muscles groaned as she leaned over to catch her breath.

A part of her knew she was only prolonging the inevitable. At some point she would have to look up above... where the sprites were. Or where they should have been. Knowing she might not like what she found, she had avoided glancing upward.

But if she couldn't fly, she had no other choice. Tension rose into her throat, crashing its way past the little warmth that still lingered there. She glanced up.

No sprites.

Ice crystals seemed to form along the sides of her throat when she tried to swallow. The sprites still hadn't returned after the fight with High Queen Alessandra the evening before.

Tension forced Elora onto the balls of her feet, but it did nothing to temper the fear and regret roiling her insides. Her fingers twitched over her sword hilt. She looked forward.

A golden enchantment continued to shimmer just ahead of her. She had flown through most of the night, but still managed to stay within the large bubble of enchantment Prince Brannick had created the night before.

The enchantment protected her and everyone else from High Queen Alessandra's enchantment of fear that still poisoned the air in every part of Faerie.

If Elora stepped past Brannick's protective enchantment, fear would press in on her from all sides. Her thoughts would writhe with memories strong enough to collapse her. She had mastered many of her emotions, but fear was clearly her weakness.

She glanced up again. The tiniest part of her heart dared to hope that a single sprite might float somewhere up above.

Tansy was her friend. If any of the sprites had dared to return, it would be her. But the familiar sparkle of pink inside a green glow was nowhere within Elora's sight.

Taking a deep breath, Elora swallowed again. She bit into her bottom lip as she scanned the landscape ahead of her. No village stood nearby.

The closest thing she saw to any kind of civilization was a male fae and a small brownie, who stood on a narrow cobblestone path across a small field.

Tightness overtook each of Elora's muscles as she forced herself to breathe.

No sprites meant she couldn't send a message. Sore muscles meant she couldn't fly.

She had to get help.

The fae on that cobblestone path could open a Faerie door for Elora, though he'd probably require a bargain or debt of some kind to do it.

But Elora *could* get help. She just had to step outside the protection of Brannick's enchantment.

She just had to let fear consume her.

Her heart skittered. She fought the urge to brush the frost from her clothes. She had already done it more than necessary. No frost even remained. As if of their own accord, her hands flicked across her leather pants anyway. At least it gave her something to do while she considered her choices again.

If she stayed inside the protective enchantment in Noble Rose, perhaps someone would eventually come for her. Brannick had been captured by High Queen Alessandra, and Vesper couldn't enter Noble Rose without a special enchantment since he was still technically banished, but maybe Lyren would come?

The little flame of hope within her snuffed out. Even if another fae did try to find her, Elora had flown so much the night before, no one would ever know where she had traveled to now.

Ice stretched over the lump in her throat as she swallowed. She took a step forward.

Her gut rolled over on itself. Sucking in a shallow breath, she gripped her sword hilt for strength.

She swallowed again.

With one last glance over her shoulder, she finally bolted forward.

Her feet flew over the frosty grass. Fear poured over her like a bucket of water retrieved from a half-frozen lake. After the initial shock, more fear needled under her skin with icy tentacles. Her breath hitched.

Her feet stumbled.

Memories poured into her mind, giving life to the ice under her skin. She remembered everything in flashes.

A sharp knife tip at her throat. Smacking lips that tasted blood. Chains that bound her so tight she couldn't even dream of escape. A breath that smelled of sour milk, one that wouldn't leave her face.

The shudder that shook through her body sent her feet sprawling forward fast. Too fast. Her knees hit a grassy knoll that sagged under her weight. She gulped in air, but it felt like she was sucking up chunks of ice.

Chains closed in around her waist. Her arms. Even knowing the chains existed only in her memories, they still seemed to weigh her down as she forced herself to her feet again.

She had to keep running.

The male fae she had spotted earlier was nearer now. Once she moved just a little closer, she'd be within shouting distance.

Her chest constricted. It felt like glass on the brink of shattering. She continued to gulp in air, but each breath seemed shallower than the last. Her feet pounded against the grassy field. She refused to acknowledge how each step sent a flurry of frost even higher up her boots.

Maybe it would help to close her eyes.

The moment her eyelids dropped, she wasn't greeted with the safety of black she expected. Instead, a pair of glowing yellow eyes appeared in her mind.

Ansel's eyes.

Her chest clenched even tighter.

The glass shattered.

Her feet stumbled so hard, it sent her sprawling. Her nose pressed into a patch of icy grass. One shoulder throbbed where it had landed on a sharp rock. Rolling to her other side, she curled her legs up until she hugged them tight against her chest.

Whatever release she expected from her tears didn't come. They pooled out of her eyes, nearly freezing before they could even trickle down her cheeks. Her body shivered as she tried to rock herself in a rhythmic motion.

Fear gnawed at her insides. It tore her apart, laughing at every victory she had ever claimed.

Ansel would capture her again. She knew it. He would steal her away, drain her of blood. He would break her. He would destroy her.

It didn't matter how many times she had protected herself in the past. She had tried to fight in Fairfrost Palace. And she had still failed.

Ansel would come for her again.

And she would fail.

If the mere memory of him sank her into a sobbing mess in the middle of the Noble Rose countryside, how much worse could he do once he brought her back to his home?

Ice trailed down her spine. Her body shook so hard, she nearly bit off her tongue. Her legs curled tighter against her chest. Her tears turned to ice on her cheeks.

She only vaguely recognized the tendrils of frost that crawled up her boots and leather pants. The frost existed because of High Queen Alessandra. The fear in the air lingered because of High Queen Alessandra. Was the frost now overtaking Elora because she had succumbed to the fear?

It didn't matter.

Only three things filled her mind, no matter how she tried to push them away.

Yellow eyes. A knife at the neck. Chains that held her still.

Yellow eyes.

A knife at the neck.

Chains that held her still.

With her eyes closed firmly, she pressed the heels of her hands into them. A thousand bursting colors filled her vision when she pushed harder on her eyes. Even those didn't remove the flashes.

Yellow eyes.

Her gut churned, sending bile to her throat.

A knife at the neck.

The muscles in her limbs locked, making it impossible to move them.

Chains that held her still.

Screams erupted from her mouth, hanging in the air around her.

No more.

A quivering breath shook through her, but she had forced some air into her chest at least. She gulped in even more. Her knees wobbled. She forced herself to her feet anyway.

One more breath.

Tears continued to slide down her cheeks, but they made it to her chin before they froze.

She had succumbed—she still succumbed—to the fear.

But she would not let it control her.

Her boot hovered for a long moment before she finally took a single step forward. The visions continued to dance in her mind.

Yellow eyes.

With her first steady breath, she took a second step forward.

A knife at the neck.

She swallowed and gripped her sword.

Chains that held her still.

It didn't matter how her muscles ached, she pushed the wings out of her back anyway. More steadying breaths calmed her as she lifted off the ground.

Fear could stab her and shock her, but she wouldn't allow it to keep her down. Her wings beat the air, forcing it into submission.

Elora flew.

By the time she reached the fae on the cobblestone path, the frost stretching over her boots and pants had melted.

Her feet landed on the grass with a little jolt. She sprinted the rest of the way to the fae. By the time she reached him, she was breathless, but not too breathless to speak. "I need your help."

The fae wore a thick red tunic belted with a cream sash. Under the tunic, he had tight-fitting, tan pants. A stiff cream collar circled his neck, poking out from the red tunic.

At the sight of Elora, the fae jumped back in fright. He clapped both hands over his mouth and ducked behind a nearby rose bush. Shoving a hand out, he tugged the little brownie behind the rose bush with him.

The bush didn't do much to hide him or the brownie, which he seemed to realize at the same moment as Elora. The fear in the air clearly affected him as much as it did her.

With his nose twitching and his forehead turning crimson, the fae jabbed a finger forward. "*You.*"

"What?" Elora's eyes opened wide at the accusation.

The female brownie peeked around the rose bush just long enough to wrinkle her short nose. "This is *your* fault." The brownie turned her face upward at the male fae in the red tunic. "She *is* the one, right, Deegan?"

Ice crystalized over the hem of Deegan's red tunic as he stood. He glanced down at his brownie before turning back to Elora with a glare. "This *is* her fault."

"What is?" Elora's words came out in a whisper.

"This." He gestured over the frosty landscape. "All of it." Now he gestured toward the air.

Despite the fear still prickling inside her, Elora folded her arms over her chest. "How is this my—"

"You helped Prince Brannick win the testing." Deegan's eyebrows twisted even closer together as he marched forward. "If High Queen Alessandra had won, we would have accepted her rule without question. She never would have controlled us with," he shuddered, "this fear."

It took far too much effort to brush the words away. Instead, Elora dropped her hands to her sides. "If you help me,

I can rescue Prince Brannick, and he can overthrow High Queen Alessandra. I just need you to open a door for me to…"

Her voice trailed off as she considered a destination. A Faerie door had to open to a place not to a person. If she told the fae to open a door to Quintus's house in Bitter Thorn, would that be enough? The fae probably didn't even know who Quintus was.

Taking a deep breath, Elora continued, "To Bitter Thorn Castle." If she went to the castle, Kaia, the dryad, would be able to open a door to Quintus's house. Hopefully, her sisters and the others would be there waiting.

The brownie's squat nose seemed to fold in on itself as it wrinkled more. "We would never help you."

It was unrealistic to expect them to help without a favor of some kind, but Elora still tripped over her next words. "I will owe you a debt."

A scoff tore from Deegan's lips. He scowled. "Noble Rose is nothing because of you. What could you possibly offer that we might want?"

The question had merit. Even as Elora's thumb stroked her sword hilt, no ideas came. But she couldn't give up, not after facing her fear.

Her head snapped up with a jerk. "I will teach you how to control your emotions. You see how I can continue even despite the fear?"

A look passed between the fae and the brownie. Deegan raised an eyebrow at her. "I saw how you crumpled once you left the protective enchantment."

She nodded eagerly. "Yes, but look at me now. I feel normal again. Can *you* do that with the fear all around us?"

16

His eyebrow arched higher. When he glanced down at the brownie, they both looked more intrigued than before. Hopefully she wouldn't need more than that.

Gripping her sword for strength, Elora rolled her shoulders back. "I propose a bargain." Tingles spread all through her shoulders and down to her fingertips. She had made several bargains in Faerie, but this was the first she had ever proposed herself. It felt special. "You must open a door for me to Bitter Thorn Castle. If you do, I will teach you later how to control your emotions."

The brownies ears flopped with a nod when she looked up at Deegan.

"I accept." His brownie's approval must have been the only thing Deegan needed. Waving one hand a circle, a swirling tunnel of red roses and white lilies appeared in front of them.

Elora started forward. Luckily, the fae had not specified *when* Elora would have to teach him how to control emotions. Truthfully, she could only barely do it herself. She probably wouldn't make much of a teacher.

But she would deal with that problem on another day. For now, she had more important tasks ahead of her.

Rescue Prince Brannick. Overthrow High Queen Alessandra.

Her fingertips tingled as she stepped toward the swirling tunnel. Maybe it was her imagination, but she sensed purple sparks bursting from her fingers just as she entered the door.

CHAPTER

2

Even before stepping out of the door, Elora knew something had gone wrong. She couldn't smell the familiar scents of wet bark or wild berries. Her feet faltered over a rocky path. The fresh, open air drifting around her sent her gut into a knotted mess.

Mistmount.

She recognized the court from its scent alone but ignored the truth until she saw the mountain ledge she had just stepped onto. The Faerie door behind her disappeared before she could dart back inside it.

For a single moment, she convinced herself to be brave. If she stood on a mountain, then Ansel's home—which had been in a valley—couldn't possibly be nearby.

In the next moment, she dropped down to the ground. Her legs curled into a shivering ball while the images of yellow eyes, a knife, and chains swirled in her mind.

Even in Mistmount, fear poisoned the air. High Queen Alessandra's enchantment stretched over every corner of Faerie, seeping into every heart.

Elora could handle grief. She could work through anger. But fear stung her the way no other emotion did because she had felt it too deeply. If Ansel and High Queen Alessandra had captured her before she had used the balance shard, she probably never would have survived the change to fae.

As she had done in Noble Rose, she took deep, steadying breaths. She could beat this.

She was stronger than the fear. Bigger than it. Even if her knees trembled, she would get to her feet. Yes, she had traveled to Ansel's court. Yes, she feared he would be hidden around every corner. And yes, she could push forward all the same.

Her gut clenched tighter as she took her first step. It rocked as she took another. But her feet moved forward still.

She focused on her location. That devious fae, Deegan, had entered her bargain and promised to send her to Bitter Thorn Castle. Why did the door send her to Mistmount instead?

The question had deeper implications once she considered it. Faerie itself forced all creatures to keep their bargains. She ran through the words of the bargain in her mind, but it didn't make any sense. Deegan had agreed to send her to Bitter Thorn. She *should* have been in Bitter Thorn.

How did she end up in Mistmount instead?

Yellow wildflowers and tufts of grass lined the rocky path beneath her feet. Questions churned in her mind while she started down the mountain.

The purple sparks.

She bit one lip while her mind whirled. It had only lasted a fleeting moment, but purple sparks had burst from her fingertips just before she stepped into Deegan's door.

Did those sparks have something to do with her ending up in Mistmount instead of Bitter Thorn?

As soon as she considered it, she flipped the thought away without hesitation. *That* was impossible. She had only used magic twice since getting it. The first time had been when a demorog attacked her, and technically, only her sword used magic, not her. The second time had been when she held the crown of Bitter Thorn, but the only reason she had magic then was because the crown enhanced her magic.

She had never used magic on her own. Not purposefully. The purple sparks couldn't have had anything to do with the door leading her to the wrong place.

Her body froze when she noticed a cave entrance near the path ahead.

Clenching her jaw, she forced herself forward. There was no sense fearing the cave until she peeked inside it. Even if Ansel was in Mistmount, what were the odds he stood inside that exact cave?

Sweat broke out across her forehead. Her hands shivered hard enough to knock into her thighs. She continued anyway. Once she neared the cave, she could sprint forward until she had passed the cave entrance. Even if fae stood inside, they wouldn't notice her if she moved fast enough. Hopefully.

Her heart jumped.

Unless she made too much noise. Without thinking, she broke into a run. If noise was a problem, she had made too much already. Better to pass the cave as quickly as possible and hope for the best.

A pair of voices drifted through the air, stilling her movements. Terror washed over her, but recognition dawned almost as fast.

By the time she reached the cave entrance, she had already stopped running. Instead of sprinting past, she turned to look directly into the cave. Two startled faces stared back at her. A female with white-blonde hair and a friendly smile held onto a male with light brown hair and ice-blue eyes.

"Tindra?" Disbelief filled Elora's voice, almost turning it into a chuckle. "Severin?"

Relief cut away most of the terror that gripped their features, but the two fae still looked distressed. They had no reason to fear Elora, though. They had helped her get into Fairfrost Palace and rescue the sprites. Even though that mission had gone terribly wrong, these two had done nothing to cause it.

High Queen Alessandra's brother stood taller, shaking another measure of fear off his face. "How did you find us?" Severin asked.

Something twisted inside Elora, right around her navel. She looked over her shoulder. "I…" Her gaze turned down toward her fingertips, but she shook the thoughts away before they could form. "I have no idea. I had no intention of finding you."

Severin and his beloved glanced at each other with a knowing look. Or maybe it was a searching look. They seemed to understand each other, but Elora certainly didn't.

"What happened?" Tindra's friendly smile returned, and this time, it only held a sliver of her earlier fear.

Without Elora's permission, her hands lifted as she glanced down at them again. She forced them back to her sides and curled them into fists. "A fae in Noble Rose was supposed to open a door for me that led to Bitter Thorn Castle. He agreed to the bargain, but when I walked through the door, I ended up here."

A crease appeared between Severin's eyebrows while he tapped his chin. At least they were as puzzled as her.

Tindra beckoned Elora toward herself. "You should come in. We have an enchantment on the cave entrance that keeps the fear out." Her shoulders gave the slightest twitch. "Well, *mostly* keeps it out."

Nodding, Elora stepped inside the cave. She didn't respond though. Her thoughts turned back to the door. "I thought no one could defy a bargain. I thought Faerie itself makes it impossible. The door should have taken me to Bitter Thorn Castle, right?"

With a gentle tug, Tindra sat Elora down on a tree stump that had a burlap-wrapped pillow on top. Allowing herself to glance around, Elora took in the rest of the cave. One end had boulders with cut and smoothed surfaces so they served as tables. Clay and glass jars of various sizes were scattered across the surface. Piles of papers and a single feather pen sat among them. A basket on one corner of the table held herbs, flowers, pebbles, and various other flora she didn't recognize.

Tindra went straight toward the rock table and began measuring liquids from the various jars. "Did anything strange happen just before or while you were going through the door?"

Severin moved to sit next to a small fire encircled by large rocks. He stoked the flames with a bendy stick, then turned to a ceramic plate with vegetables that were halfway through being chopped. Using a short knife, he continued the process.

Elora's gaze turned toward the back of the cave. Flecks of sparkly rock dotted the cave walls. It led far deeper into the mountain than she had realized at first. After a great distance, it wound into a corner. A pile of fluffy blankets and spongy sleeping mats had been tucked into a small alcove just before the corner.

They lived here. They must have been hiding from High Queen Alessandra.

A dragon with blue eyes and brilliant pastel scales peeked its head around the corner at the back of the cave. She recognized it as the same dragon they had with them with they found her in Bitter Thorn.

Turning back to the others, she shook her head. "I cannot think of anything that would have changed the destination of the door." Even while she said it, she glanced down at her hands, and something sparked inside her. She opened her mouth but immediately clamped it shut again.

"I know that look." Severin continued to chop the potatoes and carrots on his ceramic plate, but an amused glint had filled his eyes.

Folding her hands into her lap, Elora glanced at him. "What look?"

From the side of the room, Tindra grinned. Had she noticed the look too? "Do not disregard something just because it seems strange or impossible. I cannot tell you how many things I have discovered from impossible situations." Her grin rose as she shrugged. "Faerie is unpredictable."

They could tell Elora had a guess. An impossible guess.

Though it still felt ridiculous to admit, words tumbled from Elora's mouth. "Purple sparks burst from my fingertips just as I entered the door." She shook her head. "Or *maybe* they did. I could have imagined it."

Severin tapped his chin before he went back to the vegetables. "Perhaps your magic changed the destination of the door."

The tree stump tilted as Elora leaned forward on it. "Can magic do that?"

"It depends on what kind of magic you have." Tindra paired her explanation with a prodding expression. Severin donned an identical one.

Letting the stump fall back against the ground, Elora looked down at her hands. "I do not know what kind of magic I have. I have only used it twice and both times were... unusual."

Severin dumped the chopped vegetables into a cast iron pot. "Perhaps a more important question to ask is, why were you brought *here* specifically?"

Looking to the side, he shared another look with his beloved. For a moment, it seemed like his gaze shifted to the rock table and the items scattered over it. Tindra gave a tiny nod, but it could have been Elora's imagination.

Before indecision could gnaw at her, Elora jumped to her feet. "High Queen Alessandra captured Prince Brannick." She gulped. "Again." The words pricked on their way out. The air around them felt thicker too. "I have to rescue him again, obviously, but I have no idea how to do it. High Queen Alessandra stole the necklace you gave me last time, so I do not even have a way inside the palace without her sensing my presence."

Whatever expression had been on Tindra's face fell away. She blinked. "You think you can rescue Prince Brannick from Fairfrost Palace?"

Elora had never been so grateful to finally have her memories back from her first visit to Faerie. She stood taller. "Since I am the one who rescued him the first time, yes, I know I can do it." Her shoulders wilted. "But I was mortal then. I had no magic for the high queen's enchantment to sense."

Another look passed between Tindra and Severin. The high queen's brother nodded at his beloved as if she had asked him a question, even though neither of them had spoken. Were all couples this way with each other?

Tindra darted across the cave to a large bag made of blue and silver brocade. After reaching inside it, she pulled out a necklace with a string of opals and a bright pendant at the end. Elora had to temper her gasp. Tindra had given her an identical necklace when she snuck into Fairfrost Palace to free the sprites. It could block the high queen's magic-sensing enchantment.

White-blonde hair draped over Tindra's eyes as she dropped the necklace into Elora's palm. Tindra threw it a wistful look. "I thought we might need that, but you seem to have greater need."

Elora's fingers itched to close over the necklace, but she forced herself to look up instead. "Are you sure?"

A shower of embers danced upward when Severin placed the cast iron pot onto the fire. He came to Tindra's side and slipped an arm around her waist. "If Tindra's research continues to progress as well as it has been, no one will have need of such a ward necklace ever again."

A flush of red filled Tindra's cheeks. "My beloved often makes me sound more impressive than I am." The flushing continued when he pulled her closer. After a longing gaze into his eyes, she cleared her throat. "I am trying to develop a formula that will completely rid Fairfrost of all enchantments. If everything goes according to plan, my formula will also break the bargains the high queen has with her guards."

"Truly?" Elora whispered the word, but even that had been hard to get out. She ached to believe it, but such an extraordinary formula seemed too good to be true.

The friendly smile broke across Tindra's face as she glanced back at her rock table covered in jars and pages of research. Her smile went tight. "Yes, but there is a big difference between trying to do something and actually doing it."

Unable to stop herself, Elora stepped forward. "But if you succeed, all enchantments will disappear? The sprites will no longer be forced inside a bubble that destroys their essence once they enter Fairfrost? The high queen will not be able to sense anyone's magic? The guards will no longer have to do the high queen's bidding?"

Tindra frowned. "The formula must be perfect to work, but if I can figure it out, yes, all those statements will be true. Unfortunately, I am a long way from perfection."

Her gaze fixated on a jar filled with pearlescent blue liquid. Something about it made her frown deepen.

"Do not let my beloved fool you. She is closer than ever." Severin winked, but it did nothing to lift the frown on Tindra's face. She went back to her table and began measuring liquids once again.

Severin waved a hand over the cast iron pot, then used a wooden spoon to stir it. After another moment, he scooped a thick stew onto a gray ceramic plate. His magic must have cooked the vegetables faster than a normal fire. After plucking a spoon from a little basket, he pushed the food into Elora's hands.

She took it gratefully since she hadn't eaten since before the battle the day before. After tucking Tindra's necklace into her pocket, she took her first bite.

Severin went back to his earlier spot and retrieved a piece of parchment and pen from his pocket. "While you eat, I will write down everything about Fairfrost that might be useful in rescuing Prince Brannick."

The salty and sour flavors of the stew melted into Elora's mouth. If she weren't so ravenous, she could have savored the delectable food even more. Instead, she shoveled it in as quickly as possible.

Tindra spun on her heel with her mouth raised in a smirk. "The dragons are wild now. That might be useful... or dangerous, I suppose."

Severin's eyes lit up as he nodded. "Yes, I had forgotten to include that. Excellent addition."

While they continued to speak, Elora's eyes slid to the back of the cave. The dragon with pastel scales peeked its head around the corner, as if sensing her fear. The spoonful of soup on its way to her mouth froze midway there.

A kind chuckle left Tindra's lips. "You have no need to fear. All the dragons are wild, *except* that one."

Their clear lack of concern went a long way to convince Elora she had no need to fear. It would have been easier to accept if it made any sense at all. Still, fae were physically incapable of lying, so even if it didn't make sense, it *had* to be true. Maybe it just would have taken too long to explain.

Once she finished the stew, Severin handed her his parchment. He had neatly folded it before placing it into her hand. With a nod, she tucked it into her pocket. Now her gaze flitted across the entire cave. "Could you open a door to Bitter Thorn Castle for me?"

In answer, Severin waved a hand and produced a white tunnel filled with swirling icicles.

Elora just barely stopped herself from saying *thank you*. Such words would require her to give him a gift. Instead, she said, "I will not forget your kindness."

After only one step toward the door, she turned back to face them again. "When High Queen Alessandra took Prince Brannick, she said she wanted him to help her find the source of the creation magic in Bitter Thorn."

Tindra gasped and nearly dropped the glass jar in her hand. She put a hand over her chest. "If she finds it..." She glanced toward her beloved. When their eyes met, she shivered. "She will be more powerful than Faerie itself."

Severin answered in a near whisper. "She could control all of us with a wave of one hand."

Elora gulped. "So, I have to rescue Prince Brannick, but I also must do it before she finds the creation magic."

Closing her eyes for a moment, Tindra breathed out deeply. "I wish we had more to give you."

Elora bit her bottom lip. "Me too." Fate itself seemed determined to make her goals as impossible to accomplish as possible. But what else could she do except try anyway? Her lips pursed as she attempted to stand straighter. "Your necklace will be helpful though. I already know it."

The crease between Severin's eyebrows returned, but he was obviously trying to smother it with a pleasant expression. "Our thoughts will be with you."

Tindra gestured over her table. "If I perfect my formula, you will be the first to know."

If someone as close to the high queen as her own brother longed for her overthrowal, it probably should have been easier to accomplish. Despite that, Elora inherently knew it would be the most difficult thing she ever did.

Her heart lurched as she stepped into Severin's door. Once again, tiny purple sparks burst from her fingertips.

CHAPTER

3

A gnarled tree root caught Elora's foot as soon as she stepped out of the door. Her palms slapped against a clump of spongy moss. A cool breeze fluttered in the crisp air. The lush forest around her might have made her happier if the high-pitched shriek of a demorog hadn't accompanied it.

Fear hit her like a knife to the gut. The thorn creature swooped down toward her, already raising its claws for a strike. Unlike every other time she had met a demorog, true fear forced her to crouch into a ball. She threw her hands over her head and let out an actual scream.

The demorog swiped a set of claws across her leather-covered arms and another set across the back of her head. The slices left a trail of blood behind, but at least it continued flying away. Apparently, her fear had been enough to make it leave her alone.

She ran a hand over the cut in her leather sleeve. Quintus usually crafted objects, not clothing, but maybe he'd be able to repair the cut. Or maybe she'd just find another outfit to wear. Her fae healing abilities had already started working, at least. The cuts on her arm and head itched as they closed and healed.

If only she could use her magic to create an enchantment to block the fear filling the air. For now, she had to trudge through the forest with no protection at all.

At least she had arrived in Bitter Thorn this time. Severin's door hadn't taken her right to the castle, but she could see its spires ahead. It wouldn't take her long to walk there, assuming more demorogs didn't intervene. Once there, she'd just have to find Kaia's tree and then the dryad could open a door that would take her to Quintus's home.

Her boots pounded on the moist soil as she stomped forward. Memories of the battle the evening before cut into her mind, even though she politely told them to disappear forever. No matter how polite she was, the memories won.

Everything should have worked out. They had tricked High Queen Alessandra and even captured her while in Noble Rose. They had soldiers from Bitter Thorn that the captain of the guard, Soren, had gathered. The rulers of Swiftsea, Mistmount, and Dustdune were there, ready to give power to the crown of Bitter Thorn.

Doing so would have given Brannick enough power to steal the title of High Ruler from Queen Alessandra. He was poised to finally reclaim his rightful title as High King of Faerie.

And then it had all gone wrong.

Frustration boiled in Elora's stomach. Brannick had done everything he could. *She* had done everything she could. Despite the soldiers, and even the trolls Queen Alessandra had summoned, they had still captured her.

But then the king of Mistmount and the queen of Dustdune had revealed they would not give power to Brannick's crown unless he closed the portal to the mortal realm. Such an action would have shut Faerie off from all emotions.

At the time, Elora had been sick with the idea that Brannick might do it. Even High Queen Alessandra's unending fear enchantment couldn't be worse than losing her emotions completely.

But now?

Once Brannick refused, Queen Nerissa of Dustdune had revealed her soldiers, who had been hidden by a glamour that made them invisible. The soldiers released the Fairfrost queen and captured Brannick.

Not only did she and the others fail to overthrow High Queen Alessandra, they also allowed her to become Queen of Dustdune, and even worse, Queen of Bitter Thorn.

The thought twisted Elora's insides, no matter how she tried to ignore them.

A whistling shriek signaled the presence of another demorog. If the same one as before had returned, it probably wouldn't leave just because Elora showed fear. But maybe she could hide from it instead.

Grabbing onto the nearest tree branch, she hoisted herself up. Climbing was much easier while wearing a leather shirt and pants than while wearing a dress. Soon, she sat on a high branch behind a curtain of bright green leaves.

The demorog shrieked wildly as it swooped right past her. Hiding in the tree had done the trick.

Before she could make any move to climb back down, a familiar voice pierced the air.

"Elora."

It came out soft and warm like a quilt that could ease every discomfort. She pressed a hand to her heart and shook her head. Just what she needed. She missed Brannick so much, she could now hear his voice even when he wasn't near.

"Elora." It came out louder this time.

Her back shot up straight. She clutched the tree branch nearest to her. "Brannick?" Her head whipped side to side, searching for any sight of him.

"*Shhh.*" Metal seemed to land in a pile on a hard surface, but nothing in the forest could have made such a sound. "One moment." It was definitely Brannick. She'd know his voice anywhere.

She whipped her head around, searching once again. Was he glamoured to be invisible?

"Look." He whispered this time.

A moment after he spoke, a swirling motion just in front of her caught her eye. It was no bigger than the palm of her hand. In a flash, it grew bigger until a regular-sized Faerie door swirled just in front of her. She recognized the green, brown, and black whirls, the soft breeze, and the scents that smelled just like Bitter Thorn.

After one blink, the door shrunk once again. This time, it went down to half the size of her palm. Now that she knew where to look, it was easy to see it, though she hadn't noticed it before that.

Everything became clear at once. Brannick was speaking to her through his Faerie door, but that knowledge just raised a host of questions.

She sat up straight, still holding onto a branch for support. "Where are you?"

A huffy sort of noise sputtered from his door. "High Queen Alessandra's dungeon." The clanking metal sound returned. "I am in chains that block my magic."

Leaning back into the tree, Elora swallowed. "If they block your magic, then how did you open a door?"

"These chains may be powerful," he chuckled. "But I am Prince of Bitter Thorn."

She could imagine him lounging across some surface with a wide smirk on his face. The image almost made her smile. Almost. She hated to shatter his smirk in any way.

"Elora."

Her heart sputtered. She had been silent too long. Curling one hand into her lap, she finally dared to speak again. "*Are you still the prince?*"

"Ah, so I was right." His smirk *had* shattered. She could hear it in his voice. "You somehow glamoured yourself to be invisible and never went through my door to Quintus's house like you were supposed to." Even only hearing his voice through a door, she could sense how his tone shifted. His voice became gravelly. "You saw everything."

The hand in her lap gripped her sword hilt. Part of the iron pommel dug into her stomach with the way she had it positioned, but she didn't care. The leather from her shirt mostly blocked the iron from affecting her anyway. "You made me vow that I would keep myself safe. That vow prevented me from doing anything that would reveal myself." Her voice caught as a sob rose in her throat. "I wanted to save you."

"I am glad for the vow. I worried you would do something rash."

It didn't matter how much she wanted to respond, she could only clench her jaw to keep silent sobs from escaping. The stupid vow stopped her from moving at all. She had to sit

33

back and watch her beloved be captured—again—by the queen of Fairfrost.

"I do not know if I am still Prince of Bitter Thorn. Each court has always had exactly one ruler. Even if married, there is always only a king or a queen, never both. Since High Queen Alessandra is Queen of Bitter Thorn, I should not be a ruler anymore." He paused a beat before continuing. "But I still feel as powerful as ever." He let out a dark chuckle. "Although the chains make it difficult to know for sure."

"Can you leave the dungeon?"

Brannick let out a sigh that could have twisted every tree in Bitter Thorn. "Alas, I cannot. I am able to open a door, but the chains prevent me from stepping through it. The high queen does not even keep me guarded always because she knows I have no way to escape. Then again, maybe she simply needs her guards elsewhere."

"I am going to rescue you." Elora had swallowed down the last of her sobs. Now her voice came out sure.

Silence met it.

Finally, Brannick let out a long breath. "I would not blame you if you went into hiding instead."

"I would never give up like that." She reached into her pocket and pulled out the crystal that contained Brannick's essence. The sage green stone pulsed under her fingertips. He had a matching purple crystal that contained her essence now. She had been hesitant to allow him to make it, but that crystal had helped him know where to find her.

The crystal pulsed again, and somehow, she *knew*. Sensations sparked under her fingertips. The two crystals were connected almost as much as she and Brannick were. It probably sounded crazy to anyone who didn't know them, but she didn't care. She knew. Brannick was holding her crystal too. It almost felt like she was holding his hand.

"I need you to vow that you will keep yourself safe." His voice was low and husky but determined too.

"I will make no such vow."

"Elora."

She gripped a tree branch and sat up straight. "That same vow prevented me from helping you when you got captured."

"If you had done anything, you would have been captured too. High Queen Alessandra would have killed you immediately." His voice lowered again to a pleading grind. "Make the vow."

She would have refused again. She would have refused as many times as it took. But she didn't have to because a slurry of voices and footsteps changed everything.

Brannick's voice came one last time. "I must go."

Her heart sank when the tiny door vanished, but of course, if anyone in Fairfrost saw it, he would certainly get punished. While her heart sank, she almost didn't notice that not all the voices disappeared with the door. Most of them did—but some remained.

Sucking in a breath, she sat up straight and peered down at the forest path below.

Clearly, some of the voices hadn't been in Fairfrost at all. Whoever they belonged to, they were coming nearer.

CHAPTER

4

Voices continued to move closer to Elora. With fear swirling in the air, the voices probably should have raised the hairs on her arms. Instead, they offered comfort. At least they weren't more demorogs.

Gripping her sword, Elora popped the wings from her back and flew to the ground. By now, the voices had moved close enough to distinguish actual words. Hearing them shoved away the last of the fear in Elora's gut. She ran forward to meet them.

Vesper and Quintus marched down the path. When they caught Elora's eye, both of them clapped a hand to their mouths. Vesper even teared up, but maybe it was just a trick of the light that made it appear so.

By the time they stomped over to her, smiles adorned their faces. Quintus wore an expression of relief. "We are glad to see you. Your sister nearly strangled me when you never returned last night."

Even without asking, Elora guessed the *sister* he spoke of was her middle sister, Chloe.

"Where have you been?" Vesper pulled her into a hug, which only lasted half a breath. Now he gripped her shoulders and stared a little too intensely into her eyes. "Where is Prince Brannick?"

Rather than waiting for an answer, her fae brother scanned the forest. Did he think Brannick would just be standing there?

A loud shriek filled the air. Elora's stomach twisted into a knot when another shriek started before the first one ended. Demorogs. There were two at least, but there could have been more.

Without a word, Vesper grabbed her hand and yanked her through a door. He must have opened it while she searched for the demorogs. A moment later, she, Vesper, and Quintus tumbled into the middle of Quintus's home.

Her sisters tackled her before she could even stand up straight.

"You're alive." Grace already had tears streaking down her face. How had she started crying so fast? Or maybe she had already been crying.

Chloe kept going back and forth between hugging her sister and jabbing her in the shoulder and demanding she never fight in a battle again.

When they finally released her, Lyren emerged from around a corner. She clasped her hands in front of herself while her eyes grew wide. Hesitancy kept her steps uneven, but it disappeared by the time she reached Elora. Soon, even Lyren wrapped her arms around Elora.

37

The hug was probably the shortest one Elora had ever experienced in her life, but coming from a fae who only barely understood emotion, it meant a lot.

For some reason, that moment released the well of tears that had been brimming inside Elora since the night before.

With an understanding nod, Lyren placed a hand on Elora's shoulder. "Queen Noelani told me what happened. I told the others already. We know the queen of Dustdune was working with High Queen Alessandra." Her eyebrows pinched together. "But my queen left as soon as Dustdune soldiers started to appear. We have no idea what happened after that."

Maybe all the hugs had given her courage, maybe being back in Bitter Thorn did it, or maybe it was simply because Lyren had already told half the story, but Elora finally felt ready to explain.

More tears spilled as she recounted how Brannick had been captured. Even more fell when she confessed she could do nothing to help him. Everyone there annoyingly agreed that the vow had saved her life. They also thankfully agreed they had to rescue Brannick as soon as possible.

Once things settled down a bit more, Lyren managed to pull Elora away from the others. They went into the bedroom where Elora and her sisters had been staying. Another sleeping mat and blanket had been added. Lyren must have stayed with them last night instead of staying in Swiftsea.

With curls bouncing, Lyren sat cross-legged on the new sleeping mat. She waited until both of them were settled before she finally spoke. "I must tell you something." Her voice lowered. "I have never told anyone this, but I think I have waited long enough."

Elora reached a hand out. "Are you okay?"

"I killed someone."

Pulling her own hand back into her lap, Elora raised an eyebrow. "During the battle?"

Lyren tucked a curl behind her pointed ear as she shook her head. No white sea flower sat among the dark curls. "No, that would have been different." She gulped. "This happened when I was a child."

No response seemed appropriate, but Elora tried to sit forward at least. Hopefully that would demonstrate her interest.

With blue-painted fingernails pressed against her forehead, Lyren took a deep breath. When she finally lowered her hand, her brown and silver eyes had dulled. "I had been swimming and discovered a lovely island. I probably should not have explored it on my own, but I was too young to know anything about danger."

She shifted, as if a pebble sat underneath her in an uncomfortable spot. "I caught a male fae dripping blood from his palm onto the sandy beach. Even now, I do not know what he was doing, but I know he did not wish to be seen."

Lyren's gaze turned downward. When the male fae realized I had caught him, he attacked me. He tried to kill me."

"What did you do?" Elora's mind whirled with possibilities. The mermaid, Waverly, came to her mind first. Perhaps the mermaid had saved Lyren and that was how they became friends.

Lyren took a deep breath before she answered. "I killed him first."

The words cut through the air even faster than the swipe of a demorog claw. Elora could think of no response. She only muttered a quiet "Oh."

"I had no other way to escape." Lyren tapped her forehead, staring off at a corner of the room. "I was already skilled with a javelin since I grew up near Swiftsea Palace."

Finding her composure once again, Elora nodded. "You had no choice then. I am glad you could protect yourself when your life was in danger."

The words had been meant to comfort, but they seemed to have the opposite effect. Lyren looked up, her eyes wide and frenzied. "A fae's essence is greatly affected when that fae takes a life. Do you remember when Prince Brannick said he would kill Ansel for what he did to you, and the rest of us gasped at the proclamation?"

Ansel's name sent Elora's hands into tight fists. It took effort to ignore the images of yellow eyes, a knife, and chains that flashed through her mind. She tried to turn her thoughts to how Brannick had rescued her instead. After swallowing, she said, "I forgot about that."

Lyren sat up straighter, as if that would lend more importance to her words. Her pitch even raised a notch. "Taking a life would hurt Prince Brannick's essence even more than anyone else's since his greatest magic is in essence."

"What about High Queen Alessandra?" Elora raised an eyebrow. "She has killed plenty of people."

"So did King Huron, and his essence was greatly tainted. That is why Prince Brannick refused to take his magic after he died, even though the prince had earned it."

Tilting her head, Elora tried to understand. If this was true, then High Queen Alessandra's essence must have been greatly tainted too. Did it hurt her? Maybe that was why she wanted the creation magic. Maybe Faerie itself punished her for killing so many. And maybe that was why she was so desperate to be more powerful than Faerie itself.

The pieces continued to fall into place in Elora's mind. "You told me High Queen Alessandra might be responsible for the decay in Swiftsea, but not intentionally."

Something about Lyren's dark curls looked different now. They seemed to limp around her face instead of bounce when she nodded. "She has killed countless fae while in our court. My queen believes the high queen's tainted essence is also tainting our court. But my queen *also* believes High Queen Alessandra's tainted essence is only making the decay worse. She still thinks the cause is because Faerie has the wrong High Ruler and Faerie itself knows it."

Elora's fingers found her sword hilt once again. "So, if Prince Brannick becomes High King, that will fix the source of the decay, *and* High Queen Alessandra's tainted essence cannot taint your court anymore."

With one hand curled into a fist, Lyren leaned forward. "I think Queen Noelani is wrong. Faerie *is* out of sorts because it has the wrong High Ruler. When Prince Brannick becomes High King, that *will* help."

"But?"

Lyren took in deep breath. "But the decay is my fault."

"What?"

Her eyes darkened. "I killed that fae. I tainted my own court."

Elora shook her head. "But you had to kill him. Surely, Faerie itself understands that."

"You think so?" No amount of hope laced her words. Lyren followed them with a scoff. "Then why is the *source* of the decay, which we only recently discovered, in the exact spot I killed him?"

Elora had no answer for that.

Whether good or bad, Lyren didn't seem to expect an answer anyway. She kept shaking her head back and forth, which only made her curls look limper. "I have always appreciated the selfishness and lack of emotion fae have. I never felt too guilty about what I did."

She started rocking back and forth, shaking her head faster each time. "But the high queen's enchantments are filling Faerie with stronger emotion than it has ever had before. My past pains me in ways I have never known."

Reaching forward, Elora placed her hand on Lyren's forearm. She wanted to reaffirm that Lyren had only done what she had to do, but Elora instinctively knew her opinion would mean little to Lyren. Luckily, she also knew whose opinion did matter to the fae.

"What does your queen think of you?" Elora gestured toward the two seashell necklaces hanging around Lyren's neck. "Did you not earn those necklaces because of your accomplishments? If Queen Noelani believes you worthy of those necklaces, then surely you cannot feel too guilty about something you had to do to survive."

The words worked like magic. Lyren's black curls twisted into tighter spirals. The silver in her eyes gleamed. She ran her fingers down the silver chains of her two necklaces while a smile played on her lips. "I earned the first necklace for mastery of words. And of course, you know I earned the second for bravery after our fight with King Huron in Dustdune Castle."

Her eyes shimmered as her hand fell to her side. "The third necklace I can only earn by making a great sacrifice. All my life I have been desperate to earn three necklaces from my queen because then I would believe my essence had grown better than the mistake I made as a child." She glanced down. "But I still only have two necklaces. Two instead of three. If I could just earn the third, I would not feel guilty. I think the decay might finally heal then." Her voice lowered. "But I do not know if I have the will to make a great enough sacrifice."

Their conversation got cut off short when Vesper entered the room. His weary eyes didn't seem to notice the gravity of the conversation he had interrupted. He just gestured toward the sleeping mats as Elora's younger sisters came into the room behind him.

"You need to rest, Elora." He glanced back until Chloe and Grace moved over to their sleeping mats. He rubbed one eye before speaking again.

"We all need to rest. Tomorrow, we can devise a plan."

CHAPTER 5

Quiet whimpers and sniffles woke Elora from her sleep. The moment consciousness took hold of her, a strong pain gripped her heart. It pulsed and then spread throughout her limbs.

Despair.

Hopelessness curled around her insides. It didn't make any sense how physical emotions could be. This one clenched tight on her heart, gnawing until everything inside her felt raw.

While her body writhed in the pain of despair, she tried to shift her focus on identifying the whimpers that had woken her. After sharing a room with two sisters for most of her life, she had learned how to differentiate between the two of them.

Grace was crying.

Elora sat up, wrapping a blanket around herself and crossing the room.

"I want to go home." Grace sniffed after every other word. She used her own blanket to wipe the tears that wouldn't stop flowing from her eyes.

By the time Elora made it to Grace's sleeping mat, Chloe had also sat up. Her eyes were puffy, but maybe lack of sleep had turned them that way. Or maybe Chloe had been crying too.

Wrapping an arm around her youngest sister, Elora spoke in the most soothing voice she could manage. "Okay. You can go back to the mortal realm if you want to. Quintus or Lyren can open a door. We will have to choose a new place for you to live and we will—"

"No." A surprising amount of bite shook through the single word. Grace pushed her hair behind her shoulders and shook her head. "That's not what I mean. I want to go *home*."

Fresh tears welled in her eyes, but when the next sob came out, it came from Chloe. Their middle sister buried her face in her hands while another sob wracked her shoulders.

Grace wrapped her arms around her knees and pulled them to her chest. "I want to go back to *our* village. I want Mother and Father to be alive." Her head lowered. "I wish you had never come to Faerie. If you hadn't, they never would have died."

The despair in Elora's chest bloomed into something as massive and as prickly as a thorny demorog. It took effort to keep her chin from trembling.

Apparently, Grace had no such self-control. Her entire body shivered as she let out a sob. "It's your fault they died."

Though those exact words had been swimming around in Elora's mind, hearing them spoken by her sister hurt a dozen times worse. A shaky breath kept her from calming her heartbeat.

Chloe pounded the ground beside her. "I *hate* it here. I thought Faerie would be magical, but it's dangerous and ugly and…" Her eyes turned feral as she faced her oldest sister. "It *is* your fault. Why did you have to kill that troll when you rescued Prince Brannick from Fairfrost? High Queen Alessandra wouldn't have killed our parents if you hadn't killed that troll. And now Prince Brannick is captured again anyway."

The accusations from her sisters pinned Elora's heart down to where it might never be able to get back up again. But at the moment, her thoughts turned to the dead troll. Was her essence tainted because she took a life? The troll *did* try to kill her first. She wouldn't have killed it if she could have avoided it.

Did Faerie itself understand? Did Faerie itself even care since she had been mortal at the time?

"At least she did not destroy her entire court when she was only a child." Lyren spoke from the deepest corner of the room. Tears streamed down her face as well.

In a flash, everything became clear.

Elora stood to look out the window. Shimmery enchantments surrounded the outside of Quintus's house just like they had when Brannick created them. She turned toward Lyren's corner. "If Prince Brannick is weakened in Fairfrost, will his enchantments still hold here? Or will the enchantments weaken when he weakens?"

"They will hold just fine." Lyren snapped the words out, probably getting close to biting her own tongue in the process. She bared her teeth. "What does that have to do with anything?"

Now that she understood, Elora had an easier time tempering the despair that seemed intent on crushing her from the inside out. It turned to nothing more than a dull ache now.

She muttered under her breath as she left the room. "I wonder if Vesper or Quintus had to remove the enchantments for some reason then."

Grace started sobbing again. Chloe didn't *sob* exactly, but she definitely cried harder than she had been a moment ago.

Once Elora stepped outside the bedroom, she heard Vesper and Quintus bickering with each other. They had clearly been awakened by the despair as well.

"I never fiddled with the enchantments. How dare you accuse me of that?" Vesper's words could have been venomous with the right tone, but they merely sounded hollow instead.

"I saw you on the side of the house for no reason yesterday. Do not try to deceive me."

A loud scoff erupted before Vesper answered. "I told you the reason. I was looking for a flower or something to cheer up my sisters. You know I cannot lie. If I said I did not do anything to the enchantments, then you know I did not."

Their bickering continued.

Shuffling feet broke Elora from her thoughts. When she turned, Chloe's blonde hair glimmered in the light of the sprites above. "I'm sorry I said that." Tears slid down Chloe's face with each word. "I know it wasn't really your fault. I just miss Mother and Father so much."

"Me too." Despite her ability to work through the despair surrounding them, Elora still felt it clawing away at her heart.

"I'm sorry too." Grace's voice came out in a squeak, but she had stopped crying at least. "I had the most terrible dream, and then I woke up and the sadness hit me like it never has before."

After a few sniffs, Chloe wiped away the rest of her tears. Elora pulled her sisters into a tight hug. Sobs erupted from both of the other bedrooms. Elora stepped back to look at her sisters. They didn't look happy by any means, but they did look... better.

Interesting. Her sisters were doing better, but Lyren, Quintus, and Vesper all seemed to be doing increasingly worse.

Elora put a hand over her heart, looking back to her sisters once again. "High Queen Alessandra's magic caused this despair. It must have."

As she spoke, a glowing green light with a pink sparkle flitted down from the ceiling. The sight of her sprite friend put the first smile onto Elora's face. "Tansy."

The sparkly pink skirt twirled as the sprite landed on Elora's shoulder. Her velvety hair bounced but not with the same height as it used to. Her limbs still looked weak after her recent experience in Fairfrost. "We think High Queen Alessandra used another gemstone. There are no sprites in Fairfrost now, so we do not know for sure. But we are almost certain. Despair has filled every court."

"Oh." Chloe's voice came out flat. She glanced at her youngest sister. "We have never felt her magic before." She swallowed and rubbed a hand over her heart. "I can see why everyone has been so frightened by it."

Elora stared at Tansy for another moment, soaking in the sight of her alive and well and far from the imprisonment she endured in Fairfrost. An unexpected smile twitched at her lips. "If High Queen Alessandra used another gemstone, there is one good thing about it. She only has one gemstone left."

Grace's face contorted into a scowl. "But there's something bad too, isn't there?"

With a hard swallow, Elora glanced toward her shoulder. "Her magic has never penetrated a protective enchantment before, but now it has. Prince Brannick's enchantments are still surrounding the house, yet all of us feel the despair anyway."

Chloe groaned.

Grace burst into tears yet again. Since Lyren was practically wailing in the bedroom now, the noise of Grace's tears didn't carry far.

Even Chloe had a few tears slipping down her cheeks. "I know I only feel so awful because of the enchantment. I know there isn't a real cause." She sniffed. "But it still hurts. The pain is real even if the cause isn't."

Elora squeezed her middle sister's hand. "You are doing better than the fae already. Be grateful you have experience with handling emotion."

With a flop, Tansy sat cross-legged on Elora's shoulder. She wore a deep scowl. "The sprites feel it too. Sometimes our essence is strong enough to counteract the magic. Sometimes we have tokens that help us get through it." Her chin fell to her chest. "And sometimes it hurts as bad as being trapped in Fairfrost did."

Grace's sobs had turned into hiccups. "A good cup of herbal tea always makes me feel better when I'm sad." She hiccupped again. "And cake can make almost anyone smile." Another hiccup came out. "I'll make some tea and cake."

"I have an idea too." Chloe ran into the bedroom full of Lyren's wailing while Grace went into the kitchen.

Rolling her eyes, Elora turned to her shoulder once again. Tea and cake could not possibly help. She expected Tansy to wear a similar expression of disbelief. Instead, the little sprite looked intrigued.

Elora dropped into the nearest chair and retrieved Severin's note from her pocket. "I have to rescue Prince Brannick from Fairfrost. Again."

49

Tansy gave a quick nod and fluttered off the shoulder to get a closer look at the paper in Elora's hands. "Who gave you this?"

"Severin."

A spark lit in Tansy's pink and green eyes. "Good. Then it has the best information you could find. He knows Fairfrost Palace better than anyone."

The first bit of information certainly seemed helpful. Ideas already started flowing through Elora's mind before she even finished the first few sentences.

Prince Brannick will be kept in chains that block his magic. No fae has ever escaped them without help. They can be removed by a powerful fae who does not wear chains, or they can be removed with a key.

The note then explained in detail where to find and retrieve such a key.

Tansy glanced upward with a smirk. "This might be easier than I thought."

Despite the despair that still throbbed in Elora's chest, a tiny blossom of hope sparked inside it too. "I hope so."

Wailing filled the house louder than before. Chloe dragged Lyren to the table and forced her to sit down. She ran into the other bedroom and got Quintus next. By the time she was dragging a weeping Vesper to the table, Elora had already turned back to the note.

Dragons are wild.

Elora knew that one already from Tindra.

"Leave me be. I want to be alone." Vesper lashed out with one hand, nearly slapping Chloe.

She seemed utterly unfazed as she ducked to avoid it. "Sometimes when you want to be alone the most, that's the worst possible time to be alone."

Quintus swiped a handkerchief across his face. "There is no time—"

"Yes, I know there's no time in Faerie," Chloe snapped before he could finish. She sent a long glare toward Quintus. "Now shush. All of you."

She had finally managed to get Vesper into a chair. She stood at the head of the table with a poem in her hand. The edges had curled, and smudges covered the parchment in a few spots. It must have been a well-beloved poem for it to have been so worn.

Chloe cleared her throat and began reciting the poem in her most dramatic voice. It told the story of a young man in the deepest despair. His father had just been killed by a group of ruthless robbers, who only cared for money. They had pillaged his home, cut off his hand, killed his father, and left him for dead. His mother had already died the year before. Now he had nothing. No one. Except for losing a hand to a blade, the story was a little too similar to Elora's own life.

The robbers left his home and went to pillage the rest of the village. The other villagers were in great trouble. The young man knew it, but he couldn't bring himself to care enough. He wanted to give up.

"He *should* give up." A heartbreaking sob came from Vesper's throat, cutting his sentence off a hair too early.

Though Lyren and Quintus both seemed hurt by High Queen Alessandra's magic, Vesper seemed profoundly affected by the despair more than anyone else. Maybe it was simply because he had experienced love and had more to lose. He did have a beloved in the mortal realm, after all. And since High King Romany had banished Vesper from Noble Rose, Vesper also couldn't open a door to the mortal realm.

Pointing her nose in the air, Chloe folded her arms over her chest. "I am the one telling the story, not you. Now, be quiet."

When she continued, the story reached a turning point. The young man found strength in his despair. The rest of it was probably very touching, but Elora turned her attention back to the note from Severin.

The number of guards around Prince Brannick will depend on what else is going on in Fairfrost. It could be a great number of guards if the court is calm like usual. But if they are preparing for battle, there may not be as many guards.

He finished the note by explaining about some curious orbs that were hidden in a research room in Fairfrost Palace. The orbs had several fascinating abilities like making noises, shooting out blinding lights, and even exploding. Even more fascinating, no magic was needed to use the orbs. Tindra must have designed them.

At the very bottom, Severin had drawn a map of Fairfrost Palace. He labeled the dungeon where Brannick was surely being kept, the room where Elora could find a key to his chains, and even the research room that held the orbs.

Just as Chloe finished her epic poem, Grace began passing around the tea and cake she had made. She set a clay plate and a stone cup in front of Vesper first. "It's hard, and it hurts." She wiped a tear from her eye. "But life is good too."

Quintus ignored the plate and cup that Grace set in front of him. Instead, he stared at Chloe, completely engrossed, even though the story had ended now.

Lyren stroked a strand of her hair, making the curls even limper than before. Her eyes dulled. She kept shaking every few breaths.

Vesper was still crying. He looked too upset to even touch the cake in front of him.

Scanning them all one last time, Elora bent to whisper to her sprite friend. "Which fae looks the strongest, do you think?"

"Quintus." Tansy twirled her pink skirt when she answered

Elora nodded. She had already come to the same conclusion. "Quintus." His eyes still didn't leave Chloe. Elora cleared her throat. "Could you put your strongest protective enchantment around this table and around us?"

"I…" He spent one more moment staring at Chloe before finally turning. "Yes. If the enchantment is small like that, I can do it." He sent one last glance toward Chloe that was not subtle in any way, and then an enchantment shot from his fingertips.

The moment the enchantment enclosed around them, Lyren heaved with a sigh of relief. Vesper still sniffed and scowled, but he started eating his cake at least. Tansy jumped into the air and used her wings to fly to Elora's shoulder once more.

Sitting up straight, Elora looked everyone in the eye. "We need to travel to Fairfrost as soon as day dawns."

CHAPTER

6

Shimmers of gold twinkled over the table in Quintus's kitchen. Elora watched the light dance over her arms and hair. The enchantment didn't have the same intensity as Brannick's usually did, but it worked well enough.

Every tear had finally been wiped away. Grace's cake had been reduced to small piles of crumbs. Vesper still looked worse than anyone, but he ate all of his cake, at least. And he interacted with the others.

Chloe's epic poem and Grace's tea and cake helped far more than Elora ever expected. Quintus's enchantment helped too.

With a flutter of wings, Tansy flew down and landed her soft pink shoes on Elora's wrist. She glanced at the others and then flew back up to Elora's shoulder. Grabbing Elora's ear with both of her tiny hands, the sprite whispered. "Can you feel how the despair is still coming through?"

While the others finished off the last of their cake crumbs, Elora nodded. She wanted to believe Quintus's enchantment just wasn't as strong as Brannick's and that was the only reason she could still feel a sliver of despair. Deep down, she knew it was because High Queen Alessandra's magic was too strong this time. It was strong enough to penetrate any enchantment.

If they didn't act soon, everyone in Faerie would be too despondent to ever fight against the high queen.

Standing up, Elora stole everyone's attention. "I know how to rescue Prince Brannick."

Quintus scoffed. "Do you have any idea how long it took to organize *your* escape? We need a solid plan. We need to make contingencies."

"I already have a plan."

Lyren and Vesper glance at Elora before they shared a look with each other. An infuriating look.

With a forced smile, Lyren tilted her head to the side. "I know you are learning more and more about Faerie, but that—"

"I have inside information." Elora ignored how her heart thumped. She carefully unfolded the note from Severin. "The plan is simple. Someone needs to glamour me to be invisible. Then that fae needs to open a door to Fairfrost Palace for me. I will walk straight into the palace and use this map to find a key. Then I will go to the dungeons and free Brannick. Once his chains are removed, he can open a door back to here. We will return together very soon."

An open sketchbook sat in front of Quintus. He copied the map from her note into the pages of his sketchbook. His eyes never left the paper when he spoke. "You are forgetting about the enchantment in Fairfrost Palace that can sense your magic. High Queen Alessandra will know you are in her palace immediately, even if you have a glamour that makes you invisible."

Elora pulled the necklace from her pocket and draped it around her neck. "This necklace will block that enchantment. The high queen will not be able to sense my magic as long as I wear it."

"Where did you get that?" Lyren strummed her fingers on the table, but it didn't hide the curiosity in her eyes.

"Tindra made it. She is a brilliant researcher and Severin's beloved."

A beat of silence landed, but Vesper shoved it away by slapping his palms against the table. "Severin is High Queen Alessandra's brother."

Elora nodded. "I know that. Tindra and Severin helped me last time I got into Fairfrost Palace."

Quintus tapped his pencil on the table while he mused. "I wondered how you got in."

"Does that not make you suspicious?" Lyren's eyes had widened as much as they could, but she still seemed intent on opening them wider. "Are you not afraid that Severin was helping High Queen Alessandra?"

"No." Elora waved a hand. "He had nothing to do with my capture."

Vesper glanced toward the window, just like he always did. This time, it didn't fill his eyes with any mischief. He just frowned and turned back to Elora. "Are you sure?"

A tiny scoff erupted from Elora's shoulder. Tansy huffed loud enough for the others to hear. When they glanced toward her, she folded her arms over her chest and turned to face only Elora. "Ignore them. Severin is trustworthy." She turned to the others just long enough to scoff again. When she looked back at Elora, her pink and green eyes sparkled. "We would never try to deceive you after everything you have done for us."

56

Though Elora had no doubts about Severin, getting confirmation of his loyalty still eased her fears. She raised an eyebrow, ignoring how her sisters squirmed. "Who will open a door for me?"

"This sounds dangerous." Chloe rubbed a thumb over an ink smudge on the back of her hand. When she looked up, tears welled in her eyes. "What if something goes—"

Elora held up a hand to cut off her sister's words. She turned to the other end of the table. "Vesper?"

He scowled and settled deeper into his chair. "Why do you always assume I will help you with everything? I want you safe as much as Chloe does."

It took every bit of Elora's self-control to keep herself from wrapping both arms around her stomach. At the very least, she wanted to grab her sword hilt and squeeze away her worry. Desperate to appear strong, she merely straightened her spine. "We need Prince Brannick in order to save Faerie." Her hand found the sword hilt she'd been trying to avoid. "And…" Her eyes stung as she tried to keep her tears back. Her brother may have been annoyed, but he was also entranced by the sight. Elora gulped and purposefully stared straight at him. "Brannick is my beloved. Would you not do anything for your beloved if you could?"

The scowl melted off Vesper's features. His clothes shuffled when he sat up. The noise of it filled the room since everything else sat in complete silence. Quintus's enchantment continued to shimmer around them, but something different hung in the air now. Something that snuffed out the bits of despair that had seeped through the enchantment.

Hope.

With a smirk playing at his lips, Vesper threw his brown curls backward. "Fairfrost is the least thrilling of any Faerie court. The next time any of you gets captured, could you *please* end up in any court besides Fairfrost?"

He stood up and the knot that twisted around Elora's heart began to unravel. With a wave of his hand, she went invisible.

Lyren gasped while staring at Vesper. "You are really going?"

"He does not have to go at all." Elora checked that the ward necklace from Tindra was firmly in place around her neck. "He just has to open the door for me. I can do the rest."

One eyebrow quirked high on Vesper's forehead. "I *am* going with you. I will glamour myself to be invisible, and I will stay just outside Fairfrost Palace."

Tansy flitted upward, wearing a devious smirk of her own. She wouldn't dare talk now that she couldn't make it obvious she spoke only to Elora. Still, it was clear that she liked this plan. Or maybe she just liked Elora's and Vesper's daring natures.

Snatching Severin's note from off the table, Elora shoved it into her pocket. "Once I return here with Brannick, he can open a door to just outside Fairfrost Palace. Then Vesper, once you see his door, you will know the rescue was successful."

That same eyebrow on Vesper's forehead tilted even higher. "And if no door appears by nightfall, I will know that you got captured too."

Elora huffed. "That will not happen."

Grace fumbled forward, wrapping her arms tight around her sister's waist. "Be careful."

After returning the hug, Elora stepped away from the table. "Hurry, Vesper. You need to glamour yourself to be invisible as well and then we will go. The longer we wait, the harder it will be to leave."

CHAPTER 7

The air stung with a buzzing energy as soon as a door had been opened to Fairfrost. Elora curled her arms around herself, wishing she had thought to grab a cape before she decided to leave. It was probably too late now. When she stepped toward the door, the stinging energy only grew.

Worry needled its way under her skin. She told herself the emotion came because of High Queen Alessandra's manipulative magic. When the worry turned to straight fear, a part of her knew it had nothing to do with any manipulation at all.

At her side, she heard Vesper's footsteps also nearing the door. Since they both wore glamours keeping them invisible, they could not see each other. Maybe she should have offered a word of encouragement to her brother.

It seemed neither of them could manage it. They both knew how dangerous their plan was. That wouldn't stop Elora though.

Taking a final breath, she stepped into the door. When they landed in Fairfrost a few moments later, she swore the air felt colder than ever.

That thought spun away when a flying axe narrowly missed her ear. She sucked in a sharp breath and jumped to the side. While still in motion, she noticed her light brown hair fluttering in the wind.

She could *see* her hair.

But that meant... Her eyes darted and immediately fell on Vesper. She could see him too.

Their glamours had fallen away.

When a second axe came swinging toward her, she used her wings to zip into the air.

The glamour had definitely been in place when they first entered Vesper's door. She gripped her sword hilt, finally glancing toward where the thrown weapons had come from. A dozen guards in white brocade formed a circle around Elora and her brother.

When one charged, she tore her sword from her belt and swooped down for a lethal strike.

The sword sliced straight across the guard's arm. It dug in down to the bone. The guard let out a blood-curdling wail, but it didn't stop him from raising a curved axe into the air. The blade came crashing toward her chest. Her wings carried her away just in time.

Short gasps escaped her while she tried to catch her breath.

Despite the attack, her mind turned back to the glamours. Had her magic done something? Had it taken away their

60

glamours just like it had possibly changed the destination of her door?

An ice-cold hand wrapped around her ankle and yanked her toward the ground. Her blade swung in a full circle as it fought to make contact with her attacker. At last, the sword stabbed the fae's lower leg. The guard sank to the snowy ground, which was quickly stained with splatters of blood.

The victory meant nothing. Elora continued to consider the glamours. No purple sparks had erupted from her fingertips this time. Whatever happened, this was different.

Maybe High Queen Alessandra had simply put an enchantment in Fairfrost that took away any glamours immediately. After the battle in Noble Rose when High Queen Alessandra had nearly been overthrown, it made sense that she might be paranoid enough to create such an enchantment.

A guard slammed into Elora from behind. Unable to catch her fall, she hit her jaw hard on an icy rock. Pain wracked through her skull and stars burst behind her eyes.

For some reason, she could only think of her wings. Now that she had fae healing, the injuries were only inconveniences. They wouldn't last. But if anything happened to her wings...

Rolling onto her back, she kicked both feet into the chest of the fae charging her. The guard fell backward in a long arc until she finally slammed against the ground in a flurry of snow.

Elora gulped as she got to her feet. Her wings fluttered behind her back, presumably uninjured. Just in case, she folded them away into her back. When a white-clad guard charged at her from one side, she stabbed her sword into his chest without a second thought.

He crumpled to the ground in a heap, blood splattering all around him. Her breath caught at the sight.

Had she killed him?

Bile stung in her throat when his body went still.

Would Faerie itself punish her for taking a life?

Almost in answer to her question, the fae at her feet twitched. A sputtering cough erupted from the fae. He was gravely injured, but at least he still lived. His fae healing would get him back to normal eventually.

More axes sliced and spun through the air. Ignoring them, Elora chanced to use her wings again. Once high enough that no guard could grab her ankle, she sought out her brother.

Vesper's eyes had turned wild. He had pulled a pointed mace from his pocket. His arms swung wide as he hit any fae who came near him. A few fae had already fallen at his feet.

He seemed to be safe at least, but something about his demeanor frightened her more than she cared to admit. Seeing him slash his weapon, she finally accepted the truth she wanted to ignore.

Her plan had failed. Without a glamour, she had no way of entering Fairfrost Palace. Even as she accepted it, more guards spilled out the tall iridescent doors of the palace. They had to leave before things got worse.

"We need to get out of here." An icy wind carried Elora's voice across the snowy landscape. It muffled her words so they sounded like a whisper instead of a shout.

Vesper heard them anyway. He didn't acknowledge her, but he did open his misty Faerie door.

Knowing she'd have to enter the door on foot, she flew to the ground and put away her wings once again. Just as she landed, four guards stepped between her and the door.

Her brother took one look at them and shrugged. In the next moment, he stepped toward his door. The sight was too unbelievable, she didn't accept it until he almost stepped out of sight. At the very last moment, she shouted at him.

"Do not leave without me!"

When he turned back, the wild look in his eyes had returned. "Why would I help you?"

His words did more to chill her bones than the frosty landscape around her ever could. A hard lump settled into her throat. It ached and refused to be swallowed down.

He intended to leave her there.

If he did, High Queen Alessandra would kill her immediately, if her guards didn't do it first.

Desperation took hold. "Vesper." Her bottom lip trembled. "I am your sister."

He already had one foot in his door, but the words had stopped him. The guards took the opportunity to attack with greater vigor. A few slashes of Elora's sword kept them back just long enough.

Vesper shook his head. He blinked like he was finally seeing for the first time. Raising his mace, he swung it toward the guard nearest to him. After another massive swing, he locked eyes with Elora.

"Hurry."

Though his voice came out breathless, and the guards evaded most of his blows, something about him had changed. His eyes looked bright again.

They fought together against their attackers until Elora finally reached the door. She sliced a guard across the stomach, which sent a waterfall of blood to the snow. He certainly wouldn't be able to walk for a while, but at least he hadn't died either.

Mist enveloped them as they entered Vesper's door. They landed in Quintus's home like she expected. She *didn't* expect Vesper's face to turn red as if he was lifting an enormous pot full of water.

"What are you doing?" Elora asked. "Close the door, or they will follow in after us." Maybe she should have taken care to use a kind voice, but she didn't have the strength after the unexpected fight.

Even worse than the threat of guards, that same strange energy crackled in the air. It leaked out from Vesper's door, filling each corner of the house with prickles. Whatever it was, it worsened the despair all around them.

"The ceiling!" Quintus jumped toward Chloe, shielding her with his body while cracks formed above them.

Vesper's face burned a brighter red.

Lyren grabbed both Vesper and Elora with each of her hands. She jerked her chin toward the misty tunnel swirling in front of them. "The Fairfrost guards have magic to keep Faerie doors open. We need to hide and then we can open another door and escape them. If we do not hide, they will just keep the new door open too."

Grace let out a squeak from under the table. Her red hair spilled across her forehead, sticking against the tears on her cheeks. Vesper grabbed her with his free hand while Lyren pulled them into the nearest bedroom. Quintus and Chloe jumped inside the room just as Lyren slammed the door closed.

They all took a collective deep breath. After their single moment of peace, Lyren darted toward a large desk along one wall. Elora sprinted after her and soon they shoved the large desk into place in front of the bedroom door.

Chloe and Grace huddled together, both shaking so hard, their dresses fluttered around their ankles.

From outside the house, a swarm of demorogs shrieked. Their claws must have been digging into the ceiling because more cracks formed across it.

Quintus gulped as he urged Chloe and Grace into one corner of the room.

Lyren followed after him, positioning herself as far from sight of the bedroom door as possible. With a wave of one hand, her foamy blue door appeared swirling faster than ever.

A fist pounded on the bedroom door. The Fairfrost guards had entered Quintus's home.

Elora's heart leapt into her throat as she joined the others in the corner of the room.

Red and white sparkles blasted from Vesper's fingertips. They shot against the bedroom door. Despite the continued fists pounding on it from outside the room, the door seemed to stay in place better after that.

Still, it probably wouldn't be long before the Fairfrost guards broke through.

Waiting until everyone else had gone through, Elora finally stepped into Lyren's door. Hopefully they could close it before the Fairfrost guards entered the room.

CHAPTER

8

Salty air drifted through Elora's light brown hair. The salt had a way of turning her naturally straight hair into gentle waves. White sand scattered across the floor of the sea cave she stood in. Singing birds and lapping ocean waves filled the space with calming sounds.

At least it would have been calming, if everything hadn't gone wrong. Lyren had gotten them safely to Swiftsea, but now they were stuck there until Lyren decided it was safe to return to Quintus's house. She said they had to stay through the night at least.

After Lyren had gotten them food, she conjured sleeping mats and blankets made of coral-colored woven cotton. Then she disappeared with the declaration that she would make sure the area was safe for them to stay overnight.

She'd been gone too long. Vesper and Quintus both put protective enchantments around the sea cave, but the despair continued to seep through it anyway.

When the tears and forlorn glances from the others became too much, Elora stood up to leave. She said she would try to find Lyren to see what was taking her so long, but she intended to mostly just enjoy the solitude.

Her sisters had succumbed to the despair again. Vesper and Quintus couldn't help how much the manipulation affected them, but that didn't make them any easier to be around. Elora just needed to be away from everyone while they felt so down.

Sand crunched under her boots, even when she stepped slowly. After passing a few cave entrances, she heard voices. Lyren and a male fae spoke to each other inside one of the smaller sea caves. Since Elora had *said* she would try to find Lyren, she probably needed to at least check that the voice actually belonged to the Swiftsea fae.

She peeked around the entrance. Lyren stood across from a male fae. Their position made it difficult for them to see the cave entrance unless they craned their necks, but Elora could see them perfectly. Neither one of them noticed her presence.

"Why did you come *here?* Why did you not go to Swiftsea Palace?" The male fae had slightly lighter skin than Lyren, but it was still a rich shade of dark brown. He stood in front of Lyren, wringing his hands.

She bit her bottom lip and reached toward one ear. Her eyes closed when her fingers touched her tight curls. Perhaps she had been expecting to touch her white sea flower, but it was still missing. Her eyes turned downward. "I did not wish to bring danger to the palace. High Queen Alessandra's guards might have come after us. I am surprised we got away before they could catch us."

"So, you brought danger here instead?"

Lyren smirked. "No one is better at hiding than this clan. Do you deny it?"

His hands dropped. The faintest glimmer appeared in his eyes. He leaned forward but immediately jerked his head toward the back of the cave. "We are in no position to help you." A shiver shook through him. When he turned to face her again, his eyes were wide. "Something new is in the air."

Curls bounced as Lyren nodded. "We felt it in Bitter Thorn too."

"Our protective enchantments do not help."

"Not at all?"

"Not enough."

Lyren touched a hand to her forehead, breathing deeply before she continued. "We do not need to stay for long. We just need a place to sleep for the night. We will leave as soon as day dawns."

The male fae reached for Lyren, placing a hand on her forearm. Elora had no idea what sort of relationship the two of them had, but she knew it didn't feel right for her to be watching their conversation anymore.

Popping out her wings, she flitted past the cave entrance as inconspicuously as possible. When she reached the end of the sea caves, she climbed down a short rock wall to a beach with fine white sand.

Boots no longer made any sense.

She tore them off and left them by the rocks. Now her toes could dig into the delightfully warm grains of sand. She loved the warmth, but once she reached the lapping waves, the cool water felt even better.

The warm sand provided the perfect resting spot for her weary body. She stretched her toes as far forward as possible so they would catch the edges of the foamy waves as they crawled up the shore.

Despair continued to grind all around her. It did everything it could to wriggle into her heart. She didn't like how much it succeeded. Despite the beautiful beach and the magical bird song around her, she still wanted to curl into a ball and cry until her body gave out.

"Elora."

A spark of hope flared in her chest at the sound of Brannick's voice. She glanced around, finding his door much faster now that she knew what to look for. He had made the door as small as the palm of her hand.

"Why are you in Swiftsea?" He clearly meant for the question to sound curious, but it did little to hide his fear.

She groaned and pulled her knees up to her chest. She was glad he had the crystal filled with her essence. It meant he could find her and open a door to her no matter where she was. Now they could speak even while he was imprisoned, but it also meant he knew her exact location even when it was difficult to explain. At least he couldn't see her frown. "Vesper and I accidentally led Fairfrost guards to Quintus's house. We have to wait until day dawns before we go back to his house, just in case the guards are still there."

"*Fairfrost* guards?"

She gulped. "I tried to rescue you."

A rustle of fabric flitted through the door. She guessed he had probably sat down on a blanket of some kind. "I wondered. An entire squad came to guard me suddenly. I could not tell any reason why. They are finally gone now."

Trailing a thumb along the hem of her leather shirt, she let her other fingers slide through her hair. "That was simply my first attempt. I just have to figure out a different plan, and then—"

"You need to accept that rescuing me might be impossible."

She scoffed. "It is not impossible. I know I can do it." She had to do it. Faerie needed Brannick to save it. Without him, everything was falling apart.

"How do you *know?*" His voice came out soft, but it had an edge to it.

Her toes dug into the wet sand while her throat thickened. "You have to be rescued. I know I can do it because…" A burning sensation filled her throat while she tried to think of anything she could say that wasn't an outright lie. "I know I can do it—"

"Because you have done it before," he finished.

She gulped.

Responding right away might have eased tensions in that moment, but she couldn't even breathe. Her fists had curled into the sand at her sides. The grains dug into her palms while she squeezed tighter and tighter. Tight pains stretched across her chest while warnings pinged in her mind.

Silence filled the space between them, which made him feel even farther away than Fairfrost. At last, she sucked in a shallow breath. "You remember?" She whispered the words, unable to speak any louder than that while Kaia's warnings pounded through her mind.

The dryad had insisted Brannick must never find out Elora had been the one to rescue him from Fairfrost the first time he had been there. Kaia said it was his one victory and that finding out he hadn't even done it on his own would break him.

When Brannick spoke again, Elora latched onto the sound of his voice. Did he sound broken?

He cleared his throat. "I had a dream about my escape, but it was different from what I remembered. And it felt a little too much like a memory. Then, I was holding your crystal one night, and…"

"Kaia said we are connected." Maybe talking could distract him from being upset. Elora even tried to smile, hoping it would make her tone more approachable. "She said you might remember once I got my memories back."

"Kaia." He huffed, which was followed by the sound of rustling clothes. Maybe he was leaning against a wall. "I wish I could blame her for keeping it secret, but she was right."

"Right about what?" Elora had to force the words out. She couldn't help how every single one came out strained.

"You must give up." His gruff voice gave her the perfect image of the face he must be wearing. Though she couldn't see them, something in her knew his eyes had gone dull and lifeless.

Forcing her hands to release the sand they had been gripping, she placed them into her lap. "What do you mean?"

His huff came out so fast, it nearly sounded like a hiss. "Stop trying to rescue me. Go back to the mortal realm if you must. Just leave this place and all its woes. Leave before you get hurt any more."

"I will not leave." Her hands had formed fists again, but this time they pounded the sand at her sides. "And I will not give up. Just because my first plan failed does not—"

"I am not fit to be High King anyway." He started out strong, but his voice wavered now. He cleared his throat. "I am not good enough for Faerie." His voice lowered a notch and turned husky. "I am not strong enough."

Her hands relaxed as she leaned toward his door. "Brannick."

"Do not try to change my mind. You cannot."

71

She tried to keep herself from sniffing as she used the back of her hand to wipe away a few tears. She had to save Brannick so he could save Faerie, but how could he save Faerie like this?

Aches tore through her throat. "I will not give up." Her voice was so tiny, she wasn't even sure he'd be able to hear it.

He didn't answer. She swallowed and waited, but he said nothing. A sigh escaped his door. She could hear a movement, probably him shaking his head. He *had* heard her, then.

Reaching into her pocket, she wrapped her fingers around the crystal containing Brannick's essence. She held onto it like her life depended on it. His silence worried her, but he hadn't closed his Faerie door at least. Maybe he just didn't know what to say.

She sat forward, leaning closer to the door. "How is Blaz?"

Brannick let out a long, deep sigh. "They will not feed him. I share my food with him, but it is not enough for either of us. He is used to hunting on his own each morning, but now he is stuck inside this prison with me."

Her eyebrows pinched together. "If you make it bigger, can he come through your door? He could hunt here in Swiftsea and then return to you."

At those words, Blaz himself howled. He had never sounded so weak.

Brannick sighed again. "He will not leave me."

Elora jumped to her feet and scanned the beach. She found a coconut lodged between two rocks and snatched it up at once. "I need you to make your door a little bigger."

Once the door grew to the size of a plate, she tossed the coconut through.

Brannick hummed at the sight of it. "He needs meat." A beat of quiet passed, but then he hurried on to add, "But this will help."

Knots twisted inside her gut, already fearing for the prince's wolf. She ran down the beach and into the salty water. Drawing her sword, she scanned the water for any sign of fish. When something darted just ahead, she stabbed her sword at it.

Maybe it hadn't been a fish at all, but whatever it was, it got away.

She frowned and popped the wings from her back.

Brannick didn't seem to realize she had moved away from his door. Luckily, with her fae hearing, she could still hear his voice. "Blaz was with me when I was in Fairfrost before, but I was not imprisoned then."

Now that she flew above the ocean, Elora could see the fish more easily. She jabbed her sword at a few of them, but they swam away too quickly.

The prince's voice lowered. "Blaz could get out to hunt then, but now he cannot." His voice got tight. "He is wasting away."

Her eyes fluttered closed while she attempted to hold back her tears. With her chin trembling, she gripped her sword with a new energy. Maybe she couldn't help much on her own, but her sword had always been there for her. It had always been steady. She trusted it to help her now.

Taking a deep breath, she welcomed the tingling that broke out across her fingertips. She could feel the glow coming off her sword even before she saw it. Closing her eyes again, she let the sword guide her. It had magic from Faerie itself, after all. She could trust it to guide the way.

When she jabbed her blade into the ocean again, she could feel that it struck at least one target. After opening her eyes, she found two large fish speared by the sword.

The knots in her gut finally loosened.

Once she returned back to shore, she tossed the two fish through the door.

"How did you…"

She wished she could have savored the surprise in Brannick's voice just a little longer.

Sliding the sword back into her belt, she stood tall. "Do not give up yet. High Queen Alessandra is using despair to make everyone feel like giving up. Soon, no one will be able to fight against her at all." She swallowed. "It sounds like she is manipulating you in the same way."

"Despair." He whispered the word. "That describes it well."

"Maybe you do not believe in yourself right now, which is fine. Just believe in me instead. I *will* rescue you." She had to. Faerie needed Brannick to save it.

Something sparked inside his voice. It filled her chest with a growing warmth. "Then I will believe in you."

Closing her eyes, she gripped her sword hilt. If she couldn't get into Fairfrost Palace while glamoured to be invisible, she would just have to do it another way. She had gotten in easily the first time by being disguised as a servant.

That would have to work again. She'd just find some servant clothes. And if the others argued too much about her idea, she'd simply learn how to open a door and get to Fairfrost herself.

CHAPTER 9

When day dawned the next morning, Elora and the others returned to Quintus's home in Bitter Thorn. Cracks spread all through the clay and moss ceiling. Every few moments, something would slam against the roof from the outside. The entire house shuddered whenever that happened.

The whistling shrieks and black thorns that dug into the house made it clear that demorogs caused the damage. At least the Fairfrost guards had gone.

With his mouth open wide, Quintus placed a palm on one wall. "My house." His voice caught.

Stroking a finger over the purple ribbon in her blonde hair, Chloe stepped to his side. She bit her lip nervously before addressing him. "If the ceiling breaks, we can rebuild it once this is all over, right? I'm sure it will be fine."

Flashing his teeth, Quintus let out a hiss. "It will *not* be fine."

Chloe stepped back, her jaw clenching tight. "Yelling at me isn't fine either. I know you're upset, but that doesn't mean you get to yell at me."

"I miss Mother and Father," Grace whimpered as she fiddled with the purple ribbon tied to her belt.

"Go cook something, Grace." Chloe gave a flippant wave toward the kitchen. "It always makes you feel better."

With eyes turning wild, Quintus reared on Chloe. "You can yell at her, but I cannot yell at you?" He scoffed. "Such hypocrisy."

Her jaw clenched even tighter. "Don't start with me, Quintus. I—"

Before she could finish, Vesper stepped between them and placed both his hands on Chloe's shoulders. His face looked as limp as a curl that had been soaked with rain. "Stop. I cannot take it anymore."

Everyone in the room seemed to feel a jolt of guilt at the same moment. It festered along Elora's arms, reminding her of her failed rescue.

Vesper flopped into the nearest chair and buried his face in his hands. Chloe immediately sat down next to him. She whispered soothing words and patted his arm, but he acted as though she didn't exist.

Quintus scowled at the pair of them until his face twisted into a frown. He too buried his face in his hands.

On the other side of the room, Lyren shot various enchantments from her fingertips. The shimmery blue, silver, and foamy white enchantments surrounded the room, but they did nothing to stop the despair that thickened around them.

Tears welled in Lyren's eyes when she shot an ocean blue enchantment out. Her fingers shook as much as her chin did. "Why am I not strong enough?"

Tears fell then. They slipped down her dark cheeks, landing on the muted fabric of her blue dress.

They needed help. Elora lifted her hand, but she didn't reach for her sword hilt. This time, she ran a finger over the purple ribbons braided into her belt. The ribbons had once been a part of her old skirt. They were only simple ribbons now, but they were the last thing she had from her mother.

Elora wanted to help the others. She was *desperate* to do so. But what could she do?

Reaching for her sword hilt now, she straightened her back. She had to save Brannick. That was their only chance.

While the others sniffed and bickered, she snuck into the bedroom she and her sisters had been staying in. Sneaking away was easy since everyone else was too deep in their despair to notice a little movement.

The moment she entered the room, a little glowing light flew down to her. Tansy's pink dress hung as limp as Vesper's face, but the sprite's face held a devious smirk. "Maybe your rescue only failed because you have not figured out your magic yet."

Opening a wardrobe that stood against one wall, Elora sighed. "I have been thinking the same thing."

Dozens of dresses winked in the light of Tansy's green glow. Elora riffled through them one by one. Fine silks and soft gossamers formed most of the clothes. The simple suede and leathers most Bitter Thorn fae wore had no place here. Since Chloe had likely dictated to Brannick exactly what sort of clothing to conjure, it made sense that the dresses were luxurious and poufy. Unfortunately, that also made them entirely impractical for what she needed.

Tansy flitted over to the dresses, landing on a pretty mauve one. "Why do you need new clothes?"

"When we got to Fairfrost, our glamours immediately vanished. I think High Queen Alessandra created an enchantment that removes glamours. That means I need to disguise myself as a servant when I enter the palace." She crouched down and pulled out a large drawer at the bottom of the wardrobe.

Piles of more practical outfits sat inside, but these looked too Bitter Thorn for a Fairfrost servant.

Frowning, Tansy landed on a pair of brown leather pants that were much thinner than they looked. "These will not work." Her face screwed into a knot. "I do not think any of your friends are good at conjuring clothing."

Elora huffed. "I worried about that."

Tansy flitted upward, hovering near the dresses once again.

Either way, Elora's leather pants and shirt had too many scratches and holes now. She needed something new to wear. Her fingers trailed over the dresses.

She reached for the mauve dress her sprite friend had landed on earlier. Shimmery gossamer fabric formed a tight-fitting bodice with a sweetheart neckline. It gathered at the waist with line of silver beadwork trailing the waist in a belt-like adornment. Dozens of layers of mauve gossamer formed a full skirt that would land just below her ankles. Embroidery and silver beadwork adorned the skirt and over the entire bodice. The embroidery threads were mauve like the dress, but so rich in color, they almost looked like jewels. Thin, looped strands of crystal beads formed the sleeves.

She pulled the elegant dress over her head and let it flutter around her. The full skirt and many layers would allow her free movement without having to worry about revealing anything.

Best of all, the dress had deep pockets that cleverly placed embroidery hid perfectly. The dress would be easy to move in, it would hide anything she needed to hide, but it was exquisite enough to look fit for royalty.

With the new dress in place, Elora sat down at the desk her middle sister usually frequented. Chloe's books about Faerie littered the surface. Many of them were open with bits of ripped paper marking certain passages or pages.

Tansy landed on a book in the corner and then flew over to sit on Elora's shoulder. "That one might be useful if you want to learn more about Faerie magic."

Elora reached for it, but that didn't stop a twinge of embarrassment washing over her. *Of course* Tansy knew the exact reason she had sat down. Maybe every new fae was desperate to learn about their magic like she was. Even if they were, that knowledge didn't make her feel any better.

She thumbed through a few pages while Tansy offered commentary on things most fae were born knowing. Since Elora hadn't actually been born fae, she found each bit of information fascinating. She chose to keep that to herself though.

Several pages had passed when a familiar phrase seemed to jump out at her from the page.

When magic calls, you must answer.

The words stole her breath for a moment. Brannick had said those same words to her when she asked him about how to access her magic. He had something about change as well, but she only remembered the magic part of it now.

When magic calls, you must answer.

She repeated the words in her head several times, willing them to sink in deep.

Ever since becoming fae, she had always sought magic when she needed it, but maybe it went the other way around. Maybe she needed to accept the magic when it came to her instead.

Her head craned toward her shoulder. "What is the easiest type of magic to access?"

Tansy raised an eyebrow. "Every fae has a different type of magic. What is easiest for you will be difficult for another."

"That is not what I mean. There are some things every fae can do easily. You all have magical pockets. You can all open doors."

The sprite clicked her tongue. "Sprites cannot open doors."

Elora blinked. "Oh." She blinked again before shaking her head. "But you do have the magical pockets, and even if sprites cannot open doors, almost all other fae can. Are any of those types of magic easier than others?"

"I understand what you are saying." Tansy's wings lifted her into the air. She tilted her head to the side with her eyes narrowed. "Usually, when a fae purposefully uses magic for the first time, it is to open a door. But most fae do magic unintentionally a few times before they do it on purpose."

The words lit like a spark inside Elora's chest. "A door. I knew I was right to try doing that first."

From outside the room, a loud crash sounded.

Elora jumped to her feet. She glanced toward the closed bedroom door and slammed the book shut. She needed to learn how to open a door. And she still needed the right clothes to disguise herself as a Fairfrost servant. A glamour wouldn't work, but maybe she could find someone else to conjure servant's clothing for her.

Shouts rang out.

She *didn't* need a group of fae and mortals who continuously bickered until they devolved into tears. She had no energy to deal with such things.

Another crash sounded, followed by even louder shouts.

Sighing, she stomped toward the door. When she pushed her way into the kitchen, chaos was too mild a word to describe the scene.

Chloe's blonde hair whipped around her face in tear-damped strands. She held a large clay pot, which was poised to be thrown straight at Quintus's face. He glared at her with fiery eyes and clenched fists, practically begging her to throw the pot.

Vesper had curled himself into a ball, rocking back and forth on the floor. Grace cowered in a corner. She gripped a ribbon tight and closed her eyes even tighter.

Lyren sobbed as she shot more and more enchantments from her fingertips. Each one looked weaker than the last.

Elora knew she was closer than ever to accessing her magic. She had a new plan for Brannick's rescue brewing, which had a much higher chance of success than her last attempt. But the others needed help *now*. She couldn't keep ignoring them.

Stepping between Chloe and Quintus before her middle sister could throw the clay pot, Elora shook Quintus's shoulder. As she moved, a wonderful thought entered her mind.

She raised both her eyebrows, hoping Quintus would recognize her seriousness despite his dark attitude. She gripped his shoulder tighter for good measure. "Open a door to Bitter Thorn Castle."

Her fierce expression must have done it. He stared for only a moment before he shook his head. In the next moment, he opened a door.

CHAPTER 10

Decaying scents mingled with the mossy and crisp air in Bitter Thorn. Elora's fingers hadn't sparked with purple bursts when they all entered the door that took them there. They hadn't sparked when she went to Fairfrost with Vesper either.

Perhaps traveling with others had prevented the purple sparks. Or perhaps the earlier doors had changed destinations for an entirely different reason that had nothing to do with her purple sparks at all.

Even with the decaying scents, hope swelled in her chest just from being so close to the castle. She had felt useless to help the others for so long, but when she needed it, an idea had finally come.

Brannick always went to Kaia when he needed help with his essence. Maybe Kaia could help them now.

Elora's hope crashed to a halt when she saw a line of bickering fae leading up to the dryad's tree. Apparently, Kaia had a well-known reputation as a fae who could heal. Elora's mouth twisted into a knot. Would it be wrong for them to ignore the line and ask Kaia to help them first?

Chloe and Quintus bickered loudly, but they also stepped to the back of the line without any prompting. Lyren and Grace followed, both of them sobbing into their hands. Vesper's entire body wilted. He didn't cry, but he hardly moved. He looked ready to be whisked away at the lightest breeze.

It still seemed like a good idea to ignore the line and march straight to Kaia's tree for help first. They were going to rescue Brannick, weren't they? Surely, no other Bitter Thorn fae needed help as much as they did.

But at the back of Elora's mind, an entirely new thought bloomed. It sat so far back, she hardly even noticed it at all. She didn't make a firm decision to leave the others at the back of the line while she trailed ahead, but somehow, she started doing it anyway.

Her feet continued to move, almost of their own accord. She trudged forward without any thought. The slightest inkling told her she was almost there.

But where? Her mind started spinning then. Doubting. Why did she suddenly move forward like that?

Only then did she notice the purple sparks at her fingertips. Had her magic led her forward? Could it do that when she didn't even know how it worked?

In a flash, the sparks disappeared.

She wanted to believe in her magic. She wanted to accept it. But now that her mind began working, it all seemed too good to be true. She didn't even know what kind of magic she had.

She hadn't even opened a door yet. Assuming her magic had led her there was probably nothing more than wishful thinking.

Her lips pulled downward while disappointment washed over her. With her chin dropping to her chest, she spun on her heel to return to the others.

Just as she turned, a nearby voice made her feet freeze in place.

"I can conjure clothing all day long, but my mother has no need of more clothing. She just wants the purple berries my father used to bring her. Do they really exist? I have never seen purple berries before." He sniffled as he spoke the words.

With her back turned away from the mysterious fae, Elora leaned her ear toward him.

A female fae who sounded even more distressed answered his question. "I believe those berries only grow near Bitter Thorn Castle."

The rest of the conversation didn't matter. Elora grabbed a fistful of the gossamer layers of her gown and sprinted into the forest.

She knew where to find the purple berries. Her brownie, Fifer, loved them. She left them as an offering for him as often as she could. All thought of the sparks at her fingertips had vanished. Now she could only think of the berries and the fae who wanted them. A fae who could conjure clothing was exactly what she needed to get servant clothes for a disguise.

At the edge of a trickling stream, she crouched down to gather purple berries from a small bush. Soon, she had two handfuls. Carefully gathering her skirt to hold the berries, she darted back to the line of fae.

Holding her skirt out, she presented the berries to the fae who had been asking about them. His eyebrows flew upward, but then a sparkle glinted in his puffy red eyes.

"Purple berries," he said through a laugh.

For a moment, the despair that constantly bombarded the air seemed to drift away. The fae's eyes stopped drooping. A smile formed at the corner of his mouth.

He reached for the berries, but Elora took a step back. She had to tilt her head to catch his eye. "I need you to conjure an outfit for me. Once you do, you can have the berries."

He raised an eyebrow. "Very well." The fae acted as though he was getting the better end of this deal. Maybe he would have felt differently if he had any idea how desperately she needed the servant's clothes.

Now that the memories of her first visit to Fairfrost had been restored, she could describe in detail what her servant clothes should look like. He conjured them with ease, expertly making adjustments as she asked for them.

Just as she finished, shouting and shoving broke out somewhere near the back of the line. Her heart stammered as she held the berries out for the fae to take. The shouting grew louder.

Maybe an entirely different group of fae had caused the commotion, but it seemed more likely that her sisters were involved.

She snatched the servant's clothes from the fae the moment he finished them. While she ran, she stuffed them into the pocket of her gown.

Getting back to her sisters and the others took longer than it had to leave them, but maybe it only felt that way because she had more anxiety now.

Her heart stammered with each step. The bright spot of hope she felt while getting the servant's clothes snuffed out completely. She could think only of her sisters and what danger could have caused them to shout.

But when she caught up with them, they were fine.

Well, they weren't *fine*. Their hair had gone stringy because they kept stroking it too much. Tears stained their cheeks and their noses and eyes were puffy. At least they looked better than Vesper. He had curled himself into a ball once again. Now, he rocked back and forth over a patch of moss on the forest floor.

Quintus threw rocks at the nearest tree, seeming to take pleasure in how they nicked the damp bark. Lyren held her arms over her stomach and kept sniveling.

They weren't fine. But they were safe. They hadn't been injured, anyway.

Turning to Chloe since she looked the sanest, Elora asked, "What happened? I heard shouting."

Her middle sister blinked twice before answering. "Oh, that." She gave her head a hard shake before continuing. "I don't know. It came from over there."

Elora followed her sister's vague gesture toward a path that led to Bitter Thorn Castle. Another shout rang out, even more terrifying than the first. Whoever screamed stood too far away to see from there.

Should she try to find out what had happened?

Getting to Kaia and rescuing Brannick seemed much more important than finding out what some random fae was screaming about. But maybe that was just her new, selfish fae nature speaking. If *she* was in trouble, she would want someone to come for her. And that scream *did* sound terrifying.

Biting her lip, she turned to face the others once again. Maybe she'd ask what they thought. Once she looked into the devastated eyes, she realized how ridiculous that plan was. They were in no state to make any sort of decisions.

Before any other ideas could dance through her mind, her sisters disappeared. She sucked in a gasp and reached out for them.

She immediately felt their arms, which meant they hadn't actually disappeared. They had only been glamoured to be invisible. But only one thing made them turn invisible automatically.

Ansel.

Gripping her sisters' arms tight, she yanked them toward the nearest tree. Lyren and Quintus dashed after them without a word. Vesper stayed curled in his ball. Even when Elora shouted at him, he just rocked back and forth over the moss.

By the time they hid behind the tree, all of them had turned invisible. Lyren or Quintus must have glamoured the rest of them too. Glancing over her shoulder, Elora noted that Vesper had also turned invisible.

That's when she finally noticed the rocky, gray door at the edge of the forest. Ansel stepped out of it with his yellow eyes glowing. When he saw the line of fae in front of him, a wicked grin skittered across his face.

CHAPTER 11

Even standing behind a tree, even being invisible and clearly out of Ansel's sight, Elora still shook at the sight of him. She clenched her fists, her jaw, her stomach, hoping it might calm the palpitations in her throbbing heart. If she couldn't get herself under control, the slimy fae would probably hear her panting breaths.

He scanned the fae before him, his yellow eyes glowing more with each fae he spotted.

It was strange to see him when he clearly had no idea Elora stood nearby. He looked at the fae with the same greedy eyes she had assumed he only used on her. It should have been obvious considering the numerous *pets* he kept in the loft of his house. Still, the look grated on her nerves as effectively as if he were staring straight into her eyes.

While scanning the crowd, his fingers twitched at his side. A grin flickered across his lips. It wouldn't lead to anything good.

In a flash, he lunged forward and grabbed a female fae from the crowd by the wrist. When he tried to yank her backward and away from the crowd, he stumbled over his feet.

Elora's heart jumped into her throat.

Vesper.

Ansel had stumbled as if he had tripped over something, but nothing appeared to be in his way. But Elora knew Vesper's invisible body was close by. Her fists clenched tighter when Ansel threw a furious glare at the ground.

The female fae he had gripped took his moment of distraction to shove him and sprint away.

Pain trickled down the side of Elora's neck when she glanced at Ansel once again. She wanted to move. She wanted to draw her sword and slice it across every working part of his body. Instead, fear froze her in place behind the tree. Fear sent pain through her neck in all the places he had cut her to get blood.

The other fae clearly had no sense of how dangerous Ansel could be. They simply looked at him curiously while continuing to cave into the despair that plagued them.

Why didn't the despair affect Ansel?

By the time she asked herself the question, she had already found a white mountain flower pinned to Ansel's lapel next to a red gemstone. High Queen Alessandra must have imbued the flower with love or some other emotion that counteracted the despair. He probably hadn't allowed her to manipulate him as completely as all those Noble Rose fae she manipulated, but one thing was certain. He and the high queen were still clearly working together.

He scanned the crowd again, stepping forward with greater purpose. Too many tears and dropped chins existed in the crowd for anyone to properly avoid him. Soon, he grabbed a male fae and yanked him away from the others.

This time, Ansel didn't trip on anything as he walked.

Just when Elora thought someone in the crowd might try to fight against Ansel, the male fae crumpled into a ball and began rocking on the ground the way Vesper had been doing earlier.

Ansel let out a chuckle at the sight. Immediately after, he reached into his pocket and pulled out a shimmery box made of marble. A little door with a silvery latch sat at the front of the box.

The sight of it ignited a memory in Elora, but it wisped away at the edges until she had nothing left of it to hold.

Standing taller, Ansel grinned at the fae in front of him.

The grin burned into Elora's mind. It pulsed and crackled then licked out its flames.

Yellow eyes. A knife at the neck. Chains that held her still.

Elora's gut clenched so tight, she nearly doubled over. She slammed a palm against the tree at her side to remind herself she wasn't in Fairfrost anymore.

It took all her willpower just to force a shallow breath inside her mouth. She followed it with a sharp gasp that made her feel like the air was suddenly suffocating her.

"Quintus." Chloe whispered, but the sound felt like a knife stabbing Elora's ears.

"I see it," he responded.

"*Hush.*" Elora spoke much louder than she intended. Her gut immediately clenched tighter until she could peek around the tree and confirm Ansel had not noticed their whispers.

He hadn't. Or maybe he was too busy reaching for the silver latch on his strange device to care about the sound.

When Elora spoke again, she did it under her breath. "Do *not* speak again. Do not even make a noise."

Ansel flicked the silver latch on his marble box. Once moved to the side, he could open the little door in the front of his device.

The male fae in front of him started coughing immediately. Soon, his coughing turned to choking. He bent at the waist and convulsed. Red splotches crawled up his neck and into the light brown skin of his face. A moment later, the fae collapsed onto the ground.

Producing a knife, Ansel leaned over the fae just long enough to cut a small slit in his neck.

The world went black.

Elora knew it wasn't really black. She could hear her sisters breathing. Wet tree bark still sat beneath her palm. But seeing the knife, seeing the slit that produced blood, her body rebelled.

She was breathing faster than ever, unable to catch her breath. Shouts sounded all around her. Or maybe they were in her mind. Everything felt blurry. Shaky.

Someone patted her arm until finding her hand.

As she squeezed Elora's hand, Chloe whispered, "Are you okay?"

The world came back in that moment. Every breath Elora took still shuddered through her, but at least she *could* breathe.

Elora squeezed her sister's hand. She took in a deep breath that only skimmed her lungs instead of filling them. "Not yet."

Chloe moved close enough to wrap her arms about Elora's waist. Breathing came easier then. Only slightly, but it still helped.

Finally, she could peek around the tree once again.

Ansel had made an emerald gemstone from the male fae's blood. He shoved one foot against the fae's chest, keeping him tight against the ground. While holding the fae down, Ansel examined the gemstone between his fingers.

The marble device with the little door must have had an iron talisman inside it. Brannick had stolen three talismans from High Queen Alessandra already. Ansel still had the last one in his possession. He had clearly used it to weaken the fae's blood enough to draw power from him.

But Ansel didn't look as weak or as tired as he had after making the gemstones from Elora's blood. Maybe having less power also meant it took less energy to create the gemstones.

Either way, the fae's emerald gemstone would still be powerful, just maybe not as powerful as the gemstones made from her blood.

With his foot still digging into the fae's chest, Ansel waved his free hand. At first, it didn't seem like he had done any magic.

Then the shrieking began.

Loud, whistling shrieks filled the air around them. Demorogs flapped their thorny wings, each flying closer to the gathered crowd. Ansel's grin lifted when the creatures swooped toward him.

He waved his hand again.

The shrieks multiplied.

Demorogs flew at the crowd, slicing anyone with their thorns that they could reach. Many of them flew into the crowd, but most of them shot toward Ansel.

His face stayed steady as they circled around him. When two demorogs swooped down to claw at his face, he gave no reaction at all. He just grabbed one of the demorogs by its thorny foot.

Two new demorogs attacked, clawing at Ansel's shoulders, head, and arms. He continued to ignore everything except the demorog's foot he held tight in his grip. With a sharp punch, he thrust his other fist into the demorog's stomach.

It didn't make any sense. The demorogs had no innards. They were made from the black thorns that infested Bitter Thorn. They were part of the curse on Brannick's court. What did Ansel think he could accomplish by punching the thorn creature?

Just as the question flitted through Elora's mind, she noticed he had pushed the newly made gemstone into a bed of thorns. Now it sat embedded in the demorog's stomach.

As if Faerie itself knew something sinister was about to happen, the air thickened with the scent of decay.

Elora's stomach twisted. She sucked in a breath, trying to convince herself it wouldn't be so bad.

Ansel grabbed the demorog's foot again, curling the thorns backward until the demorog's claws pointed inside its stomach along with the gemstone. With its other three feet and with its wings, the creature beat at Ansel from every angle possible.

The other demorogs around him fought with equal ferocity. Their actions did nothing to stop him.

Ansel twisted the thorns until the sharpest one could reach the gemstone embedded in its stomach. Once it got close enough, he shoved the thorn deep until the demorog itself crushed the emerald stone.

Blinding light exploded out of the gemstone. It filled the air with an energy that stung everything it touched. Elora had to grip the tree in front of her to keep from collapsing.

The light then turned to a whipping wind that blasted Elora's hair back. The wind blew so fast a part of her worried it might rip her clothes and even her hair right off her body.

Leaves got ripped off every tree around them. Half of the leaves flew off at once. It would only take another moment until the other half joined.

When the wind finally died down, a thick mist crackled around them. It carried a stinging energy that sent Elora's nerves into a fit. The mist eventually faded, but the stinging sensation worsened.

Most of the fae in the crowd had fallen to their hands and knees. The male fae at Ansel's feet wailed and rocked his body back and forth.

A malicious grin worked across Ansel's features. The four demorogs that had been attacking him suddenly curled in on themselves. They faded until their black thorns turned to a sickly gray. With a snap of his fingers, the creatures exploded into bits of ash. They must have had some kind of magic inside them still because they hovered in the air, refusing to fall to the ground.

Something had happened, but no one seemed to understand exactly what. Elora did understand one thing perfectly well though. Ansel had forced the demorog to crush his gemstone. Ansel had scratches across his skin from the demorog's attacks, but those were already fading. Since he hadn't actually used the gemstone, he wasn't weakened at all by crushing it. In fact, he looked stronger than ever.

Whimpers broke out followed by harrowed whispers. Some of the stronger fae got up and ran deep into the forest.

Ansel ignored them. He scanned the crowd again, probably for his next victim.

Fear shook through every limb in Elora's body. Her nerves were like jagged shards of ice. But something hot and prickly burned through the fear. Devoured it.

Something snapped.

Her icy fear transformed into a seething, fiery anger.

Being ruled by anger could lead to trouble, but this was different. She had *earned* this anger. After everything Ansel had put her through, she deserved to have anger burn away the last of her fear.

She *needed* this anger.

Clenching her fists tight, she allowed the anger to engulf every last ice crystal that tried to cling to her heart. She embraced it. She let it fuel her.

When she took another deep breath, it wasn't too shallow. For the first time since Ansel appeared in the forest, she breathed in deeply.

Ansel marched forward with his eyes on a female fae who shivered in a heap on the ground.

Burning flames seemed to lick Elora's fingertips as she gripped her sword hilt. She knew exactly how it felt to be hurt by Ansel. She could no longer sit back and let another being feel the same way.

She stepped out from behind the tree. The glamour keeping her invisible stayed in place, but suddenly, she didn't care anymore. Even without a glamour, her actions would have been the same.

Drawing her sword, she charged forward. The purple glow it emitted had almost become familiar, but it let out showers of purple sparks as well.

The crackling must have been loud enough to hear because Ansel jerked his head toward her. His eyes narrowed while he scanned what looked like an empty space ahead of him.

Baring her teeth, she let out the fiercest growl she could manage.

His eyes widened. His feet stumbled backward while his eyes darted back and forth trying to find his attacker.

He could look all he wanted, but it wouldn't stop her from slicing him open.

Maybe he could feel her anger even without seeing her. With a quick wave of one hand, he opened a door. Just before she could reach him, he stepped inside it and disappeared.

She almost went after him, eager to plunge her sword inside his chest, but the door vanished before she could.

Her heart sank at his disappearance, but she was grateful for one thing.

She was ready to face him now. Fear would not control her anymore.

CHAPTER

12

With fists clenched tight, Elora slammed her sword back into her belt. Bright leaves scattered across the mossy forest ground. Even with half the leaves still on their branches, the trees looked empty and sad. The moss didn't look spongy either. It wilted with a brownish hue.

Demorogs circled the air above, shrieking louder than ever. They did not swoop down to attack, but that likely wouldn't last for long.

More than half the fae who had been there before had already run off into the forest. Most of the others were getting to their feet to do the same. A handful of fae sat on the ground in heaps of leather and glossy black hair.

Those fae hugged against the ground, apparently with no desire to leave it. A few of them let out soft whimpers, but some of them didn't move at all.

Gulping, Elora turned toward the dryad's tree that seemed much closer with the rest of the fae gone. Someone had made Elora visible again. She didn't even notice until she tripped over Vesper, who had also been turned visible.

He glanced up at her when she offered him a hand, but he didn't take it. He didn't look sad. He didn't even look desperate. His face held no expression at all, which sent a jab right to her heart.

Turning toward the dryad's tree again, she shook her head. She'd have to deal with Vesper later. Once she rescued Brannick and they overthrew the high queen, the despair in the air would vanish. Then Vesper would be okay.

After traipsing over piles of fallen leaves and mounds of moist dirt, Elora finally reached the tree with emerald-green moss.

"Kaia." Elora wanted to reach out to the touch the bark, but her fingertips stopped before she could reach it. Was it rude to touch a dryad's tree?

After a moment, brown and green eyes appeared in the bark. They held none of the splendor they usually did, but they still managed to look older than ever. Water glinted against the bark. It almost looked like tears.

"My child. I never thought Bitter Thorn would be reduced to *this*. I wish you did not have to see it."

A lump bulged inside Elora's throat. Swallowing it down did nothing. "What was that?" She gestured over the forest. "The light, the wind."

None of Kaia's body was visible except her eyes, yet she still managed to look downcast. "It is the curse on Bitter Thorn. I do not understand how Ansel did it, but he made the curse stronger here. Our court will be reduced to nothing before long."

Swallowing still did nothing for the lump in Elora's throat, but maybe she could ignore it. Reaching into her pocket, she grabbed the servant's clothes she had secured just before Ansel arrived. In the next breath, she tore the mauve gossamer gown off her body.

Kaia raised an eyebrow, although the eyebrow was actually a striation in the bark. At least the action had distracted the dryad from her pain.

Elora reached for the white top embroidered with red and blue flowers the fae had made. She buttoned it as fast as she could before pulling on the full skirt that came to her ankles. "I need you to open a door for me. Have it open in the ice forest near Fairfrost Palace but not directly in front of the palace."

Pattering footsteps indicated the others in her group had finally caught up to her.

"Where did you get those clothes?" Lyren's voice came out more strained than curious.

Grace jumped forward. Her red hair glistened as she grabbed her oldest sister's arm. "Don't go to Fairfrost." She shuddered as she sucked in another breath. "You almost got caught last time."

"Last time?" The eyebrow-like striation in the bark curved even higher above Kaia's eye.

"That was only because I used a glamour and Fairfrost has a new enchantment that takes glamours away." Elora tightened the belt over her white linen and red wool skirt. She couldn't look in her youngest sister's eyes or she might lose her nerve. "I have a disguise now. I do not need a glamour to sneak into the palace. As long as the high queen does not see me, I will be safe."

Kaia stepped out of her tree. Her hair had vines and leaves growing through it. Her dark skin had the same striations as the bark behind her. She needed to be in her tree right now. If the vines and striations were so thick, she needed the magic of her tree to recover. But maybe she just felt her next words were so important, she had to say them in her fae form. The dryad gulped. "High Queen Alessandra will know as soon as you enter her palace. She will sense your magic."

Elora lifted the ward necklace from Tindra that still hung around her neck. "Not with this she won't." She tucked the bright pendant under the high collar of her white blouse until it was hidden completely.

Though distress still warped the brightness in Kaia's eyes, the dryad stepped back into her tree with a nod.

Quintus pointed upward, capturing everyone's attention. "The demorogs." Before he could even finish speaking, two demorogs flew downward with their claws out.

Chloe gasped.

With her servant clothes in place, Elora reached for the braided belt that normally held her sword. The belt sat in her hands for only a moment before she realized it couldn't be hidden without a glamour. And it would probably be suspicious for a servant to wear a sword.

Before she could dwell on that fact, a demorog swooped down toward them.

Grace screamed and covered her head with both hands. The demorog flew back, but another took its place.

With eyes blinking inside the bark again, Kaia hissed at the thorn creatures.

Glancing down at Elora's sword, Chloe grabbed her sister's arm with both hands. "Don't go, Elora. What if we need you?"

Though the thorn creatures had yet to attack them, that probably wouldn't last. Nerves split into frayed edges inside Elora. She had to rescue Brannick as soon as possible, but she couldn't leave her sisters defenseless either.

Making the decision in a split second, Elora lifted her weapon toward her middle sister. "Take my sword. It has magic that can destroy the demorogs if they try to attack."

Lyren sniffed. Her knuckle caught a tear just before it fell from her eye. "Magic does not work that way."

"Yes, it does. Mine does." Without thinking about what she intended to do, Elora popped the wings from her back and flew into the sky. Her sword's purple glow and shower of sparks erupted as soon as her feet left the ground. Reaching the nearest demorog, she jabbed her blade inside it.

Creaking erupted from the thorn creature as it curled into a ball. Once the thorns had created a tight ball, they faded to a sickly gray and erupted into a shower of ash. Unlike the ash from Ansel's demorog that still hung in the air, this ash fluttered gently to the ground below.

Landing on her feet again, Elora shoved the sword into her middle sister's hands. Chloe took one look at the purple glow and immediately handed the weapon off to Lyren.

No matter. It would work just as well for Lyren as for anyone else. With her javelin training, Lyren was probably the most capable to use it anyway.

Elora turned to Kaia expectantly.

The dryad's eyes made a movement that looked almost like a nod. She stepped out from her tree once again. Her emerald hair looked shinier now, with only a few stray bits of branches and leaves. The bark-like striations in her skin had faded significantly. Waving her hand, a door appeared to the side.

Grace started saying something, but Elora didn't wait to hear it. She'd probably just ask her sister to stay, which would only delay things further. If Ansel had a way of amplifying the curse in Bitter Thorn, they needed Brannick back more than ever.

Elora's breath caught when she stepped onto a blanket of soft snow. Though it was soft, her feet still stung from the cold. Maybe she should have kept her boots instead of changing into the delicate shoes she had asked the fae to make her. The shoes matched her servant's attire perfectly, but they didn't go well with the snow.

Why did Fairfrost servants wear such impractical shoes anyway? A hard sigh escaped her when she realized the reason. It probably prevented them from running away.

Trees covered in a glass-like encasing of ice surrounded Elora on all sides. They glittered each time they caught the light. Shivering filled her limbs as she stepped forward.

Just like she remembered it, the Fairfrost air felt thick with silence. Billows of snow muffled any sound, which may have been peaceful in some circumstances. Now, it put her on edge knowing it would be more difficult to hear if anyone snuck up on her.

She took another step forward and snow collapsed all around her foot, covering it with an icy chill. Huffing, she shook the white flakes off her delicate shoes. Luckily, an idea sprang to her mind at that same moment.

Wings popped from her back. She stayed low to the ground to keep from calling any attention to herself, but at least she wouldn't have to trudge through the snow anymore.

She fluttered through the ice forest much faster once she used her wings. Soon, Fairfrost Palace came into view.

The tall white spires topped with dollops of golden ceilings were hardly the first thing she noticed. Soldiers in white brocade stood guard around the palace walls. *Hundreds* of soldiers. Her breath hitched as she found a stray ice tree to hide behind.

The guards didn't just form one row either. Craning her neck, she counted one, two, *three* rows of guards surrounding the palace. They didn't look especially attentive, which was probably the only reason she hadn't been caught yet.

Still, if she moved closer to the palace, at least one of them would notice her eventually. And since they all had a bargain with High Queen Alessandra that demanded they follow her every order, Elora would probably be captured or killed as soon as they spotted her.

Throbbing prickles worked through her chest every time her heart pounded, but she did her best to ignore them. Maybe this side of the palace had more guards than ever, but she should check the other sides before giving up.

Using her wings once again, she flew back into the ice forest slightly. Then, she began circling the entire palace. From the farther distance, she couldn't see the guards as clearly as before, but she could still make out three rows of guards along every side of the palace.

Refusing to let her heart sink, she continued to fly.

There had to be a way in.

She just needed a hidden door or even a small window that she could climb through. Her eyes strained as she stared at every nook and cranny of the palace. Eventually, she made it back to the side of the palace she had started on.

Three rows of guards surrounded the *entire* thing.

Clenching her jaw, she flew a little higher. She had wings, didn't she? Surely some of the windows near the top of the palace weren't as fiercely guarded as the lower windows.

That hope got dashed as soon as her eyes lifted. Soldiers in white brocade stood just inside every window.

Hope continued to flicker in her chest while her eyes darted across the palace a few more times. Faerie needed Brannick. There had to be a way to save him.

It only lasted another moment before Elora put away her wings and dropped onto the ground in a heap. Hot tears burned her cheeks as they slid down.

She couldn't do it on her own.

Even with wings, even with a disguise, she couldn't possibly sneak into a palace that heavily guarded. Her fingers curled into fists as she let the truth wash over.

She needed an army to save Brannick.

An army she didn't have.

For now, she'd just have to go back to the others. Hopefully Kaia had left her door open so Elora could get back to Bitter Thorn.

Getting to her feet again, she brushed the snow off her servant's clothes. She waved her hand through the air, thinking about the clearing near Kaia's tree. When she stumbled across a door with brown and green swirls and small splotches of purple, she walked straight through it without thinking to check that it looked like Kaia's door.

But who else could it have come from anyway?

After a few steps, her feet landed on the mossy ground of Bitter Thorn. Black thorns creaked under the weight of her delicate shoes. She landed in the clearing in the exact spot she had been imagining.

Soren and Fifer stood next to Kaia's tree now. Kaia stood with them, but her skin looked like bark once again.

Lyren, Quintus, Chloe, and Grace all stood nearby. They looked stricken. None of them even seemed to notice Elora and the door she had just walked through.

A pile of ash indicated they had used Elora's sword to destroy at least a few demorogs. None of them spoke to each other. They hardly looked like they were breathing.

Narrowing her eyes, Elora scanned the landscape, eager to find the reason for their demeanor. When she saw nothing but empty forest, it suddenly hit her all at once.

She gulped. "Where is Vesper?"

Several pairs of eyes glanced up at her question. It didn't look like any of them wanted to answer.

Stepping forward, Elora repeated her question with more force. "*Where* is Vesper?"

Grace burst into tears first, but Chloe followed soon after. Even Lyren shook with a sob.

Digging fingers into her matted red hair, Grace shook her head back and forth. "He left. He opened a door and left."

Chloe sniffed, trying to wipe away the sheet of tears on her cheeks. Her voice shook over every word. "He wouldn't tell us where he was going. He said he never wanted to see any of us again."

Elora took a step back, placing a hand over her open mouth.

Dropping a hand onto Chloe's shoulder, Quintus shook his head. "He looked… despondent. It was like he had no life left in him."

With knees shaking, Elora gripped the nearest tree. This was the exact opposite of what she needed. It would take an army to rescue Brannick. And now her brother had disappeared.

How much worse could things get?

CHAPTER

13

When despair slid under her skin, Elora had to fight harder to keep it out of her heart. She clutched the tree at her side. The bark dug into her palm, reminding her what was real and what was not. Vesper had disappeared. They had no idea where to find him.

She repeated the words in her head, but they didn't sink in. She could only think of the guards around Fairfrost Palace. She could only think of how her beloved was *still* trapped.

But with Vesper gone, every other problem seemed worse by tenfold.

Still in her fae form, Kaia dropped to the forest floor. Her shoulders hunched. Her hair lost its shine. "We are doomed."

Soren clutched his spear and hit the end of it against the ground. If he had kicked a rock or complained about the thorns crawling across the forest floor, it might have been easier to breathe. Instead, his face fell. He spoke under his breath. "I may never lead another army." He gulped. "The demorogs might kill us first."

With ears wilting, Fifer looked down at his spindly fingers.

Stepping toward him, Elora tilted her head to catch his eye. "Can you create an enchantment that—"

"No." Fifer's voice had never come out so low. His large eyes seemed to get smaller as he gestured toward the castle without looking. "My home is destroyed, my magic along with it."

She turned away from the brownie then. She turned away from everyone. She refused to even look at Chloe, Grace, Lyren, and Quintus. She already knew what she would see.

Dejected eyes. Fallen faces. She couldn't bear to see them now.

Someone had tossed Elora's sword onto the ground. Elora snatched it back up again. The sparks were gone, but a faint purple glow still emanated from the blade. She snatched up her braided belt next. Hoping it might give her courage, she trailed a finger along the purple ribbons from her mother, then she squeezed her sword hilt.

"We need an army." She cleared her throat but refused to face the others. "There are too many guards around Fairfrost Palace for me to sneak in. We will have to fight our way in instead."

The mauve gossamer gown sat in a small heap near the edge of the clearing. She shook it out, assessing it for damage. It still looked as enchanting as ever. Maybe she could head deeper into the forest and change back into it. That would give her the space she needed to think.

She shoved it into her pocket before she remembered the servant dress she wore didn't have any pockets. Yet the pocket still existed. A magical pocket.

Suddenly, another epiphany sparked in her mind.

The door. Had Kaia really left her door open or had the door come from someone else? Had Elora done it? Had she opened her *own* door?

A thousand ideas shoved against each other, all fighting for the front of her mind. But maybe she didn't want any thoughts in her head right now. Maybe acting would be better instead.

Without thinking, she raised one hand and gave it a gentle wave. Shimmery sparks of sage green erupted from her fingertips. The sparks twinkled with a purple hue. They rose high above the clearing and then began falling down around them. Once finished, a dome of enchantment sparkled around them.

The colors surged, but then they faded slightly, making the dome nearly transparent. Even better than the sparkly, translucent color, the enchantment also gave off warmth. It warmed them like the sun on a bright day. After a few moments, the air felt less suffocating. The conflicts they faced seemed bearable. The despair had weakened.

Shuffling footsteps sounded next to Elora. When she glanced to her side, Lyren was eyeing the enchantment with her jaw hanging open.

"What is it?"

Elora's question seemed to snap Lyren out of whatever trance held her. The Swiftsea fae tucked a curl behind her ear. "I have never seen magic like yours."

The fact that Elora even had used magic at all still seemed unreal. She couldn't deny it had happened, but she worried thinking about it too much would somehow make it vanish.

"Do we have any clues about where Vesper might have gone?" she asked. "We know he cannot go to his home court of Noble Rose ever since High King Romany banished him. He cannot go to the mortal realm to his beloved either. Does he have any other favorite places?"

Picking herself up off the ground Chloe dusted away the moist dirt that stuck to her dress. "I never asked him about that. Why didn't I ever think to ask where he liked to go?"

Grace pulled a handkerchief from her pocket and wiped under her eyes. "He has traveled all over Faerie. Maybe everywhere is his favorite place to go."

With his eyes turned upward, Quintus took in a deep breath. It was as if he tried to soak in whatever warmth the enchantment gave off. Under its twinkling light, his skin did seem richer than before.

When he finally spoke, it wasn't in the dejected tone he had used for days. His words came out more musing than anything. "Prince Brannick knew him the best. I wish we could ask him."

He hadn't spoken the words like he'd given up, but they only reminded Elora of yet another reason they needed to rescue Brannick as soon as possible.

"I can build us an army." Soren spoke through a grumble, which was like music to Elora's ears. When he kicked a rock away, she had to keep herself from smiling. He gestured upward. "But we will need an enchantment like this one during the battle or no one will have the will to fight."

Kaia got to her feet, smoothing a tangle out of her emerald hair. "High Queen Alessandra likely has an enchantment in Fairfrost that will remove any protective enchantments like this one."

Elora tried to not let the words upset her too much. "Fine." She let out a long breath. "We will have to find a way around that then."

She fastened her braided belt around her waist and tucked her sword back inside it. Everyone else sat down, most of them stretching out their legs. At least they seemed to be enjoying themselves instead of looking like they were ready to simultaneously sob and vomit.

In her head, Elora ticked off everything she could remember about Severin's note. "The dragons in Fairfrost are wild now. There must be a way we can use that."

Quintus chuckled as he settled his back against a mossy boulder. "The dragons cannot be wild. They have been domesticated since before High Queen Alessandra became Queen of Fairfrost. Why would they suddenly be wild now?"

It did seem strange once he pointed it out, but Tindra had said it, and fae couldn't lie. Whatever the reason for it, they could probably find a way to take advantage of wild dragons.

Chloe's mouth dropped in a long yawn that quickly spread to the others. She already sat with a tree against her back, but she settled her head against it now. "It's awfully nice now with the enchantment."

Grace had been sitting at Chloe's side, but now she settled her matted head of red hair into her middle sister's lap.

When her youngest sister's eyes closed, Elora realized every other pair of eyes in the group fluttered with the longing to close them too. Now that her enchantment blocked them from the despair in the air, their exhaustion seemed to catch up all at once.

"We should rest."

At least three of them closed their eyes immediately after Elora's suggestion. It almost made her smile. "The despair has made it impossible to relax and even to sleep properly." She swallowed and gripped her sword hilt. "We can look for Vesper in the morning."

Kaia stepped into her tree. Soren and Fifer spread out on soft patches of moss. Lyren hummed to herself while curling into a ball at the base of a tree. Quintus was already snoring. Grace and Chloe wouldn't be far behind.

It was good they had all been able to rest so easily, but that didn't make it any easier for Elora. Since the despair didn't affect her much, she left the protective enchantment and changed back into her mauve gossamer gown.

Now she just needed a tall tree to climb so she could put her problems into proper perspective.

After a bit of searching, she found a tree with a thick trunk and more leaves than the others. Hoisting herself up, she made it to the top in only a few breaths.

"You feel energized this evening."

"Brannick." Tears welled in her eyes at the sound of his voice. Her voice caught when she continued. "I tried to rescue you again, but there are too many guards now. The entire palace is surrounded by three rows of guards. There are even guards standing in the windows so I can't fly into one of the upper levels. I had no way back to Bitter Thorn. I had to open a door."

A beat of silence followed, and then, "You opened a door?"

"Wait." She sat up higher on her tree branch. "I just had an idea. I can open a door that leads straight inside the palace. I can open it to the dungeons where you are."

"No!" His voice came out as a shout, which he probably regretted because he tried to cover it up with a cough. When he spoke again, he whispered. "Do not ever open a door inside of a house unless you have been invited. Faerie does not take kindly to such impoliteness."

Scowling, she sat back against the tree. "Faerie considers the dungeons part of a house? That does not seem fair."

"Every part of Fairfrost Palace is protected in that way."

Her chin dropped to her chest, but before it could get there, it snapped back up again. "But you can open a door inside the palace because you are already inside, right?"

"That is correct." He didn't sound nearly as excited as her.

She sat up straighter. "Then open a door just outside your cell. I will come through it and can go find a key for your chains. Once I find the key, I will free you, and you can open a door for us both to leave."

It took too long for Brannick to answer. When he did, his voice came out low. "That will not work."

Elora huffed and folded her arms over her chest. "Yes, it will. I have servant's clothes to disguise myself, so I do not need a glamour. No one will look twice at a servant. And I know where the keys are kept."

"That is not what I mean."

Her spine curled as her shoulders drooped forward. "What do you mean then?"

"While I am imprisoned, any door I open will be imprisoned too. I cannot open a door outside my cell for you to come through. Any door I open will be inside my cell with me."

She reached into her pocket, stroking his crystal as if it could give her life.

Though she spoke to him through a door, she sensed a shift in his energy.

He cleared his throat. "I do not think you should rescue me right away."

Her eyebrow raised. "Are you just telling me that to make me feel better?"

A chuckle fluttered through his door toward her, and she wanted to hold it in her heart. He chuckled again. "High Queen Alessandra is keeping me here so that I can give her information on the creation magic. I am telling her things that... well, they are *technically* true."

His words brought a chuckle to her own lips.

When he spoke again, she could hear the smile in his voice. "While I am here, I can lead her astray. Once I leave, she might be able to find the creation magic faster."

Elora ran a thumb over the ribbons in her belt. Her mother definitely would have approved of Brannick's devious idea. But now her heart sank knowing her mother would never meet Brannick. She gripped her sword hilt.

Neither would her father.

She embraced the pain that stabbed her chest, knowing it would hurt worse if she tried to ignore it. Finally, she leaned back against the tree. "That will give us time to build an army, I suppose."

The moment she used the word *time*, her fae senses sparked and churned with disgust. How strange that she had slipped up after being fae for so long. She expected Brannick to chide her with a reminder that time didn't exist in Faerie. Instead, he latched onto a completely different part of her declaration.

"If you bring an army to Fairfrost, that will put Bitter Thorn fae at risk. They could die."

She nearly rolled her eyes but worried he might hear it through her voice. "Good thing you are not here to stop us then." She shook her head. "You were fine with an army when we fought in Noble Rose. Why are you suddenly against it now?"

He swallowed loud enough for her to hear it through the door. "I am not worth all that."

The words sent her stomach into a knot. She scanned the forest around her. Creaking black thorns and leaves fallen from their trees blanketed the landscape. She gulped. "Yes, you are, Brannick. Bitter Thorn needs you. Faerie needs you." Her voice caught. "I need you."

A shuffling noise drifted through the tiny door, which she recognized as Blaz moving around somewhere. Hopefully the wolf had gone to comfort Brannick in some way.

Jumping off the tree, Elora released her wings. She shouted with her neck craned back so that Brannick could hear. "You are only feeling hopeless because of High Queen Alessandra's manipulation. Do not let her win. Bad things are here but good things still exist too."

By the time she finished speaking, her sword glowed. It almost seemed to move of its own accord, dragging her toward the ground where it speared a small forest animal. As soon as she landed back on the tree, she tossed the animal through the door.

Brannick let out a noise that twisted her chest. "You remembered food for Blaz." He sucked in a breath. "This will help more than you know."

Hanging her head, she pressed her back into the tree once again. "The dragons in Fairfrost are wild now. There has to be a way we can use that, right?"

He didn't answer.

Just as well, because she knew those words were just to delay the conversation she didn't want to have. But she needed to have it. Even if it hurt. "Vesper is gone. He left and said he did not want to see any of us again." Her voice lowered. "The despair affects him more than the others. I do not understand why."

"Perhaps because he has more to lose than the others."

"I thought the same thing. Do you know where he might have gone? We have no idea where to look."

Brannick considered for a moment before he answered. "I do not know, but your sprite friend might."

Sucking in a short breath, Elora got to her feet on the tree branch. "Tansy." Her mouth cocked into a smile as she looked upward. This time, she spoke to the air above her. "Tansy."

Except, the sprites were gone.

Her stomach dropped. She had to grab the tree for support.

"What is it?"

Brannick must have heard her gasp.

She tried to swallow but failed miserably. She jumped from the tree and let her wings pull her high into the air. After a moment, she finally found a cluster of glowing green sprites. The sight only eased her tension for half a breath.

The sprites hovered nearer to the castle. They all avoided the translucent enchantment Elora had created earlier. The realization sent knots through her gut. Was her enchantment hurting them?

"Elora, what happened?"

She hated the worry in Brannick's voice. The last thing she wanted was to make him feel worse when despair already hit him so hard.

Forcing herself to speak felt like forcing out a cough when a lump tried to keep it in. "I have to go."

Her voice came out smaller than she intended.

"Elora."

"I have to go." She repeated the words louder. For good measure, she flew far away from his door, so she couldn't hear his voice even if he spoke again.

How foolish of her to believe she had truly found her magic. How silly to think she could actually control it. As if recognizing her thoughts, her enchantment flickered. She gasped again.

Closing her eyes, she lifted the enchantment she had created to keep the despair away. Now she could only wait to see how the sprites reacted.

CHAPTER 14

The others slept through the night, but Elora kept waking up to check on them. With her enchantment gone, despair oozed through the air around them. Despair had woken the others before, but hopefully sheer exhaustion would keep them asleep until day dawned. If they got at least one night of rest, surely that would help them face the despair again.

And they needed to face it. She gripped her sword hilt. Because she wasn't going to create another enchantment. Her eyes drifted upward. She knew better than to hope to see sprites floating up above. She had checked all throughout the night every time she awoke.

Even with her enchantment gone, the sprites still refused to fly over the clearing. Her gut lurched just like it had every other time she had checked. The sprites *still* hovered near the castle. How badly had she injured them with her enchantment?

As soon as the first wisps of dawn appeared in the sky, the others began stirring. Chloe woke with a scowl on her face. She stretched and groaned, probably trying to work out a knot in her back.

Grace shivered as she wrapped her arms around herself. "It's cold."

Chloe's scowl deepened. "It wasn't this cold last night."

Letting out a near growl, Quintus kicked at a rock in front of him. "The air is full of despair again."

Everyone glanced up at the sound of his words. Kaia even stepped out of her tree before doing so. Their examination of the empty sky above them sent Elora's fingers into fists.

Lyren peeled herself off the ground, not quite removing the frown that darkened her expression. "What happened to your enchantment?"

Elora swallowed. "I do not know."

She had practiced that answer. It wasn't *technically* a lie. The enchantment had flickered just before she lifted it, and she *didn't* know what had caused the flicker. Of course, she knew Lyren meant to ask where the enchantment had gone, and Elora knew full well that she had lifted it. But she didn't want to admit what she had done to the sprites.

From the edge of the clearing, Fifer cleared his throat. "I need to get back to the castle." His big ears drooped even more today than they had the evening before.

Nodding, Elora gestured toward a path. "We should all go. We can get weapons or clothes or anything else that might be useful for a battle against High Queen Alessandra."

The others followed her without question when she began marching forward. Would they be so trusting if they happened to notice how the sprites avoided that area?

119

With each step closer to the sprites, Elora took a shallower breath. When they had nearly reached them, she held her breath entirely. Would the sprites fly away once she walked underneath them? Would they continue to avoid her for what her enchantment had done?

Her steps must have faltered because Chloe jogged up to her side. "Are you alright?"

Elora did her best to look confused as she cocked her head. "What?"

"You seem... worried. Is the despair getting to you?"

"No." Elora waved the questions off with as flippant an expression she could manage.

Unimpressed, Chloe narrowed one eye. "I only believe you because you are fae now, and fae cannot lie."

For good measure, Elora smiled.

It did nothing to convince her middle sister. A moment later, Grace asked Chloe for help with tying a ribbon around her wrist. Chloe pierced her oldest sister with a searching look and then then darted back to help Grace.

The moment her sister left, Elora muttered under her breath. "I only worry that my enchantment hurt the sprites."

"What?" Both Lyren and Quintus spoke the same word at the same time.

Elora sucked in a breath. She hadn't realized they were walking right behind her. With their fae hearing, of course they heard her even when she spoke under her breath.

Quintus's eyebrows raised. "Is that why they won't fly over the clearing where we slept?"

It took too much effort for Elora to keep her chin from trembling, so she just turned away from Lyren and Quintus instead. Her eyes stung with tears when she glanced upward.

The sprites floated around with their normal glow. It did little to offer comfort.

But then a light with a pink sparkle came zooming downward. Tansy didn't bother hovering in the air. She just flopped right down on Elora's shoulder. "Your enchantment did not hurt us."

Apparently, the sprites had heard Elora's confession too.

A shiver shook through Tansy's shoulders. She wrapped her arms around her stomach. "Ansel's enchantment is what injured us."

Before a breath of relief could fully escape Elora, her stomach clenched. "So, you *are* injured then. What happened?"

The little sprite shivered again. "We do not know exactly. We only know that we cannot abide the residue of his enchantment. He mixed it with the curse on Bitter Thorn in a frightful way." Her velvety hair bounced as she shook her head. "Even worse, the residue is spreading. We must avoid more of Bitter Thorn now than we had to last night."

Elora wanted to flop to the ground, but with the sprite on her shoulder, she just frowned instead. "We already lost Vesper to the despair. I worried I had lost you too."

A very Tansy-like snort erupted from the sprite. "Despair is not what took your brother away."

Jerking her head toward her shoulder, Elora blinked. "What?"

"He has been touched by ice."

Narrowing her eyes, Elora tried to make sense of the words. Nausea churned inside her when understanding dawned. "High Queen Alessandra hit him with a shard of ice. It melted into his chest during the battle in Noble Rose."

Tansy nodded, but she didn't make eye contact. She stared at her fingers, which fiddled with a puff on her pink shoes.

121

"Her ice magic slowly pulls all emotion out of any creature it touches. She used her ice magic on all the trolls in Fairfrost shortly after she killed her father and became queen."

Horror leapt across Elora's chest until it landed in her heart. She had to swallow before she could speak again. "Why has she never used the ice magic on us before?"

"Her greatest magic is in emotion. After using ice magic on the trolls, she realized she could never manipulate them with emotion again. She made another bargain with them, but she almost never uses ice magic now. It weakens her ability to use emotions against creatures."

Lyren marched forward, staring intently at Elora's shoulder. "But why Vesper?"

With a huff, Tansy scooted herself closer to Elora's ear. She moved herself so it was clear she would look at no one but Elora. Only then did the sprite speak again. "I am also surprised the high queen used her ice magic on Vesper. I thought she would use it on you once she found out Brannick loves you."

"She tried to use it on me." Elora's heart skittered, making it difficult to breathe. "Vesper jumped in front of me and caught the magic instead."

Elora's eyes narrowed. But why hadn't the high queen used ice magic while Elora was imprisoned in Fairfrost? She gave a resigned sigh. The high queen probably thought using the ice magic might interfere in some way with making the gemstones.

Either way, it would probably be the first thing High Queen Alessandra tried to do if she ever saw Elora again. If she didn't kill Elora first.

Biting her lip, Elora turned to her shoulder once again. "Can you find him, Tansy? I worry what Vesper will do on his own. He is not himself right now."

"We will find him." Tansy jumped into the air and glanced over her shoulder. They had nearly reached Bitter Thorn Castle by now. The sprite turned and faced Elora again. "In the meantime, we believe it will be mutually beneficial if you try to stop Ansel from creating more enchantments. He has already done it in a few other spots in Bitter Thorn. But," she hovered closer, "we believe we know where he will attack next. I can take you there."

Just when Elora went to nod, Quintus marched up to her side. He glanced at Chloe before turning back again. "Before we go, I have an idea for how to neutralize his device that carries the iron talisman."

Soren stomped forward and spoke in a grumbling voice. "How could you know how to do such a thing?"

"Because." Quintus smirked. "I designed that device."

CHAPTER

15

O n the other side of Bitter Thorn Castle, the forest looked
completely different. Thorns still choked through bushes
and crawled up tree trunks. The air still oozed with thick
despair. But at least the trees still had all their leaves. The moss
still looked spongy and lush. The scent of crisp rain still drifted
around.

Elora stood behind a thick tree trunk, peeking around it
every few moments.

Tansy sat on her shoulder, making herself quite at home.
"It should not be long now."

Almost as soon as she finished speaking, a rocky gray door
appeared in the clearing just past Elora's tree. Not for the first
time, she questioned whether she should be glamoured to be
invisible. They had all discussed it, and they all agreed Elora's
part of the plan would work better if Ansel could see her.

Even though she agreed, her body still protested about only having a mere tree between her and the fae who had nearly broken her.

His yellow eyes glowed when he stepped out of his door. He glanced over the forest once before shaking his head. Then he stepped right back inside his door.

He was gone.

Narrowing one eye, she turned to the sprite on his shoulder. "Why would he leave like that?"

Tansy rolled her eyes. "If anyone could figure out why he does the things he does, all of Faerie would probably be a better place. Sometimes I wonder if that fae has any mind at all."

Elora snorted, surprised that a smile pricked at her lips.

"What do we do now?" Grace's tiny voice sounded from only a few steps away.

"Grace!" Elora whipped around to face her sister. As before, everyone around her wore a glamour to make them invisible, except for the sprite. But she could still attempt to turn in the right direction based on the sound of her sister's voice. Elora glared at the space in front of her. "You are not supposed to be out here. You are supposed to be inside the castle with Soren."

A small giggle escaped Grace.

The invisible gnome grumbled only a few steps away from Grace. "There is too much snow inside the castle still."

Folding her arms over her chest, Elora glared harder. "Then find a different clearing to hide in. Go anywhere but here."

"Fine." Soren let out a string of grumbled words under his breath. "I suppose we should do that."

She knew very well that when Soren said he *supposed* they *should*, it merely meant that he would not.

125

Just when she opened her mouth to scold him, the rocky gray door reappeared in the clearing.

Grace let out a tiny gasp and then two pairs of feet shuffled for a moment. Once Ansel came out of his door again, Grace and Soren had stopped moving. At least the others who were glamoured to be invisible knew to stay quiet.

Ansel's yellow eyes glowed with a sickly hue. He had two fae with him now. A female fae on his right side shrieked and fought against his grip. A knife stabbed deep into her thigh, but Ansel's grip wouldn't allow her to remove it.

On Ansel's other side, a tall fae stood who looked exactly like the fae Ansel had forced Elora to kill back when she was still staying in Bitter Thorn Castle. She knew now that the tall fae was probably a mortal who just wore a glamour to look like a fae. After discovering the loft in Ansel's house, she knew that he glamoured all of his mortal pets to look like fae. The same fae. All the females wore the same maroon skirt, white blouse, and even the same face. All the males had white-blonde hair and crooked teeth.

Still, this one looked taller than Ansel's other pets. He held himself like he could withstand great weight. If she had to fight him, it would be a lot harder than just fighting Ansel. Fear tingled at her fingertips when she grabbed her sword hilt. She did her best to ignore it.

Grinning, Ansel shoved the injured female fae to the ground. She let out a wail, which he ignored. He pulled Quintus's iron device from his pocket, and Elora held her breath.

She had never actually seen the device they used against High Queen Alessandra during the battle in Noble Rose, since it had been glamoured to be invisible along with Chloe. While planning this attack, they all wondered if Ansel had found and repaired the same device they used on High Queen Alessandra, or if he had simply created a new one that was similar.

It didn't really matter now. They just needed to neutralize it.

When Ansel reached for the silver latch at the front of the device, a whistle came from the opposite side of the clearing. Sucking in a breath, Ansel pulled the device close to his chest.

"Who is that?"

A shout came from another part of the clearing.

Shivering, Ansel checked his lapel for the white flower that must have been protecting him from the emotions in the air. He shook his head.

When the third sound erupted—a strange hoot—Ansel nearly jumped out of his shoes. He clenched his jaw and shot an enchantment toward the noise.

Elora bit her lip, trying to remember who had been hiding in that spot. It sounded like Lyren, but fear muddled her surety.

Luckily, the noise came out again after Ansel's enchantment faded away.

With Ansel turned completely away from his victim, Elora's moment had come. She drew her sword and jumped out from behind the tree in the same breath. Tansy flitted upward with the other sprites, but Elora knew her sprite friend would stay nearby.

She charged forward, preparing to plunge her sword right into Ansel's heart.

Just before she reached him, the tall fae with white-blonde hair produced his own sword. Their blades clashed, sending hers far from its intended target.

"Ah, my pet. I am always glad to see you." Ansel's words slithered under her skin until she shivered.

Ducking beneath the other fae's sword, she sliced hers forward once again. She only managed to nick his shoulder with the tip of her blade.

While she blocked another blow from the tall fae, Ansel gripped her other wrist. He moved close enough to leave the scent of sour milk in her face. "Your blood is exactly what I need."

Without thinking, an enchantment sparked from her fingertips. It blasted him in the chest, sending him several steps backward. He didn't seem affected except to frown at the spot where the enchantment had hit him. "You can access your magic now." After a moment, he shook his head. "No matter. Once I break you, your magic will fade away again. Then your blood will be more powerful than ever."

The tall fae lunged toward her with his sword aiming straight for her heart. She had to slice his shoulder just to keep him from succeeding. A wail leapt from his lips, which immediately twisted her insides.

She didn't want to hurt the tall fae. He was nothing more than a puppet in Ansel's hands. And he was likely a mortal who would not heal from injuries as quickly or as completely as a fae like Ansel. Still, she couldn't let the tall fae kill her either.

With another jab of her sword, the tall fae collapsed to his knees. The female fae with the dagger in her thigh continued to scream and wail at every opportunity.

Elora lunged forward, her sword aiming for Ansel's chest again. When he stepped to the side at the last moment, she kept her momentum and tackled him to the ground instead. Her knees dug into his chest and her sword pressed near his throat. Ansel only smiled.

"I invite you to my home, my pet."

Her iron sword moved close enough to make his neck sizzle with steam. His grin never faltered. "Now that you can open your own door, you may come to visit me whenever you like."

She dug her sword into his neck, but before it could sever too much of the skin, a pair of thick arms yanked her backward. The tall fae threw her onto the ground.

Holding her sword hilt firmly, she kicked the tall fae with both feet. The weight of his body stood unaffected by her action. He knocked her back to the ground in a flash. Momentarily ignoring him, she turned to Ansel.

Anger burned within her, lighting every crystal of fear that dared rear its head. She gritted her teeth. "If I went to your house, you would lock me in chains the moment I arrived."

A smug grin fell across Ansel's lips when the tall fae stepped on Elora's sword wrist. Brushing the dirt off his clothes, Ansel raised an eyebrow at her. "Yes, but someday you will choose to stay, even without the chains. You will not be able to live without me. You will do anything I say." He gestured toward the tall fae. "Just like all my pets do."

Potent fury exploded inside her then. Despite the tall fae's strength, she managed to shove him off her. Her sword finally stuck Ansel uninhibited.

He tried to jump away, but the blade still stabbed him through the stomach. She took a single breath to withdraw and position her sword, then thrust it forward once again.

Just before it could touch Ansel, he crushed the red gemstone on his lapel. It exploded in a stream of red and cream shimmers. The enchantment pinned her down against the ground. She couldn't even lift a finger.

Luckily, blood and innards spilled out of the wound in Ansel's stomach. As a fae, he would eventually heal from such an injury, but he clearly couldn't do any more to capture Elora now. And he was also greatly weakened after using the gemstone. Even the tall fae looked weaker than before.

With one hand pressed against his stomach wound, Ansel used his other to retrieve a small knife from inside his jacket. He slit the female fae's throat all the way though. Even with one hand, he managed to capture her blood.

Elora shoved against the enchantment that held her down. Even though Ansel had used a gemstone, which were supposedly extremely powerful, she could feel his enchantment fading. It pressed her deep into the forest floor, but she managed to lift one finger. A few moments later, she could lift another finger.

Ansel waved a hand, which called a demorog toward him. While Elora shoved and pushed against the enchantment, he still managed to use the demorog to crush the gemstone just like he had done before.

The same stinging cold and wind and fog as before seeped into the air around him. Once it vanished, he hobbled over to the device holding his iron talisman. Using his free hand, he went to flick the latch to close it. Just before he did, his face twisted into a scowl.

"You think taking my iron talisman will stop me?"

At least their plan had worked. Chloe had clearly stolen the talisman while Elora kept Ansel distracted. It might have felt better if Ansel hadn't been wearing such a sure expression of victory.

He chuckled darkly. "My plan is already in motion. It is too late to stop me now."

When he opened a door, the tall fae limped in after him. The moment his door disappeared, the enchantment holding

Elora down faded away completely. She grunted, but mostly she just wanted to scream.

The others became visible again. The enchantment must have been holding them down too because they were all on their backs, just starting to sit up.

Lyren sat in a heap right across from Elora. She glanced at the blood on Elora's blade and raised an eyebrow. "You were only meant to distract him." She gave a pointed glance at the blood again. "You tried to kill him instead."

"He deserves it." Elora refused to apologize. She wiped the blood onto a patch of moss before shoving it into her belt. It angered her that she hadn't succeeded.

When Lyren came closer, she placed a hand on Elora's shoulder. Her voice came out thick and daunting. "But do you want to deal with the consequences of taking a life? Killing for revenge will taint your essence."

Considering Lyren's own history with taking a life, Elora couldn't blame her for giving such advice. It didn't temper her desire to kill Ansel though.

Maybe refraining from responding would be better. Gesturing forward, Elora turned to the others. "We need to move closer to the castle where the sprites are."

She tried not to think about how much the sprites had been injured by the residue of Ansel's latest enchantment. Maybe since they knew what would happen, they had flown away before the residue could hurt them.

Chloe sprinted to Elora's side and took her arm in a death grip. Her face had lost almost all its color. Even though Ansel had never known she was there, Chloe had surely never been more frightened in her life than when she stole the iron talisman.

She shook her head, her shoulders still shaking. "I can't believe he invited you to his house."

The words sent a shiver down Elora's spine. "I know. I cannot imagine what sort of desperation would lead me there."

Once they passed the stinging residue, Tansy flew down and hovered in front of Elora. Her pink and green eyes sparkled. "We found your brother. He is in Swiftsea."

Elora sucked in a gasp. Their other plans would have to wait. First, they needed to find Vesper.

CHAPTER 16

S alty Swiftsea air fluttered through Elora's hair. Like usual, she left her hair down, free to drift in the wind. The layers of her gossamer gown fluttered too. The embroidery and beadwork sparkled in the light. She had never fawned over clothes the way her younger sisters did, but the outfit did give her more confidence than she expected. And she needed that extra bit of confidence right now, perhaps even more than ever.

Her fingertips sparked with magic. She tried to embrace it but swallowed instead. Only after two deep breaths did she finally open her palm. When her hand shot into the air, a translucent dome formed over her and the others around her. The enchantment flickered just like her other one had before she lifted it.

The sight sent her heart stammering in her chest.

Maybe she could do magic now, but it seemed fickle. Inconsistent. The more she thought about the enchantment overhead, the more it flickered away.

Chloe sighed at the magic around them. When she noticed the sound had drawn her oldest sister's eye, she quickly forced a smile. "It's still strong. It's definitely keeping the despair out. Don't worry."

Now Elora wanted to sigh. If it *definitely* kept the despair out, her sister wouldn't have had to say anything about it. It would have been obvious.

Everyone else in the group ignored the two of them. They all gazed at the sea ahead.

Lyren huffed. "I hate crossing this sea. The sea monsters get more aggressive every time."

"Sea monsters?" Chloe sucked in a sharp gasp. "I thought Vesper was on an island by the source of the decay. Why do we have to worry about sea monsters?"

Pulling a small sketchbook from his coat, Quintus flipped through the pages until he found a drawing of one of the sea monsters they had encountered last time they had crossed this sea. The long snake-like creature had the head of a dragon. It soared over a ship and tore apart a mast with its teeth.

He had perfectly captured the most frightening moment of their last trip. Chloe gasped at the sight of the image.

Wincing, he tucked the sketchbook back into his coat. "You should probably stay here."

"And me?" Grace's wide eyes made her appear more child-like than ever.

"Yes, Grace, especially you." Elora's fingertips sparked again. Why did her magic seem perfectly fine whenever she didn't think about it?

Sighing, Lyren turned to walk toward the nearby Swiftsea Palace. "I will go speak to Queen Noelani about letting us borrow a ship. We cannot get to the island without one."

Quintus grumbled under his breath. "I cannot believe she put an enchantment over an entire island that prevents fae from opening doors there."

Lyren turned on her heel and grabbed him by the collar. "The source of the decay is on that island. We had to do something to keep random fae from going there and possibly destroying things."

He raised an eyebrow, making no move to back away. "It did not stop Vesper from getting there."

Scowling, she shoved him away. She turned toward the palace once again and spoke over her shoulder. "I cannot imagine how he managed it. Only a few ships are strong enough to travel through these waters."

The interaction between Lyren and Quintus struck Elora as strange, though she couldn't immediately pinpoint why. They had shown more emotion than usual. That must have been it. After all the manipulation from High Queen Alessandra, maybe they simply couldn't be completely emotionless anymore.

Sparks danced across Elora's fingertips. In a flash, she whipped herself toward Lyren. "Wait." She had an idea. Had the magic given it to her? Shaking that thought away, she stood tall. "I can do it."

"Do what?" Chloe shivered as she glanced over the sea. The surface of it rippled with scales hiding just beneath it.

Elora gestured toward the island across the sea. "No one can open a door *to* the island, but fae can open a door once they are over there, correct?"

Lyren nodded, but she narrowed both eyes as she did it.

Popping the wings from her back, Elora lifted herself into the air. "The rest of you wait here. I will go get Vesper on my own."

If any of them protested, she flew away too fast to hear it. Once she flew over the rippling surface of the water, sea monsters immediately started jumping out of the waves. Her muscles no longer strained each time she flapped her wings. When the sea monsters snapped their teeth at her, she just flew higher.

The change had been gradual, but somewhere during her time in Faerie, she had become an expert at flying. She could rise high above the sea monsters now without any trouble. Her fingertips didn't even spark with magic. She did this on her own.

When she landed on the beach of the island, her heart felt lighter than it had since Brannick got captured. It immediately plummeted once she caught sight of Vesper.

He didn't just stand near the source of the decay. He sat right on top of it. The bubbling goo of the decay splashed over his pants. It covered his hands. His face showed no expression at all.

Reaching for her belt, she ran a finger over her mother's ribbons as she marched toward him.

As soon as he noticed her presence, his face twisted into a snarl. "I told them I never want to see any of you again. That includes you."

"You are not yourself right now. You do not get to make that kind of decision."

She grabbed his wrist, but he just pulled it out of her grip. When she reached for it again, he growled at her. Actually growled.

"Leave me." He hissed the words through his teeth.

She allowed herself one huff and then she sat down next to him, as close as she could get *without* touching the source of the decay. Magic sparked at her fingertips again. Cocking her head to the side, she lifted her mouth in a grin. "Since we are just sitting here, I will tell a story."

"I would rather you did not." His voice sounded empty.

Ignoring him completely, she continued. "Once there was a fae who had the spirit of adventure."

"I hate this story already."

She raised her voice to talk over him. "The fae traveled all throughout Faerie, learning about the courts and the people at every turn. But Faerie could not satiate his desire for adventure anymore."

Vesper groaned and dug his hands deeper into the oozing goo of the decay.

She continued to ignore him. "He traveled to the mortal realm and met a lovely mortal girl named Cosette."

Something snapped inside him at the mention of his beloved's name. He sucked in a sharp breath and pulled his knees to his chest. "No."

Hopefully his reaction proved her idea would work. "He visited her often. Soon, their time together grew dearer to him than their time apart."

"Stop." His body shook. He kept clenching his fists as if that would help. He shook his head so hard, his curls tumbled over his forehead. "I cannot." His entire body shook. He nearly fell over. "*Please* stop."

It hurt to see him in such great pain, but she couldn't help a quick smirk over his last phrase. Her plan had worked after all.

His eyes went wide when he realized what he had said. He clapped a hand to his mouth, but the damage had already been done.

Getting to her feet, she brushed the sand from the embroidery in her gown. "You said *please*, which means you now owe me a favor." She gestured across the rippling water. "I want you to open a door to the others across this sea. You must come with me through the door and then stay with us after that."

He flashed his teeth at her and shook his head. "I do not want to go."

She shrugged. "You owe me a favor. You must do what I ask."

"Fine." He spoke through clenched teeth when he stood from the oozing decay. "I know that I must, but I hope your mortal guilt poisons your insides for what you are making me do."

Since she only wanted to help him, she knew no amount of guilt would touch her at all. She did ache at seeing her brother's pain, though.

After he waved a hand and opened a door, she touched his arm. "You only need to stay with us until we figure out how to counteract the ice magic High Queen Alessandra hit your heart with. After that, you can do whatever you want."

Then again, once he was back to his true self, he would surely choose to stay with them anyway.

He seemed to notice the hope in her eyes. It made him scowl. "I only owe you one favor. I opened the door, and I will come through it with you. That is all."

He stepped into his door so fast, she had to dart in after him. When they stepped out of the door, Chloe and Grace practically tackled him.

138

"Don't leave us again." Grace buried her face in chest, squeezing him as tight as she could. "We were so worried for you."

While he tried to extricate himself from Grace's grip, Chloe tied a purple ribbon around his wrist. His body froze once she got it into place.

"What is that?" he asked with a scowl.

Chloe wrapped one hand around his wrist, just under the ribbon. She pointed to it with her other hand. "This ribbon is a token, which means its essence has been changed by emotion." She opened her mouth again, but the words caught in her throat. Her chin quivered instead.

Elora finished for her. "High Queen Alessandra's ice magic is drawing all emotion out of you. But if you have a token tied around your wrist, it will not be able to draw everything away."

"The ribbon will help you!" Grace's red hair bounced as she jumped excitedly. Suddenly, the jumps stopped. "At least we hope it will."

Vesper yanked his arm away from Chloe. "This is not even *my* token."

Chloe pointed her nose in the air. "Yes, but it is Elora's. By mortal terms, Elora is your great-great-great-great granddaughter. That means your blood is in her veins, but your beloved's blood is in it too. I know we don't have anything of Cosette's to give you, so a token from one of her descendants will have to do."

He scowled at them and reached for the ribbon. Before he could touch it, Elora wrapped her hand over the ribbon. She thought of how desperately they needed him to keep it on until they could figure out how to help him. It was the only way they could ensure he didn't lose all emotion completely. She hardly noticed when sparks lit from her fingertips and sank into the ribbon.

Taking a step back, Vesper's eyes went wide. He brought the ribbon up to his nose, and his eyes grew even wider. When he tried to remove the ribbon again, the tie wouldn't budge. "What did you do?"

She huffed before answering. "We want to help you, not hurt you. You can remove the ribbon eventually. We just have to figure out how to help you first."

He tried to remove the ribbon again, but Elora's magic kept it in place no matter what he did. His face turned red as he curled his hands into fists. At least he didn't look as angry as he had while on that island. Maybe the ribbon was helping already.

Lyren opened a door and turned toward the group. "Come. We can stay at the sea caves again this evening. When day dawns, we will have to start planning our next move."

CHAPTER 17

Taking a deep breath, Elora concentrated on the enchantment she prepared to create. But the more she concentrated it, the more the magic seemed to slip through her fingers. The sea cave in front of her wasn't even that big. The mouth of it was even smaller. If she had created other enchantments that kept the high queen's emotions out, why did this one seem so difficult?

"Elora, come tell Grace her rice is delicious." Chloe sidled up to the cave entrance and shook her head. "She keeps saying the fire wasn't hot enough and that the rice is crunchy." Her voice lowered to a whisper. "It *is* crunchy, but I can't be the only one who doesn't care. I'm so tired, I just want to eat and go to sleep."

Nodding, Elora started toward the back of the cave. After a few steps, she remembered the enchantment. With her mind already half on the crunchy rice that probably still tasted delicious, she waved a hand over her shoulder. An enchantment burst from her fingertips with no effort at all.

It wasn't until she had eaten half her dinner that she thought about the magic again. Her eyes darted to cave entrance where her enchantment shimmered with brilliant translucence. It didn't even flicker this time. It worked perfectly once she stopped thinking about it. Again.

Soon, dinner had been cleaned and everyone settled into the sleeping mats and blankets Lyren had found. With Elora's enchantment in place, everyone could finally relax without the despair plaguing them.

As they settled, Elora slipped out the cave entrance. The moment she stepped outside, her thoughts turned to Brannick. Would he know she wanted to speak to him? His door had always appeared at the perfect moment before.

She reached the rocks that separated the sea caves from the beach. Maybe she could just pull out her crystal and hold it tight. He might be able to feel it if she thought of him hard enough. Once she reached the beach, she would do exactly that.

For now, she needed to climb over the rocks without ruining her gossamer gown.

"Blaz is gone."

Brannick's voice *had* come at the perfect moment yet again, but his words froze her foot in midair. The words were difficult enough, but his tone sounded strained. His voice came out rough. Had he been crying?

Her body teetered over the rocks while she tried to find her footing once again. *"Gone?"*

"Not dead." Brannick huffed. A noise came through the door that sounded like him falling onto a pile of blankets. "At least, I do not think he is dead. He just…"

She had to swallow before she could speak again. Maybe she needed to sit down as well. "Tell me what happened."

He sniffed, which felt worse than a knife twist to the heart. "The high queen, she found him. She knows he is always with me, but he has a glamour to make everyone look anywhere but at him. She came down to the dungeons, opened my cell, and dropped piles of fresh meat outside it. And then she left. I could not escape because of my chains, but the cell door stood wide open."

Elora had to place a hand over her beating heart before she could answer. "Blaz ate the food?"

"He refused at first, but I finally convinced him." The prince's voice broke and he sniffed again. "As soon as he started eating, guards emerged from the shadows and tackled him." A sputtering noise erupted from the prince that sounded like a half cough, half sob. "They took him from me. I do not know where he is."

Elora clutched at her heart. It did no good. She squeezed her hands into fists. She clenched her stomach. Nothing helped. Sucking in a sharp breath, her eyes opened wide. Her back straightened. She checked that the ward necklace from Tindra and Severin was still in place around her neck. Then, she forced herself to her feet.

"Brannick."

He groaned.

"Make your door bigger." At least her voice had come out steady.

"What?"

She rolled her shoulders back. "No guards are around you, right? No one will see it. Just make your door bigger."

"Why?"

He asked, but he did it anyway. At her side, his door grew from the size her palm to the size of a large, swirling tunnel. She took a deep breath and then... she stepped through.

Maybe walking right into a locked cell inside Fairfrost's dungeons was the stupidest thing she had ever done. If so, she didn't care. Brannick needed her.

"Elora." He said her name like it held Faerie itself together. His eyes opened wide at the sight of her, but relief filled his features too. Golden chains wrapped around both of his ankles, securing him to the cell but keeping his hands free. His black hair hung to his shoulders with a stringy quality it didn't usually have. It still mostly shined, though. His eyes had never been so dull. His coat had been tossed into a heap in a corner of the cell. His pants hung limp and wrinkled. Even his light brown skin looked dull.

Still, the sight of him sent a flush into Elora's cheeks.

The relief that had flashed in his eyes immediately plummeted. Stark horror replaced it. "This is dangerous. The high queen will sense your magic. You must—"

"Look." She stepped toward him, which made him suck in a breath. She lifted the bright pendant so he could see it clearly. "Severin's beloved made this ward necklace. It blocks the high queen's enchantment so she cannot sense my magic. She will not know I am here. I used a necklace just like this when I came to Fairfrost Palace last time."

He blinked. "Severin has a beloved?"

"Yes."

"No one in Fairfrost is allowed to love except the high queen and her guards. No wonder he defied her and escaped."

The words left his mouth, but it didn't even seem like he was talking. He acted unaware of his surroundings for another beat until he locked eyes with her once again. His eyes widened as if he were seeing her for the first time.

Bursts of colors swirled in his irises. He reached out to her with an expression that said he wanted to smile but his grief wouldn't let him. She didn't say another word then. She just stepped forward and pulled him close.

Another half cough, half sob sputtered from his mouth. He buried his face in her neck, pulling her closer with each breath.

"Elora."

He whispered the name into her hair. She held him as tight as she could, but it never seemed tight enough. His breaths came out erratic. She tried to soothe them by rubbing a thumb across his bare shoulder.

He melted into her at the touch, and it suddenly seemed like a good idea to get off their feet. He didn't seem to realize how heavily he leaned on her. Guiding him gently, she pulled Brannick over to a pile of yellowing blankets that must have been his bed.

She sat with her back against the white marble wall.

Brannick knelt in front of her with his body at an awkward angle. His hands hovered in the air as if he didn't know what to do with them. "Blaz has been with me since my childhood. I had not discovered magic yet, so I was not quite an adult."

Grabbing his hands, she pulled Brannick toward her. When he got close, she helped him settle his head into her lap. Laying on his back, he gazed at the ceiling while she stroked his hair.

"How did you meet him?" Even after asking, it seemed like a strange question to ask about a wolf. Then again, Blaz had never been typical.

The colors in Brannick's eyes pulsed. "I used to explore the forest in Bitter Thorn more often than I have since you met me. Once, I was out seeing how fast my fae legs could carry me when I heard an animal whimpering."

"Blaz."

Even with his head in her lap, Brannick still managed to nod. "A tree had fallen, and he got caught underneath it. The animals in Faerie are like us. They do not die unless they are killed. Their healing ability is just as strong as the fae."

She brushed a lock of hair off his forehead and circled it around her finger. "He was not badly injured then?"

"He was gravely injured. He had clearly been trapped for far too long before I found him." His eyes narrowed and the colors in them swirled even faster. "But I felt something inside him. It was almost like I could feel his thoughts, except it was even deeper than that. It was the first moment I sensed any kind of essence. That experience helped me discover my magic." His eyes closed as he gave a quick shake of the head. "I could tell he did not want to die." He shrugged. "So, I saved him."

She nodded, admiring the strong line of his jaw and the brilliance of his eyes. When she trailed a finger across his cheek, it seemed to give him strength.

He swallowed and continued. "I stayed with him through many dawns and nightfalls because his injuries made it impossible for him to move. When he needed food, I hunted for him. I would not leave his side until he had fully recovered. He finally did, and by then, I had discovered my magic and become an adult fae. He has stayed with me ever since."

She gazed into his eyes while he continued to stare at the ceiling. "I always thought you could read his thoughts and he yours."

"Not thoughts. Just his essence. But it often communicates the same as thoughts might."

"That makes sense." His hair felt softer now, and his presence warmed her. Of course, she had missed Brannick, but she hadn't realized how much until this moment. Even the tiniest things, like running her fingers through his hair, filled her with hope. She only wished they could have met under less unfortunate circumstances. Her ached for Brannick and for his wolf.

She brushed a thumb over the pointed tip of his ear. "Blaz is the reason your greatest magic is in essence then?"

His eyes flicked over to hers. "Perhaps. Or perhaps he just helped me discover my magic faster than I would have on my own. After sensing his essence while I tried to save him, it became much easier to sense it in other things."

She nodded.

He sighed and closed his eyes for a moment. "When I returned to the castle with a wolf by my side, Soren and Kaia were not happy. They would not even let me tell my father, though he was so old by then, he probably wouldn't have remembered anything I said anyway." He shook his head. "Soren said I only saved Blaz because of my mortal weaknesses. Kaia said I should have let him die, that he was not worth my effort. Maybe it was because I had finally grown into a full adult fae, but I laughed at them both. I told them Blaz would save my life someday. And he has. So many times, he has. If he had not been with me when I came to Fairfrost the first time, I never would have survived." His lips stilled for a moment. His eyes dulled. "And now he is gone."

A shudder shook through him as soon as he finished speaking. He covered his face with both hands just as a sob escaped him. "I cannot imagine what has happened to him." His body shook again.

She gripped his shoulder, tilting him until he looked up at her. "Do you think you could feel it if he died? Can you sense his essence even from far away?"

"I think so." He swallowed and his shoulders shook again. "But maybe I just hope I can."

"I think you are right."

His eyes flicked over to hers once again.

She found his hand and gave it a gentle squeeze. "If you believe he is still alive, then he must be. Blaz is as strong as you are. He will be okay."

Brannick nodded, but a stray tear slipped from his eyes. When she caught it with her thumb, he pulled her down and into his arms.

Every moment she stayed in Fairfrost meant another moment she could get caught, but she didn't care. She wasn't about to leave her beloved now.

CHAPTER 18

When Elora woke, she had an ache in her neck from sleeping on a hard surface. Once she recognized the hard surface was the marble floor of Brannick's dungeon cell, her eyes snapped open with a start.

Her gossamer dress had rumpled after sleeping in it, but a few brushes with her hand smoothed out the wrinkles. Only then did her eyes drift across from her.

Less than an arm's length away, Brannick stared at her with his head propped up with one hand. His coat still sat in a heap in one corner, but his pants didn't look any more wrinkled or limp than they did the day before. He lay with his body parallel to hers. A crooked smile filled his face. "You are so beautiful."

Heat blossomed in her chest, and suddenly her expression matched his. "Beautiful? You have never called me that before."

His mouth gaped open. He put an affronted hand to his chest. "Surely I have."

She shook her head, then turned her attention to a tangle that had formed in her hair.

He reached for it, gliding his fingers through the tangle with ease. "Then I will have to say it even more often." He met her eyes. "To make up for when I did not say it."

Her cheeks filled with instant heat, which made Brannick grin.

When she shook her head again, it was an attempt to get some of the heat out of her cheeks. The attempt failed miserably, but at least her mind started working again. She ran her fingers through another section of her hair. It didn't have any tangles at all.

"I probably only look beautiful now because I am fae." She fluffed her hair to illustrate the point. Ever since changing, her hair never needed more than a simple comb through with her fingers to look perfect. And it always looked shinier, thicker, and even longer than it had ever been when she was mortal. She raised an eyebrow. "But I looked dreadful as a mortal, right?"

"No."

Her eyes snapped up to meet Brannick's. He continued to grin at her with his head propped up with one hand. He hadn't moved much closer, but he leaned forward enough that she had to crane her neck to look into his eyes.

He stroked a hand over her cheek. "Vesper and Quintus say you look different now that you have changed, but I cannot see it. This is how you looked before." He let out a sigh, which brought his face even closer to hers. "You have always entranced me."

150

When he leaned in closer, she held her breath. Her toes curled while she waited for him to kiss her.

But he didn't. Instead, he cleared his throat and backed away. "Vesper told me about the customs at your place in the mortal realm." He sat up and crossed his legs.

One eye narrowed as she watched him carefully. "What customs?"

His eyes trailed over her body for the briefest moment before he glanced away. "He told me marriage is very important there. He said we should not share a bed until we are married." He glanced through the side of his eye at the space between them. "Although, I am fairly certain it is not the sleeping part that is the problem."

Heat filled her cheeks as she sat up with a start. "Oh." She tried to smile, but it probably came off as an unattractive slant. "Yes, the sleeping part is not the problem. We do wait until marriage for..." Trailing off, her eyes snapped to his as realization hit. "Do fae not have that same custom?"

Brannick put a hand through his hair, which perfectly ruffled his glossy black strands. "No, but Vesper was very firm with me. He sat me down and insisted I wait." One corner of his smile lifted. "I am surprised he was brave enough to threaten me the way he did, actually."

Grabbing the corner of a threadbare blanket, she tugged at the strands along its edge. "Ironic that Vesper was so firm with you when he did not follow that same advice himself. He only married his wife because she carried his baby. He knew she would be punished for getting pregnant out of wedlock if they did not get married fast enough. He did not even fall in love with her until later."

151

"I thought it ironic also." Brannick's eyes narrowed as his gaze turned downward. "I know it did not bother him at first that he ignored the customs, but it did bother his beloved. I believe he wishes he had followed them, or at least respected her upbringing more than he did."

"That makes sense, although he still married her. He probably cared for her a lot more than he realized." When she glanced up, Brannick's eyes sparked and glimmered. He stared with that intent gaze that had a habit of making her forget to breathe.

His eyebrow lifted. "You know the bargain I made with High Queen Alessandra was supposed to be a marriage bargain. She made me promise to follow her every order. But then, she betrayed me and never made a similar bargain with me. I soon found out she had tricked numerous fae into the exact same bargain and all of them were her palace guards."

Tilting her head down, Elora bit her lip. "I forgot that was a marriage bargain. Of course I knew, I just forgot it was—"

"That experience made me see marriage as entrapment. Many fae see it that way too, and they always have. Perhaps it was my mortal father's doing, but I always found the idea of marriage romantic." His voice turned rough. "But not after what High Queen Alessandra did to me. Any fae can have a beloved. They never need to be married. After my experience in Fairfrost, I thought I would never love again. And I *knew* I would never marry."

Her breath caught as she reached for his hand. "I would never dream of entrapping you. If you do not wish to marry, I will not try to persuade you otherwise. I could not ask you to give something that might hurt you."

A subtle smile passed over his lips as he brought her hand closer to his face. He pinned her with that magnetic gaze again as he kissed her hand. "That is precisely why I want to give you everything."

She melted. The way he kissed her hand, the surety with which he spoke. All of it melted her until it sparked into a tingling that spread over every surface of her skin.

His lips lifted in a grin, but he quickly looked down with a more serious expression. Using one finger, he traced circles over the back of her hand. "We do not celebrate marriage with a ceremony in Faerie. Each fae simply makes a selfless bargain. After that, each fae makes a vow. It can happen anywhere." He moved closer until his knees met hers. "It can happen whenever the two fae choose." With his free hand, he stroked his thumb across her jaw. He leaned in until his breath rustled her hair. "We could do it now if you like."

Her heart had never pounded so hard in her life. It was extremely inconvenient because she was struck with the very intense desire to kiss him, which might have been interrupted if her heart pounded so hard it left her chest.

Dozens of thoughts floated in and out of her mind. *Yes* was the only word she needed to say, but it wouldn't come out with all the thoughts bombarding her.

It didn't seem to matter though. Brannick must have seen the answer on her face.

But when his lips brushed against hers, the sound of a creaking door came from down the dungeon hallway. Brannick sucked in a sharp breath and pulled Elora to her feet. "Someone is coming." He waved a hand and opened a door while he glanced over his shoulder toward the dungeon.

Just before Elora stepped into the door, he pulled her into his arms and kissed her fiercely. It was as passionate as it could be with the half moment they had. Neither of them spoke again before she stepped through the door.

Her feet landed right back on the rocks near the Swiftsea beach she had left the night before. Instead of his door vanishing completely, it merely shrank down to even smaller than her palm. The height and position of it made her think he was hiding it behind his back.

Instead of a guard, or even Brannick, the next voice Elora heard came from High Queen Alessandra. "What happened to your eyes?"

"Whatever do you mean?"

Elora grinned at the flippant way he answered.

High Queen Alessandra huffed loud enough that it traveled through the door. "You look happy. I just took your wolf. You should not be happy."

A puff of air escaped the prince. "I thought you came here to talk about Bitter Thorn's creation magic. You want to talk about Blaz instead? Very well. I would rather talk about him anyway." Though his voice came out as flippant as before, it had a sharp edge to it.

"You have always been too sentimental." High Queen Alessandra was probably rolling her eyes. "You cannot blame me for using it against you. Now, tell me what happens when a fae touches the creation magic. What does—" Her voice cut off unexpectedly. "Are you hiding something behind your back?"

Brannick's door vanished immediately. Though Elora would have liked hearing more of the conversation, she certainly didn't want the high queen to discover Brannick had a way of communicating with his beloved. It was best that he closed the door when he did. Soft light lit Elora's path as she headed back to the sea caves. Day had already dawned.

When she reached the cave with her enchantment over it, she tried to slip in unnoticed. With only one foot in the cave, Chloe stood right in her path. She jammed one hand onto her hip and narrowed her eyes. "Where have you been?"

"Um." Heat filled Elora's cheeks *again*. "I was just—"

On the other side of the cave, Vesper looked up. He eyed her a little too knowingly.

She cleared her throat, attempting to sound as flippant as Brannick had. "I just came from the rocks by the beach." She gestured vaguely at the cave entrance behind her.

Chloe narrowed her eyes to even tinier slits and jammed her other hand onto her other hip. "And was it morning when you went *out* to the rocks?"

Elora very nearly sighed in relief at the question. "Yes." Technically, it *was* morning since she had unintentionally spent the night in Fairfrost. Morning just wasn't the first time she went out to the rocks.

Chloe continued to keep her eyes trained on her oldest sister while she used a ribbon to tie her hair into a bun. Vesper must have lost interest in the conversation sooner than Chloe because he had already turned his attention to the lace in his boot.

Donning what was supposed to be a casual smile, Elora stepped farther inside the cave. Grace stoked a fire that licked the bottom of a pot. On the other side of the cave, Quintus fiddled with a palm leaf, a piece of rope, and a silver piece of metal. He must have been crafting something, but Elora couldn't guess what.

She scanned the cave once more. "Where is Lyren?"

Quintus looked up from his materials for only a moment before he looked back down again. "Her friend came and said fae from another clan were preparing for battle."

Possibilities pounded in her mind as Elora reached for her sword hilt. "Are they building an army?"

Every fae she had ever met from Swiftsea always fought on Brannick's side. If they were already preparing for battle, perhaps they would help when she and the others went to rescue Brannick from Fairfrost.

Shrugging, Quintus bent over his work again. "I have no idea."

Vesper shoved his wrist in Elora's face. She hadn't even noticed him getting up. "When the battle is over, and you have won, *then* will you take this ribbon off me?"

When Elora stepped back, she caught Chloe's eye right away. Both of them glanced toward Grace after that. The three of them shared a look that held a little guilt but mostly the desire to help their brother.

It only lasted a moment before Grace got to her feet. She brushed a strand of red hair from her face and gestured at the pot over the fire. "Breakfast is done. You will like it, Vesper. It has cassava creamed with coconut milk and seasoned with cloves. I know how you love coconut."

Huffing, he trudged across the cave and slumped into the spot he had been before. "I do not love coconut." When she handed him a plate, he yanked it into his hands with a scowl. "I do not love anything now."

Pressing her lips together, Grace spooned some of the cassava onto plates for everyone else. No one said a word while they gathered their things.

Just when Elora prepared to spoon some of the creamy mixture into her mouth, Lyren rushed into the cave.

She panted and clutched her chest, her curls shaking. "We must leave now."

"But I just finished breakfast. We haven't even started eating." Grace whined the way only a twelve-year-old who sometimes forgot she wanted to be a grown up could.

Gasping for breath, Lyren looked over her shoulder. She waved a hand to open a door and glared at everyone. When she spoke again, she left no room for argument. "NOW!"

At least Elora had her sword. No one had time to take anything else before Lyren forced them through the door.

CHAPTER 19

Elora ended up in Swiftsea Palace before she understood the reason for it. Lyren waved her arms and shouted about a clan in Swiftsea who wanted to close the portal for good. Apparently, that same clan had helped Vesper get to the island with the source of the decay. But when Queen Noelani sent soldiers after the clan, something else had gone wrong. Something Elora still didn't understand.

It wasn't until Elora stepped foot in Swiftsea's sandstone palace that she realized the gravity of the situation.

Lyren yanked them all into a corner while she examined the area around them. Quintus and Chloe spoke in hushed tones that pulsed with energy. Soon, Quintus opened a door and Chloe and Grace stepped through it. Elora probably should have been the one to send her sisters somewhere safe, but at least someone had done it.

Soon, Lyren returned and beckoned Elora, Quintus, and Vesper to follow after her. Water gushed from ornate fountains and through the aqueduct system that trailed through the entire palace. Seashell and reed wind chimes sounded from nearly every corner and hallway they passed. Apart from those two sounds, silence filled the entire rest of the palace.

Vesper, Lyren, and Quintus kept their footsteps as quiet as the rest of the palace, but Elora had to fly to keep from making any noise.

"Where is everyone?" she whispered to Lyren.

The dark brown curls around Lyren's face wound as tight as the worry filling her eyes. "I told you, most of the soldiers left to deal with that clan who wants to close the portal for good."

If fear hadn't seized Lyren so completely, she probably would have been more annoyed by the question.

Quintus held his breath each time his foot touched down on the floor. He glanced at Lyren through the side of his eye. "But the palace wasn't left completely undefended, correct? Some of the soldiers stayed behind with Queen Noelani."

"Of course." Lyren replied in such a fast whisper, it nearly sounded like a hiss. "Who do you think contacted me?"

Vesper slumped against the wall for no apparent reason. His eyes were a hollow shell of what they had once been. Quintus sighed and went to help Vesper back to his feet again. Even Quintus's movements looked labored.

Shaking her head, Elora waved her hand in a circle. A translucent enchantment formed around them, blocking out the despair. If they hadn't left so quickly, she might have remembered the enchantment earlier.

The purple glow around them did wonders for Lyren and Quintus. Unfortunately, Vesper's face held even less expression than ever. He needed more than a protective enchantment. With everything else going on, they would just have to worry about the ice shard in his heart later.

Elora's wings fluttered silently as she hovered just behind the others. "If some of the Swiftsea soldiers stayed here, then where are they? And why are we here?"

The answer came even before she finished asking. They had reached the same large dining room where she and the others had eaten with Queen Noelani not so long ago. They stood just outside the room, peeking around the doorway into the room. So far, no one inside had noticed their presence, though that could change at any moment.

Bits of sandstone and rock scattered across the floor. The large fountains in each corner of the room had been smashed to crumpled heaps. The long table that stretched across the length of the room had been overturned. Wooden chairs sat on their sides or upside down. All of them had holes in the back where pearls had once been embedded.

Broken wind chimes and smashed plates littered every flat surface. Dozens of fae ducked behind the overturned tables. Most of them sported hair colors that ranged from white-blonde to chestnut brown. None of them had the rich black hair of Swiftsea fae.

She had to crane her neck to see deeper into the room. Across from the overturned table, a line of guards in crisp blue uniforms were chained against the wall. Their blue javelins lay at their feet, many of them snapped in half. A line of Fairfrost guards in their white brocade held curved axes that were aimed at the Swiftsea soldiers before them.

When Elora gasped, Lyren clapped a hand over Elora's mouth. The dark-skinned fae pressed a finger to her lips. Then she tilted her head toward the hallway. Her eyes landed on a bit of wall that looked slightly more decorative than the rest of it.

Trusting Lyren, Elora and the others followed her when she stepped toward the decorative spot in the wall. Lyren tugged on one of her curls as she traced a finger over the swirling carvings in the wall. At last, her blue-painted fingernail found a notch among the intricate patterns. When she waved her hand over the notch, a shimmer of blue appeared in the wall, revealing a door that hadn't been there before.

Lyren opened it and then shoved everyone inside. She whispered under her breath. "We use this wall for storytelling." She gestured toward small slits in the wall that opened into the room with all the soldiers and guards. "We use it to put scents, mist, and other things into the room that go along with the story. Since none of our enemies know this area exists, it also provides tactical advantage in situations like this."

She beckoned them forward. "This hidden area will give us the element of surprise, but we must attack at the same exact moment."

Even while she spoke, Faerie doors began appearing inside the Swiftsea dining room. Fairfrost guards pushed the Swiftsea soldiers through the doors. Whenever a fae from Swiftsea tried to protest, one of the guards from behind the table would attack.

Elora's heart jumped into her throat. She reached for her sword, but quickly released it. That weapon would do no good from inside this hidden compartment of the wall. Instead, she pushed her palm to one of the open slits, ready to release an enchantment through it.

Both Lyren and Quintus pulled her arm away from the slit before any magic could be released.

Lyren's eyes drooped when she watched the Swiftsea fae taken through doors. After a hard swallow, she whispered under her breath. "We are not here for them."

Elora wanted to scowl at Lyren's lack of concern, but then she caught a far worse sight through a slit in the wall. At the very edge of the room, far from the door they had peeked through earlier, High Queen Alessandra stood towering over a chained Queen Noelani.

The queen of Swiftsea wore a shimmery light blue dress. Her hair had been completely shaved, showing off her smooth brown skin. The silver and seashell crown glinted on her head. Something about it looked as defiant as the Swiftsea queen herself.

Not that being defiant helped her much. She had been forced to her knees with golden chains holding her arms behind her back. More chains held her to the ground so she couldn't escape. Just like the chains holding Brannick, these chains prevented Queen Noelani from using any magic. Despite that, the Swiftsea crown kept sparking and glowing, as if trying to provide the queen with the magic she couldn't use.

The crown on High Queen Alessandra's head looked even more powerful and even more menacing than ever. The high queen looked down her nose at the Swiftsea queen. She smoothed out her white brocade gown and then steepled her fingers under her chin. "How shall we do this? You can give your crown to me willingly." She shrugged. "Or I can kill you and take it by force. I will have it either way."

The Swiftsea queen huffed in response, which gave Elora the opportunity to whisper. "We have to do something."

Vesper sneered and attempted to remove the light purple ribbon still tied to his wrist.

Quintus leaned in close to the rest of them. "We need a plan."

"No." Elora made a fist. "We need to act. Now."

Lyren chewed her bottom lip before she finally nodded. "We will send enchantments through these slits and direct them at the high queen. We *must* do it at the same time. Otherwise, she will know our location and be able to avoid our attacks more easily. The element of surprise is the only advantage we have over her."

Everyone nodded in response.

With stricken eyes, Lyren looked through the slit nearest to her and put her hand over it. "When I nod, send the most powerful enchantment you can directly at the high queen."

Her head tilted upward. She took a deep breath to prepare. The rest of them held their breaths. Waiting.

But did things ever go according to plan? Of course not.

Vesper flinched and sent his enchantment before the others were ready. His enchantment flew into the room and slammed directly against High Queen Alessandra's chest. It rattled her enough to make her step back, but it had no other affect.

"What was that?" Quintus hissed the words under his breath.

Lyren dug every single one of her blue-painted fingernails deep into her curls. "You gave up our position. We were supposed to attack at the same moment."

Vesper flashed his teeth at both of them. "You should not have brought me here. You should have left me alone."

The lack of light in the wall compartment made it difficult to read his expression. He certainly sounded remorseful or guilty at least, but Elora still saw something funny in the face

163

he made. Had he done it on purpose? Was he *trying* to sabotage them?

A blast of enchantment slammed into the thin wall separating them from the high queen and Queen Noelani. When a second one slammed against it even harder, it became clear the wall itself wouldn't last long.

Good.

Facing the high queen head on would be better than cowering behind a wall.

In the short moment they had before the wall crumbled, Elora grabbed Vesper's arm. She purposefully wrapped her fingers around the ribbon on his wrist. He cringed at the touch, but he still looked toward her.

"We need you, Vesper." She gave his wrist a gentle squeeze. "I need you. You can do this."

He stared at her blankly until a spark lit in his eyes. His expression shifted so subtly she almost didn't notice it. But then his other hand found hers. He squeezed it.

She had no idea how long it would last, but for that moment at least, Vesper—the real Vesper—had come back to her.

Then the wall crumbled.

Yanking Vesper to the ground, Elora fell into a roll to break her fall. She let go of him and shot an enchantment from her fingertips, trusting her magic to know what to do. Whenever she felt the urge to duck, she did it, even if she didn't see a reason for it right away. Every time, ducking helped her narrowly avoid a blast of shimmery white enchantments.

Magic burst from Elora's fingertips as if it had been doing so her entire life, which of course it hadn't. In a way, using magic felt more natural than sword fighting did. Despite the feeling, once she got close enough to the high queen, she immediately drew her sword.

The blade sang as it whipped and sliced through the air. After a few unsuccessful jabs, she finally pierced the high queen's skin right along her collar bone.

High Queen Alessandra shrieked and sent an enchantment that knocked Elora off her feet. Lyren and Quintus sent their own enchantments, but the high queen blocked them easily. With her nostrils flaring, the high queen shoved Queen Noelani to the ground.

"I will deal with the rest of you later." The high queen's ice blue eyes narrowed to tiny slits. "I have someone more important to deal with at the moment."

In a sword fight, waiting could be an advantage sometimes. Other times, striking fast and hard gave an even stronger advantage. Without thinking, Elora sliced her sword as close to the high queen's neck as she could get.

The magic of Faerie crowns was simple. Once the crown touched a fae's head, that crown bonded to that fae. High Queen Alessandra had already taken the crown of Fairfrost, Noble Rose, Dustdune, and even Bitter Thorn. That meant only one thing.

To beat High Queen Alessandra, they had to kill her.

Elora held back nothing as she sent her glowing sword toward the high queen's flesh. She measured every strike as a killing strike. Even with enchantments to protect her, the high queen clearly didn't have the same endurance Elora had.

A huff tumbled from the high queen's lips when she sent an enchantment to block yet another sword strike. She immediately had to follow it with three more blocks in quick succession to fend off the enchantments from Lyren, Vesper, and Quintus.

She must have known what Elora was only daring to hope. Without reinforcements, the high queen couldn't hold off all of them forever.

No sooner had that hope sparked in Elora's chest than everything changed.

High Queen Alessandra sent a large blast, which knocked them all off their feet. It caused her to huff even harder, clearly taking more energy than she had previously been willing to expend. But apparently, that didn't matter now.

Once she pulled a glittering opal axe from her pocket, they all knew why.

In perhaps the most desperate attempt in her life, Elora threw her sword with its tip aiming for the high queen's chest. Powerful enchantments shot out at the same moment, also aiming for the high queen's chest.

None of their attacks met their mark.

In one swift motion, the high queen ducked and then swung her axe hard. With a sickening crunch, the weapon crushed Queen Noelani's ribcage. Blood spurted from the wound as the high queen yanked her axe free.

A hard lump grew in Elora's throat. The queen of Swiftsea, the queen who had helped them so often, now sat in a pool of her own blood on the palace floor. When the last breath left her lips, a shudder shook through her.

Screams wracked through the room, mostly coming from Lyren.

Enchantments shot from Elora's fingertips without any thought or aim. High Queen Alessandra blocked them as she ripped the silver crown off the ground and placed it on her own head. It glowed bright blue. The high queen laughed as its power seemed to fill her.

When she looked toward the others, she spoke in a voice that was probably more for herself than anyone. "I am Queen of Swiftsea."

Lyren screamed again, louder than before. Vesper slammed his fist against his chest as if his own chest pained him.

Stomping across the blood and broken wind chimes, Elora snatched her sword off the ground. High Queen Alessandra smiled at the sight of it, apparently now excited for the challenge.

Before Elora could lift the sword, someone grabbed her by the wrist and yanked her through a door. Swiftsea Palace disappeared, but Elora's grip on her sword only tightened.

CHAPTER

20

Writhing against the grip on her wrist, Elora stumbled out of the door. They landed in Bitter Thorn back in the clearing where her two sisters and Kaia waited for them. Sucking in a deep breath between clenched teeth, Elora turned to the fae who had forced her through the door. She didn't expect to find Quintus had done it.

Vesper and Lyren had come through a few steps ahead of them. The door disappeared before she could go back through it.

With a grunt, Elora shoved Quintus as hard as she could without actually making him fall. "What was that for?"

"She would have beaten us." No apology laced Quintus's voice.

"We were tiring her out!"

"She put the crown of Swiftsea on her head. Do you have any idea how much magic a crown has? She would have killed you."

Momentarily stunned by his word choice, Elora narrowed one eye. "Since when do you care whether I live or die?"

Quintus folded his arms over his chest. "Since I made a vow to your sister that I would not let you die in Swiftsea."

It took a moment for the words to sink in, but once they did, Elora immediately rounded on her middle sister.

Chloe's blonde hair looked wild and untamed. She tipped her nose in the air. "You're too impulsive. If you refuse to be careful during these battles, I have to protect you in other ways."

Clenching her jaw tight, Elora whipped around to face Quintus again. "Why are you conspiring with my sister?"

He only smirked and edged closer to Chloe. A smile danced across her lips once his shoulder bumped hers. Color flushed across her cheeks. Quintus's smirk grew.

Elora's teeth ground as she shoved Quintus again. It didn't even matter now if she made him fall. "I told you to stay away from my sister."

He didn't flinch once he regained his balance. He simply raised one eyebrow. "Just like you stayed away from Prince Brannick?"

A strangled scream erupted from her throat. She shoved him back again, even harder. He still didn't fall. "She is too young." Her voice did sound a little crazed, but she couldn't have been the only one to think they paid each other a little too much attention.

"Vesper." She whipped around again, searching for the brother who would surely be as protective of Chloe as Elora was.

He wasn't. He sat at the bottom of a tree with his knees curled up to his chin. His body rocked back and forth.

Lyren sat in a similar slump right at the base of Kaia's tree. Tears streamed down Lyren's cheeks. Her curls hung limp and stringy.

"Kaia took us to your house while you were gone, Quintus." Chloe's tone tuned soft. Her eyebrows pinched together. "It's not..." She gulped. "I don't think we should go back there. The walls are falling apart and demorogs keep attacking it."

The smirk Quintus had been wearing earlier vanished at once. He leaned against a tree and sank to the forest floor.

Despair crashed in all around them. Queen Noelani had died. High Queen Alessandra was now Queen of Swiftsea. And they couldn't even go back to Quintus's home.

Everyone had already erupted into tears or started moaning, at the very least.

Kaia stepped out of her tree. Branches and leaves grew among her emerald hair. Her skin had striations and a rough texture.

"Why have you not been staying in your tree?" Elora probably didn't need to scold, considering the dryad had been around a lot longer than her. But still, she looked as though she had been away from her tree for much too long—and now she was stepping out of it again? Fear forced the scolding out.

Kaia only sighed in response. She twirled a bit of emerald hair around one finger, but even that looked duller than usual. "I *have* been in my tree. The despair makes me distressed. When I am distressed, my tree cannot work its magic like it should."

Elora nodded, ignoring how her gut twisted in on itself. She closed her eyes and sent an enchantment into the air with as little thought as possible. Soon, a dome of purple sparkles surrounded them. Her voice caught when she spoke. "Hopefully the enchantment around us can help you now."

The dryad nodded, but it did nothing to lift her expression. "It should." She lifted both her arms into the air and breathed in, as if the enchantment gave her strength.

"Where are Soren and Fifer?"

Kaia's face fell as she brought her hands to her sides again. "They are trying to make the castle livable again. Do you remember the snowflakes filled with anger that High Queen Alessandra sent to Bitter Thorn Castle? The snow is still falling. They cannot figure out how to remove it. And black thorns are infesting the castle more than they ever have before."

Even the embroidery on Elora's gossamer gown looked duller when she flopped onto the ground.

The dryad sat beside her and lowered her voice. "What happened?" Using her chin, Kaia pointed toward Lyren, who sobbed the loudest of anyone.

Elora brushed her thumb over a silvery patch of beadwork on her mauve gown. "Queen Noelani is dead. The high queen took the Swiftsea crown for herself."

Kaia closed her eyes and pressed a hand to her forehead. She appeared more resigned than surprised. Truthfully, it shouldn't have been a surprise to any of them. High Queen Alessandra clearly wanted all the crowns. Now only the Mistmount crown remained.

Clearing her throat, Kaia glanced toward the castle. "When Soren and Fifer return, I will tell Soren to find King Jackory and keep him safe. We cannot allow the high queen to get the last crown. She would become unstoppable."

"What about building an army?"

As Kaia shook her head, several thin branches appeared in her hair. Her skin looked more bark-like than ever. "We will just have to find another way to rescue Prince Brannick."

No matter how Elora tried, she could not think of a single thing to say. Even with the enchantment surrounding them, despair sank into her chest. Her arms felt too heavy even hanging at her sides. She leaned her back against the tree behind her and did her best not to cry.

But what did it matter now anyway? They had already lost so much. Could any of them really believe they had any chance at all?

Kaia stepped back into her tree. The others continued to sob. Elora tried to find any reason to not give up completely. When she found none, she allowed her mind to drift and think of nothing instead. For a long while, they all just sat there.

Perhaps resting could give them the peace they needed. Maybe then they could formulate a new plan.

CHAPTER 21

Without time, Elora couldn't explain how long she had sat in the forest clearing with the others. But maybe it didn't matter how long it had been. Her heart didn't feel as tight or strained now. No one cried anymore. Joy did not fill the space, but devastation didn't fill it either.

Didn't that matter more than the time that had passed?

Faerie had changed when Queen Noelani died, but they were learning how to continue on anyway.

Elora cleared her throat and glanced at Lyren. "Can you tell us more about that clan in Swiftsea that wants to close the portal for good?"

With her nose twitching, Lyren ran a hand over her arm.

"Close the portal for good?" Chloe asked. "Can they do that?" Her blonde hair draped over her shoulder as she prepared to braid it.

Lyren's eyes stayed downcast as she chewed on a fingernail. "I do not think so. The only fae with strong enough magic are Prince Brannick and High Queen Alessandra. Prince Brannick already refused to close the portal. Since High Queen Alessandra relies on emotion to control people, I doubt she will close it either."

"That's a relief." Grace sighed and pointed her face toward the enchantment protecting them.

Elora turned back to Lyren. "Is there a way to close the portal without magic?"

Vesper rolled his eyes. "Of course there is." His eyes went wide when the words tumbled from his mouth. He immediately pressed his lips together and looked down.

When the others tried to ask what he meant, he wouldn't answer.

Quintus stuffed a hand into his pocket for no apparent reason. "Why do they want to close the portal anyway?"

By the time his hand emerged from his pocket, he had retrieved a single harp string. Perhaps it had been left over after the harps he had crafted for Elora and her sisters. He handed the harp string to Chloe, leaning a little too close to her as he did.

She stared at it and then glanced up at him. Her fingers held the end of her hair that she had just finished braiding.

He pushed the harp string toward her again. "To tie off your braid." He shook his head. "Never mind. I can do it for you. It might be too difficult with only one hand."

"Oh." Chloe's cheeks turned pink when he took her blonde braid and wrapped the harp string around it several times. When he finished, he caught her eye and gazed intently.

Elora's fists clenched, ready to remind Quintus that her sister was only fifteen and not an adult and not fae and *definitely* not someone he should ever look at in such a way.

Before she could open her mouth, Soren and Fifer appeared at the edge of the clearing. Soren's beard shook as he cleared his throat. "There is something you should all see." His eyes flicked upward at the dome of magic surrounding them before he turned to Elora. "Just make your enchantment follow us and come this way."

Anticipation fluttered in her belly when Elora got to her feet. She turned to ask Kaia to join them, but the dryad had stepped out of her tree already. By the time they all started down the path Soren indicated, Elora only half noticed she had done some kind of magic to make her enchantment follow them. Even Vesper joined them as they moved deeper into the forest.

Once they moved past the clearing, Tansy floated down from among the sprites above. She landed on Elora's shoulder with a short nod in greeting.

Soren stopped only a few steps later. His bug-like eyes widened when he placed a palm against a trunk with thorns crawling up its side. The entire tree had bent over. It had a wide trunk that Elora wouldn't even be able to reach both her arms around, but still, the tree bent over at its middle with the branches now pointing toward the ground.

The sight of it gnawed at Elora's insides. A lump formed in her throat, though she couldn't explain why. An overwhelming sense washed over her that the tree was in pain.

A similar expression of pain stretched across Fifer's face His floppy ears drooped as he glanced at ground. "There are more. We will show you."

When they continued walking, Quintus turned to Lyren. "*Why* does that Swiftsea clan want the portal closed? You never said."

She rubbed a hand over her forearm while her lips pulled to a deeper frown. "There are groups in Mistmount and Dustdune that want to close it because it will keep High Queen Alessandra from manipulating them. But the clan in Swiftsea thinks it will fix the decay."

From Elora's shoulder, Tansy let out an impressive snort for someone her size. Her furry green wings shook as the sprite chuckled. She muttered under her breath, "If they hate the decay so much, they have no reason to close the portal."

"Exactly." To Elora's surprise—maybe to *everyone's* surprise—Vesper had been the one to respond.

Lyren's expression turned sour.

"What does that mean?" Turning to her shoulder, Elora raised her eyebrows at the sprite.

Tansy rolled her eyes before sitting down. "The *decay* is not a decay at all. It is only a place in Faerie where the portal is closed."

Elora's feet stopped in place while the words sank in. Shaking her head, she tried to force understanding where it didn't exist yet. "Are you saying that if Prince Brannick had closed the portal, the decay would have spread throughout all of Faerie?"

The sprite shrugged. "Yes. That is how Faerie looked before the portal was opened. The land changed gradually, which is why most fae do not remember." She raised an eyebrow. "But sprites remember all."

Though Soren and Fifer lead them in the opposite direction, Lyren turned and marched toward Elora's shoulder. Both of Lyren's hands clenched in tight fists. "You knew that

176

for how long, and you never bothered to tell anyone?" A loud huff erupted from her lips. "Do you have any idea how long we have been trying to find the cause of the decay?"

Pointing her nose toward the sky, Tansy let out an even louder huff than Lyren had. The sprite got to her feet and spun away from Lyren so fast, her sparkly pink dress twirled out around her.

Lyren clenched her teeth and stomped even closer. "If I had known that I could have told my queen." Her voice faltered as she reached for the two silver necklaces hanging from her neck. "Maybe I could have gotten a third necklace. Maybe I could have righted my past. Maybe…" Sucking in a breath, she gazed at the ground. "Now my queen is dead, and I will never get a third necklace. You should have told us about the decay."

After flying to Elora's other shoulder, Tansy landed close enough to grab onto Elora's ear. She spoke loud enough for the others to hear, but her body language made it clear the words were just for Elora. "We sprites see everything in Faerie. We know *all* secrets. Surely, you must agree that it is better to reveal nothing, rather than to reveal *everything*."

Puffs of air burst from Lyren's nostrils. Her dark curls shook with each one.

Elora folded her arms over her chest, which drew Lyren's notice exactly as she had hoped. "The sprites have good reason to not speak to fae except to deliver messages. Would you like all *your* secrets spilled?" When Elora threw a pointed glance, Lyren's puffing finally calmed. Elora continued. "At least we know the cause of the decay now."

"Here is another one." Soren's voice came out gruff as he gestured toward another tree. This tree was even bigger than the first. Just like the other, it had been bent right in half.

Thorns wrapped around its base, but they crawled upward too. At least half the tree trunk had been covered in the black, creaking thorns.

Biting her bottom lip, Elora placed a palm against the trunk. Crackling energy seemed to spark just under the bark. It wasn't the sparkling, exciting kind of crackling either. She recognized the feeling even without wanting to.

"Ansel did this." She pulled her hand away without ceremony. "He used a gemstone to do it."

"How do you know?" Quintus stood too close to Chloe, but that didn't stop his voice from dripping with skepticism.

"I just do." Even if she wanted to give one, Elora had no other explanation.

"But why would he do such a thing?" Grace's big eyes worked as a reminder that she was both too young and too innocent to be dealing with Faerie's problems.

"That is not all he has done." Tansy spoke in a low whisper, so only Elora would hear. The sprite closed her eyes and gulped before she spoke again. "When Ansel used those dark enchantments and tainted the air with his residue, we could not figure out his motive. He never spoke of his plan to anyone." Her eyes snapped open. "But we finally figured his plan out on our own. He has made a complete circle of enchantments all around Bitter Thorn. The residue from his enchantments continues to spread outward. It will continue to spread until it reaches magic strong enough to hold it back."

The glint in Tansy's pink and green eyes went dull when she raised an eyebrow.

Elora blinked twice before she understood the significance of the words. Finally, she gasped. "Creation magic."

Tansy nodded. "Ansel knows he cannot touch the creation magic. He learned that long ago, but he never told anyone. Not even High Queen Alessandra. Once he finds the creation magic, he knows he can't touch it, but that won't stop him from finding a way to control it."

Since the others hadn't heard Tansy's words, they all looked from Elora to Tansy expectantly.

Only after attempting to swallow the lump in her throat could Elora speak again. "Ansel is trying to find the creation magic in Bitter Thorn." She shook her head, forcing herself to use even more correct words. "He is not just trying, he is succeeding. His residue keeps the sprites away."

She gestured upward showing how sprites flew up above them, but not over another part of the forest. "The sprites cannot abide the residue." She gulped. "And the residue will only stop when it hits the creation magic. So, wherever the sprites start congregating, he will know that is correct spot."

No one had any response to that. Ansel would find the creation magic, and he would do it soon.

Whatever happened, they had to stop him from taking control of it.

CHAPTER
22

On the way back to Kaia's tree, Elora noticed another bent tree deeper in the forest. The mystery needed solving, but her ideas had been spent trying to find a way to rescue Brannick and trying to figure out how to work her magic. Now she had to figure out how to stop Ansel too. At least her protective enchantment seemed to be helping the others.

When they returned to the clearing, Kaia and Soren spoke to each other quietly. Soren would probably leave soon to help protect King Jackory from the high queen.

The others began conjuring sleeping mats to lay onto the forest floor. Elora stayed as busy as she could while everyone worked. If she gave off the appearance that she would stay, hopefully no one would notice when she slipped away.

Just before she stepped outside her dome of enchantment, Grace grabbed her oldest sister by the hand. "Where are you going?"

"Um." Elora swallowed. Her eyes turned straight to her middle sister, hoping Chloe might help to distract their youngest sister. Except Chloe stared too deeply into Quintus's eyes to notice either of her sisters.

If she hadn't been in such a hurry, Elora would have stomped over and pushed the two of them apart. For now, she simply waved her youngest sister off instead. "I need to study those bent trees more. Go lay down and try to get some rest. You will need it after everything we have been through today."

Grace responded with a huffy burst of air. Her nose scrunched up as she folded her arms over her chest. But when Elora stepped outside the enchantment that protected them from the despair, Grace could not follow.

After only a few steps down the path, Tansy fluttered down to Elora's shoulder again. "You are getting better at deception."

Elora sucked in a breath. "I *am* going to study the bent trees. I need to figure out why Ansel would do something like that."

"Hmmm." Tansy tapped her chin with exaggerated curiosity. "And will your *study* involve a conversation with the prince of this land?"

"Maybe." Elora tipped her nose in the air, but it did little to hide her true motive, since she also pulled out the sage green crystal from her pocket.

Tansy gave one look at it before she snorted. Her furry green wings lifted her into the air until she hovered just in front of Elora. "We sprites know when to afford privacy." Her expression dimmed. "But if you go through his door again." A wince twisted across her features. Her pink and green eyes lowered to the ground. "Just be careful."

The sprite floated upward so fast Elora had to shout her response. "I will."

With the crystal in her hand, she trudged over bundles of thorns until she reached another bent tree. Her fingers tingled when she touched the trunk. Once again, she felt the same magic that had stolen her essence to create the gemstones. She couldn't put into words why she knew the magic came from Ansel, but that didn't make her any less sure of the fact.

"Elora."

She spun around, more eager than perhaps she should have been considering everything she had to speak to Brannick about. His door swirled just behind her. Unlike every other time he had used a door to contact her, the door swirled as large as a usual door. Big enough for her to step through.

Her heart leapt in her chest. She lowered her voice to a whisper. "Are you alone? Is it safe for me to come through?"

"Yes." His answer sounded just as eager as she felt.

Letting warmth spread through her arms, she stepped into his door without hesitation.

He stood on the other side, eyes expectant. The moment her feet touched the marble floor of his cell, he took both her hands into his and held them against his chest. "Blaz is safe."

Her lips curled upward as she glanced over the cell. "Is he here?"

"No. I still do not know where he is." A crack in Brannick's demeanor appeared, but he quickly smiled it away. "But I thought about what you said before. You asked if I could feel his essence, so I tried to do it." He took in a deep breath that sent a gleam into his eyes. "It worked. He is alive, and he is safe. He escaped High Queen Alessandra somehow. I am certain of it."

Elora touched a hand to her chest, taking a moment to let the good news fill her. "I am glad to hear it."

Before she could open her mouth again, he leaned forward and squeezed her hands, which he still held. "You would be so proud of me." He stood a little straighter. "I convinced the guards to plan an attack."

"An attack?" Fear caught hold of the spot of joy she had dared to allow inside her. She swallowed. "Against High Queen Alessandra? Is that safe?"

His chuckle might have alleviated her fears if he hadn't suggested something so dangerous. "It is not safe now. How much difference could an attack make?"

It could make plenty of difference, specifically between the high queen working with her guards and killing them, but maybe now wasn't the best moment to point that out.

He shrugged. "It is not truly an attack anyway. Because of their bargain with her, they cannot physically injure her, but they *can* trick her. Remember how you told me the dragons in Fairfrost are wild now? We think we might be able to use that."

She wanted to praise him. She wanted to tell him it was the most splendid plan and that he would most certainly succeed. Instead, she frowned. "Are you sure this is a good idea?"

Though the prince still looked supremely proud of himself, his face took on a more serious quality. "We cannot let her have every victory. If her own guards devise a plan against her, she will realize her standing is not as sure as she wishes it to be."

His head tilted then, which flipped Elora's stomach into a knot. He leaned down, bringing his nose almost close enough to touch hers. His eyes shimmered and pulsed as he gazed at her. "When did you start calling her *high* queen instead of just *queen?*"

If he had just stood there staring into her eyes, maybe she could have answered. Except right then, he reached out and ran his fingers through the hair framing her face. Suddenly, she was leaning into him without even realizing it.

He met her eyes just long enough to raise questioning eyebrows but quickly glanced back at her hair.

She had to slam her eyes shut just to remember what he had asked in the first place. "I cannot remember." By the time she opened her eyes again, pain had cleared her mind. "I think it was when I started to believe she might actually win."

Those words broke Brannick out of his own trance. His eyes dulled as he let out a hard breath. "She will *not* win." Once the words left his lips, a carefree gleam lit in his eyes. He slipped his fingers deep enough into Elora's hair to reach the back of her head. Now, he smirked. "A prince never accepts defeat."

It didn't matter if she had any retort. Once his lips met hers the retort fluttered away into nothing. He wrapped his other arm around her back, pulling her close enough to meet his chest. His kiss came gentle, but with an eagerness that searched for more. Her body melted against his. It suddenly seemed very important to enjoy every moment because soon, everything could change. She needed to be with Brannick now.

Just in case.

At that thought, she immediately pulled away. Her cheeks were hot. She could feel them burning while she tried to catch her breath. "Stop distracting me."

She had meant to scold, but her voice came out a little too breathless for it.

Brannick only smirked in response.

An identical smirk played across her own lips, which refused to disappear even when she bit her lip. "I came here because I have questions." She forced her gaze away from his mesmerizing eyes just long enough to smooth nonexistent wrinkles from her gown. "What happens when a fae touches the creation magic in Bitter Thorn? I heard you talking to High Queen Alessandra about it."

His smirk only faded slightly at the mention of the high queen. He kept staring at Elora with a gaze that could probably control her. "The fae loses his or her magic."

"What?" Elora shook her head. If the words had been even a smidgeon less shocking, she probably would have continued staring at Brannick forever. But now her eyebrows were raised, and she had taken a step back.

He raised a conspiratorial eyebrow. "I am careful to avoid that particular piece of information no matter how many questions the high queen asks. I hope she will think the creation magic is safe and touch it herself."

Elora's expression turned playful. "How devious."

Brannick ran his fingers through his hair with an arrogant eyebrow raise. "I have been known to be brilliant when it is needed most."

The arrogance quickly faded into an intense gaze that heated her cheeks once again. "Or perhaps only when I have the most beautiful fae in Faerie to impress." When he stepped forward, his gaze fell to her lips.

"You are distracting me again." If she hadn't stepped even closer to him, her scolding might have meant more. "I need to tell you what happened in Swiftsea. And also about something Ansel did to the—"

Before she could finish, they both heard a door creaking open followed by a pair of marching footsteps.

Brannick's shoulders stiffened with tension. "The guards are on our side, but they cannot stop themselves from following the high queen's orders." His jaw clenched. "They will tell her if they see you."

He waved a hand and gestured at the door he had opened. She nodded, already stepping toward it. "I will go, but I need to tell you something. Open a door to me again as soon as it is safe."

He leaned close, as if to send her off with one more kiss. But then the footsteps grew louder, and they both knew the moment had passed. She hurried through the door and returned back to the forest of Bitter Thorn once again.

The visit had been worth it just to see Brannick, but it hadn't given her anything she sought. She still had many mysteries to uncover. Her eyes flitted upward to the sprites who avoided the residue from Ansel's enchantments.

If she didn't find out more information soon, Ansel might find the creation magic first.

CHAPTER 23

Heart beats thundered inside Elora's chest, but just when it got too powerful, the beats turned to flutters. It left her feeling both too much and too little all at the same time. The residue from Ansel's enchantments was closing in. *Someone* needed to save Faerie before it was too late, but how could she do it on her own when she had no idea what needed to be done?

When a glow of green light floated down and onto her shoulder, Elora let out a sigh. "Prince Brannick told me Blaz escaped High Queen Alessandra." She took a breath before turning to face the sprite on her shoulder. "Can you find him?"

Tansy took her time brushing her sparkly pink dress before she folded her arms over her chest. "If he is still in Fairfrost, we cannot. No sprites are there to see him."

Elora nodded, her stomach twisting at the words.

The expression on Tansy's face darkened. "And if he wears his glamour, we also cannot find him."

With a huff, Elora kicked a nearby rock.

Wind tickled across her face when the sprite lifted into the air to hover in front of her. Tansy opened her eyes wide, filling them with a sort of hope that had been absent a moment ago. "But if he leaves Fairfrost *and* he removes his glamour, you will be the first besides us to know."

Tremors worked through Elora's fingers as she formed them into a fist over her heart. Her lips pressed tightly together, doing everything they could to keep herself from saying *thank you*. But gratitude burned so fiercely inside, even her lips wanted to disobey.

Would it really matter being indebted to the sprites? Would it matter when they were willing to do so much for her?

As if sensing the debate in Elora's head, Tansy fluttered even closer. "It is the least we can do after you sacrificed so much to rescue us."

When a twig snapped near them, Elora's stomach muscles clenched. She reached for her sword and whirled around in a flash. Her hand had automatically started drawing her sword, but it stopped when she saw who had come upon them.

Wilting ears hung on either side of Fifer's head. He stumbled over the thorns and moss on the forest floor without any clear direction. He didn't even seem to notice Elora.

Mutters whispered under his breath. "A home. I just need a home until the castle is repaired."

"Fifer."

The brownie froze in place, blinking up at Elora with his great big eyes. He stared at her, but he didn't seem to see her. Maybe her protective enchantment hadn't protected him as much as the others. Without his home, he just kept getting worse.

She shook her head and crouched down to the nearest berry bush. It didn't have his favorite purple berries, but he still liked the red ones it grew. After gathering a few, she pushed them toward him expectantly.

He blinked at the berries with the same blank expression as before, but he also licked his bottom lip.

When she brought one of the berries closer to his mouth, he opened it without hesitation. It took at least three berries before he made any indication of being aware of his surroundings.

Sighing, Elora continued to gather berries for him.

While she worked, Tansy plopped onto her shoulder. "Did you gain the answers you sought from the prince?"

A twitch worked through Elora's nose as she plucked a few more berries from the bush. "No. A guard started coming, and I had to leave before I could tell Prince Brannick about the bent trees or about Queen Noelani. He is planning an attack with the Fairfrost guards, but that seems dangerous when the guards still have to follow the high queen's every order."

"Hmm."

Tansy's lack of concern only brought Elora's worry right to the surface. She took a breath, trying to calm herself. "They have bargains they must follow." She kept pushing her hand toward Fifer, noticing too late that he had already eaten all the berries there. She shook her head. "How can they fight her when they must follow her every order?"

Tansy twisted her hips, which sent her sparkly dress in a twirl around her knees. She looked even less concerned than before. "If only you knew someone with a formula that could destroy the high queen's enchantments and possibly break her bargains too."

Sucking in a breath, Elora got to her feet. "Tindra." She grabbed her sword hilt and glanced around. But how could she get there?

Fifer had gone to the bush and began plucking off his own berries now. He didn't look great, but at least his ears didn't droop so much.

Still gripping her sword, Elora began talking to herself. "I have been to the place where Tindra and Severin are hiding. I do not know the name of the location, but I know that it is in a cave in Mistmount." Her brown hair flung out behind her as she whipped her head toward her shoulder. "Is that close enough to open a door to them? I know I have to open a door to a location, but is it enough to open a door to their cave, even if I do not know the name of the cave?"

Tansy scrunched her nose. Even her eyes seemed to wince. "Do not open a door to the cave itself. That is their home. You should not open a door inside a home unless you have been invited."

The sprite had meant to send a warning, but one word stood out more than the others.

Home.

Elora mouthed the word as she glanced downward. Fifer continued to stuff berries into his mouth, but somehow, she knew food would not be enough to cure him of whatever ailment weakened him now.

He needed a home.

Even if it was temporary until Bitter Thorn Castle had been repaired, he needed a place to call home. Without one, he might never recover.

Elora took a deep breath, holding onto her sword for strength. When that didn't help enough, she used her other hand to touch the purple ribbons from her mother in her belt.

She had to open a door. Just because she knew it didn't mean it would be any easier. But she had done it once before when she had to leave Fairfrost. Then again, she had assumed it was Kaia's door. She hadn't realized until later that she opened the door herself. But she *had* done it. Maybe *not* thinking about it would help.

Glancing down at Fifer, she focused on him as much as possible. Her hand waved through the air, but she did her best to ignore it. Fifer and the berries. That's what she needed to focus on.

Taking an unsteady breath, Elora finally allowed herself to glance up. She feared what she might or might not see. Her stomach clenched as she held her breath.

But a door swirled just ahead. She knew now that it was her own door, not Kaia's. It still had the signature browns and greens of someone who came from Bitter Thorn with small vines of black twisting through. It gave off the scent of fresh wildflowers, spongy moss, and crisp rain. It also had tufts of purple wildflowers dotting through the swirls of the tunnel.

Her own door. It proved she was Bitter Thorn, even though she hadn't been born there. The purple wildflowers looked exactly like the ones Brannick had given to her many times. Maybe he knew all along that the wildflowers were like her. Perhaps she and the wildflowers shared a similarity in essence.

It still seemed strange that her magic worked best the less she thought about it, but she couldn't afford to worry about that just before using the door. Tansy settled herself onto Elora's shoulder, apparently ready to go with her.

A moment later, Elora stepped onto the same mountain path she had visited once before. A white, iridescent enchantment shimmered over the cave entrance, but other than that, it looked exactly the same as before.

Both Tindra and Severin hunched over the stone table at the edge of the cave. They had built a small fire right on top of it with a strange contraption made of wire hanging above it. A glass vial filled with pearlescent blue liquid hung suspended over the fire. The two of them held their breaths as Tindra dipped a glass skewer into the liquid and began stirring.

Nothing happened.

They must have expected something because both of their shoulders slumped.

From Elora's side, Fifer nudged her with his shoulder. Nodding, Elora cleared her throat. "May we come in?"

CHAPTER
24

Elora bit her bottom lip as she stood at the cave entrance waiting.

A wave of white-blonde hair flew as Tindra whipped around to face the cave entrance. Fear crinkled the edges of her eyes, but something even deeper lingered inside them. Severin turned too, his face drawn and tight.

Once they realized it was Elora standing outside their cave, fear lifted from their shoulders. They both still shuddered though. It probably had something to do with the despair in the air. Apparently, the white enchantment over the cave entrance didn't help enough with it.

After the pair of them took in Elora's presence, their eyes then shifted in different directions. Severin glanced toward Elora's shoulder where Tansy still sat in her sparkly, pink dress. His lips twitched up at the sight of her.

Tindra's gaze turned downward to the floppy-eared companion at Elora's side. Quirking one eyebrow up, Tindra asked, "Did you bring a brownie?"

"Yes." Elora looked down at her feet, itching to move them forward. "He needs a home. I thought maybe he could stay with you until his real home is repaired."

When she took another pointed glance toward her feet and into the cave, Tindra understood at once. She waved them all inside. "Come in. We would be happy to house your brownie friend for now." She looked down into his big eyes. "If that is all right with you?"

Fifer stood tall and pointed his squat nose upward. At his highest height, he stood only slightly taller than a rabbit. "I require an offering every evening if you expect me to help with meals and cleaning."

"Of course." Severin dashed away from the stone at the edge of the cave and knelt next to the fire at the center of the cave. He dug through a large burlap bag until he drew out two drawstring bags made of leather. "Do you prefer berries or cheese? Once you tell us what you like, we can find more of it."

Severin's words came out as quick and excited as usual, but his movements did not. His muscles seemed to strain under the lightest moves. And his face looked more drawn by the moment.

Fifer had the same drawn expression on his own face. He lumbered over to Severin, clearly eager to discuss his preferences for offerings. Both acted as though a heavy weight pressed down on their chests.

With fluttering wings, Tansy lifted off Elora's shoulders and flew over to Severin as well. She momentarily glanced back at the cave entrance and shuddered at the sight of it.

Not allowing herself to think, Elora waved her hand and shot an enchantment from her fingertips. The moment it covered the cave entrance, everyone in the room let out a heavy sigh. After that, both Tindra and Severin gaped at the glittery purple enchantment Elora had created.

"Remarkable." Tindra's jaw dropped more even after she finished speaking.

Severin placed a hand on his chest and took in two deep breaths. By the time he finished, his face looked brighter than ever. "None of our protective enchantments have worked so well against the despair."

Words buzzed at the back of Elora's throat, but she didn't know whether to share them or not. Running a thumb over her leather sword hilt, she glanced toward her sprite friend. Tansy landed on Severin's knee. She nodded graciously when he offered her a small hunk of cheese. After digging through his bag, he found another drawstring bag full of white nuts for Fifer.

The sprites saw everything in Faerie. A large cluster of them floated overhead, filling the cave with a soft green glow. Elora knew for herself how much it took to become a friend to the sprites. If the sprites trusted Severin, surely, she could trust him too. Besides that, something deep in her gut told her to trust Severin and Tindra.

And with Brannick unavailable, she needed someone else to talk to.

Swallowing hard, Elora finally forced the buzzing words from her lips. "My magic works better when I do not think about it." She gulped. "Is that normal?"

Shrugging, Severin popped a berry into his mouth. "Everyone's magic is different."

Tindra had gone back to her worktable. She stirred the pearlescent formula, leaning a little closer to it with every breath.

Perhaps she shouldn't worry about her magic now anyway. Elora cleared her throat again. "Prince Brannick is planning an attack with the Fairfrost guards. I could not speak to him for long, but I thought your formula might help him. You said it could destroy the high queen's enchantments and possibly break her bargains too, right?"

Whipping around, Tindra bit into her pink lips. "Once it is finished, it will be able to destroy the bargains and *almost* all enchantments." She frowned. "I do not think I can get it to destroy the enchantments she made using Ansel's gemstones, unfortunately." Her nose wrinkled at the cave entrance. "Those are too powerful."

Churning filled Elora's stomach as she fought to stand still. Maybe Tindra and Severin didn't know why those particular enchantments had so much power, but Elora did. They had been made with her fae blood back before she had access to her magic. The gemstones had all the power from fae blood. Without magic, her fae blood hadn't been able to resist being taken and used in such a way.

Even now, the thought sent a shiver down her spine.

Tindra turned back to her worktable. "My formula needs more tweaking, but I am getting close."

Severin stoked the fire at the center of the cave. By the time he finished, a light seemed to spark in his eye. At the same moment, he and Tindra jerked their heads toward the cave entrance. Considering the conversation, they probably looked at the glittery purple enchantment covering their cave entrance. *Elora's* enchantment.

Elora swallowed. She had to change the conversation. She couldn't have them asking any questions about her magic because she didn't even know how to use it properly. She didn't even know what *kind* of magic she had. It wasn't enough that she got it to work occasionally. If they wanted her help, they needed dependable magic. The last thing Elora needed was an entire realm depending on her when she didn't even know why or how her magic worked.

Another question flitted into her mind, and she asked it immediately. She just needed to change the subject. "What do you know about Ansel?"

They both flinched. In Severin, the flinch happened more around his mouth and nose. In Tindra, it happened in her shoulders and in her eyes. Regardless, neither of them had any pleasant expressions to give at the mention of his name.

"Too much." Disdain curdled Severin's words.

"Same as me then." Elora let out a sigh. "He set off enchantments in Bitter Thorn that will soon reveal the source of the creation magic. He is also using gemstones to bend trees in Bitter Thorn, though I have no idea why."

Fifer and Tansy continued to munch on the food Severin had found for them. Severin, however, sat completely still. His eyes stared a little harder than they ever had. "You seem more concerned about Ansel than you do about High Queen Alessandra."

"Do I?" It wasn't until then that Elora realized she held her sword hilt in a death grip. Her other hand formed a fist around a portion of her gown. Even the muscles in her neck clenched tight. She shrugged and took a few steps nearer to the worktable to ease some of the tension inside her.

She regretted the action at once because Tindra stared at her steadily, clearly eager to continue the conversation Elora had been trying to avoid. Tindra gestured toward the glass vial. "If you can create an enchantment strong enough to block the despair, your magic might be strong enough to break the enchantments created with those awful gemstones. You might need a gemstone to do it though."

"I cannot do that." The words came out of Elora harsher than she meant them. Instead of trying to temper them, she stepped back.

Still perched on Severin's knee, Tansy looked up in surprise. If it had only been surprise that would have been one thing, but disappointment shimmered there too.

Elora gulped.

Tindra and Severin shared a look with each other and then they both sent unforgiving gazes at Elora. Placing a hand on top of her worktable, Tindra raised an eyebrow. "Why not?"

"I cannot." Elora stepped back again. At least her words hadn't come out harsh again. Instead, they came out as small as a single berry compared to all of Bitter Thorn Forest. She shook her head. She gulped. None of it made any difference.

Near panic roiled in her gut. She gripped her sword hilt again, as if that would help. "I am nobody. I know I am spectacular with a sword and decent with a harp, but that does not make me good at everything."

Once the words started spilling from her lips, they wouldn't stop. All the fear, all the pain she had been ignoring came to surface. The words stung her throat on their way out. "I was born a mortal. I was not meant to fight a war in Faerie. I was meant to marry a man who only barely tolerated my sword skill. I am glad I escaped that life, but what right do I have to put all the fae in Faerie at risk?"

Again. Her head spun as she remembered how her bargain with King Huron had nearly destroyed Faerie and how her blood had made the gemstones that were currently destroying Faerie.

Her voice came out tiny again. "I was not born for greatness."

"That is true." Severin nodded from his spot by the fire.

198

Tindra shot him a deathly glare.

He raised both hands, as if that would act as a ward against her glare. "I have heard of the way mortal women are treated in her place in the mortal realm. Their greatest destinies are usually in a strong marriage and nothing more."

"What does that matter?" Tindra spit the words out, still glaring at Severin a little.

By the time she whipped her head toward Elora, her expression turned gentle. She gestured toward her worktable. "Do you think a simple palace researcher like me was ever destined to create a formula that could take down the most powerful high queen Faerie has ever known?"

Elora's throat continued to sting with the pain of her earlier words, but at least the lump inside it started shrinking.

Tindra shrugged. "So you were not born for greatness. Who cares? Be great anyway."

A dumbfounded expression must have filled Elora's face. The grip on her sword hilt had relaxed so much that her arm fell to her side. She blinked.

Sweeping her blonde hair behind one shoulder, Tindra smiled. "I am certain you have it in you."

It took another beat before Elora could find a response. When she did, she subconsciously leaned forward to share it. "But I do not even know what kind of magic I have."

They all snorted at that. Even being the smallest, Tansy snorted loudest of all. She glanced up at Severin and flashed a wide smirk. Fifer chuckled as he rolled a berry between his spindly fingers. Tindra shook her head and turned back to the worktable.

Only Severin found it necessary to explain *why* they all found her response so hilarious. He glanced up at her with a twinkle in his eye. "You think too little of yourself."

"What does that mean?"

Bent over slightly, Tindra stirred her formula. She didn't turn around, but she used her other hand to vaguely gesture toward the enchantment covering the cave entrance. "If you can do magic like that, then you already know what your magic is."

"I do not know." Elora had to use all her self-control to keep from stomping her feet. "I have tried to pinpoint it. I have—"

"You said it works best the less you think about it, correct?" Tindra turned around. "What does your gut say?"

Even before she finished speaking, the blue formula began hissing and spewing splatters of formula out of the glass vial. Severin bounded over to the worktable where he and Tindra began chopping herbs and adjusting the fire.

As her hands flew across the worktable, Tindra shook her head. "It got too hot again. We will be up all night correcting this."

Tansy flew over and landed on Elora's shoulder. "You should go."

Severin whipped around and nodded. "I will have the sprites update you on our progress. They will send me word if you have anything to tell us as well."

Elora nodded and opened a door back to Bitter Thorn. She wondered about her magic, but something rumbled even deeper in her gut. Words she had never dared to think of on her own. Yet now they burned inside her, filling every empty crack and space.

Be great anyway.

CHAPTER 25

Spongy moss met Elora's feet when she returned to Bitter Thorn. Decaying scents nipped the air, but it still smelled mostly like rain, bark, and flowers. A whistling shriek sounded nearby. Moments later, a demorog with creaking black thorns zoomed in near her.

By the time she drew her sword from its hilt, a strong purple glow crackled off its blade. The demorog shrieked even louder than before and then flew in the opposite direction. Perhaps the thorn creatures had learned to avoid fae after how Ansel had used them.

Her sword fell back into her belt with a thud. She stomped over broken twigs and moist soil, wishing for a better way to release all the tension inside her. Pacing had never worked for her, but maybe she should try it anyway.

Tansy fluttered away from her shoulder and hovered just in front of her nose. The sprite eyed her carefully before donning a grave expression. "You are on the verge of discovery." Even her voice sounded grave. "I will leave you to it."

As the sprite floated upward to join her fellow sprites, Elora finally knew exactly how to release her tension. Her wings burst from her back so fast it blew wind through the leaves around her. Before they could settle, Elora climbed high into the air.

Her stomach did cartwheels as she flew even higher than the sprites. Once well above the trees, she stopped flying upward and started flying over the trees instead. Wind tickled her cheeks and waved through her hair. The layers of her gossamer gown brushed against her legs. When she flew faster, the wind turned colder.

She needed it.

The chill helped to clear her mind. It helped her to focus on the multitude of problems that so far, had no clear solutions.

Brannick had to be rescued.

Ansel had to be stopped.

High Queen Alessandra had to be killed.

Brannick had to become High King.

Even that list of four items wasn't really such a small list at all. Each item had multiple steps, most of which Elora didn't even know yet. For now, she decided to focus on just one.

Stop Ansel.

In order to do that, she had to figure out why he had bent those trees in the forest. And what he intended to do with the creation magic. According to Tansy, he knew he couldn't touch the creation magic, but he still might find a way to control it. How could she stop him when she didn't even know his plan?

Her wings beat harder then. She pushed herself against the wind, letting it sting her skin. Her muscles protested flying so hard, but she ignored them.

What would Brannick do?

If he found the bent trees and knew that Ansel had a way to find the creation magic, how would Brannick react?

Her heart faltered. When it did, she flew a little lower. A little closer to the trees.

Brannick should have been there. He should have been the one to save his own court.

Not her.

The conversation with Tindra and Severin rushed into her mind, but it didn't offer comfort. Maybe Elora could be great anyway like Tindra suggested. Maybe she could finally figure out what kind of magic she had and then use it against Ansel and High Queen Alessandra.

But Bitter Thorn was still *Brannick's* court. Not hers.

Something shifted in the air. Whether the actual air or a thought deep within her, she didn't know.

Either way, it caused her to stop midair. Her wings held her in place instead of bringing her forward or backward or even up or down. She hovered above a tree with her boots nearly brushing the leaves at the top.

Her hand waved in a circle. A twirling Faerie door opened in front of her. Even though she had opened it herself, she had no idea where it led. The destination didn't matter. Not right now.

The only thing that mattered was how that door looked. *Her* door.

Brown and green swirls undulated through the tunnel. Thin vines of black twisted through them, almost like the black thorns that twisted through the forest below her. Tufts of purple wildflowers bloomed from random intervals throughout the tunnels. She could smell the wildflowers too, along with crisp rain and spongy moss.

Every fae in Faerie could open a door, and every fae's door was unique. It represented who they were.

And her door was unmistakably Bitter Thorn.

Her eyes prickled while tears welled inside them. Maybe she hadn't been born a fae. Maybe she hadn't been meant to save anyone in Faerie while she lived out her dull existence in the mortal realm.

But things had clearly changed.

As Faerie itself had told her when she got her fae magic, she was a part of this conflict now. Faerie was molding its history around her.

Tears continued to well in her eyes. Warmth spread throughout her chest while she embraced what she had been too afraid to believe.

Bitter Thorn *was* her court.

And she was capable of saving it.

The back of her hand brushed a tear from her cheek. She started flying again. Wind continued to sting her cheeks and rustle through her hair. She welcomed the feeling while she focused on her problems with more clarity than before.

Brannick was planning an attack with the guards in Fairfrost. As someone who had once been a guard in Fairfrost, he could probably do that better than any other fae. He understood them. He knew them. And he was clever enough to figure out a way around the bargains.

A smile twitched at Elora's lips as she flew even faster.

Instead of moaning that she wasn't enough to save Bitter Thorn, maybe she needed to focus on taking care of his court while he couldn't.

e great anyway.

The words acted like fuel, helping her surge forward even faster. She eyed the trees beneath her. The glowing green of the sprites lit most of the forest, but she could see where they had gathered to avoid the residue of Ansel's enchantments.

They were closing in. It wouldn't be long before they revealed the creation magic. She needed a plan for when that happened.

After spying another bent tree, she flew down to land on top of it. The arc of the tree trunk made it difficult to balance properly, but her wings made up the difference.

That's when she noticed a second bent tree right next to the first. They tilted toward each other, almost forming a bridge with their trunks. She placed a hand on the trunk. Closing her eyes, she felt the magic. More of Tindra's words filled her mind.

What does your gut say?

Once she chose to listen to it, apparently it said a lot.

All at once, Elora's eyes flew open. She stumbled off the tree trunk and caught herself midair with her wings. Nothing in the air had changed, but something inside her certainly had. It crackled and buzzed, sending sparks all along her limbs.

She knew.

For so long she had fought and struggled and ached over what her magic could possibly be. The answer had been there all along. It had been waiting deep inside her, waiting for the moment when she would finally choose to believe it.

Intuition.

She had the gift of intuition. Her magic worked best when she trusted it to do what she needed. It worked best when she believed.

It made sense, really. All her life she had been impulsive, but how often had such behavior gotten her into trouble? It

205

had gotten her into trouble of course, but not nearly as much as it should have.

Because deep down, she always knew when to act. Deep down, she had always trusted her gut. It had only been when the other fae told her she wasn't really fae that she doubted herself. That doubt had deepened when Ansel and the high queen used her to defeat Faerie.

Her breath hitched as a smile played at her lips. Too bad for them, that wouldn't happen again. She knew her magic now, and *nothing* would stop her from using it.

Energy buzzed along her fingertips as she touched the bent trunk again. Purple glowed out from her palm. She stared at the two bent trees carefully considering what she already knew.

Ansel could not touch the creation magic or he would lose his own magic. Maybe High Queen Alessandra didn't know that yet, but Ansel did. He needed the creation magic, but maybe he also needed to figure out a way to use it without touching it.

If he didn't know how to use it yet, then he must have needed a way to protect it from everyone else. Or at least everyone else besides the high queen.

Elora's eyes roamed over the brown bark of the bent trees. Pieces of the puzzle tried to fit together in her mind, but they weren't quite the right size yet. Her eyes narrowed as she stared even harder at the trees.

How could Ansel ensure that no fae could get to the creation magic unless he specifically invited that fae?

The word *invited* struck loud in her mind like the booming lower strings of a harp.

A home. He planned to bend trees around the creation magic and create a home with them. Then no fae could enter unless that fae had been specifically invited.

Tingles spread across her fingertips while purple sparks burst out of them. Any victory she might have felt at guessing his plan got swallowed up in the brilliancy of the plan itself.

If he succeeded, he would have unlimited access to the creation magic, and no one could get inside his new home to stop him.

The sprites would reveal the location of the creation magic soon. But what if Elora found a way to make it happen sooner? Maybe she could force Ansel into action before he was ready. Maybe she could stop him.

CHAPTER 26

Landing on the forest floor, Elora dug deep into the pocket of her gossamer gown. She vaguely noticed the pocket was actually her magical pocket that she had now that she could access her fae magic, but she really only cared about the sage green crystal at the bottom of it.

Her fingers closed over it while every piece of her plan fell into place in her mind. Since the plan was slightly—or maybe extremely—insane, she wanted to get Brannick's opinion on it first. And she still hadn't told him about Queen Noelani's death.

Brannick.

She thought his name while holding the crystal tight.

No door opened.

She thought his name a dozen more times.

Eventually, she pulled the crystal from her pocket to make sure she had the right one. But of course it was the right one. She only carried one crystal. Squeezing her fingers tight over the crystal again thought Brannick's name a dozen more times. When that didn't work, she said his name out loud.

Nothing appeared.

He had promised to open a door to her when he could, but he still hadn't. Did it mean guards surrounded him? Or had something else gone wrong?

Bringing her closed fist to her chest, she attempted to keep her breaths steady. Worry would do nothing to help her. But each breath only sent another clench through her chest. What if something had happened to him?

Brannick.

Still nothing.

Just when tears started welling in her eyes, the tiniest whoosh sounded in front of her. She held her breath, scanning the forest around her.

After several uneven heart beats, she located his door. It wasn't big enough for her to walk through now. In fact, it twisted and swirled the smallest she had ever seen it.

The tiny door hovered an arm's length in front of her, just smaller than a thumbnail. Her shoulders hunched, but she tried to shrug it off. At least he had opened a door to her. Finally.

"Can you leave the dungeon for a bit?" Brannick's voice drifted through the door to her, but he clearly spoke to someone else.

A gritty male voice responded. "I have orders to keep you in my sight until High Queen Alessandra returns here in person. Faerie is allowing me to blink, but that is all I can offer." A slight pause. "And no, I cannot blink extra long either. I already tried."

"Hmm." Brannick's tone sounded tilted. "I do not suppose you could—"

"I also have orders to report back to High Queen Alessandra anything you ask me."

Brannick huffed. "I see." A noise came next that sounded like a fist against a marble wall. "She may be close to guessing our scheme then. I probably will not have any privacy until it is over."

The door disappeared.

Elora blinked at the spot it had been, scarcely able to believe it had already vanished. Of course it made little sense to expect conversations with Brannick since he sat in a dungeon in Fairfrost Court. Yet she had come to expect them all the same. At least she knew nothing had happened to him. Yet.

Letting out a sigh, she glanced upward. The sprites had flown above that area earlier in the day, but now they avoided the spot. The residue from Ansel's enchantment had driven them away.

The location of the creation magic would be revealed soon.

Marching across the damp soil and patches of moss, she moved to a spot where the sprites still flew. Once she reached it, Tansy immediately flew down and landed on Elora's shoulder.

"Can you lead me to the source of the creation magic?" She glanced toward the sprite hopefully.

"Yes, but what will you do once you get there?"

Sweat prickled across Elora's palm when she gripped her sword hilt. "I will kill Ansel before he can make a house from the trees around the creation magic."

Raising one eyebrow, Tansy pinched her mouth into a knot. "That is not a very good plan. Ansel is powerful. You might not succeed."

Elora huffed and turned away. "He is coming either way. At least if I am ready and waiting, I will have a chance at stopping him."

"You should not go alone." Tansy twirled her sparkly pink dress around her knees, but she glanced a little too intently through the side of her eye to appear truly indifferent.

Nodding, Elora traced a finger over an embroidered flower in her mauve gown. "I will ask Quintus and Lyren to come. Is there any way I can make Ansel come before he is ready?"

The sprite flew off Elora's shoulder to hover in front of her. "One of his gemstones is embedded in the belly of a demorog. The thorn creature escaped him before he could force it to crush his gemstone. If you find the demorog and crush the gemstone, the residue will be too great for us to resist any longer. It will reveal the location of the creation magic and Ansel will come."

Elora's hand slipped upward until she pinched the neckline of her dress. "That would hurt you and the other sprites."

"Yes." Tansy's wings shook as she flew closer. "But as you said, it will happen anyway. Is it not better that it happens on our terms instead of his?"

Turning her head down, Elora bit her lip. "What happens after that? If I stop him from making a house around the creation magic, what then?"

Tansy sighed as she flew back to Elora's shoulder and flopped down on top of it. "We will be trapped. The residue of Ansel's enchantment will keep us near the creation magic with no way to escape."

"Trapped again?" Elora stomped across the forest floor, which sent her skirts swishing. "I cannot do that. You sprites only just escaped Fairfrost."

"Do you want Ansel to gain complete control over the creation magic, then?"

Elora stopped in place and jerked her head toward the sprite. "No."

Shrugging, Tansy folded her arms over her chest. "Then you know what you must do."

After a long blink, Elora sighed. "Fine." She huffed and kicked the nearest rock with a little too much gusto. "How do I find the demorog?"

"You must send an enchantment that calls the thorn creatures to you."

A bitter chuckle spilled from Elora's lips. "You make it sound so easy."

Knowing she had no other choice, she waved her hand through the air. Showers of sparks burst from her fingertips, releasing a faint purple glow into the air. At first nothing changed.

The forest looked no different, and even worse, it sounded the same too. If any demorogs flew nearby, their whistling shriek would surely herald their appearance.

Chuckling, Tansy floated off Elora's shoulder and closer to the air. "Your magic is too gentle. It welcomes the creatures instead of hurting them."

"Ansel's beckoning magic hurts them?"

Tansy nodded.

Rolling her eyes, Elora sank to sit at the bottom of the nearest tree. "I should have known."

She glanced ahead at the faint pulsing glow of her beckoning magic. She could sit and worry about how her magic

212

might not be strong enough or fast enough, but that would solve nothing. Instead, she decided to trust her magic.

The demorog would come. She could wait until it did.

Night closed in all around her.

Tansy flew upward to join the other sprites.

She didn't notice drifting off to sleep until she woke with a start. Her body snapped up like something had woken her, but nothing in the forest looked any different than when she had first curled up and gone to sleep.

The distant shriek of a demorog forced her to her feet. She swallowed and glanced every which way, trying to decipher the demorog's location.

But even as she did, her gut told her to ignore the demorog for now. Her fingertips began sparking with magic. Gripping her sword hilt, she stepped deeper into the forest, ready for anything.

Even though she held the sword hilt, she didn't anticipate danger. She couldn't explain why, but she knew she had to hurry.

Her wings popped from her back. She flew over the forest path, covering more distance that way.

Eventually, she noticed a rustling bush with no wind to account for the movement. Still flying above the ground, Elora darted behind a tree. The rustling returned, but it shook a bush a little farther away. Something was in the forest. Something hidden.

Ansel.

Her stomach clenched tight at that thought. While her fingers curled, visions of knives and blood and chains flooded her mind. It took a moment, but she pushed them away.

It wasn't Ansel.

Just like she had known when she first woke, she knew danger did not await her in this part of the forest.

Her fingertips sparked with even more magic. She took in a slow breath and let her wings guide her to the ground. Once they slid into her back, she leaned forward.

"Hello?"

Her voice came out shaky. A beat of silence followed it. But then heavy steps bounded toward her. The owner of those steps came into a view half a moment before the black-furred creature toppled her over.

"Blaz." Her back hit the forest floor, but she didn't care. The wolf nuzzled his snout against her face. His paws pressed against her shoulders in the closest thing to a hug a wolf could offer.

She buried her face in his fur and wrapped her arms around him tight. "Blaz." Just saying his name sent an ache through her throat. "You do not know how much I have worried for you."

He gently stepped off her, still pressing his body as close to her as possible. But something wasn't right.

She placed a hand against his side, feeling how his breathing came labored and erratic. "Are you hurt?"

Of course, he couldn't answer. If Brannick had been there, he would have been able to read the wolf's essence at least. Since Elora had no such ability, she had to rely on what she did have. She scanned the wolf once more.

His bones protruded more than she had ever seen before. He looked gaunt.

Without a word, she jumped to her feet. He fell into step beside her at once. Her fingertips sparked with magic again. After only a few steps, she found a small forest animal.

Blaz bounded forward, attempting to catch the creature. His legs collapsed beneath him before he could get to it. He let out heavy pants, burying his nose in the damp earth beneath him.

She sucked in a breath, her throat aching again.

Stretching out her fingers, Elora waited for her magic to spark at her fingertips again. Following its direction, she soon found another small animal. Jabbing her sword forward, she speared it without hesitation.

When she brought it back to Blaz, he feasted on it like it was the first meal of his life.

He had already gobbled down the entire thing before she could find him another animal. He only started slowing down on his third animal. She got him a fourth just in case.

She knelt at his side while he devoured the meat. Her fingers trailed through his soft black fur, wishing she could have done something for him earlier.

"I have been trying to speak to Brannick, but there are too many guards around him now." She buried his face in his fur once again. This time, it caught a few tears. "He will be so happy you are safe." She sniffed. "*I* am so happy."

He nuzzled close to her for a moment, but immediately went back to his animal, eating it ravenously.

Soft light started to spill between the trees. The faint pulsing glow of her magic hovered nearby. Had Blaz sensed her beckoning magic? Had he found her because of it?

She only had a moment to ponder the question before a shriek cut through the silence. Jumping to her feet with a gasp, she reached for her sword.

Thorny wings beat hard as the demorog swooped down toward her. Resisting the urge to reach for her sword, she held her hand out for the creature instead.

Blaz's legs quivered as he forced himself to his feet. He growled at the demorog when it came nearer.

Not wishing to upset him while already weakened, she released her wings and flew closer to the demorog.

Blaz continued to growl but had apparently drained himself of the little energy he had. He collapsed onto the ground, chewing his food once again.

The demorog let out a wild shriek and clawed its thorns across Elora's neck and cheek. She flinched at the pain but still managed to grasp one of the demorog's wings. Her breath stilled while she peered inside the creature's belly.

Bitter Thorn had many demorogs, but somehow, her magic had summoned the exact one she needed. Just as Tansy had promised, a yellow gemstone sat in the demorog's belly, ready to be crushed.

Even though the creature swiped its thorns over every surface of her skin that it could reach, she still managed to curl a sharp thorn toward the gemstone. But just before the thorn met the gemstone, an entirely new kind of shriek erupted from the demorog.

It didn't sound wild or senseless. It sounded afraid.

With a gasp, she jerked her hand away from the creature and let it escape her grip.

Did it know what she intended to do? Did it know that crushing the gemstone would make it burst into a pile of ash?

Every demorog she had ever encountered acted senseless and wild. They attacked without abandon. They acted exactly like a cursed enchantment and nothing more.

But maybe they only acted like a curse because they had never been treated as anything different. When Ansel used them to fill the air in Bitter Thorn with his residue, maybe it had changed the demorogs.

Without thinking, Elora thrust her arm forward and snatched the gemstone from the demorog's belly. The gemstone still had to be crushed, but maybe she didn't have to use the demorog to do it.

As soon as she pulled the gemstone out, the thorn creature let out a shriek and flew out of her sight.

Day began to dawn just as she landed back on the ground. Blaz came to her side, his legs carrying him stronger than before.

She tucked the gemstone into her pocket and gestured toward the path that led to Kaia's tree. "We need to return to the others."

His nose dipped in a nod. He padded after her when she started down the path.

She had Ansel's gemstone. Now she just had to get Lyren and Quintus and bring them to the source of the creation magic. Then, once they crushed the gemstone, they could ambush Ansel.

CHAPTER 27

The urge to sprint coursed through Elora, but she managed to keep herself to a brisk walk. Blaz matched her speed, but he panted through every step. The meat had given him strength. She could only hope it would be enough because he likely wouldn't leave her side no matter how weak it made him.

Slipping a hand into her pocket, she squeezed the sage green crystal. Brannick probably couldn't open a door to her still, but Blaz had found her. *Blaz.*

Even if she only had the slightest chance to talk to Brannick, she had to try.

To her surprise, a tiny swirling tunnel appeared before her eyes. Her feet froze in place, gripping the ground while she tried to hold her breath. Blaz's ears perked up straight.

After a hard gulp, Elora glanced down at the wolf and pressed a finger to her lips. His head immediately dipped in a nod.

"Are you certain?"

When Brannick's voice drifted through the small door, Blaz's eyes brightened. Luckily, the wolf reacted without making a sound.

Another voice came next. Elora recognized it as the same guard who had been with Brannick the night before. "Our plan *must* begin now. This is our only chance."

"I had hoped for a moment of privacy beforehand." He let out heavy sigh. "But yes, I am ready."

The door vanished immediately after that.

Whatever joy had been in Blaz's eyes vanished along with it. He howled at the spot in the air where the door had been. Fear dug into Elora's insides while Brannick's words sank in.

The attack. Whatever he and the Fairfrost guards had planned, they were doing it now. Her breath shuddered as she tried to swallow.

Blaz howled again and covered his nose with his paws. He whimpered and turned his nose downward.

Dropping to her knees, Elora slid her fingers through Blaz's soft fur. "Brannick can take care of himself. He will be all right." Her breath hitched as she buried her face in the fur. "He has to be."

She allowed herself a few moments of worry, a few moments to hope for his success. And then she stood.

"We must stop Ansel before we do anything else. We have to trust Brannick to be okay."

She and Blaz started forward again, but a sickly taste settled on her tongue. Even saying the name *Ansel* affected her. She could almost taste the sour milk on his breath that he so liked to breathe in her face.

Was she truly ready to face him again? Lyren warned that Faerie itself would not take kindly to Elora killing for revenge. But maybe it wasn't about revenge anyway. Maybe it never had been.

By the time she made it back to the clearing with the others, her two sisters practically tackled her.

"Where have you been?" Chloe held her arms fast around her oldest sister's shoulders. She sniffed and ran her fingers over her braided blonde hair.

The harp string from Quintus still secured the braid, but Elora chose to not mention it.

A wild poof of red hair encircled Grace's head. Her messy bun had become several times messier since last Elora had seen her sisters. "Is that Blaz?"

Kaia, Lyren, Vesper, and Quintus all stepped forward. Questions began spewing from their mouths all at once.

"How did you find Blaz?"

"Why is he not with Prince Brannick?"

"Did something happen to Prince Brannick?"

They spoke so quickly, Elora couldn't decipher which question came from which fae. Instead, she just waved a hand at them. "Hush."

That stopped the questions, but it did not stop them from looking at Blaz suspiciously. The wolf moved closer to Elora, offering comfort right when she needed it.

She took a deep breath. "Prince Brannick is still in Fairfrost. Right now, we have to stop Ansel. I have a gemstone that will reveal the location of the creation magic. Once Ansel comes to the right spot, he plans to bend the trees around it to make a home. We need to be there waiting for him when he comes."

Kaia gasped. Her emerald hair shook, causing the leaves inside it to flutter. "That's why he bent the trees? To practice making a home with them?"

Elora nodded. "If he builds a house around the creation magic, no one else will be able to access it or stop him from whatever else he plans to do with it."

Quintus stepped forward, standing entirely too close to Chloe. His eyebrows drew together. "We need a plan."

When Elora got the urge to grab her sword hilt, she decided to pet Blaz's head instead. If the prince couldn't be there himself, she would do her absolute best to care for Blaz exactly as he would have done. "Chloe and Grace, you two will stay here."

As if on signal, every eye in the group wandered over to Vesper. He had a stick, which he dug into soft soil near his feet. Each time it went deeper, his eyes glazed over a little more.

Elora lowered her voice. "I think we should leave Vesper here too."

Lyren's jaw clenched. "We should tie him to a tree before we go." Now her fist clenched. "Otherwise, there is no telling what trouble he could cause."

The three sisters shared a look. Afterward, Chloe stood tall. "Grace and I will look after him. We'll make sure he doesn't get into any trouble."

Lyren threw a side eye that reeked of doubt. Rather than wait for her to voice any more concerns, Elora grabbed Lyren and Quintus by the hands and pulled them away from the clearing.

"I know where the sprites are gathering," Elora said. "We need to go near them and then I will crush the gemstone that

221

will reveal the location of the creation magic. Ansel will come soon after that."

Quintus glanced back at the clearing, but he kept walking.

The same could not be said for Lyren. She moved forward, but she didn't walk exactly. It looked more like a slump with dragging feet and hunched shoulders.

Elora's hand went into Blaz's fur without thinking. He nudged her leg with his head once and continued. Again, he offered comfort right when she needed it. Not that she ever doubted his reasons, but she understood even better now why Brannick cared so much for his wolf.

"Lyren." Elora tried to throw some optimism into her voice. "No one is better with words than you are. Do you think you could convince Ansel to stop his plan?"

Lyren huffed, hunching her shoulders even more. "Ansel listens to no one."

Elora scowled at the truth in those words. "Maybe you could distract him though. Even if you do not convince him of anything, it might be enough to capture his attention while Quintus and I attack."

"I could distract him. Maybe." Lyren's head dropped. "But I was not able to save my queen, so maybe there is nothing I can do anymore. Maybe I have earned as much redemption as I deserve." Her fingers slipped over the silver chains of her two seashell necklaces. The curls in her hair fell looser around her face.

At first, Elora wanted to roll her eyes. And then she wanted to smack her forehead. The despair. It hung thick in the air now that the others had left her protective enchantment. She had learned to live with it so completely, she had forgotten it even existed.

Though Quintus kept from moaning or complaining, he dragged each foot when he stepped forward. His lips pulled downward, and his messy black hair hung down over his eyebrows.

After a quick enchantment, a translucent purple bubble surrounded them. Both Lyren and Quintus perked up at once. They took a few deep breaths and almost seemed back to normal. Lyren kept running a finger over her necklaces, but her eyes had brightened, at least.

Blaz marched forward the same as ever. He did seem to be gaining strength, probably from the meat he had eaten, but the despair didn't seem to affect him. At least she had one companion she could rely on if her protective enchantment failed.

"What are you going to do when Ansel gets there?" Lyren spoke to Elora in a hushed tone. Since Quintus could clearly hear the words, Lyren had probably only spoken in such a way to demonstrate the gravity of her question, not because she was trying to hide the words from anyone.

Matching the hushed tone, Elora answered without hesitation. "I am going to kill him."

"But—"

"I know." Elora swallowed but kept her head high. "You fear that Faerie itself will punish me if I kill for revenge." She shook her head. "But this is not about revenge. It is not because of what he did to me, it is because of what he *will* do to others. Nothing except death will stop him. Do you disagree?"

Instead of answering, Lyren just slumped even deeper into herself.

Quintus turned toward Elora with his mouth pressed into a knot. "I believe you are correct. Ansel has always caused trouble, but he usually only ever hurt mortals. Now that he is hurting fae too, it is clear he has no conscience at all. I do not know of any way to stop him except death."

Lyren probably would have protested more except they had finally reached the spot with the sprites.

Tansy flew down from above and landed on Elora's shoulders. The sprites had gathered even tighter together since Elora had seem them last. Once she used the gemstone, they would have to fly even closer together still.

Trapped again.

But like Tansy said, it would happen either way. At least this way, they could make sure Ansel appeared when they were ready for him.

"Did you find the demorog?" Tansy's wings continued to beat, even though she stood on Elora's shoulder.

"What demorog?" Quintus narrowed his eyes.

Lyren glanced upward.

Blaz ducked his head under Elora's fingertips. She ran her hand through his fur while a hard lump lodged in her throat. With her other hand, she reached into her pocket and retrieved the yellow gemstone.

Tansy raised an eyebrow at her. Her pink and green eyes flashed when she glanced at Elora. "You did not capture the demorog?"

"I..." Elora gulped. "I think the demorogs are becoming sentient. I did not want to use a sentient creature in that way."

She didn't add that it seemed too similar to how Ansel had used her.

Rolling her eyes, Tansy shook her head. "If you do not have the demorog, then one of you must crush the gemstone." Her velvety hair tilted as she leaned forward. "Be careful who you choose because crushing a gemstone weakens the one who does it."

224

CHAPTER 28

Silence stretched through the forest while Elora held the gemstone close to her chest. She had intended to crush it herself, but if it weakened her as much as Tansy claimed, that didn't seem like the best idea anymore. Had it been stupid to let the demorog go? Maybe she had only imagined that it seemed different than before.

"I will do it." Quintus turned his eyes downward as he dug his toe into the moist soil below them. "What use am I during this fight anyway? You both have skills with weapons, but I am just a craftsman. At least this way I can be useful."

Both Tansy and Lyren sighed in relief.

Elora just narrowed her eyes. "Are you sure?"

He scoffed and plucked the gemstone from her hand. "Do I need to do anything special with it? How do we know it will reveal the creation magic like we expect?"

Flying off Elora's shoulder, Tansy began moving upward. "Ansel magicked that particular gemstone with an enchantment already. You only have to crush it to make it work."

By the time she finished speaking, she had flown high enough to join the other sprites in the air.

Nerves made Elora anxious to hold her breath, but Quintus crushed the gemstone before she could.

As before, a blinding light flashed out of the gemstone. Whipping wind came next, which was followed by a stinging mist.

Quintus collapsed onto the forest floor. He clutched his chest and let out hard breaths. Elora knelt at his side. "As soon as you are able, go back to the clearing with Kaia. She will know how to strengthen and heal you."

Tight coughs erupted from his mouth before he could answer. "What about you two?" He glanced at her and Lyren.

Getting to her feet again, Elora gripped her sword. "Do not worry about us."

She checked the position of the sprites before turning her eyes forward again. She and Lyren marched ahead.

It wouldn't be long now. Soon they would find the creation magic.

After a few moments, she glanced upward once again. "Wait."

Lyren stopped and raised an eyebrow.

Pinching her eyebrows together, Elora gestured upward. "I just checked our position, but as soon as I looked away from the sprites, I went the wrong way."

"Interesting." Lyren wrapped the chain of her necklace around one finger while her eyes narrowed. "I thought we were going the right way too, but now I see we have not moved closer to the sprites at all."

"Do you think Faerie itself is intervening?"

"It is probable." Lyren tapped her chin. "If what you told us about the creation magic is true, fae lose their magic when they touch the creation magic. Perhaps Faerie itself wants to lead us away from it, to protect us."

Elora ran her fingers through Blaz's fur. "That explains why no one has ever found it before."

With a huff, she glared at the sprites above and stepped forward. Now that she watched the sprites *and* stepped forward at the same time, she began moving closer to them.

Lyren did the same.

Once they reached the small gathering of sprites, Tansy's sparkle of pink floated down until she hovered right in front of them. "I can lead you to the creation magic now. Hopefully it takes Ansel a little longer before he figures out that he has to look up to be able to reach the right spot."

Elora nodded, but she didn't respond. What could she say?

Now that the residue had fully trapped the sprites, the creation magic sat completely unprotected. Ansel would be there soon.

Anticipation buzzed across Elora's limbs. She gripped her sword hilt and wished she had a better plan than to attack Ansel unexpectedly and hopefully kill him. At least they had the element of surprise.

When the buzzing in her limbs grew more insistent, she wondered if it wasn't anticipation after all. Maybe something in the air buzzed. Something like the creation magic.

The first flicker of a strange light flashed in Elora's vision. Even without seeing it completely, she knew it came from the creation magic. She and Lyren both bounded forward until they came even closer.

A clearing sat past a small cluster of trees. When they finally came close enough, they could see the entire clearing. At the center of it, a twisting net of magic pulsed with radiance.

Creation magic.

No words could accurately describe the sight before her. The pulsing magic was slightly bigger than a bush. It moved with swirls and twists and bounces. The color didn't even look like a proper color. It looked like every color, any color, and no color at all. It kept pulsing from colorful to colorless and back to colorful again before she had finished a single breath.

It flashed with brilliance. It mesmerized and entranced.

It looked like Brannick's eyes.

A small smile tugged at the corner of her lips. Now that she had made the connection, she couldn't unsee it. The creation magic pulsed and swirled in tight nets of magic. It sparkled and changed colors exactly like Brannick's eyes.

Not that there had ever been any doubt, but this proved how tied to Faerie Brannick was. Even without a crown, Faerie itself had clearly intended for Brannick to be powerful. He must have had his own creation magic inside him.

Once the initial shock at seeing the swirling magic passed, Lyren glanced to Elora. "What do we do now?"

"First, we get behind the trees to hide until Ansel gets here. After that..." Elora sucked in a deep breath. "I have an idea for after that."

They didn't have long before Ansel arrived. Once he did, Tansy flew up to join the other sprites. Blaz hid himself with his glamour. Elora's stomach flopped in on itself.

Glancing toward her body, Lyren bit her lip. "Are you sure about this?"

"You do not have to do it."

A quiet chuckle spilled from Lyren's mouth. "*I* do not mind at all. I just worry you might not like me stealing your appearance."

Elora shrugged. "You will only wear the glamour for one fight, and we have no other ideas anyway. What choice do we have?"

With that, Lyren waved a hand over herself. A glamour shimmered into place. Now she looked exactly like Elora, even down to the mauve gossamer gown and the heavy boots. Her cheeks were pinker than Elora expected and her skin more brilliant. Apparently, being fae really had improved Elora's appearance.

Nodding, Elora waved a hand over her own body. The glamour she wore turned her invisible.

Ansel stepped into the clearing with his wide eyes gazing into the creation magic. Behind him, three females and four males stood among the trees. All the females looked identical to each other, and all the males did too. More glamours. He must have brought some of his mortal pets with him.

Her jaw clenched tight. She reached for her sword, more determined than ever to end Ansel's life. He kept mortal pets and used them to do his bidding whenever he chose. She happened to know from her visit to his house that he had even more pets waiting for him at home.

Killing him no longer had anything to do with how he had used her. Now, she had to kill him to save his pets.

While Elora clutched her sword, Lyren tumbled into the clearing. She gathered several layers of the gossamer skirts into her arms. A sharp gasp escaped her lips.

"Ansel. What are *you* doing here?" Her eyebrows that currently looked exactly like Elora's, rose high on her forehead.

In a flash, they pushed tightly together. She gave the most exaggerated glare Elora had ever seen.

Is that what Lyren thought Elora's expressions looked like? For a fae who only knew minimal emotions, Elora's face probably did seem more expressive than any fae. Still, Lyren exaggerated a bit more than necessary.

Ansel didn't seem to notice at all. His gaze immediately turned from the creation magic to the gossamer gown. His yellow eyes glowed at the sight. "My pet. You got here just in time."

He reached into his pocket and pulled out a sapphire gemstone.

Before he could crush it, Lyren stomped.

Her glamour made it look like she wore boots, but since she didn't actually wear them, the sound didn't come out quite right. Still, her eyes shimmered with hate. "Pet? Did you just call me a pet?" Her facial expressions now looked even more exaggerated than before. "If you say that again, I will gouge your eyes out with my bare hands."

Fully drawing her sword, Elora edged closer to the clearing. As long as Lyren kept him distracted, Elora could attack without Ansel ever noticing her presence.

Ansel quirked an eyebrow up at Lyren. He cocked his head, looking at her more carefully than he had a moment ago. Did he finally notice something strange about Lyren's mannerisms?

Whether he did or not didn't really matter. Elora had moved close enough to strike. She focused on his chest, right at the same level as his heart. Her arm moved back.

His eyes narrowed at Lyren. "Imposter."

Just when Elora jabbed the sword toward him, he ducked and rolled to the side.

Her teeth gritted together as she sprinted after him. She raised her sword and sliced it forward again. The tip of it caught Ansel on his thigh, but he leapt away before it could cause damage to his skin. Only his pants got scraped. They didn't even slice completely.

Even if he couldn't see her with the glamour making her invisible, he knew someone was attacking him. Watching the ground for footprints, he soon guessed her position.

While her feet stumbled into a good stance, he lunged toward her. In a flash, he pinned her to the ground. Her glamour fell away at once. It didn't get ripped away like when High Queen Alessandra removed glamours. In those instances, the high queen used magic to evaporate the glamour. This was different. Elora simply got too startled to keep the glamour in place.

It fell away the moment her back hit the forest floor.

Yellow eyes glowed back at her when Ansel grinned. "There you are." He traced an ice-cold finger down her cheek.

Jerking her knee upward, she caught him between the legs as hard as she could. He flinched, and she could have sworn his eyes watered a little, but he managed to keep her pinned to the ground.

Of course, when Blaz growled and bit a chunk out his leg, he lost all control at once.

Elora scrambled to her feet, while Ansel attempted to kick Blaz with his good leg. Ansel reached into his pocket again, huffing through his clenched teeth. "I *hate* that wolf."

He had gotten too far away for her sword, but she had other means of attacking now. She blasted an enchantment from her fingertips and sent it straight for his chest.

It hit him but not with as much force as she would have liked. A moment later, Lyren tackled him to the ground. Her glamour had vanished now too.

Lyren slammed her palms against his shoulders, holding him tight against the soil. He couldn't have escaped, but for some reason he grinned.

Gulping, Elora rushed forward to offer support to Lyren.

Still, Ansel grinned.

Even with Blaz at her side, a sick churning filled Elora's belly. Confusion danced across Lyren's features at the sight of Ansel's grin.

By the time they finally realized why, it was too late.

He had slipped a gemstone underneath one of Lyren's fingers. When she pushed him harder against the ground, the gemstone exploded.

Energy drained from Lyren's face as sapphire dust burst out from the crushed gemstone. The magic immediately began bending one of the trees at the edge of the clearing.

Ansel was making a home.

Huffing, Lyren tried to get up. Her arm shook under the weight of her upper body. A moment later, she fell back onto the forest floor.

Elora broke into a charge, shouting as she ran. "Find Quintus and get back to the others."

"But..." Lyren's body shuddered as she forced herself to her feet. Once she got up, she immediately collapsed to the ground again.

If Lyren got in the way, Ansel wouldn't hesitate to kill her. Elora could try to pretend he might spare her, but she knew that was wishful thinking. But if she left while he focused on Elora, then Lyren had a good chance of getting away.

With a hard swallow, Elora flicked a hand toward the forest. "Crawl if you have to, just get out of here."

She couldn't wait to see if Lyren listened. She just charged toward Ansel with her sword pointed straight at his chest. He blasted her with an enchantment just before she could reach him.

At almost the same moment, he tossed a gemstone to one of the mortals behind him.

The mortal crushed the gemstone and slumped to the ground. Another tree began bending over the clearing.

When the second tree grew closer to the first tree, their branches intertwined to start forming a solid wall.

"Lyren!" Elora used her glowing sword to block an enchantment.

"I am going. Just be careful."

The fae's black curls bounced before she disappeared into the trees on her hands and knees. Ansel sent an enchantment toward her, but Elora jumped in front of it and took the blast herself. Air escaped her chest in a rush.

Her knees slammed against the forest floor. When Ansel stepped toward her, she jabbed her sword at him.

He jumped back just fast enough to miss her blade.

Momentarily ignoring her, he threw two more gemstones to the nearest mortals. A third and fourth tree began bending over the creation magic.

Elora's heart jumped into her throat.

Only a few more gemstones and Ansel's home would cover the creation magic.

CHAPTER 29

Moss and soil littered Elora's gossamer gown. A few of the looped bead strands that formed her sleeves had snapped. She attempted to swing her sword at Ansel once again, but he blasted her with an enchantment that knocked her onto her back. Blaz bounded to her side, growling hard whenever Ansel stepped closer.

If her heart hadn't been beating so fast maybe she could have caught her breath.

Forcing her body up, she tried to suck in enough air.

Ansel had forgotten her momentarily, or maybe he just chose to ignore her. He must have seen her weakened state and determined she wasn't a threat.

He tossed a gemstone to one of his mortals and instructed her to crush it immediately. Another tree began bending over the clearing. But Elora had gotten her breath back now. Soon, she got back to her feet.

She gripped her sword and sprinted toward Ansel. Blaz ran right at her side. When he sent an enchantment toward her, she blocked it with her glowing sword. Before he could shoot another enchantment her way, she shot one from her own fingertips.

The cluster of purple sparkles hit him square in the jaw. He stumbled back toward a tree. That only got him closer to one of his mortals. Even while his chest heaved, he tossed another gemstone to a mortal.

And now, another tree added to the home he was creating. The branches intertwined and grew into each other.

She lifted another hand to attack, but a rock slammed into her stomach. Both she and Ansel wore the same surprise at the sight of it. One of his mortals must have thrown it.

Before he could lift a hand to form another enchantment, Blaz swiped his claws down the side of Ansel's leg. A strangled hiss left his mouth. Ansel tried to grab the wolf by the throat, but Blaz bounded away before he could reach.

Elora came nearer now. She swung her sword in a circle, eyeing her enemy as she determined the best attack.

His eyes darted around the clearing. More than half of the trees had bent to form his house, but he still needed a few more. He backed away carefully. Stuffing a hand into his pocket, he pulled out what looked like a handful of gemstones. He tossed them toward the nearest mortal and then shot an enchantment from his fingertips.

The sight of the gemstones sent Elora's body into an expected lunge. Instead of trying to slice open Ansel's chest, she found herself reaching out for the gemstones instead.

Almost as if Faerie itself helped, her fingers tightened over every single gemstone Ansel had thrown. She allowed herself a grin when she glanced back at him. "How will you make your home now?"

A disturbing chuckle fell from his lips. Without even batting an eye, he stuffed his hand into his pocket and retrieved an even bigger handful of gemstones. "With these."

Blaz jumped onto Ansel's back, attempting to tackle him to the ground. Ansel slammed a fist into the wolf's stomach. Blaz flew over the forest floor until his body hit hard against a tree trunk.

Her breath hitched, but Elora managed to stuff Ansel's gemstones into her pocket without accidentally crushing any of them. If she accidentally crushed any of them, she would be weakened just like Lyren and Quintus had been.

She ran for Blaz first. He shook himself and rushed to her side before she could even reach him. Now another tree bent over the clearing, and another mortal was slumped onto the ground.

She itched to swing her sword and drive it deep into Ansel's chest.

But then her fingertips sparked. She slammed her sword into her belt and got to her knees.

When she pressed both her hands against the forest floor a moment later, she didn't even understand what she was doing. But she knew better than to question it.

She trusted her magic and her intuition.

Her fingertips continued to spark as she pressed her palms deeper into the moist soil.

When Ansel noticed her actions, he winced and charged toward her. Blaz answered by digging his fangs deep into one of Ansel's legs.

She closed her eyes, trusting Blaz to protect her while she worked.

"What are you doing?" Terror shook Ansel's voice.

How funny that he expected an answer when even she didn't know what she was doing. But just when that thought passed through her mind, the answer came. It was almost as if the soil itself spoke inside her mind.

Her eyes snapped open. She looked right into Ansel's yellow eyes. "You used blood magic to control these trees, but I have a greater magic than that."

He scoffed, side stepping when Blaz tried to attack him again. He moved backward, probably hoping to incite less of the wolf's wrath. Still, the intensity of his glare never changed. "No fae has greater magic than my gemstones."

Purple sparks shot out of her fingertips, but she could feel energy and buzzing all the way up her arms and into her chest. Her lips curled upward as she took in a deep breath of the crisp air around her. "The magic is in the trees themselves."

She had gotten too caught up in the conversation to notice how he had slowly crept closer to her. When she did notice, it was too late.

He slammed his elbow against her chest. Then, he grabbed her shoulders to throw her across the clearing. Blaz immediately attacked. Judging by Ansel's screams, the wolf had probably taken a chunk of flesh from somewhere off his body.

Regardless of the wolf's loyalty, Elora's body still rolled across the clearing. She held her breath and tried to stop herself, but it did no good. The momentum carried her right toward the creation magic.

Her heart stopped completely while she watched the hem of her gown flutter inside the twisting net of pulsing energy. The moment the hem touched the creation magic, that part of it turned white. Her boot would reach it next. And then her foot.

Maybe holding her breath had helped because she managed to dig her knees into the ground. Her boot narrowly avoided the creation magic. Her shoulder slammed against the forest floor next. The momentum would have hurtled her right into the center of the pulsing net, but she dug her fingers into the soil and stopped herself.

Just barely.

Her heart continued to stall, as if afraid to beat. Finally, she let out a heavy, weighted breath. She was safe. Magic continued to spark at her fingertips.

Ansel must have given another gemstone to one of his mortals because another tree started bending over the clearing. It didn't matter. She just had to stop him before the house fully formed. He still needed at least two more trees.

Taking one more deep breath, she rolled away from the creation magic. Blaz stood at her side, helping her up as much as he could. Once she got to her knees, she pressed her sparking fingers deep into the soil once again.

From across the clearing, Ansel smirked at her as another one of his mortals crushed a gemstone. His yellow eyes glowed as horrifying as ever. "I know what kind of magic you are attempting to access." His smirk grew. "But you cannot do it. Only a fae of Bitter Thorn can reach the trees of this court."

Her jaw clenched as she dug her fingers deeper into the soil. "I *am* a fae of Bitter Thorn."

He chuckled, drawing a gemstone from his pocket and rolling it between his thumb and forefinger. Taunting her. "You are a mortal pretending at being a fae."

Dropping the gemstone into the palm of one of his mortals, he began stepping toward Elora.

Blaz moved in front of her, growling louder each time Ansel stepped closer.

She couldn't move. The magic wouldn't work unless she kept her fingers deep in the soil. Ansel must have known how easy it would be to stop her. The smug look on his face made it clear.

When Blaz tried to leap toward him, Ansel sent an enchantment that knocked the wolf off his feet. He whimpered and got back into position in front of Elora a moment later. But now Ansel had moved closer than ever.

His mouth formed a twisted grin. "My pet, it is senseless to stop me. I invited you inside my house, remember? You are welcome inside it whenever you like."

Ansel turned back and nodded to the mortal who held the last gemstone.

Just as the mortal crushed it, Ansel leaned in close enough to leave his breath on Elora's forehead. "You cannot stop me."

The scent of sour milk felt like knives on her skin, but she couldn't stop now. Her fingers pressed into the soil while the last tree bent to finish forming the house. Magic buzzed and skittered along every limb in her body now. She breathed in deeply and looked into his eyes. "I am no pet." She dug her fingers deeper, letting the magic wash over her. "I am a fae of Bitter Thorn!"

Each of her syllables increased in volume until she shouted the final word. Once it left her lips, the trees started shaking. Shimmers of purple and green drifted away from the trees. Every bit of bending and intertwining stopped, as if the trees had been paralyzed.

The first look of fear sparked in Ansel's eyes. He waved his hand to open a door and instructed his mortals to go through it.

Leaves fell from the trees the more they shook. Soon, even the ground itself started shaking.

Ansel took a step back.

She ripped her hands away from the soil. When she did, every tree around the clearing snapped upward, stretching toward the sky once again. Branches untwisted and pulled back until they moved to their original spots.

Elora stood to her full height, ready to finally kill the fae who had done so much damage to mortals, to Faerie, and to her.

With a snarl, he waved his hand in a circle. Wind-like shrieks immediately pierced the air around them.

Demorogs.

Their shrieks grew louder as they swooped down. Thorns twisted and writhed, slicing Elora's skin without abandon. She shoved the nearest demorog away just to glare at Ansel. "You are hurting them."

Demorogs attacked him too, but it didn't stop him from moving closer to his door. "I do not care as long as they hurt *you*." He reached into his pocket.

Her gut tightened into a knot at the sight of it.

He had a plan. Instinctively, she knew that whatever he pulled from his pocket could spell doom. But with at least a dozen demorogs digging their thorns into her skin, she couldn't do anything about it.

Instead, she raised her hands high into the air. The creatures shrieked. Thorns wrapped around her arms, drawing blood at every turn. She ignored them.

Her fingers stretched upward, searching. Closing her eyes, she reached out more. She felt for magic just like she had when her fingers pressed into the soil.

After another moment, she found it.

She gasped. For the briefest moment, the demorogs stopped.

"You were made from Bitter Thorn," she whispered.

Their attack began again, even more ferocious than before. But it didn't matter now. She already knew she could call on the magic of her court.

Reaching her hands up high, she shouted loud enough for every demorog to hear her. "You were made from hate, meant to terrorize your own court." Her fingers curled into fists while magic showered from her hands. "I release you from that hate. You are free to roam your court as you please. May you live in peace for the rest of your days."

The shrieking stopped. Silence followed. Then the demorogs began whistling. Their thorny wings beat as they flew high into the air. As they disappeared, a weight seemed to lift from Elora's shoulders. Except it wasn't just her shoulders that felt it.

The air itself seemed to lighten, to spark with greater magic than before.

At that exact moment, Ansel pulled his hand from his pocket. A flash of silver flew across the clearing until a short dagger caught Elora square in the chest.

Her breath rushed out with a grunt. Blood seeped from the wound, staining her gossamer gown.

Before she could even think to react, Ansel had stepped into his door and disappeared. She stumbled across the clearing, trying to find the path that would take her to the others. Pain burned through her chest.

If she had been mortal, the wound would have killed her by now. Even with her fae healing abilities, she probably didn't have long before death would take her.

Her back slammed into the forest floor, but she couldn't feel it. She felt nothing except the dagger in her chest.

Nothing but pain.

Blaz nudged his head against her shoulder and then against her cheek. She tried to smile at him. She tried to lift a hand to run it through his fur one last time. But pain wracked through her arms now. Her skin. Everything prickled and stung. Everything burned.

Maybe the pain itself would take her.

She tried to breathe, but it came out as a cough instead. Splatters of warm blood dotted her face when she coughed again.

Blaz nuzzled closer to her. At least she had that small comfort.

Pain stroked her skin with needles and knives. It hammered her down. Her lips moved, but no sound left them. The question she asked was spoken only in her mind.

How am I supposed to rescue Brannick now?

Would he be stuck in Fairfrost forever? Would he survive after he found out she had died?

Blaz got to his feet.

Another blood-splattering cough erupted from her lips.

She assumed the wolf had simply gotten up to readjust, but then he sprinted out of the clearing.

"No!" For the first time since the dagger struck her, she managed to speak. Her voice came out too small. Too small and too breathless. Somehow, she finished anyway. "Do not leave me. I do not want to die alone."

242

CHAPTER 30

Black and white spots appeared in Elora's vision. Her muscles ached to curl into a ball, but the pain in her chest kept her from moving at all. She wondered if she could even breathe. Sometimes, it felt like she didn't.

Back and forth, her mind wandered between hoping she would somehow live and being frustrated she hadn't died yet.

It hurt too much.

Pain bloomed inside her bones, along her pores. It burned and clashed against every sense of peace she had ever known.

Maybe Ansel knew this would happen. Maybe he purposefully intended to injure her enough to immobilize her but not quite enough to kill her. If he had done it on purpose, that meant he would be back. What would he do to her then?

The dagger blazed in her chest. Even sitting still, it felt like it cut away bits and pieces of her muscles the longer it sat inside her.

Why couldn't she just die?

Leaves rustled nearby. At first, she assumed wind had created the noise, but when it sounded again, it was more deliberate.

Was it Ansel?

Her muscles tensed, which didn't even seem possible given how much she already clenched them.

She heard padding footsteps next.

Blaz? Had he come back for her?

Another pair of footsteps accompanied the padding ones. A moment later, Blaz did return to her side. He nuzzled close and touched her cheek with his nose.

Someone gasped. Hard.

She couldn't guess who it was, but soon a voice answered that question for her.

"I will *kill* Ansel for this."

"Brannick." She attempted to sit up, desperate for confirmation.

He rushed to her side in a single bound. "Careful." He scooped her into his arms effortlessly. "Kaia can heal this, but we must hurry to her."

His light brown skin glowed under the light of the sprites. His black hair hung a little limper than usual around his shoulders, but it still shined as black and as glossy as ever. And his *eyes*.

"How…" Blood splattered from her lips when she tried to force more words from her lips.

Brannick pulled her closer. His eyes shimmered. His chin trembled. "Save your breath."

He didn't say *please*, but she could see the word in his expression.

Blaz let out a small yip. Her eyes went blurry before she saw anything else.

Brannick waved a hand underneath Elora's back. When he finished, he pulled her even closer to his chest. He had opened a door, which he and Blaz stepped through at once.

On the other side, Elora recognized another clearing in Bitter Thorn. He had taken them near Kaia's tree, right where the others waited for them.

"Brannick!"

Several voices shouted the name, but Brannick only glared. "No questions right now." He lowered Elora to a mossy spot on the forest floor.

With her on the ground, the dagger in her chest must have been visible because the earlier voices now gasped.

Pressing one hand around the outside of her wound, Brannick ripped the dagger from her body. He immediately tore off his coat and used it to press into the wound. "Hurry, Kaia. She is fading."

The black and white spots filled Elora's vision. Pain bloomed so bright inside her, breathing felt like a joke. Heat and rage churned in her chest.

She could only vaguely take in her surroundings.

Kaia smoothed something cool over Elora's chest that took the slightest edge off the pain. Brannick held Elora's hand tight, squeezing it every time she moaned. Blaz sat nearby, nuzzling closer to her whenever he could.

Worried voices whispered and muttered above her.

An object of some sort got thrust into her dagger wound. She gasped. But then...

Pain receded into the object and away from her limbs. Away from her chest. The object absorbed the pain until nothing but a dull ache was left behind.

She could breathe.

In.

Out.

Finally, she could *breathe*.

When her eyes fluttered open, Elora watched Kaia pull a clear but now bloody crystal from the wound in her chest. The dryad smoothed a gritty, green concoction over the wound, which healed the skin, muscles, and bone.

Nothing had ever felt so glorious.

Brannick slipped his fingers into Elora's hair and kissed her forehead.

Well, almost nothing.

"You should rest." Kaia folded a blood-soaked cloth into a tight square. When finished, fire sparked from her fingertips and burned the cloth to ash.

Now that she could breathe, Elora placed a palm on Brannick's chest. He felt real, but she couldn't be sure. "Is this a dream?"

"No, my beloved." He took her hand and brought it to his lips for a gentle kiss. His eyes. They pulsed and swirled. The colors in them flashed and went colorless before turning colorful again. Just like the creation magic. He touched her fingers to his lips again. "You rescued me from Fairfrost already, I thought it fitting for me to rescue myself for once."

"But how?"

He pulled her back into his arms and carried her over to a nearby tree. Once he leaned his back against the tree, he gently settled her so she could rest all her weight on his chest and on his arms. Now she could relax. Rest.

"I think we would all like to know how." Lyren pulled herself forward, leaning against her own tree.

Quintus nodded, forcing himself closer. "I certainly do."

"No, not there." Grace ushered him toward a different nearby tree. "Form a circle." She gestured toward a spot next to Quintus, and Chloe took it. Vesper took the final spot she pointed out, but he grumbled while he did it.

Nodding at the circle of them, Grace dashed back toward a fire on the other side of the clearing. "I made soup for everyone. It will be easier to talk and eat if we all sit in a circle."

While she moved toward the fire, Brannick tilted his chin toward the air. "Who created this enchantment? It blocks out the despair perfectly."

"Elora did it." Chloe smiled proudly, which would have felt nicer if she hadn't scooted closer to Quintus at the same time.

But Brannick didn't notice that. His eyes gleamed as he glanced down into his arms. "You discovered more of your magic."

Heat flushed in Elora's cheeks when she nodded. "Intuition."

Grace's red hair had fallen out of her bun in several places. She tucked a strand behind her ear before bending down to hand a bowl and spoon to Elora.

Quintus licked his lips at the sight of it, but then his gaze turned toward the prince. "How *did* you escape Fairfrost Palace?"

Warm, herbed liquid trailed down Elora's throat. She had never tasted such perfection. But maybe almost dying had given her stronger appetite.

Brannick sighed at Quintus's question. "My escape is a thrilling tale to be sure, though I fear I will not do it justice when I am so eager to hear about what happened in that clearing with Ansel."

The second bite of soup tasted even better than the first. Elora shrugged, eager to speak fast so she could continue to eat even faster. "Ansel tried to bend the trees to make a house over the creation magic so no one else could get to it." She snuck in a quick bite before speaking again. "But I called on the magic inside of the trees, and they went back to standing straight. If he tries to bend them again, the trees will not listen. Oh, and I freed the demorogs, so they will not terrorize anyone anymore."

Brannick held his hand out when Grace went to hand him a bowl, but now his arm stayed outstretched. His eyes had opened wide.

No one else around them moved either.

Elora glanced across the clearing at Kaia, Lyren, Vesper, and Quintus. All of them stared open-mouthed at her.

"What?" If they wouldn't speak, at least that gave her more time to eat.

Finally, Lyren tilted her head. "You called on the magic *inside* the trees?"

"Yes." Elora shrugged.

Brannick chuckled and finally took the bowl that Grace had offered. Elora glanced toward him, hoping for an explanation. He smiled wide. His eyes were even more mesmerizing than the creation magic itself. "Bitter Thorn has accepted you as its own."

It felt good to smile back at him. "I know."

"Did you really free the demorogs too?" Quintus leaned forward.

She nodded before taking another bite.

Kaia touched a hand to her chest as she leaned on her tree. "Then the curse on Bitter Thorn is lifting."

Only now did Elora freeze. Her mouth hung open too long before she finally said, "Really?"

Brannick chuckled. "Yes, really. And now I can tell you about my escape because my heart is light again." He pulled Elora closer before he continued. "The Fairfrost guards must follow every order from the high queen, but occasionally, she gives orders without thinking them all the way through."

Quintus grinned and started shoveling soup into his mouth.

With a smirk, Brannick said, "One of the guards kept asking the high queen tedious questions about the wild dragons in Fairfrost. The high queen knows why all the dragons are wild now, but she will not explain it to anyone else. The guard kept insisting the dragons had to be dealt with. He was careful to only bring it up when the high queen was extremely busy."

Now that everyone had a bowl, Grace finally flopped onto the forest floor in between Chloe and Vesper. Grace took a bite, but she seemed more anxious to hear the story than to taste her food.

Brannick took a small bite. "The guard asked so many questions that the high queen finally gave an order in a fit of frustration." A devious smirk played across his lips. "She ordered the guard to take care of the dragons himself. When he insisted he would need help, the high queen ordered him to take whoever he wanted with him."

A puffy breath escaped Lyren's mouth. "*Whoever* he wanted?"

Brannick nodded.

Elora chuckled at the sight of it. "Let me guess. He chose to take *you* with him?"

"Of course." Brannick's smile turned wide. "He also took all the guards whose names the high queen cannot remember. If she does not remember their names, she can only give them an order when they stand in front of her. But now that they are deep in the ice forest of Fairfrost, she cannot order them back to the palace. Their bargain requires them to take care of the wild dragons, which they will do... eventually."

Everyone in the circle snickered, even Vesper. It was probably the most emotion he had shown since they found him on the island in Swiftsea with the source of the decay.

Brannick chuckled to himself as he swallowed his latest spoonful of soup. "The high queen knows the names of many of her guards, unfortunately. Those guards we put in chains and hid in rooms she never uses. They have food and water and a place for waste. It is not ideal, and she *will* find them eventually. But for now, even when she orders them into the throne room, the chains will keep them from coming. She will have to find and free the guards herself before she can order any of them again."

Elora had scraped down to the bottom of her stone bowl. After pouring the last of it into her mouth, she glanced up at the prince. "Why did they need your help with everything?"

"The guards could not chain up fellow guards. It is one of their long-standing orders. So, I had to chain them all up—and then I opened a door and left."

With a smile on her lips, Elora rested her head against his chest. "Even with all your magic, you managed to escape with cleverness alone."

He trailed a finger down her arm, which sent heat tingling under her skin. "It is amazing what I can accomplish when I refuse to accept defeat."

His arms enveloped her as he brushed his lips across her forehead again. Before she could fully enjoy it, he scanned their group again. Now his gaze turned toward the dryad. "Where is Soren?"

Instead of answering, she squirmed and stared at the bowl in her hands.

Brannick sat up straight, his face darkening. "Is Soren dead?"

Kaia's emerald hair whipped out when she shot her eyes upward. "No, my prince. He is…" She stared down at her soup once again. "He has disguised himself as a dwarf."

"In Mistmount?" Brannick asked.

She nodded.

The prince's eyes narrowed. "Why?"

"He is trying to help protect King Jackory."

Brannick closed his eyes, the muscles in his face growing taut. After opening his eyes again, his gaze slowly turned toward Lyren. "High Queen Alessandra is already Queen of Fairfrost, Noble Rose, Dustdune, and Bitter Thorn. Is—"

"Queen Noelani is dead." Lyren's voice shuddered over the words, but she still forced them out. "High Queen Alessandra is Queen of Swiftsea too."

Brannick sighed. The weight of it pressed down all around them. The joy of being reunited got snuffed out by a single revelation.

His eyes continued to swirl and pulse but not with the same brilliance as before. "I suppose we have avoided this conversation long enough, but we cannot put it off anymore. We must make a plan to overthrow the High Queen of Faerie."

CHAPTER
31

In the end, they decided to rest first. Night had fallen, and everyone in their group wanted nothing more than to sleep away the aches and bruises of the day they had just experienced. They all slept in the same circle they had been sitting in for dinner.

Elora slept close to Brannick. For her sisters' sake, she managed to keep a bit of space between them.

When day dawned, Grace had another meal ready before most of them had even opened their eyes. While they ate, Brannick kept glancing at Elora. His eyes suggested he thought the space between them throughout the night had been wholly unnecessary. He seemed eager to correct it as soon as possible.

Chloe groaned loudly as she stuffed a handful of berries into her mouth. Talking over them, she said, "Can you two stop staring at each other for a moment while we figure out how to save Faerie?"

Brannick did turn away from Elora, but he also wrapped an arm around her waist and pulled her as close to his side as she could get. When he spoke, his hand on her waist wandered lower. "We need fealty from all the courts in order to defeat High Queen Alessandra. Even if the fae are not physically fighting with us, their fealty can give us strength during the fight."

Kaia stepped out of her tree. Striations still stretched over her skin and a few vines still lingered in her emerald hair, but she looked less tree-like than the last few times she had come out of her tree. "That is the same as when rulers swear fealty to the High Ruler of Faerie. By swearing fealty, their magic lends support to the High Ruler."

"Exactly." Brannick nodded.

"But High Queen Alessandra is already more powerful than any ruler Faerie has ever known." Lyren scowled at the pile of berries in front of her.

Grace nodded as she tried to tuck stray hairs back into her bun. "And her despair is everywhere."

At Elora's waist, Brannick's hand wilted. "I forgot about the despair. The fae have no reason to believe in me when they are so greatly distressed."

Quintus nodded as he stuffed the crumbs of corn muffin into his mouth.

A spark lit in Elora's chest. Without thinking about it at all, she jumped to her feet. "I know what to do."

The others squinted and cocked their heads at her. Everyone except Brannick. His face transformed back into one of wonder.

"Excellent," he said. "What do we do?"

253

She gestured upward. "So far, no enchantments have been able to block out the despair completely."

"None except yours." Brannick flashed a lopsided grin.

Her cheeks prickled with heat. She had to grip her sword hilt to remind herself not to smile too wide. "Right. But maybe that is only because I can overcome the despair even without magic."

Brannick nodded, his eyes swirling and gleaming. "Excellent." His face froze in place for a moment. "How does that help us?"

She gestured toward him. "You learned how to overcome the despair too, did you not? At the beginning of your imprisonment, you could barely think with the despair all around you. But now it hardly affects you at all."

He nodded slowly, the pulsing in his eyes growing faster by the moment.

Quintus raised an eyebrow. "You want to teach everyone in Faerie how to overcome the despair, and in exchange, they will give Prince Brannick fealty?"

"Why not?"

Lyren scoffed. "Because it will not work."

Elora managed to temper her scowl when she turned to look at Lyren.

The fae wrapped one finger in the silver chains of her necklaces. "The despair is getting stronger. When I came back to this clearing, I barely made it because of how thick the despair filled the air."

"Same with me." Quintus wore a solemn expression.

Chloe pressed a hand to her lips. "You almost couldn't get back?"

He grinned back at her. "Luckily, I had a strong enough reason to return."

She bit her lip and brushed away a hair that had fallen across his forehead.

"What is this?" Brannick gestured between the two of them, his nose wrinkling the longer they gazed into each other's eyes. "When did you two start looking at each other like that?"

Elora huffed loudly. She folded her arms over her chest, glaring at the pair of them.

Brannick turned toward her with his hand still pointing to the others. "Are we not happy about this?"

Maybe it was more exaggerated than necessary, but Elora shook her head hard. "Not happy at all."

With a nod, Brannick immediately knotted his eyebrows together in a tight glare. "Quintus. This is wrong because…"

His voice faltered for a moment, and his gaze turned back to Elora with a question in his eyes.

"Because Chloe is too young."

"Right." Brannick's glare returned as soon as he turned back to Quintus. "Her life experience may make her seem your equal, but she is still a child by mortal standards."

Chloe stood up, her braid whipping behind her. The harp string from Quintus still held it in place. "I am *almost* an adult."

At her final word, Quintus gulped and scooted away from her.

Chloe's mouth dropped at the sight. She pressed a hand to her chest as if him scooting away had physically pained her.

Lyren rolled her eyes. "We are getting side-tracked. If overcoming despair was easy, why have we not tried it already?"

The words were like a knife to Elora's gut. She swallowed. "I should have tried to teach you. I was so consumed with discovering my magic, I never stopped to think if the solution even needed magic at all."

"I'll try it." Grace used the back of her hand to wipe away the last of the crumbs on her face.

Their mother would have had a fit seeing her precious daughter use her *hand* instead of a *napkin* to wipe away crumbs. It still hurt to remember such things, but at least the memory made Elora smile.

Without any warning, Grace took a deep breath and left the safety of the enchantment around them. Her face scrunched in a wince as soon as she reached the part of the forest with the despair. "What do I do?"

Instinctively, Elora stepped toward her sister. She wanted to make it easy and just extend the enchantment to take the pain away, but that would have defeated the purpose.

After another gulp, Elora finally had an answer. "First, do not try to stop feeling the despair. You must embrace it."

Grace nodded bravely, but she burst into tears another moment later. "Done," she said through a sniff.

Elora had to curl her hands into fists to keep herself from extending the enchantment over her youngest sister. Just when she almost faltered, Blaz bounded to her side and rubbed his head against her leg.

She patted his head, and soon, Brannick had come to her other side. They both offered comfort right when she needed it. With a deep breath, she finally addressed her sister again. "Now, feel the despair and accept that it is a part of you. Do not try to set it aside or pretend it does not matter to you. Just embrace it and continue on anyway."

Tears streamed out of Grace's puffy red eyes. Her shoulders bunched up tight just beneath her ears. Even the muscles in her face had gone rigid. Nothing about her stance looked promising.

Inside the protective enchantment, Vesper snarled at the purple ribbon around his wrist. He dug at it with his fingernails and then attempted to tear it away with his teeth.

Brannick narrowed his eyes at Vesper.

"I..." Tears still slipped from Grace's eyes, but her shoulders had relaxed. "I think it's working." She sent her hand across her cheeks, and with a dainty swipe, wiped the tears away. "I can still feel it, but it doesn't sting as much."

The tiniest smile twitched at her lips.

"Let me try." Chloe marched toward her youngest sister. She had grabbed Quintus by the wrist and pulled him after her.

He dug his heels in the ground, trying to stop her from bringing him outside the enchantment. "I do not think I am ready."

"Then *get* ready." Chloe continued to drag him forward. "We are not hiding from this anymore."

Once they both joined Grace on the other side, Lyren stood up. She stared at them for a few moments before stepping outside into the despair too.

Nodding to herself, Kaia followed soon after.

Vesper was using his teeth on the ribbon again. When he noticed Elora staring at him, he hissed and flashed his teeth.

Raising an eyebrow, Brannick turned toward her. Under his breath, he whispered, "Is something wrong with Vesper?"

"I forgot you were not here when we found out." She touched a hand to her hairline and shook her head. "High Queen Alessandra struck him with an ice shard."

Brannick kept his gasp silent, but he could not help raising his eyebrows high.

She let out a sigh. "Vesper wants to close the portal to the mortal realm. He also sabotaged us in our last encounter with High Queen Alessandra."

257

Folding his arms over his chest, Brannick raised the same eyebrow again. "But he still travels with you?"

"We want him with us." Her eyes turned downward. "We are hoping once we defeat High Queen Alessandra, we will find a way to repair his heart."

"It is not so bad now." Quintus stood outside the enchantment with his eyes and fists both squeezed shut. He took in a deep breath, which only made him clench his fists tighter.

At his side, Chloe reached out and took one of his hands in hers.

Every muscle in Quintus's body relaxed at her touch.

She gave him a gentle nudge. "You're doing great." Her shoulders shook as she winced. "It takes some concentration to keep it back though, doesn't it?"

When Elora glared at her middle sister, Chloe just glared right back.

Huffing, Elora turned back to Brannick. He stared at Vesper. "I do not know if he should be with us while we discuss our plans. Not while he is like this."

Elora waved off the words. "He mostly ignores us anyway. And we know better than to take him with us during fights, so what harm could he do?" She reached into her pocket. "Look at what I got when we fought against Ansel."

She opened her fingers, showing off the glittering colors on her palm.

Brannick's eyebrows rose again. "Ansel's gemstones." His eyes narrowed. "These are dangerous."

She couldn't help but chuckle. "I have no plans to use them, but it made me think. What if we found and took all his gemstones? Without them, his magic is probably not very impressive."

Whatever response Brannick might have had never came out.

Somehow, Vesper had sprinted across the clearing without either of them noticing. He tackled Elora to the ground, shoving her head into a patch of moss. Once she was down, he snatched most of the gemstones from her hand.

Brannick shouted and reached for him, but Vesper sprinted away too fast. He opened a door and vanished before they could even take a breath.

It hurt that they had no idea where he had gone, but an even greater fear slithered into Elora's belly.

How much damage could he cause with those gemstones he had stolen?

CHAPTER 32

Fear crawled down Elora's throat, seizing her heart in an iron fist. She embraced it, which made it easier for the fear to consume her. Breathing became a chore. She forced herself to take in heavy breaths both in and out. Finally, she could speak again.

On the outside of the enchantment, Chloe and Grace stared with jaws hanging wide. Quintus, Lyren, and Kaia looked less affected, but they were still surprised. Clearly, they had all seen Vesper disappear through the door.

Spinning on her heel, Elora stepped toward Brannick. Her voice caught, but she still managed to speak. "How do our crystals work?"

He blinked at the place where Vesper's door had disappeared before facing her. "What?"

"The crystals." She heard how crazed her voice came out, but she couldn't do anything about it. "Whenever you opened a door to me, you could find my location with the crystal. Remind me how it works."

He nodded, placing his hand on Blaz's head. "The crystal holds a piece of your essence. With magic, I can use the crystal to sense the rest of your essence."

Her hand flew to her sword hilt. She chewed on her lip, as if that might help her to think. It didn't. At least it gave her the illusion of doing something though.

The others began stepping through the enchantment and back into the clearing.

Elora dug her hands through her hair, inadvertently pulling out several strands as she did. "That ribbon on Vesper's wrist came from my mother's skirt. It became a token for me a while ago. Do you think it holds my essence?"

"Yes." Brannick's answer came quickly, but it sounded anything but sure.

She stepped toward him. "Enough of my essence to sense his location? Can you open a door to him?"

From the other side of the clearing, Lyren scoffed. "Why bother?"

Elora whirled around to face the Swiftsea fae. "Excuse me?"

"Vesper has brought us nothing but trouble ever since that ice shard pierced him. We would be better off leaving him on his own."

Straightening her spine, Elora sneered. "That ice shard is not his fault."

"So?" No amount of sympathy filled Lyren's eyes. Then again, maybe fae were not capable of feeling such a simple thing as sympathy.

"He's our brother." Grace's voice trembled. She had crept closer to Chloe, with her shoulders slumping forward with each step. Despite that, she still spoke loud enough for Lyren to hear.

Curls bounced around Lyren's face as she shook her head. "And he hurt you. He hurt *all* of us."

Chloe closed the distance between her and her youngest sister. She linked an arm through Grace's and pointed her chin in the air. Then she flashed a glare toward the Swiftsea fae. "How would you like it if we abandoned you when you needed help the most? Is that what you expect us to do to our brother now?"

Lyren's eyes narrowed to small slits. "He is not *my* brother."

Grace winced.

Chloe's nose wrinkled. She jerked her head toward Quintus. "Is that how you feel too? Are all fae really this selfish? You only care about yourselves?"

She stepped closer and closer to Quintus with each sentence. Now she had moved close enough to jab him in the chest.

Before she could, Brannick spoke in a commanding voice. "Perhaps we should split up."

Everyone turned toward him in surprise.

"Quintus and Lyren." He gestured toward them. "You two go to Swiftsea and begin teaching others to overcome the high queen's despair. Be sure to request their fealty in return for teaching them." He raised an eyebrow and leaned forward. "Do you think you have learned enough to teach others?"

"Uh." Quintus took a step back.

Lyren shrugged. "Maybe." Her face gained a more focused expression. "But I do want to return to my court." Her voice lowered. "I fear the state of it now that Queen Noelani is gone."

Brannick nodded. "Understandable. Quintus, I need you to go with her."

"But…" He glanced toward Chloe who looked back at him with an almost tangible longing. For a moment, his body swayed back and forth between her and the prince. At last, Quintus's gaze turned downward. "Yes, my prince."

While he moved toward Lyren, Grace stood tall, clearly trying to look older. "What about Chloe and me?"

Now the prince gestured toward the tree at the edge of the clearing. "You two will stay here with Kaia."

The dryad nodded. "And where will you go?"

When he turned back to Elora, he pinned her with a gaze that spoke more than words ever could. "Elora and I will go after Vesper." He glanced back at the others before turning back to Elora again. "He took some of Ansel's gemstones."

Too many gasps followed to be able to tell who they had all come from.

Rather than try to differentiate them, Elora only made a statement of her own. "We cannot afford to let him escape us."

Brannick nodded and then waved off Quintus and Lyren. "Meet us back here when you can."

Once they left through a door, Brannick beckoned Elora toward a deeper part of the forest.

She, Brannick, and Blaz all left the protective enchantment and trailed down the path until the others were out of earshot.

While the prince scanned their surroundings, Elora dug her toe into the soil. "Do you really think Quintus and Lyren can teach others how to overcome the despair?"

From his pocket, Brannick pulled out the purple crystal with a green stripe around the top that perfectly mirrored hers. "They might or they might not. I do think they have a small chance. And at least if they are separated from us, they cannot complain about what we decide to do about Vesper."

"True."

He closed his eyes then, so she closed her mouth. His fingers twitched at his sides. Even standing still, she could sense his concentration.

She dropped to her knees and wrapped her arms around Blaz's neck. The wolf moved in closer while they both waited.

Eventually, Brannick's demeanor shifted. He stood in the same spot with his eyes closed, but his shoulders had slumped forward.

"Did it not work?"

His eyes flickered open for half a moment. "No, but I will try again."

He kept his eyes closed longer, but the second attempt must have failed as well.

While running her fingers through Blaz's fur, Elora stood. "Maybe we do not need to use the ribbon to find his location. He is probably trying to get back to the source of the decay in Swiftsea."

"Back to..." Brannick blinked at her. "Why would he go there?"

"The decay is not actually a decay. It is just a place in Faerie where the portal to the mortal realm is closed."

His eyes opened wide, but his mouth opened wider. His jaw twitched like he wanted to say something, but his mouth just hung open instead.

Never had she seen such befuddlement on his face before.

She shrugged. "Tansy told us."

He blinked several times before he finally spoke. "I cannot believe that never occurred to me." He shook his head. "No wonder stories work so well at keeping the decay at bay."

"Why?"

"Stories are full of emotion. The emotion in them must have strengthened the connection to the mortal realm, and thus opened the portal further."

Waving her hand in a circle, she nodded. "I never thought about it like that, but that does make sense."

She hadn't even noticed opening her own door until Brannick grinned at it. He turned toward her with his head tilting toward the door. "It has your wildflowers."

A matching grin fell across her own lips as she stepped toward the door. "It smells like them too."

On the other side of the door, they arrived on the beach of the sea that separated them from the island with the source of the decay.

Brannick scowled at the beach. "I forgot we could not open a door straight to the island itself. We will need a boat to get across. With Queen Noelani dead, the sea monsters will likely be even more merciless than ever."

"I do not need a boat." Popping the wings from her back, Elora lifted herself high into the air. "Stay here. I will return as quickly as I can."

Salty air stung against her cheeks as she flew across the sea. She made the trip to the island even faster than the first time she had done it. But Vesper did not sit in the black goop of the decay. He wasn't on the island at all.

She flew back to the beach quickly, but a harrowed expression had fallen across Brannick's face. His hand stroked his wolf's fur a little faster than usual. Even before she landed, he started speaking.

"Great magic—even greater magic than Vesper has—is needed to close the portal." His face fell. "But there is another way to close it too."

She gulped. "How?"

"A life sacrifice will do it. If Vesper is so consumed by the ice shard in his heart, he may give his life to free himself from the pain of the emotions in Faerie. It would only work because the portal is partially closed right now."

Her fingers trailed across the ribbons in her belt until she gripped her sword hilt. "Can you open it permanently then? Now that you know it is the portal."

He lifted his hand from his wolf's head and dug his fingers through his own hair. "I do not know. Maybe. It has been partially closed for so long, it will take more than magic to open it fully. A sacrifice is still needed. It does not have to be a life sacrifice, but it will have to be a great one."

After digging his fingers through his hair once more, he met her gaze. "I think it has to be a token that is sacrificed. A strong token."

At the same moment, both of their eyes drifted downward to her sword. She gulped. She wanted to help Vesper, but could she sacrifice the only items she had left from her parents?

A glowing green light zoomed toward them. She probably should not have been so grateful for the distraction.

The sprite that flew toward them had sparkling yellow-green eyes and a brown coat.

She knew the residue from Ansel's enchantment kept Tansy stuck in Bitter Thorn, but she still ached at the sight of a different sprite instead of her good friend.

At least she had met this sprite before.

"Finally." Thisbe shook his head several times while his wings glowed brightly behind him. "We thought you would never leave that residue in Bitter Thorn."

"What is it, Thisbe?" Elora leaned toward the little sprite.

"Severin and his beloved would like you to visit them. They have news."

CHAPTER 33

Gravel crunched under Elora's boots. Open breezes fluttered through her gossamer gown. The mountain smelled of dirt, rocks, and plants, but the scents were nothing like Bitter Thorn. These scents were wide and exposed.

As much as she loved Bitter Thorn, she had to admit Mistmount had grown on her. As long as she stayed in the mountains, far from Ansel's house, she could see the appeal of living in such a court.

The narrow mountain path only had enough room for two people to walk side by side. Blaz had to trail behind them.

When they arrived at Tindra and Severin's cave, Elora and Brannick glanced inside.

Tindra's cheeks flushed with excitement at the sight of them. "I believe my formula is ready. I just need—"

Elora had stepped inside the cave, which for some reason, had caused Tindra to stop midsentence.

"Prince Brannick." Severin wore the same surprised expression as his beloved, the reason for it now becoming clear. "We thought you were imprisoned."

"I was. Luckily, it did not last long as my first imprisonment." He stepped into the cave, placing his hand on the small of Elora's back while he scanned the area.

She leaned into him, suddenly conscious of how much she had missed having his hand at her back.

Grinning, Severin turned to his beloved. "See? My sister's defenses are already failing. Your formula will finish things off."

Elora leaned close to Brannick and spoke under her breath. "Tindra's formula can destroy all enchantments and even the bargains that entrap the high queen's guards." Elora's gaze turned back to the Fairfrost fae. "If it truly works."

A friendly smile fell across Tindra's face. She gave an eager nod. "It can destroy any enchantments we create, but I am eager to test it on an enchantment created by High Queen Alessandra. As I already explained, it will not work on any enchantments she created with the gemstones, but it should destroy all others." Her mouth twisted into a knot as she rubbed the back of her leg with her foot. "We were hoping to travel somewhere with a place that already has one of High Queen Alessandra's enchantments."

Reaching into her memories, Elora tried to think if she knew of any such place. Her mind supplied the answer right away. "Bitter Thorn Castle. High Queen Alessandra created snowflakes filled with fear, but she did it without a gemstone. The enchantment should still be there."

Severin swiped a tuft of light brown hair off his forehead and tilted his head toward the back of the cave. "That is what Fifer suggested as well."

"Fifer?" Brannick went to give Elora a questioning glance, but before he finished, the brownie appeared from around the corner at the back of the cave.

His large ears pointed up toward the ceiling. His big eyes sparkled brighter than ever. Even his light brown skin had more freshness than it had since the snowflakes had first fallen inside Bitter Thorn Castle. A smile wrinkled his squat nose as he nodded at Brannick. "My prince. It is good to see you again."

Reaching for a section of her white-blonde hair, Tindra stepped forward. "Fifer told us how the curse in Bitter Thorn poisons the castle walls. If the curse has taken too much hold, it might affect the formula."

Brannick tapped his chin while his eyes narrowed. "The curse is lifting now. I should be able to push it out of the castle completely. My essence is stronger than it ever has been." As if to punctuate the statement, his eyes swirled with their mesmerizing bursts.

Tindra's smile turned even friendlier. She glanced toward the back of the cave where Fifer stood. "Then you can return to your true home."

The brownie gave a delighted shriek and scurried forward.

"We will have to travel on our dragon to get to Bitter Thorn Castle." Severin gestured at the back of the cave. "High Queen Alessandra has magic to track any doors I create *and* any doors I step through. But she cannot track our dragon. It is the only one left that hasn't turned wild."

Tindra had gone over to her worktable where she started dropping vials and herbs into a large basket. She spoke over her shoulder. "Before we leave, we need to gather more sage and even some of those little white pebbles. There is a whole pile of them at the end of the path outside."

"We will get them." Brannick spoke quickly, but not as quickly as he pulled Elora out onto the mountain path.

Soon they moved out sight of the others. Even Blaz had stayed back.

After a few steps down the path, Brannick ran his fingers through his hair. He pinned Elora with a gaze as mesmerizing as his smirk. "I thought we needed a moment alone."

Her lips twitched upward. "Did you now?"

Rather than answer, he slipped an arm around her waist and pulled her in close. He leaned down until his nose hovered just in front of hers. "I remember how it felt when I could not touch you." His free hand found her cheek and then his finger traced the line of her jaw. "Now I am overcome with the desire to memorize your every line." His finger trailed down the bend of her neck. "Every curve."

His touch sent heat under her skin.

She had to raise onto the balls of her feet to reach his lips. Once she did, he pressed himself even closer to her body. The kiss sent a tingle into her lips that spread to her tongue and the rest of her mouth until it seemed to fill every space inside her.

He caressed the curve of her neck, her jaw, and even up to her ear. His hand seemed eager to do exactly as he had said and memorize her every feature. When his hand slid into her hair and reached around the back of her neck to pull her closer, her heart skittered and melted into a puddle.

His hand at her back had an entirely different purpose from the other. It seemed intent on pulling her closer with every breath.

271

By the time he pulled away, her fingers ached from gripping his coat so tight.

He brushed his nose against hers and stared into her eyes without blinking. "We should probably find that sage and those pebbles, but we can continue this later, yes?"

She stole a small kiss before rocking back onto her heels. "Definitely yes."

"Good." Flashing a suggestive smirk, he kept his arm around her waist and led her down the narrow path.

Gravel crunched under her boots again, but her toes felt like they stepped on air. Her heart probably wouldn't settle for days, especially if Brannick kept his arm around her waist like he did now.

If they had any hope of retrieving the sage and pebbles, she needed to give herself something else to think about.

"How did you make your door small whenever you contacted me? Every time I have opened a door, it has always been big enough to walk through, but you were able to make your door as small as a thumbnail."

He brushed a hand over her elbow before bending down to gather some sage. "It took extra concentration, nothing more. Try it. I am certain you could do it too."

She did not concentrate. Since her magic was intuition, she feared too much concentration would only get in the way of things. But she did imagine a door the size of a thumbnail when she waved her hand in a circle.

Soon, a tiny door appeared right in front of her nose. It might have been cause for celebration except a foul voice drifted out of it.

"She will be here soon. Hurry up to the loft. Make no noise."

272

Brannick stood up with a start. He glanced at the tiny door and then flicked his eyes to Elora. He whispered under his breath. "Where did you open your door to?"

She replied in an even quieter whisper. "Ansel's house."

With eyebrows raising, Brannick's eyes flashed. "Ansel's..." Fear seized the muscles in his face. He lowered his voice even more. "Why?"

She bit her bottom lip, not quite able to shrug when she tried to. "I have no idea. I just did it. I did not think about it."

The necklace at his throat bulged when he gulped. He stepped closer to her. "You should not open a door to a home where you have not been invited. There are consequences that—"

She held up a hand to silence him. "I *have* been invited." Her head tilted toward the door. When he opened his mouth, she held up her hand again. "Listen."

Ansel spoke louder now in a more commanding tone than before. "The invitation I gave you is for this visit only. You are not invited to my house whenever you like after this."

Someone snorted in response. "Why do you think I would *want* to return here?"

Elora's blood chilled when she recognized the second voice.

High Queen Alessandra.

Brannick met Elora's gaze. Then they both leaned closer to the tiny door.

Ansel responded in a mutter. "I know how to protect my house."

The sound of swishing fabric suggested High Queen Alessandra had started pacing the floor. "We need more gemstones. I still have one more purple gemstone from that... *girl*." She spit the last word out. "But if those other fae were

273

able to get to the creation magic like you claim, we need more gemstones. We need to be prepared for another battle."

"That *girl* stole some of my gemstones too." Ansel sounded equally annoyed and impressed. "I only have a few left in my collection. I can make more, but my pets are running low on energy. They are nearly used up."

The high queen scoffed. "Then go to the mortal realm and steal another mortal if you must."

"Something funny is happening with the portal. I fear that if I leave now, I may not be able to return."

"I had forgotten about that." Even without seeing High Queen Alessandra's face, her words sounded like a scowl. "Come back to Fairfrost Palace then. I am certain I have a mortal servant somewhere. You can use it to make another gemstone."

"Once you use the creation magic for the final enchantment, I will not have this problem anymore. I will be able to use fae for my gemstones instead of mortals." He paused for a beat. "Unless you fail to find your vessel."

The high queen huffed. "I will find him."

Ansel did not sound convinced. "Remember what I told you. If you touch the creation magic yourself, you will lose your magic."

"I remember." She spit the words out.

"If Prince Brannick touches the creation magic and then you touch *him*, you will be able to channel the creation magic through him and create your final enchantment. You can make every creature in Faerie love you just as you wish." He paused. "But you *need* a vessel."

"He is not a prince anymore." She huffed. "*I* am Queen of Bitter Thorn."

"The crown never changed its appearance. It has not accepted you as its ruler." Ansel sounded bored.

"Its appearance never changed for Prince Brannick either."

"If you cannot find him, it will be difficult to find another vessel strong enough to withstand the channeling of the creation magic."

High Queen Alessandra responded with a haughty laugh. "And what about the girl? You said she is the only other who might be strong enough to be a vessel, yet you lost her too."

A foot stomped. "She should not have been able to move after what I did to her." He grunted. "But at least I did not have her in chains inside my own dungeon when she escaped."

"Enough." The high queen's voice came out shrill. "I have a plan to find him again. You come with me now to Fairfrost Palace and make new gemstones. I will worry about the rest."

"Fine."

The whirring sound of an opening Faerie door drifted out. Footsteps muffled their voices and then they vanished completely.

Elora gulped when she waved a hand to close her own tiny door.

"I cannot believe Ansel told her about the creation magic." Brannick's eyebrows knitted together as he dug both his hands through his hair. "That was my one advantage over her, and now..." His jaw clenched tight. Breaths puffed from his nostrils while his eyes swirled with dangerous sparks. "I will not hide from her, but I will not let her use me or you as a vessel either."

Elora nodded, the truth sinking into her slowly. "Whatever happens, I think one thing is clear. A battle is coming."

CHAPTER 34

The mountain air had more bite as it whipped through Elora's hair. She stood in place, still trying to make sense of everything she had just learned. High Queen Alessandra and Ansel were running out of gemstones. The high queen had some final enchantment planned that required creation magic and a vessel.

She intended to use Brannick as the vessel.

Elora's breath hitched when she turned to her side. The prince had a clump of sage under his arm and two handfuls of white pebbles in his palms. The carefree expression on his face suggested he didn't have the same fear writhing in his belly like she had.

He even managed a half smile in her direction when he stood. "Come. After we give Severin and Tindra these items, we can return to Bitter Thorn Castle." He started down the path. "I do want to send a message to Soren while we are here though."

He had gone halfway to the cave entrance before he realized she didn't follow. When he turned around to face her, he raised a questioning eyebrow.

"I..." She sucked in a breath, still trying to settle the thoughts hurtling through her mind. "I just need a moment." She waved him on. "You go ahead. I will be right there."

His body didn't move as he held her gaze. He stared without speaking for a long breath. Then his lips parted, as if to speak. He must have changed his mind at the last moment because he nodded and turned away instead.

Once he entered the cave, her thoughts hammered inside her, refusing to be ignored for another moment.

Ansel was not at his house.

She knew with certainty that he had just left and that he would be gone for a while at least.

Even with his invitation, she never intended to actually enter his house. But now he was gone. Her magic of intuition had clearly helped her find that out.

And his mortal pets were still there. His pets that, according to him, were *nearly used up.*

A hard lump formed in her throat. It refused to be swallowed.

After fleeing his home, she once promised to herself that she would rescue those mortals. She intended to free them from the despicable existence Ansel provided them.

Somehow, that promise had gotten lost among all the other things she had done for Brannick and for Faerie.

But now Ansel was in Fairfrost.

And the mortals were alone in his house.

So were the other gemstones.

The lump stung in her throat, crawling deeper inside it.

She didn't know where the gemstones were hidden, but maybe the mortals knew. Maybe she could convince them to help her. Maybe...

The thoughts collapsed as she let out a sigh.

She had never been good with words. Her idea of a solid negotiation tended to involve her sword skill. The other fae had only ever found her impressive because of her ability to feel emotions. But those mortals had emotions just like her.

They would not be impressed by her. How could she dream of convincing them when she had no great words to persuade them with?

Her hand formed a fist over her sword hilt when three words burned in her mind.

Be great anyway.

She gripped the sword hilt tighter. Words had never been her strength, but maybe that didn't matter. Maybe she just needed a strong enough resolve.

The words marched through her mind.

Be great anyway.

Without another thought, she opened a door and stepped through it.

Her feet landed on a familiar wooden floor. A table topped with gray ceramic dishes sat to the side of her. Glass light fixtures hung over the table, adding to the light the sprites in the room gave off.

Every muscle in her body seized, but her stomach clenched tightest of all. She had known the door would lead her here, but seeing it churned her stomach into knots. The slightest movement would send its contents spewing from her mouth.

It took several deep breaths before she could take a step. She turned and saw a navy plaid couch with a gash that had been sloppily repaired.

Her stomach clenched tighter at the sight of it. She had made that gash with her sword. She had escaped.

Forcing herself to remember the escape, she edged deeper into the room. Once she reached the wood and glass cabinet against the wall, she flung open one of its glass doors.

Originally, she intended to find the mortals first and to ask for their help. But being in Ansel's house again made her skin prickle and her mouth thick with a bitter taste. Since the cabinet stood right in front of her now, perhaps it would be best to search for the gemstones first.

The door she flung open revealed a candle and a glass figurine. She tore them both off the shelf and threw them over her shoulder. Throwing open a small drawer, she discovered more glass figurines and long chisel. Those got thrown onto the floor as well.

Each movement her body made came jerky and erratic. No matter how often she reminded herself that she was safe as long as Ansel was in Fairfrost, she could not shake away the chill that had settled into her bones. She flung open another door and found a few worn books.

Drawer after drawer, shelf after shelf revealed none of the gemstones she sought.

When she yanked open the last drawer, footsteps sounded behind her.

"What are you doing?" A female voice had spoken, but it sounded raspy and harrowed.

Elora whipped around to meet the eye of a familiar-looking fae. Of course, Elora knew from experience that appearance of the female before her was nothing more than a glamour. Ansel used glamours to hide the true appearance of all his mortals. Even though this female looked fae, she was surely a mortal.

Standing up straight, Elora tried to use the greatest words she could think of. "I am here to help you."

From behind the couch, a male with blonde hair emerged. "Help us?" His voice was rough and raspy like the female's, but it held defiance too. "By destroying our master's things?"

After swallowing, Elora glanced at the ground. She frowned, but it couldn't take back what she had already done. Rolling her shoulders back, she tried again. "I need to find Ansel's gemstones. Do you know where he keeps them hidden?"

The two mortals looked at each other. The glamours over them probably hid their true expressions, but they still shared a look that communicated something.

When the female looked back at Elora, one side of her mouth raised. "We know what we must do with you."

They both stepped forward in unison.

The hairs on the back of Elora's neck stood on end. She sucked in a breath. "I want to help you. I can take you away from here."

"Away?" The male scoffed. "But this is where we belong. We could not survive anywhere else." His shoulders hunched forward. "We must not upset our master."

They continued stepping closer. With the cabinet at her back, Elora had nowhere to go. She told herself they meant no harm. But then they both lunged and reached for her arms.

Her body reacted instinctively. The wings popped from her back and lifted her into the air away from their reaching hands. "I know Ansel hurts you. He uses you. Come with me, and you will finally be safe."

Both mortals jumped into the air, reaching for Elora's ankles. The female's face twisted with determination. "Ansel *loves* us."

The male nodded. "He *needs* us."

Elora's throat thickened at the sound of the words. She wanted to scream at them, but that probably wouldn't help them understand. Instead, she tried to plead. "He does not care about you. He only cares about what you can give him."

Beating her wings, she flew high enough to reach the loft she had discovered during her first experience in Ansel's house. Just like her first visit, the loft didn't appear until she flew high enough.

As before, mortals sat on cushions and sprawled out on the ground. Their bodies looked wasted. Their eyes looked lifeless. She swallowed hard and landed on the loft. Her eyebrows pressed together tight enough to cause an ache across her forehead. None of the mortals on the loft noticed her appearance until she started speaking.

"I can help you, but you have to come with me."

The sound of her voice acted like a signal. Suddenly, their heads lifted. Their eyes focused in on her. One by one, they pushed themselves up and lumbered closer to her. "We must do what our master says. We cannot leave him."

When they started reaching for her, she stepped back. One of them caught a handful of her gossamer gown.

She gasped and took another step back. But she had reached the edge of the loft. Her foot met air, pulling the rest of her down with it.

The mortals tried to reach for her, but they could not stop her from falling. At least in the air, her wings could lift her once again. They beat hard against her back as she hovered in front of the loft.

"I want to help you."

Even with lifeless eyes, the sight of all their faces curdled her stomach. Just like sour milk. She flinched.

Before she could decide what to do next, a net of scratchy rope got flung at her body. She had to swoop nearly into the wall to miss it. Whatever breath she had rushed out of her now.

Another net flew through the air. This one landed over her head.

Her hand waved automatically.

She wouldn't get caught. No matter what, she refused to be a prisoner in Ansel's home again. The mortals could try to catch her, but they couldn't stop her from going through her own door back to Mistmount.

Once her feet hit the gravel of the mountain path, she sucked in as much air as possible. Rope scratched at her arms. The net had traveled through the door with her. She gasped and ripped it away from her body.

It tumbled down the mountain side while she tried to catch her breath. At least her door had closed now. Stitches formed in her sides. She clutched her sword hilt, eager for anything that might ground her.

Tindra and Severin's cave entrance stood only a few steps away, but she couldn't move toward it. She could barely even breathe.

When she sucked in another breath, Blaz bounded out the cave until he stood close at her side. The sight of him helped her lungs to fill a little more. Touching his fur gave her enough strength for another deep breath.

Brannick left the cave entrance and locked eyes with her at once. He stared, perhaps trying to guess what had happened without having to ask.

Before she could even dream of opening her mouth, Severin and Tindra spilled out of the cave entrance behind Brannick.

Severin's eyes went wide at the sight of her. "Your face has gone as white as marble."

Tindra bit her lip. "Are you okay?"

They all must have seen the terror in her eyes, but Brannick acted first. He strode toward her confidently and opened a door. As he moved toward her, he glanced over his shoulder at the others. "We will be expecting you and your dragon at Bitter Thorn Castle. If that sprite returns before you leave, let me know what message he brings."

By the time he finished speaking, he had reached Elora. He wrapped an arm around her waist. She immediately leaned into him, still trying to catch her breath.

She would feel better once they returned to Bitter Thorn. At least she hoped she would.

CHAPTER 35

Decaying scents shattered the peace that used to fill Bitter Thorn Castle. Elora stumbled over vines and briars of thorns. Snow piled in the hallways, bringing a chill to the air. Cracks through the walls sent stone crumbling onto the snow every few steps she took.

Brannick held her tight around the waist, guiding her movements. Blaz walked with them, but he stood on the opposite side of her, offering support whenever she stumbled.

Eventually, they trudged through the snow and entered Brannick's bedroom inside the castle. Since he had removed the snow clouds from only his bedroom, it was the only room that didn't have snow piling on the floor.

Thorns still stretched over his walls and up the furniture. Stone crumbled off the walls, creating a few holes. At least thorns hadn't overrun his bed. Aside from a few ripped blankets, it looked the same as it ever had.

A crease formed between his lowered eyebrows. He stepped toward the bed with unerring focus. At one point, trudging through all that fear-filled snow in the hallways would have broken him. Now, he had better control of his emotions.

When he reached the bed, he gently helped her onto it. She didn't lower herself all the way down. Instead, she partially sat up with a mound of pillows at her back. Blaz jumped onto the bed and rested his furry head in her lap.

She ran her fingers through his black fur while Brannick sat next to her on the edge of the bed. His eyes gained that intense quality they always did when he stared a little too long.

He brushed a strand of hair out of her face, letting his fingers linger on her cheek. "What happened?"

Even in a half-sitting position, it still brought her comfort to reach for her sword hilt. She squeezed it with one hand while the other continued to pet Blaz's head. "I went to Ansel's house."

The words hung in the space between them. Brannick blinked. His face stayed mostly still but for the slightest tension along his jaw. He continued to stare, probably wanting to clench his jaw but also not wanting to appear angry.

It didn't matter. She knew he was angry, and it was probably best to let him get it all out. Her fingers tightened over the sword. "I wanted to save the mortals he has in his house. I thought it would be safe since we know Ansel is in Fairfrost right now."

A vein pulsed in Brannick's jaw. His teeth clenched together tight. "Why did you not tell me?"

Blaz let out a soft howl and pressed his head deeper in Elora's lap. His pain echoed the prince's.

Air burst from Brannick's nose as he turned away. "Why did you not take me with you?"

She sank deeper into the pillows, eyeing her sword hilt so she wouldn't have to look at the prince. "Ansel invited me to his home. I can go inside it without consequence. You cannot."

Another puff of air burst from Brannick's nose. He shoved himself off the bed and began pacing. "What happened while you were there?"

Her fingers trailed along the leather of her sword hilt while she tried to form the right words. Even then, her voice came out shaky. "The mortals attacked me. I tried to explain that I wanted to help them, but they would not listen." A chill slithered down her spine, sending icicles through her veins. "They tried to trap me with a net."

Brannick's feet froze in place. His entire body stilled, except for his eyes, which opened wide, wide, wide. He clenched his jaw again and turned away from her. "*Why* did you go at all?"

"Because of how he treats them." She sat up higher now, finding her first bit of courage. "He did the same things to me, and…" Her throat hardened with a lump. The sword hilt offered no help now, so she released it and flopped her arm down by her side. "*Someone* has to save them."

Stepping closer to the bed, Brannick held his arms out slightly with the palms facing up. "Can you not wait to do it until after I kill Ansel?"

Silence thickened as she stared back at him. She waited one beat. And then two.

When she opened her mouth, her gaze dropped downward. "Lyren says it will taint your essence if you kill him."

Even from the corner of her eye, she noticed him wince. He shook his head and started pacing again. "Lyren is…" His voice trailed off. He continued pacing but didn't seem eager to finish his sentence.

"Right?" Elora supplied.

He winced again. "Only a murder will taint my essence. Faerie itself will not punish me if the killing is justified."

"Is it justified?" Her voice came out smaller than she meant it.

His gaze flicked to hers in a flash. He stared for a moment before giving a hard swallow. When he answered, his voice had lowered to a gravelly, hardened tone. "Yes."

Something passed between them then. He stood a few steps away, but she could sense his conviction. Feel his heart swell. Even if she wanted to, she couldn't have pulled her gaze away. But why would she want to when he looked at her like that?

Blaz let out a quiet whimper and nuzzled his nose against her hand that had stopped petting him. She swallowed and ran her fingers through his fur once again.

She watched her fingers now as they parted the soft, black fur. "We have to kill High Queen Alessandra too. Five crowns have bonded to her. The only way to break that bond is to kill her."

"I know." Brannick went back to pacing. "Once she is dead, I also have to appoint new rulers for each of the courts she stole crowns from. I hope King Jackory is not dead because I do not know many Mistmount fae besides him." His nose wrinkled in a snarl. "Except Ansel."

Her body flinched at the name.

"I *will* kill him." Brannick stood at the edge of the bed, his eyes more fiery than usual.

Elora sighed. "I think I would rather kill him myself."

He nodded, his nose wrinkling again. "I would not stop you if you got the chance to do so, but if I get my own opportunity, I will take it."

When her eyes met his, another shift filled the space between them. She pushed herself to her feet so she could stand in front of him. Only a small amount of space separated their bodies, but it still felt like too much.

He brushed a strand of hair away from her face. His fingers lingered on her cheek with apparently no intention of dropping.

She took a step forward, tilting her head up to look into his eyes. "I tried to find his gemstones too. I think we might need them to have any chance at all."

His fingers brushed the pointed tip of her ear as he tucked hair behind it. "I think you might be right."

Biting her bottom lip, she felt her eyebrows come together. "Then *I* have to retrieve them. I am the only one who can go into his house without consequence."

Pain contorted his face. He dropped his forehead until it met hers.

Her eyes darted to his lips, but she quickly looked up to his eyes again. "Do we need to find a way for you to come with me?" Her voice lowered. "I will not go alone if you cannot support it."

He closed his eyes, pressing more of his forehead against hers. When he breathed deeply, it warmed her face. "I will always support you. Always." His eyes opened then. He moved back just enough to ensure they could look into each other's eyes. "But is it really support if I make you feel like you cannot do anything without me?"

Blaz jumped off the bed and quietly padded out of the room, but Elora couldn't pull her gaze away from Brannick's. He touched her cheek, flushing it with heat. Swirls pulsed in his eyes, filling the entire room with magic. "You are stronger than anyone I know. I do not like it, but you can find those gemstones." He swallowed and continued with a rougher voice. "I know you can."

He held her gaze until she nodded. As soon as she did, he spread his hand across the back of her head and pulled her in for a kiss.

Just like the room itself seemed to shift during their conversation, something in the kiss had shifted too. Brannick leaned into her, he pulled her close, but it felt deeper than any other kiss they had shared. He stepped toward her, sliding his other hand down her back where it could press into her.

She had reached her arms around him, hugging tight and kissing hard.

But it wasn't enough.

He moved closer to her again. And again. His hands roved over more of her until he had her pressed up against the tree standing at one corner of his bed. Her skin felt hot in every spot he touched.

He reached around her and lifted her off the ground. Never once did his lips pull away from hers. For a moment, she thought he might lay her onto the bed, but then he pulled away.

His arms untangled from hers as he took a step back. He closed his eyes and breathed in deeply. She could see how his fingers twitched at his sides, eager to take her into his arms again. Somehow, he held back.

Her own breaths came out heavier than she expected. When he glanced toward her, heat filled her cheeks with a tingling burn. She bit her bottom lip, but it didn't hide her grin.

He grinned back with hunger flashing in her eyes. But then he closed his eyes and turned away. "I know Vesper told me about your customs, but I never asked how you feel." When he faced her again, his eyebrows pinched together. "Does marriage matter to *you?*"

She sucked in a breath. A part of knew this question was coming, but she still wished it hadn't come so soon. Lifting one foot, she rubbed it across the back of her leg. "Yes." Her eyes lowered to her sword hilt so she wouldn't have to see his reaction. "But I understand why it seems like entrapment to you. I feel unworthy to ask for it when I know how much you suffered because of your marriage bargain with High Queen Alessandra."

The silence might have been easier to bear if she could force herself to look into his eyes. Instead, she continued to stare at her sword.

When he spoke, his tone revealed nothing. "We should go to the castle entrance. The others might be here by now."

She followed him when he moved toward the hallway. Once she got to his side, he slipped his hand into hers. It didn't tell her how he felt about what she just admitted, but at least he hadn't given up on her. They should probably wait to discuss it until after the battle anyway. They had other things to worry about at the moment.

Faerie itself needed saving.

CHAPTER 36

Snow piled so high, Elora had to lift the layers of her gown just to trudge through it. Brannick conjured a thin piece of metal to push the snow out of the way, which did help. But the snow kept the air around them icy and wet.

They rounded a corner, moving even more slowly than before. Each step brought them closer to the castle entrance.

"Brannick." Her voice didn't tremble, but it felt weighted coming out of her mouth.

He stopped and looked straight into her eyes.

Blaz had found them again. He wriggled his body between the two of them, rubbing his head against each of their legs.

She swallowed. "If a fae touches the creation magic, is there any way for that fae to gain his magic back again?"

The weight in her voice transferred across the distance and into his eyes. His chin lowered when he took a deep breath. "Just one. But it only works if Faerie itself chooses to help."

Her eyebrow cocked up. "How is it done?"

He opened his mouth, but no words came out. He stared at her, but he seemed to be looking at something else entirely. Thoughts probably tumbled through his mind. He shook his head. "It does not matter because neither of us will touch the creation magic."

When he stomped forward down the hallway, she could do nothing except follow him. Though she still had questions about the creation magic, she could tell the conversation had ended.

By now, they made it to the large doors at the entrance of the castle. Brannick gripped the thick leather straps of the door handles and flung the doors open wide. The forest winked back at them as lush and as crisp as ever.

It felt good to be back in the castle again, even if they stood knee-deep in snow to do it.

Tindra and Severin stood just outside the doors with the pastel-hued dragon standing at their backs. They weren't the only ones standing there.

"Have you seen this, Elora?" Chloe stroked the dragon's tail, her eyes open wide. "It's a dragon." She touched the creature again and let out a disbelieving chuckle. "A *dragon*."

She'd probably be less impressed with the creature if she had seen how High Queen Alessandra used a dragon to steal a chunk of Bitter Thorn Castle. Still, the dragon *was* quite a sight to behold.

Grace stood next to the dragon's head, rubbing it between the eyes. Her own jaw had dropped as well. "Look how it sparkles."

Even Kaia admired the dragon. Her emerald hair looked shiny and bright. Not a trace of bark-like striations colored her dark brown skin.

Severin chuckled at the three of them before turning back to the castle entrance. "We got a message from Soren. He is alive and has found King Jackory. They are in hiding and will stay that way as long as they can."

Patting her pocket, Tindra flashed a friendly smile. "May we come in?"

Brannick nodded and stepped back to give them room. Before Tindra or Severin could move forward, Fifer scurried toward the doors. His floppy ears bounced. Just before he stepped over the threshold, his foot hovered in the air.

He had almost touched the snow, but now his foot hung without moving. His shoulders shook as he stared at it. But then his head snapped up with a start. He took a step back and turned to glance at Kaia. "How are you not affected by the despair all around us?"

Even as he spoke, his body trembled. His ears drooped.

Grace nuzzled her cheek against the dragon's with a grin forming on her face. Though the brownie's question had been directed at the dryad, Grace answered it instead. "Elora taught us how to withstand the despair."

Fifer's big eyes opened wide. Tindra and Severin both whipped around to stare wide-eyed at Grace.

Elora waved a beckoning hand toward them, drawing their attention back to the castle. "I can teach you how to do it too, but should we try the formula first?"

Brushing a hand over his nut-brown hair, Severin nodded. "Good idea."

When they entered, Brannick used the thin metal he had conjured to clear away a spot for them to walk. Sparks formed

293

at Elora's fingertips until she shot an enchantment over their heads to block them from the falling snow.

Despite the enchantment, and despite the snow Brannick had cleared away, they still shuddered with every step they took.

Tindra wrapped her arms over her stomach, pulling them close to her body. "We should start with a small area first. A single room would be best."

Nodding, Brannick led them to the council room. The long table that sat in the middle of the room had thorns twisting up its legs and along its edges. Twelve trees grew on one side the table, but they wilted with faded colors. Snow covered the branches so thoroughly, the leaves on them were buried.

Everyone piled into the room, standing mostly along the back wall. Brannick gestured around him. "Will this room work?"

Tindra nodded, shivering all the while. "Yes, but the curse needs to be gone or it might interfere with my experiment."

"Right." Brannick knotted his eyebrows close together. His eyes narrowed as he lifted his hand. Stretching his fingers out, he sucked in a deep breath. While he did, the vague scent of decay curled inward from around the edges of the room. It slithered on the air until it gathered close around the prince.

When he sucked in another breath, he pushed both his hands toward the exit. Though the curse itself was not visible, Elora could feel how it clung to the air. When Brannick shot his hands forward, it flew out of the room in a single burst.

His face relaxed for a moment until he caught sight of the thorns that still twisted around his throne at the head of the table. They crawled away from the tree merged with stone, leaving the seat and arms bare. But the thorns still stretched down the side of the throne and up the tree trunk.

Taking a quick glance at her beloved, Tindra then turned to the prince. "Is… the curse gone?"

"Yes." Brannick reached a hand out. He rubbed his finger and thumb together, as if touching the air. "It no longer infects this room."

Severin threw his own glance toward his beloved before his gaze fixed on the throne. "I thought the thorns were part of the curse. Why did they not wither or slide away?"

Dropping his hand to the side, Brannick sighed. He narrowed his eyes at the thorns twisting over his throne. He glanced over at the table where thorns still grew along the legs. Finally, he shrugged. "I do not know. Maybe we have embraced them. Maybe they are no longer a part of the curse but are simply a part of Bitter Thorn. Either way, the thorns will not interfere. I am certain of it."

Tindra and Severin glanced at each other once more before both of them shrugged. Pushing her white-blonde hair behind one shoulder, Tindra pulled a glass vial from her pocket. She held her breath as she pulled the stopper out of it. The pearlescent blue formula clung to the long post of the stopper.

Her eyes narrowed when she lifted the stopper away from the vial until she held it an arm's length away from her body. She held her breath while the blue formula slithered down the post until it collected in a heavy drop at the end of it. She leaned forward, waiting for the drop to fall away from the stopper.

At the same moment, everyone else in the room leaned forward too. They waited. No one made a sound.

Finally, the blue liquid pooled into a large enough drop that it fell away from the glass. It dropped with a splash onto the snow below. Tindra immediately slid the stopper back into her glass vial.

Icy blue smoke swirled out from the splash. The smoke puffed and glittered with iridescence as it spread throughout the room. It continued to swirl faster with every breath. While it worked, the snow began to vanish. It didn't melt. If it had melted, the snow would have left puddles of water behind. Instead, it simply puffed into smoke and ceased to exist.

When the smoke and glitter finished swirling through the entire room, it curled back in on itself. It moved quickly, gathering back into the spot on the ground where the drop had first splashed. Once it all moved back into that spot, every trace of the ice-blue magic vanished in a flash.

A light breeze drifted in through the window, filling the room with the scent of crisp rain, wet bark, and fresh wild berries. The branches on the trees curved back toward the ceiling looking as strong and sturdy as ever. The leaves turned a brilliant green as they fluttered in the gentle breeze.

No one had to ask if the formula had worked. The spongy moss, gentle breeze, and even the sturdy trees made it clear. It *had* worked. The council room looked as lovely as it ever had.

Everyone in the room let out a collective sigh. Elora gripped her sword hilt as tears pooled in her eyes. Maybe they still didn't have any protection against enchantments created by the gemstones, but they did have a way to defeat any other enchantments.

They had a chance.

Brannick swallowed hard, this throat tightening against his necklace. The tiniest smile dared to linger beneath his lips. When he glanced toward Tindra, his eyes seemed to sparkle. "It only takes a single drop?"

She nodded. "For a space this size, yes."

He eyed the glass vial in her hands, probably trying to determine how many drops it held. "Is that all you have of the formula?"

Severin slid a hand through his hair as he glanced toward his beloved. "She can easily make more now that she knows the recipe."

While Severin spoke, Brannick's eyes drifted past them toward the door that led out to the rest of the castle. Longing filled his eyes.

Tindra seemed to understand the look, even without a word. Her expression turned calculating as she pulled the formula close to her chest. She glanced at Elora, then at Brannick, then out toward the rest of the castle. "If you teach us how to withstand the despair, I will use my formula to clear out the enchantment from the rest of the castle."

Brannick started to nod, but he stopped almost as soon as he began. His gaze flicked over to Elora. A question sparked in his eyes.

"Of course I will teach you." Her chest loosened when she saw Brannick let out a sigh of relief.

She quickly explained just as she had done for her sisters and for Kaia, Lyren, and Quintus. After asking a few questions, Tindra and Severin went into the hallway to practice among the fear-filled snow. Fifer joined them and caught on much more quickly than either of the Fairfrost fae.

Maybe it had helped that he had spent days around Elora. He must have had more experience with emotions than either of the other two fae.

Still, it didn't take long before they had the basic concept down. Brannick joined Tindra and Severin as they went room to room throughout the castle to clear away the last of High Queen Alessandra's destructive enchantment.

While they worked, Elora and her sisters helped Kaia and Fifer to tidy the castle as much as they could. When Brannick pushed the curse out of the castle, it repaired the cracked and crumbled stone. Thorns still grew along walls and over furniture, but it looked brighter than usual. It nearly glinted in the light with a glossy shine.

Still, plenty of broken spears, torn books, and other stray items littered the rooms and hallways of the castle. They worked hard to clear it all away.

When the first tendrils of night started wisping inside the castle, Fifer and Grace returned to the council room to cook a meal for everyone.

Just as Elora wandered back into the council room, Lyren and Quintus stepped in behind her.

"The snow." Lyren reached for her curls. "It is gone. We went to the clearing and saw no one there, so we thought we would check the castle, but…" She pressed her blue-painted fingernails to her lips. "It looks like Bitter Thorn Castle again."

Quintus ran a hand over the nearest stone wall. Before he could say anything, Chloe bounded in from the hallway and took his hand in hers.

Her cheeks flushed with pink. "Quintus. I thought something must have happened to you. Why were you gone so long?"

He answered with a half smile. Reaching up, he brushed a thumb over the harp string that still secured the end of her blonde braid. When he looked back up, his half smile grew. "It is working."

After deliberately stepping between her sister and Quintus, forcing them apart, Elora glanced toward Lyren. "What is working? Were you able to teach other fae how to withstand the despair?"

Lyren nodded eagerly.

Quintus shrugged. "Some are better at it than others."

Pride sparkled in Lyren's eyes as she brushed a wrinkle from her blue dress. "The Swiftsea fae caught on much more quickly than those in Noble Rose and Dustdune. We have not been to Mistmount yet, but a group of fae from Noble Rose agreed to travel there and teach any Mistmount fae they could find."

Donning a devious smirk, Chloe leaned to the side to flash a smile at Quintus. Then she turned to Lyren. "I bet the Swiftsea fae learned the fastest because of all those stories you tell. The stories probably helped you to embrace emotions even before you realized that's what you were doing."

Elora trailed a finger across her belt, touching the ribbon from her mother that she had braided into it. On a whim, she opened a door to Noble Rose and quickly stepped through it just to send a message.

When she returned back to the council room, Chloe slammed her hands onto her hips. "Where did you just go?"

Waving away the question, Elora stepped closer to Brannick's throne. "I promised a fae in Noble Rose that I would teach him how to control his emotions. I made a bargain with him about it. I just sent a message to tell him he could come to the castle to learn how to do it."

Night darkened the corners of the room when Brannick, Tindra, and Severin returned. Brannick slid a hand through his glossy hair and strolled into the room with a grin. He moved to Elora's side. "It is done."

Grace ushered everyone into a circle while Fifer passed out plates of herbed squash and spiced beans. Once Elora sat down, Blaz rested his head in her lap. She and Brannick sat close enough for their shoulders to touch.

"You got the enchantment and curse out of the whole castle?" she asked. "Even the throne room?"

Brannick started to nod even before she finished speaking. But once she asked about the throne room, he paused. He opened his mouth to speak, but then took in breath instead. When he did speak, his eyebrows pushed together. "The throne room still has thorns everywhere." He shook his head. "But the thorns are different now. Shinier. They do not fight against me. They just... exist."

Her eyebrow raised when Fifer pushed a plate into her hands. She nodded at him and took a bite of the squash. After chewing slowly, she glanced at Brannick again. "This seems like more proof that the curse on Bitter Thorn is lifting."

Brannick's eyes pulsed with magic as he nodded.

From across the room, Lyren frowned at her plate. "Vesper would have loved to see the castle like this."

Just like that, their large group suddenly seemed too small. The hole Vesper's absence left filled up more space than the trees in the room.

Elora swallowed, her eyes prickling with oncoming tears.

Brannick took her hand, pulling it close to his chest. "We will find Vesper, and we will melt that ice shard in his heart."

He spoke with conviction, but her heart couldn't settle completely. They *would* find Vesper—she had no doubt. But while preparing for a battle with the high queen, they had more important things to worry about first.

As soon as day dawned, she had to figure out how to steal those gemstones from Ansel's house.

CHAPTER 37

When Elora woke the next morning, the scent of rot thickened in the air. She sat up with a start, scanning the council room in a single breath. The trees drooped, their leaves had turned sickly and gray. Dark smudges of oozing rot spread across the stone floor and walls. Every patch of moss had crusted over.

She gasped. "The curse is back."

At her side, Blaz whimpered and covered his nose with his paws. Brannick lay on the other side of his wolf, rubbing his eyes as he sat up. The rest of their group formed the same circle they had night before, except now they sat in various states of sleep and wakefulness.

Brannick rolled out his shoulders and forced his eyes open wide. He stroked his wolf's fur as he scanned the room. "It is not the curse."

With his head still on the small pillow he had conjured, Quintus squinted at a smudge of rot that oozed just next to his head. "What is it then?"

Lyren sat up with a start. She sucked in a breath, swallowing hard at the sight before her. "This is the decay."

Elora's hand flew to her sword hilt, which she squeezed a little too hard.

Chloe shivered under the thin blanket that covered her. "The what?"

"But I thought that sprite said the decay isn't really a decay. It's just a place where the portal to the mortal realm is closed." Grace's voice sounded even younger while the remains of sleep still clung to it.

Elora whipped her head toward Brannick. "Vesper has gemstones from Ansel. He must have used them to close the portal."

Brannick shook his head. "The portal is not fully closed yet. The gemstones are powerful but not powerful enough to close it completely. Only a life sacrifice can do that."

"Vesper said..." Grace's voice sounded even younger still. She bunched her blanket up under her chin and bit her lip. "Before he left, Vesper said he would give his life to close the portal if he had to."

The words oozed into the room just like the smudges of rot.

Chloe's nose wrinkled as she sniffed. "At least we know where he is."

Jumping to her feet, Elora marched toward her middle sister. "What do you mean? Where is he?"

Chloe raised an eyebrow. "On that island. The one with the source of the decay."

Before she had even finished speaking, Brannick had opened a door. Whatever sleep lingered in their eyes got slapped away. Elora marched forward and followed Brannick into his door. Two figures followed after them, probably Lyren and Quintus.

"We're coming too." Grace's tiny voice drifted through the door just as Elora started stepping through it.

Once in Swiftsea, Brannick and his wolf moved forward and out of the way for the others. Elora stepped to the side instead. Lyren and Quintus stepped out next, which was fine. Good even. Elora held her breath, watching the door steadily.

Just as she feared, Grace came through the door next, gripping Chloe's arm tight in hers. Once they stepped onto the sandy beach, Chloe reared on her youngest sister. She pulled her arm free and sucked in a breath. "What are you thinking? This is going to be dangerous."

Grace stood up tall. "Who cares about danger right now? Vesper could *die*. Don't you want to help save him?"

Chloe gasped as if someone had just punched her in the gut. Her face stayed still for a beat and then she nodded quickly. "You're right."

Even though she came through the door, Lyren now stood at the edge of the group. She stepped away from the others, rubbing a hand over her arm. "We need a boat to get across. Even then, the sea monsters are more troubled ever since Queen Noelani was murdered."

Before she finished, Brannick waved his hand and conjured an entire ship right before their eyes. His jaw clenched tight, suggesting that sea monsters were the least of his troubles. "Everyone get on quickly, and I will take care of the rest."

Popping the wings from her back, Elora gestured across the sea. "I will meet you over there." Flapping hard, she flew

303

over the sea faster than the boat. Still, Brannick crashed his boat through the water much faster than any other boat ever had. When the sea monsters tried to attack, a few well-placed enchantments kept them back.

Elora threw one last glance over her shoulder to make sure the others would get to the island without trouble. Once certain they were safe, she landed on the beach. Her boots sank into the sand with each step, but she still managed to run.

Vesper sat in the same oozing pile of rot he had been sitting in the first time they found him there. Except now, half his body slumped to the side while his other half tilted up at a sharp angle. His eyelids shuddered, and his chest barely rose with his breaths.

Heart leaping into her throat, Elora darted to his side. "Vesper." She shook his shoulders, which didn't affect him at all. "Vesper, wake up."

His body went from hanging slack to winding tight in a flash. He lunged for her sword, nearly grabbing the hilt.

Once she realized his intention, she jumped to her feet and backed away. His fingers brushed the leather of the hilt, just missing it.

A snarl twisted his face. "Never mind." Using one hand, he pushed back his brown curls. Somehow, he had removed the ribbon she had magicked to his wrist. Maybe he had used a gemstone. It left behind a thin scabby burn around his entire wrist.

Each movement he made came a little too slow. A crazed look filled his eyes when he stuffed his hand into his pocket. "I have my own weapon, though it will not kill me as quickly as yours."

Just as he pulled a mace from his magical pocket, the boat arrived, and the others ran to join them. Vesper snarled again, backing even deeper into the puddle of ooze. Though she had come to rescue him, Elora couldn't bring herself to step into that same puddle.

Not yet.

Chloe fell to her knees at her oldest sister's side. She clasped her hands together under her chin, pleading with every muscle in her body. "Vesper, don't do this."

When Grace joined them, she stood with her toes at the edge of the rot and reached across it toward him. "We love you."

Elora nodded, claiming her youngest sister's words as her own. She stepped forward, swallowing one too many times. "Put your weapon down."

"Love?" Vesper scoffed and eyed the burn on his wrist. "Love does nothing but hurt."

"That's not true." Grace's eyes turned a puffy red. She placed a hand over her heart while her chin trembled.

Standing taller, Elora did her best to ignore the sharp sting in her throat. "We do love you. All of us." Her eyes flicked over to Brannick, begging him to agree.

It only took half a breath before he understood her look. With an eager nod, he turned to Vesper. "You have been my friend through many difficult moments. I do not wish for you to die."

Getting to her feet, Chloe elbowed Quintus in the side.

He blinked in surprise, but then, he too turned to Vesper. "I do not want you to die either. Think of all the adventures you will miss."

After he finished speaking, they all turned to Lyren. She stared at them for a beat. She blinked. Then her lips pressed into a thin line, and she turned away.

They didn't have time to react to her display because Brannick shot a golden enchantment from his fingertips. The line of shimmery gold curled around the handle of Vesper's mace. When Brannick yanked his hand back, the enchantment pulled the mace back too. But Vesper held on tight to his mace, still keeping it in place.

Sucking in a breath, Elora shot a shimmery purple enchantment from her own fingertips. It curled around the mace, tightening over Brannick's enchantment. On cue, they pulled their enchantments back together.

Even with both enchantments, they still weren't strong enough to pull the mace from Vesper's grip.

Without any provocation, Quintus sent his own ribbon of enchantment to join the other two. All three of them pulled, but they still weren't strong enough. Vesper gripped hard, glaring at them while he struggled to keep hold of the mace. They just needed a bit more strength, and surely they would get it.

Holding tight to her enchantment, Elora angled her head to the side. "Lyren, we need your help."

The Swiftsea fae's nose pointed higher into the air. "Why should I? I gain nothing by helping you."

Elora clenched her jaw and nearly lost grip of her enchantment.

Stomping across the beach, Grace gestured toward Vesper. "If he uses that weapon, the portal will close permanently."

A flinch worked across Lyren's features as she stepped away from the rest of them. Her feet slid across the sand and ooze until she stood several steps behind Vesper. "*I* do not care if the portal closes. Open or closed, my life will not change."

Chloe let out a strangled scoff. "You are the most selfish fae I have ever met."

It might have helped for Elora to say something, but she was too shocked to think of any words at all.

With a huff, Lyren folded her arms over her chest. "I am not more selfish than other fae. We are *all* selfish. This is how we act."

Chloe threw her hands into the air. "Then stop acting like a fae and learn to care about someone else for once."

"I tried that already." Lyren nearly shouted the words. She reached the chains of her necklace, twisting her fingers through them. "I tried to earn my redemption, but I failed. With Queen Noelani dead, I am doomed forever."

While they argued, no one noticed Vesper slipping a hand into his pocket until it was too late. An orange gemstone glinted between his thumb and forefinger for a breath.

And then he crushed it.

Showers of energy knocked Elora and everyone else to their backs. A thick orange barrier formed between them and Vesper. Only Lyren stood close enough to reach him now. Though it didn't seem likely she would even try.

Coughing out a grunt, Vesper fell to his knees. The gemstone had weakened him, but he still gripped his mace and eyed the part of his chest he wanted to strike.

Grace screamed. Chloe joined half a moment later.

Brannick punched a fist at the barrier, trying to infect it with his own magic to tear it down. Elora's scream came out softer than her sisters. She dug her fingers into the orange enchantment too. Hopefully with her and Brannick working together, they could destroy it more quickly.

With his body swaying and jerking, Vesper managed to get back to his feet. He swung his mace, which missed horribly and landed in his shoulder and arm. He hissed in pain. While he yanked the nails from his body, he stumbled backward.

Right into Lyren.

All around them, decay bubbled and oozed. Brannick slammed his fists harder against the barrier enchantment. A look of terror seized his face when he glanced at the landscape before them. "The portal opening is growing weak. We must open it soon or it may never open properly again."

Shocks buzzed up Elora's arms while she dug her fingers deeper into the barrier enchantment. She spoke through clenched teeth. "You said only a token would be strong enough to open it, right?"

Wincing, Brannick shook his head. "I was wrong. We need two tokens. Two *strong* tokens."

Vesper finally freed the mace from his shoulder, but he stumbled even harder against Lyren. When he swung the weapon again, she grabbed his handle and held it back.

"Stop." Her voice caught, trembling on the wind. She stood as sure as before, except now, a tear formed in her eye.

She tried to blink it away but failed. "I like being selfish." She sniffed. "I thought I could forget my past by ignoring it." Her head shook side to side, ruffling her curls. "But then Elora taught us how to embrace emotions, and..."

The tear forming in her eye pooled, broke away. It slid down her cheek and dropped off her chin to the sand at her feet.

Vesper tried to yank the mace out of her grip, but Lyren hadn't been weakened by a gemstone like he had. She ripped it from his hands and threw it far from where they stood. When he tried to lunge for it, she tackled him to the ground.

Her knees pressed into his chest. She curled both of her hands into fists, still trying to hold back the tears that welled in her eyes. "I have no reason to help you. It will not help me earn another necklace. It will not change my past."

Her chin shook, slow at first until trembled even faster. Vesper's head fell back onto the oozing rot. Exhaustion finally took hold of him.

She loosened her fists now and grabbed him by the shoulders. "But you are my friend. I want you to be yourself again." A second tear slid from her eye. She pressed her lips together and swallowed. "I want you to be reunited with your beloved. Maybe *that* is enough of a reward. Maybe I can still earn redemption without a necklace from my queen."

Once the tears started, she couldn't seem to stop them. Now, the slightest smile tugged at her lips. Vesper tried to shove her away. He fought and wriggled. In his weakened state, the movements didn't do much.

She held on tight to his shoulders. Tears continued to stream down her face. Soon, they fell off her jaw. Drip after drip fell, landing on Vesper's chest. Right over his heart.

A magical wisp of blue light drifted out of his chest.

He stopped struggling. His body froze, except for his eyes. He watched as each tear dropped from Lyren's chin and onto his heart. His face relaxed another measure with each tear that fell.

Finally, Brannick and Elora forced enough of their magic through the barrier enchantment that they could break through it.

Elora and her sisters sprinted to Vesper's side, all kneeling next to the oozing puddle of rot. They worked quickly, finding two spare ribbons that had once been part of Elora's skirt. With both of them in her hand, she looked up at Brannick. "Do we drop them into this puddle? Will that open the portal completely?"

He winced as he shook his head. "That is how, but those ribbons are not strong enough. The two tokens must be irreplaceable."

Sucking in a sharp breath, Elora glanced at her sisters. They all seemed to understand at the same moment. Elora gulped.

Quintus knelt down by them, his eyebrows pinched. "Do you not have any tokens that are strong enough?"

It took everything inside Elora to keep from sobbing. "We have them." Her bottom lip quivered as she began to undo the belt braided with her mother's ribbons. The sword from her father was tucked neatly inside it. Her fingers shook so hard she could barely lift the belt and sword.

Lyren made a strangled noise that was probably meant to sound like a word. She shook her head and looked down at Vesper again. "I do not love you the way Elora loves Brannick or the way you love your wife, Cosette, but maybe I do love you after all." She sniffed and sat up straight. Her gaze moved across the puddle of ooze. "All of you." She gulped. "Maybe I can do something selfless without any chance of reward."

Without another word, she yanked both her seashell necklaces off her neck and dropped them into the oozing puddle.

The black goo bubbled and popped and sparked when the necklaces touched it.

Elora still held her braided belt and her sword when a bright light flashed out of the puddle. It burned so bright, she could see nothing but white.

The light burned through the landscape, spreading warmth and tingles through the air.

By the time it faded away, everything looked different.

Sand glittered beneath their feet. The nearby sea sparkled in the light of the sun. A warm, salty breeze fluttered through the lush palm leaves of the trees.

Lyren had done it.

She opened the portal using her seashell necklaces, which must have been tokens of her own.

Elora glanced down at the sword and belt in her hands, wanting to cry at the sight of them. She hadn't had to sacrifice them after all.

Vesper kneaded his chest right over the heart. His eyes had changed again. The glazed look in them had diminished. They didn't have the same spark and adventurous gleam that usually filled them, but they weren't so crazed either.

And the decay was gone.

Forever.

Brannick helped Elora to her feet. He spoke to her under his breath. "If the portal is fully open, Ansel may realize he can safely travel to the mortal realm."

She nodded, buckling the belt around her waist once again. "Then I better leave now to steal whatever gemstones he has left."

CHAPTER 38

Bitter Thorn Castle looked even more magical than it had before the decay ever touched it. Despite the beauty, Elora had no chance to enjoy it. She and the others brought Vesper back to the council room. Kaia tended to the wounds in Vesper's arm and shoulder. Quintus and Lyren stood nearby, helping whenever they could.

Fifer, Tindra, and Severin worked in one corner of the room, probably making more of the formula that could destroy the high queen's enchantments and bargains.

Chloe and Grace moaned at Elora while they tried to grab her hands. They didn't want her going to Ansel's house. How funny that they were so adamant when they didn't even know half of what Ansel had done to her. And they knew nothing of what he had done to others.

Elora checked her sword, grateful again that she still had it hanging at her side.

Blaz trailed after Brannick as he paced the room. Every few steps, he would stop and ask another question. The latest question pinched his eyebrows together. "But how do you know Ansel is not at his house? He could have left Fairfrost by now."

"I do not know." Elora ran her fingers through her hair, quickly working through the small knots it had. "It does not matter though. If he is there, I will kill him."

A tight expression hardened the prince's face. She could see how he worked hard to swallow his retort. "But you will keep your door open the whole time, yes? At the first sign of trouble, you promise to come right back?"

She nodded and then bent to check the laces on her boots.

He started pacing again. "And what about the mortals? What if they do not want to go through your door?"

Her nose wrinkled as she stood up straight again. "Just make sure they do not try to come back through the door once I send them over here." She winced. "They might be... combative."

Chloe stepped in front of the prince, stopping him in the middle of his pacing. She glared at him. "How are you okay with this? You have to tell her to stay here."

Ignoring her, Brannick turned and walked to Elora's side. He took her hand and pierced her with one of his most intense stares. "You *must* be safe. I know you have to do this, but nothing matters more to me than your safety."

Wrapping her arms around his neck, she pulled him down for the kiss he deserved after such a declaration.

Chloe groaned so loud Elora could practically hear her middle sister's eye roll. Just because of that, she kissed a little longer. Brannick lost himself in it until Vesper cleared his throat.

Both Elora and Brannick stepped away from each other at the same moment to glance over at Vesper. He raised an eyebrow at the pair of them, which looked so... Vesper. Was the ice shard in his heart melting?

She shook it off and waved her hand to open a door. Her heart skittered at the sight of it. She knew what would be on the other side, which tangled her belly even more. Anxiety danced down her limbs as she took a deep breath.

It would be different this time. She would approach the visit from an entirely different perspective. Nodding to herself, she ignored the last pleas of her sisters and stepped through the door.

Instead of opening it to the same place as her first and second visit to the house, she chose to open the door right onto the loft with the mortals. Her heart thumped, but she tempered it with a steady breath.

People first.

That was what mattered. Before, she had tried to find the gemstones first and then only worried about the people when they became a problem. But as Lyren had just learned for herself, this fight wasn't about the conflict. It was about the people.

The mortals stared slack-jawed at her, at least the ones that noticed her presence. The rest of them were draped over chairs, pillows, and even the floor. Most of them stared straight at the ceiling with drool sliding down their cheeks.

Taking a deep breath, she reached for the nearest mortal. The female tried to twist away, but she didn't have much strength. Gripping hard on her arms, Elora pushed the mortal through the door she had left open. A shout of protest erupted from the mortal's mouth, but soon she had gone through the door.

The sound of rustling fabric came through the swirling tunnel. Elora bit her bottom lip, listening carefully.

"We have her secured." Brannick's voice offered assurance just when she needed it.

A male lunged toward Elora, but she pushed him through the door even more easily than the first mortal. It didn't take long before the prince confirmed that the mortal had been secured.

She worked more quickly now that she had a system in place. Each mortal tried to fight, but she relied on her strength to shove them through the door anyway.

By now, more of the mortals had noticed her presence. Many stayed completely still except for their eyes watching her, but most of them had gotten to their feet. Their hands all sought Elora's arms and her sword.

As weak as they were, it was difficult to fight off so many hands at once. She shoved another mortal through the door, but three of them acted at once and managed to tackle her to the ground. It didn't take much effort to push them off.

But when she tried to stand, another two mortals tackled her to the ground again.

She grunted, reaching for her sword automatically.

"Elora." Panic laced Brannick's voice.

She caught her breath and shoved the mortals off again. "Ansel is not here. It is just the mortals."

"Then enchant them to stay still."

She shot a silvery enchantment from her fingertips. Magic pooled around the feet of each mortal. It froze like ice around their shoes so they could not lift their feet off the ground.

When she got close enough to grab the elbows of the nearest mortal, she released the enchantment binding his feet. He yelped when she shoved him through the door, but it didn't stop her.

She hated forcing them to leave when they didn't even want to go. She hated forcing them to do anything after the way they'd been treated. But what other choice did she have? Ansel himself said they were nearly *used up*. She had to get them out of that house whether they liked it or not.

After they overthrew High Queen Alessandra, she'd figure out how to help them recover from Ansel's treatment.

Sweat glistened along her brow when she finally lifted the last mortal off the floor and threw her toward the swirling door. Just in case, Elora checked all the bedrooms and corners of the loft. As far as she could tell, not a single mortal remained.

Taking a deep breath, she moved toward her door. "That was the last one."

"We had to tie most of them up."

Her shoulders jerked after hearing such a thing, but she tried to ignore it. What choice did she have?

Brannick spoke again, a little softer now. "Any sign of Ansel?"

"No." Elora closed her eyes, allowing her magic of intuition to flood through her chest and down her arms. "I just have to find the gemstones and then I will come back to the castle."

Even through a door, she could hear Brannick gulp. "Hurry."

When magic began sparking at her fingertips, she popped the wings from her back. She flew off the loft and down to the lower level. No thought filled her mind as she moved. Somehow, her swirling Faerie door followed after her. It stayed just behind her as she landed on the lower level.

Her feet touched the ground, and she pulled her wings into her back again. Magic sparked at her fingertips, leading her into the kitchen. She expected to reach for a drawer in the cabinet along the kitchen wall, but she reached for a plate on the table instead.

Lifting a gray ceramic plate off the table, she noted that nothing sat underneath it. Now she moved to the next plate, which also had nothing underneath it. The plates were right, but the location was wrong.

Whirling around, she flung open the nearest cabinet door. Glass cups and saucers sat behind it. She closed that cabinet and tried another. Here she found a pile of ceramic plates. Sparks burst from her fingertips at the sight of them.

Her heart fluttered in her chest, knowing she had found the right cabinet. She held her breath, checking underneath the first plate. Nothing sat under it except another plate. Undeterred, she set the plate on the ground and lifted the second plate. When that revealed nothing, she lifted the third and fourth plates.

She had still failed to find any gemstones, but it didn't matter. She *knew* they were there.

Over and over, she set the plates on the ground in a small stack. Finally, when she reached the very last plate, an entirely new sight winked back at her from underneath it.

A pile of sparkling gemstones in several colors sat at the bottom of the cabinet. She couldn't help smile when she swept the gemstones into her palm. After tucking them into her pocket, she turned to go back through her door and leave this awful house for good.

But when she turned around, Ansel stood only a few steps away from her.

She sucked in a gasp, clenching her hands into fists. The hairs on the back of her neck stood on end while she tried to force herself to breathe.

In.

Out.

She could face him. She could beat him.

She just had to trust herself.

Despite the reassurances, her chest burned with the memory of his dagger.

She swallowed hard.

His yellow eyes glowed as they roamed up and down her body. The look felt intrusive even though he hadn't moved closer to her. He raised an eyebrow. Once again, he seemed impressed by her, which she hated.

Even more than that, she hated the dagger he held in one hand. The fingers on his other hand kept trailing up and down the flat side of its blade. When she made the slightest movement toward her door, he jabbed the dagger in her direction.

She stepped back, gasping involuntarily.

He glanced toward the door and pressed his lips together. Did he know she had people waiting for her on the other side? He must have known it was a possibility or he probably would have said something by now. Either way, he moved closer, gripping his dagger tighter with each step.

Her heart rebelled against her, trying with all its might to break through her rib cage. The magic from her fingertips had long since vanished. Her throat thickened with a sickly lump.

She allowed herself three whole breaths to be frightened. Three whole breaths to cower.

And then she made her move.

She drew her sword and lunged forward in a single motion. Ansel's dagger clashed against her blade as he leapt away. She jabbed her sword at him again, which he only barely blocked, this time with his forearm.

They darted over the kitchen floor, slicing and striking at every opportunity. Despite the dance, Elora knew it wouldn't last long. With the long length of her sword, she had a clear advantage. Plus, the tournament they had already participated in proved she also had more sword skill.

Ansel punched his dagger toward her, and she allowed it to leave a gash across her arm. She even ducked as if the pain had taken hold of her. Just when he braved another step toward her, she landed the fateful blow.

Her sword pierced him straight through the chest and into the heart. When his eyes went wide and he dropped to his knees, she ripped the sword from his chest.

He fell backward then. Blood spurted out of the wound, already staining the leather of his shirt. When he tried to breathe, he coughed up blood instead.

With her jaw clenched tight, she used the navy plaid couch to wipe the blood off her sword.

Her body shook with each step. Every hair on her body stood on end. She had to clench her sword hilt to keep herself from turning back to look at Ansel's lifeless body.

He had to be dead. He *had* to be. Her sword had iron in it, plus she sliced him straight through the heart. Even with great healing abilities, no fae could possibly survive such an attack.

But even as she stepped through her door back to Bitter Thorn Castle, a thought haunted her mind. A thought that might have been fear, but it might have been intuition.

Ansel would survive.

Once in the castle, she fell into Brannick's arms, closing her door behind her. She couldn't look at Ansel's mortals, who must have been tied up. She couldn't even breathe properly. She just buried her head in Brannick's chest and cried the tears that wouldn't stop.

He had to be dead. He had to be, because she couldn't do that again.

CHAPTER 39

Tremors rocked in and out of Elora's arms. Her legs. Her heart. Brannick held her tight, which helped to control some of her shaking. But it wasn't enough. Her fingers clenched tight around Brannick's coat while images flashed in her mind.

Ansel's yellow eyes glowing while they roamed over her body too intently.

His dagger scraping her arm and leaving a gash behind.

A different dagger sinking into her chest, stealing away her breath.

She gasped.

Instead of simply holding her closer, Brannick lifted her off her feet and lowered both of them to the ground. He leaned with his back against a wall and settled her on his lap with her head against his chest.

In the new position, it was easier for Blaz to lower his head into her lap. He stuck his nose under her hand, nuzzling it gently. Already, she could breathe easier.

The light breeze and crisp scents of Bitter Thorn curled in around her, offering comfort like a crackling fire on a cold night.

Her arm shivered under the heated touch of Brannick's hand. He trailed a finger along the edge of the gash Ansel had left in her arm. She jerked her head toward it. "I almost forgot he cut me."

Brannick threw a look across the council room. Kaia immediately jumped to Elora's side and started healing the cut. Chloe and Grace knelt close enough to gently pat Elora's hands. Chloe didn't even say one word about her oldest sister sitting on Brannick's lap. They must have been even more shaken than Elora.

Everyone else came toward her too. Lyren and Quintus stood back but had lowered eyebrows and flinched every time she moved. Tindra and Severin stood to the side, sometimes reaching their hands out as if they wanted to help.

Even Vesper stepped forward. He didn't act like himself, but he stared at Elora. He wore a curious expression that seemed to care about her, but like he wasn't exactly sure why he cared.

When the cut had been healed, Brannick lifted a hand to brush his thumb across Elora's jaw. His eyes swirled and pulsed with every word he spoke. "Did you kill him?"

"I..." Her shoulders shook as she tried to catch her breath. "I do not know for sure."

Everyone around them leaned or stepped forward.

Brannick narrowed his eyes. "What happened?"

She had to close her eyes to recount the story. Her fingers buried themselves deep in Blaz's fur. "He found me right after I got the gemstones. He attacked, but he only had a dagger, and I had a sword." She squeezed her eyes tight, her entire face squishing up with it. "I stabbed him in the chest, straight through his heart."

"Did your sword go all the way through him?" Brannick's voice had never sounded gentler.

For a moment, the muscles in her face relaxed. "Yes. The tip of my sword came out through his back. I am certain of it."

"Did you twist your sword while it was inside him?" As he asked, Brannick brought a hand to her lower back and drew soft circles with the tips of his fingers.

Her eyes finally opened. "No. But he coughed up blood after I pulled my sword out of him."

The circling fingers at her back paused as Brannick let out a sigh. "He is dead then."

She jerked her head toward him. "But what if he survived?" A chill prickled at her spine. "I should have cut his head off. He probably lives."

Brannick drew circles on her back again before he continued. "Even with a regular sword, a wound like that would kill almost any fae." His eyebrow quirked up. "But your sword has iron in it. He is certainly dead."

Lifting her hand from Blaz's fur, she curled both her arms over her stomach. No matter how she tried to find comfort in Brannick's words, her gut refused to believe. She swallowed hard. "But what if he is not?"

"Worrying will not change the outcome." Brannick whispered the words into her ear.

She nodded, but it didn't settle the writhing of her gut.

Keeping his arms around her, Brannick sat up straight. His expression took on that regal quality it always did when he acted as a prince. Even without a crown, he had always seemed like more of a ruler than any other ruler in Faerie.

"We need to make our final plans," he said. "The final battle is nearing."

As if he had commanded it, every other person in the room sat down. Lyren nodded to herself, trailing a finger along her neck where her two necklaces used to hang. "I can feel it too. The battle is almost here."

From her pocket, Tindra pulled out a glass vial with the pearlescent blue liquid. "I made more of my formula. It will destroy all enchantments except the ones made using gemstones. Once it is used, the high queen or any other fae can still create more enchantments to replace the old ones."

With a weighted nod, Severin put his arm around Tindra's shoulders. "We want to make more, enough to have two vials of the formula. We can use the first to release the high queen's hold over her guards. We assume she will create more enchantments after that. We will save the second vial for as long as we can until we feel it must be used. Then we can destroy any of her newest enchantments."

Tindra nodded solemnly. "And since we will likely be in the forest near the creation magic, *and* since we are trying to break the enchantments over *all* the guards, we will need much more than a single drop. We will probably need the whole vial."

"Good." Brannick reached into his pocket and pulled out a long, wooden spear. A thick leather cloth wrapped around the top of the spear where the tip of it would have been. Leather strings tied feathers to it at different heights.

He ran a finger down its edge. "I inherited this spear from my mother, but I have never dared to used it." Now he reached for the thick leather cloth at the top. With a quick swipe, he pulled it away. Underneath it sat a glinting silver tip.

Elora's stomach immediately churned. Stinging prickles crawled up her arms. Even before Brannick explained, she knew exactly what metal formed that silver tip.

Iron.

The prince quickly covered the tip with the leather cover again. "The iron in this spear is potent. It will kill a fae more effectively than even Elora's sword." His throat bulged against his necklace as he slid the spear back into his pocket. "As most of you know, High Queen Alessandra has stolen crowns from the courts of Noble Rose, Dustdune, Bitter Thorn, and Swiftsea. To win this fight, she must be killed. My weapon will make that possible."

While every fae in the room nodded solemnly, Elora glanced around. "Where are the mortals from Ansel's house?"

She hadn't noticed their absence at first since she had been too busy shaking and sobbing. But now she glanced around and didn't see any of them there.

Everyone shifted uncomfortably. They all stared at their hands or at the ground. Clenching her jaw, Elora flashed a glare in the prince's direction.

He flicked his eyes toward Blaz, but the wolf offered him no support. Blaz just dropped his head into Elora's lap and nuzzled her hand with his nose. Shaking his head, Brannick looked up again. Instead of making eye contact, he stared at the trees lining the council room table. "Fifer is taking them somewhere more... secure."

Her eyebrows flew up her forehead. "A dungeon?"

"*Not* a dungeon." His answer came fast and defensive. "He is just taking them to a room." He rubbed the back of his neck as his gaze turned downward. "And he will put a barrier enchantment around the room so they cannot get out."

Clapping a hand over her mouth, she gasped.

He lifted his hands up with the palms out. "Fifer is getting the mortals food and bedding. They will be comfortable." He leaned closer to her, nearly pleading. "What else can we do? The battle is coming, and we must prepare." He gave a feeble shrug. "It is only temporary."

With a huff, she leaned back into him. She knew they didn't have any other choice, but she still hated it.

Maybe he was just trying to change the subject, but Brannick launched into a new topic. "We know High Queen Alessandra can remove glamours, so we should probably not have any of our plans center upon glamours. We may be able to get away with one or two glamours as long as we do not call attention to them."

Quintus sat up straighter. "Like if we glamour Chloe and Grace to look like fae, but we do not alter their appearance too much?"

Elora clenched her fists as she jerked her head toward Quintus. "Chloe and Grace are not coming."

Grace narrowed her childlike eyes and folded her arms over her chest. "Yes, we are."

Matching the expression, Elora folded her own arms over her chest. "No. You—"

"Yes, we are, Elora." Chloe sighed and ran her fingers down her braid of blonde hair. Her fingers lingered over the harp string at the bottom of it.

Elora had to blink several times before she could respond. "You *want* to come? To the *battle?*"

Chloe sighed again, squishing her mouth into a knot. "Prince Brannick said that having fealty from others will help you in the fight. I did some research, and it's going to help even more if we are physically present. We don't even have to fight. We just have to be there."

With her hands still folded over her chest, Grace bounced her head in a dramatic nod. "We won't fight if we can help it. We'll just stay at the edges and offer support where we can."

Once again, Brannick jumped into a new subject before Elora had time to protest. The prince turned his gaze toward Lyren and Quintus. "We need fae from every court if possible, anyone who is willing to offer fealty."

Quintus squeezed Chloe's shoulder and then got to his feet. "Lyren and I will gather fae and bring them back here. I know we can find fae from Swiftsea, Dustdune, and Mistmount who will help."

After standing, Lyren gripped Vesper by the elbow and forced him up as well. "We will take Vesper with us." Once they both stood, she pointed a finger toward his face. "If you promise to behave, that is."

He blinked at her. His demeanor shifted, and his eyes flashed. He reached for his wrist, which still sported a faint burn from the ribbon he had removed. When he nodded, he almost looked like himself. "Yes. I will help."

Quintus opened a door for the three of them.

Just before they went through, Brannick raised a hand to stop them. "We need Nerissa as well."

Stealing a quick glance at Chloe, Quintus turned back to the prince with his eyebrow raised. "The former queen of Dustdune? The one who gave her crown to High Queen Alessandra?"

"Yes." Brannick got to his feet, offering a hand to Elora once he stood. "Make sure you bring her here."

The three of them nodded and then stepped through Quintus's door.

From the entrance of the room, Kaia cleared her throat. Her emerald hair shined, and her skin looked vibrant and fresh. She must have just come from her tree.

Her head dipped toward the prince. "I will gather weapons from the armory, though it is strange to do so without Soren."

Brannick nodded. "Soren is busy protecting King Jackory. We need him where he is."

Grace jumped to her feet, her red hair trailing behind her as she raced to Kaia's side. Her cheeks flushed. "I can help you gather weapons. I want to be useful."

Dragging her feet across the floor, Chloe wandered over to the pair of them. "I will help too, but I better not have to use any of those weapons."

They all turned to leave, but Kaia quickly glanced over her shoulder at the prince. "I almost forgot. Someone is here to see you."

Though she looked at Brannick, Elora felt the visitor had come to see her. She and the prince went straight to the castle entrance, her fingers setting off short sparks all the while. Once they reached their destination, she immediately knew why.

"Deegan." Elora rushed forward to greet the fae who had helped her get away after the fight in Noble Rose.

He recognized her at once, and a small smile formed at his lips. "I got your message. I came here to learn how to withstand emotions like you can. You did promise to teach me, after all."

Elora dispensed with any other pleasantries and jumped right in to explaining how to beat the high queen's manipulation.

While they practiced, both Brannick and Blaz stepped around them and eyed Deegan carefully. It didn't come across as predatory or protective. Instead, Brannick almost seemed impressed.

When they finally finished, Brannick glanced toward Deegan. "I know who you are."

"Um." Deegan raised both his eyebrows. "Is that good?"

Nodding, Brannick continued. "You and High King Romany's son were close. I heard how you and Prince Fabian once saved the fae of your court from a great plague."

A sad smile fell across Deegan's lips. "Yes. It is a shame High King Romany blamed his son for poisoning him. Prince Fabian never would have knowingly murdered his father."

Brannick's eyes narrowed, watching Deegan closely again. "You are right about that. I remember how Prince Fabian loved his court. Some said he did more to protect it than his father did. They also said you protected the fae as well, but I am curious, did you do it for your court or did you do it for Prince Fabian?"

Deegan took a step back. "What a strange question." He blinked and worked his jaw up and down as he thought. "I did do it for Prince Fabian, of course, but I still love my court. I would do anything to help the fae of Noble Rose."

A knowing smile raised Brannick's mouth upward. "I hoped you would say that. Would you be willing to join us in our fight to overthrow High Queen Alessandra? We could use your support."

His jaw worked up and down, but he didn't answer. Before he could muster a response, Lyren and Quintus ran down the castle hallway to the castle entrance. They panted while trying to catch their breaths.

"We received a message from Soren." Quintus let out a puff of air and glanced toward Lyren.

She bounced her head with an eager nod. "He says he is with King Jackory, and they are by the creation magic in Bitter Thorn." Now she gulped. "And they need help."

Elora sucked in a breath, jerking her head toward Brannick. "No one can get to the creation magic unless they know to look up at the sprites." Her lips pressed together. "Do you think this is a trap?"

With a carefree shrug, Brannick swept into the castle, walking back to the council room with the others. "Of course it is, but we knew this battle was coming. All the high queen has done is chosen when to begin it."

Elora's hand went straight for her sword hilt. When they got to the council room, fae from multiple courts filled it to the brim. Deegan must have decided to help because he pushed his way into the room as well.

They were ready now. The final battle had arrived.

CHAPTER 40

Thorns creaked in the wind, twisted over trees, and through bushes. They gave off that subtle scent of decay that had been swept clean from Bitter Thorn Castle. Moist soil covered the forest floor, punctuated by patches of moss, trees, and other greenery. Elora's heart pounded with a steady beat. For once, it did not race or skitter or pound too slow.

The battle was nigh, but this time, she was ready.

They all were.

After traveling through several clusters of trees, they had finally neared the spot where the sprites gathered over the creation magic. Elora automatically tipped her head up, watching the glowing lights with each step.

"Do not watch the ground while you walk." Brannick stood tall, his voice as sure as his step. "Keep your eyes on me or Faerie itself will try to lead you away from the creation magic."

He sounded so sure Elora hated to correct him. She leaned in close. "We had to keep our eyes on the sprites in order to find the creation magic. Are you certain everyone will be able to follow if they keep your eyes on you instead?"

He shrugged. "I never looked at the sprites when I found you in that clearing. I used the crystal to find your location and open a door to you, but I ended up too far away from the creation magic to see you. Blaz had to lead me there. I had no trouble getting to the clearing while watching him. If you and I watch the sprites, I am certain everyone else can watch us and still get there."

If they hadn't been marching toward a battle, she might have smiled. She had wondered how Brannick had found her in that clearing. And she wondered why Blaz had left her when she had Ansel's dagger in her chest. Now she had answers for both.

The steady beat of her heart returned. Every noise in the forest sounded twice as loud because the fae all around walked in such silence. They had a plan. Everything would work out.

Since she and Brannick were the only ones who could be used as vessels, they would enter the clearing first. While they kept the high queen busy with trying to capture one of them, Tindra and Severin would sneak into the clearing and use the formula.

Once the formula freed the high queen's guards from their bargain, the high queen would have an army no more.

Then they would kill her.

Easy.

The first tangle of anxiety threaded through Elora's fingers. Of course, no one expected the plan to go as smoothly as she'd just laid it out in her mind, but at least they had a plan. And when things went wrong, she'd use her magic. She'd use her sword. She, Brannick, and everyone else would do whatever it took to make sure High Queen Alessandra never saw another day dawn.

Sparks burst from her fingertips each time she stepped closer to the clearing. Unlike the last visit, she made no attempt to hide behind any trees. They *wanted* the high queen to know they had arrived.

It looked much the same as before. The trees growing at the edge of the clearing grew tall, stretching toward the dusky sky. Splinters and cracks in their bark showed the damage from when Ansel had tried to use them to make a home over the creation magic.

The light of the sprites above set a green glow off every surface below them.

Right in the middle of the clearing, King Jackory and Soren sat back to back. Golden chains were clasped around their wrists and ankles. More chains wrapped around their middles, chaining them both together and in place.

Elora tried not to notice the bruises coloring Soren's face. His black eyes bugged out with red rimming around them. His beard hung limp and stringy. It even looked shorter than usual.

King Jackory didn't look much better. His crown with braided bands of gold and silver no longer sat on his head. He wore a navy shirt, but it had been ripped and worn in several places. Bruises and burns covered his face and hands.

But he was breathing. He was alive.

Footsteps stomped behind Elora until the fae from every court that they had brought marched around to form a circle around the clearing.

A shimmer of iridescence wavered just behind the chained Soren and King Jackory. After another moment, the shimmer fell and High Queen Alessandra appeared. Her eyes narrowed as she looked over those who had gathered.

"Where are you, Prince Brannick? I know you would not send fae here to fight in your place."

No guards in white brocade stood in the clearing or nearby it. They had expected that. They were not naïve enough to believe the guards were not actually there. Just like the high queen herself, they must have been hidden by a glamour.

Brannick took Elora's hand and turned toward her. She nodded at him, ready to do her part. When she did, Blaz let out a quiet yip. Then, he bared his teeth and a low growl built at the back of his throat.

One more squeeze from Brannick's hand and they both stepped into the clearing.

Their hands drew apart at once when weapons suddenly appeared, flying across the clearing. The invisible Fairfrost guards must have thrown them. Brannick waved his hands, calling on roots and branches and even the soil to fend off attacks.

Popping her wings from her back, Elora lifted off the ground and eyed the clearing below. When a curved axe hurtled toward her from behind a nearby tree, she flew toward it at once. Her sword hilt fit perfectly in her grip. She jabbed the sword, hoping to merely injure her attacker since the Fairfrost guards were not truly enemies. They simply had to follow orders.

When footsteps bounded toward her, she turned just in time to strike at the axe aiming for her back. She knocked it away. A Fairfrost guard must have fallen to the ground because the soil puffed up and a loud grunt followed.

Using her foot, she shoved the invisible guard to the ground and then went to fight off another one.

Heat slithered up her arms and across her brow. Fighting invisible guards was not her idea of a winnable fight, but they wouldn't have to do it for much longer.

Through the tree, she glimpsed Tindra holding a glass vial high in the air. She stumbled as if someone had shoved her, but Severin immediately tackled the unseen guard. Raising her hand high again, Tindra tipped the vial and poured every drop of the formula to the forest floor.

Ice blue smoke swirled out from the spot, filling the entire clearing and even far past it with glittering puffs. One by one, the glamours hiding the Fairfrost guards vanished as they popped into sight.

The high queen fought against Brannick now, but she froze when the ice blue magic filled the space. It didn't take her long to recover. She glared at the nearest Fairfrost guard and gestured toward Elora. "Stop standing there. Kill that girl and capture Prince Brannick."

After a quick nod, the guard took a step forward. But then he stopped. His arms hung at his side while he stood in place.

High Queen Alessandra let out a shriek. "I order you to kill the girl and capture Prince Brannick." Her eyes darted over the rest of her guards who also stood in place. "I order all of you."

But they didn't move. None of them moved.

Amidst the confusion, Brannick backed away into the trees. Knowing the high queen's plan required her, Elora did the same. She backed up until she had nearly reached Tindra and Severin. Tindra ducked behind a tree, a smaller vial of the formula tight in her fist.

High Queen Alessandra continued to shriek at her guards, but none of them moved. Since Brannick stood on the other side of the clearing, Elora couldn't see him, but he was probably pulling out the spear from his mother.

It wouldn't be long now, and the high queen would die.

At her side, Severin placed a kiss on his beloved's forehead and then he stepped into the clearing. Elora sucked in a breath and reached for her sword hilt.

That wasn't part of the plan.

When he stepped out under the light of the sprites, High Queen Alessandra's eyes went wide. And then they softened. "Severin?" she whispered.

He stood at just enough of an angle that Elora could see him smile. He placed a hand over his heart. "My sister."

The Fairfrost guards started backing into the edges of the clearing, but the high queen didn't react to their movement. She stared at her brother like he might vanish at any moment.

"I know what you want." Severin's voice came out gentle as he gestured toward the ball of creation magic swirling just next to King Jackory and Soren. "If you create an enchantment that makes every creature in Faerie love you, then every creature will be easy for you to control. They will all follow your every command without any question. They will adore you."

She scoffed at him, but must have decided that wasn't good enough because then she stomped one foot. "If everyone would just swear fealty to me, I would not need the enchantment."

"I know power and control is not what you really seek."

Her arms dropped to her sides, more affected than she probably wanted to be by her brother's words.

He continued. "Our father never loved you. He loved me and not you, though you deserved it as much as I did. All your life you have tried to regain that love."

"I have…" She scoffed again, brushing a wrinkle from the shimmery white brocade of her gown. "How preposterous. Why would I care if our father loved me? He is dead."

Severin cocked his head to the side. "If you did not care, then why did you kill him?"

Heat flushed her cheeks as she clenched her fists. "Fine, maybe I do care, but it is his fault if I do. It is his fault that I killed him, his fault that I killed others."

"No." Severin spoke the word loud enough that it resounded off the trees. "Being damaged does not excuse you from damaging others. Life hurts us all. It was your choice alone to react with destruction. Now you must pay for what you have done."

By the time he finished speaking, he had pulled out from his pocket a curved axe with light blue sapphires studding the handle. He raised it, as if to strike. When he threw it, she ducked the blow.

Hiking her skirt up, she darted across the clearing. Elora had never seen the high queen run or even walk quickly. She always expected everyone to come to her. But now she sprinted into the trees and shot one hand out. She snatched Tindra by the hair and dragged her closer to the clearing.

"You will not take this from me, Severin. Not when I am so close." Before, the high queen's voice had held anger and frustration. Now it came out unnervingly calm. Frost formed on the fingertips of her free hand. The frost quickly turned to icicles. She pointed them straight at Tindra's heart.

Several fae must have decided now was the moment to attack. Elora lunged forward. So did Severin and several others.

Elora got a handful of the high queen's dress in her fists. Someone had tried to tackle the high queen. Many others sent blasts of enchantments. Someone tackled Tindra to the ground to get her out of the way.

Despite all the simultaneous attacks, High Queen Alessandra still had something the rest of them didn't. She had the high crown of Faerie. She had crowns from all six courts. She had power the rest of them could only dream of.

She flicked her attackers away and aimed the icicles at Tindra's chest once again.

If she succeeded with this, after so many people tried to stop her, they had no chance of stopping her from taking over all of Faerie.

CHAPTER
41

Elora knew if the high queen caught sight of her, it would certainly distract her enough to stop trying to stab ice shards into Tindra's heart. But what would happen then? The high queen would simply grab Elora, drag her to the creation magic, and use her as a vessel to take over Faerie.

Swallowing hard, Elora tucked herself behind the nearest tree. Her throat ached as she watched the icicles pointing toward Tindra's heart.

Severin leapt toward his sister again. He reached out, clearly eager to save his beloved from losing all emotion. High Queen Alessandra used her free hand to throw an enchantment that knocked Severin off his feet.

She then shot her icicles forward while her jaw clenched tight.

But she had been too busy stopping her brother, she did not notice the other fae who had also leapt.

The shards of ice burrowed deep into a chest, but not Tindra's. Vesper's curly hair shook in the wind while the ice shards melted into his heart. He revealed no expression of pain. He didn't even look surprised.

His eyebrow raised as he gestured toward himself. "You cannot freeze my heart again, not after it has already melted."

Elora gasped at the words. *Melted?* Lyren's tears must have done it then. Her tears and maybe even her sacrifice too. He was free of the ice magic.

Vesper's blue and gray eyes glinted in the light as he stepped forward. "My healed heart just proves how narrow-minded you are. Your father should have loved you, and he did not, but I am certain others did. Why was their love never enough?" His voice broke over the final words. He placed a hand over his heart and swallowed hard. "Even a friend's love can be powerful."

"I am sure this is supposed to be touching." High Queen Alessandra rolled her eyes. "But you forget that I do not care."

She lifted her hand again, forming another enchantment at her fingertips. It didn't boast frost or ice, just white sparkles that could probably sting and burn.

Just like that, the fight started again. Vesper lunged for the high queen's feet. Fae from other courts fought toward her too. Even Tindra sprinted forward to try to stop the high queen. Severin found Tindra in the crowd and grabbed her hand for a quick squeeze. Then they both rejoined the fight together.

Elora reached for her sword and went to step forward, but a shimmer of blue caught her eye. She glanced down and saw a small vial full of Tindra's blue formula. She must have dropped it during the fight.

Reaching down, Elora grabbed it and stuffed it into her pocket. She'd return it to Tindra when she could, but for now, she needed to get closer to the high queen. The creation magic in the center of the clearing seemed to grow. It pulsed and twisted amidst the battle, as if drawing power from those who fought.

It didn't seem to weaken anyone. Instead, every fae seemed to fight with more vigor, more endurance than they should have had.

Now that the bargains entrapping the Fairfrost guards had broken, many of them joined the fight against her. Some hung back, clearly afraid to defy their queen, even if they didn't have to follow her every order. But most of them did work to take her down.

When Elora reached a tree that bordered the clearing, a glowing green light from above zoomed down toward her. The sparkle of pink would have made her smile if she hadn't been in the midst of a battle for Faerie.

Tansy landed on Elora's shoulder. Her velvety hair stood tall and bright. "You must free us from the residue of Ansel's enchantments."

Elora's heart squeezed when she glanced toward her sprite friend. "I cannot. I am not strong enough to do something like that."

Tilting her head down toward Elora's pocket, Tansy spoke again. "That formula you picked up can destroy enchantments."

"I know." Biting her lip, Elora's heart squeezed even more. "But it cannot destroy enchantments that were created with gemstones. That is why the residue from Ansel's enchantment is still holding you in place right now."

Tansy's velvet hair wilted when she looked down.

341

Elora reached toward the little sprite to lift her chin. "I will find a way to help you as soon as I can. You know I will."

Tansy nodded. "We are safe now, and we are not in pain like when we were trapped in Fairfrost. But we are still eager to be free."

"I will find a way, Tansy. Once we defeat the high queen, I will find a way."

Even with the sprite on her shoulder, Elora wanted to jump right back into the fight. She began to draw her sword and went to sprint into the clearing.

Just before she could lift a foot, someone grabbed her wrist and held her back. When Blaz came to her side, she knew whose hand had grabbed her. She whirled around to face him.

Brannick held a finger to his lips and tugged her back a little more. "We must fight from farther away. If we go into the clearing and she reaches either of us, she will use us as a vessel and take over Faerie."

Glancing over her shoulder, the same tightness squeezed her heart again. Of course Brannick was right, but she hated having to go anywhere except into the thick of things.

It turned out that she could still inflict damage even from a great distance. Her sword bounced at her hip unused, but her fingers shot enchantments that blasted into the clearing. Several of the enchantments hit the high queen hard enough to make her stumble back.

The high queen may have had the power of six crowns, but even *she* lost energy when every fae in the forest fought against her. She needed reinforcements, but she had none. Maybe if she had brought trolls, it might have evened things, but she must not have thought she needed them for this battle.

A curl escaped from the perfect bun in her hair. When the curl bounced against her forehead, she seemed to realize the same thing Elora just had.

High Queen Alessandra was losing.

With her jaw clenched tight, the high queen scanned the crowd before her. She found one of her guards and grabbed him by the shoulder. Her voice came out raspy, but still loud enough for all to hear. "Help me or I will kill you."

While she spoke, she drew her axe with the opalescent handle out from her pocket. She held the curved blade close enough to kiss his neck.

The guard sucked in a quivering breath. He glanced around at the fae surrounding them. The high queen had to use her hand holding the axe to block several enchantments in just the few moments while she held him.

He took courage when a strong blast shot from Elora's fingertips hit the high queen in the jaw. Jerking hard, he ripped himself out of her grip. "I will not help you."

No sooner had the words left his lips than her axe slammed into his chest. His bones cracked as blood gushed from the wound. She yanked her weapon out of him and stomped over to the next nearest guard. By the time she gripped his shoulder, the guard was already shaking. "Help me or I will kill you."

"Yes, my queen." He didn't hesitate. He immediately turned on the fae he had just been fighting beside and swung his own axe toward the fae.

With a smile playing on her lips, the high queen continued to block enchantments as she stomped over to another guard. "Help me or I will kill you."

Hearing the words a third time sent a tingle across the back of Elora's neck. She kept throwing enchantments at the high queen, but High Queen Alessandra gained more power with every moment that passed.

The third guard showed the slightest hesitation at her command. But when she lifted her axe, he immediately threw his hands over his head and began nodding profusely. "Yes, my queen. I will fight for you."

It took almost no effort after that. She only had to look in the eye of another guard, and he immediately started to fight for the high queen instead of against her.

Her smile curled up tight. She used one hand to block every enchantment that shot toward her as she glanced around the clearing. "Fairfrost guards, you know what I will do to you unless you start fighting for me now."

She didn't need any other words. Every guard wearing white brocade immediately turned on anyone attempting to hurt the high queen. The change happened so fast, the other fae barely had time to react. Many had been fighting side by side with the Fairfrost guards. Now the Fairfrost weapons cut them down.

A frightening chuckle fell from the high queen's mouth. Her grin looked just as wicked. "Enchantments may be efficient, but they are not the only way to manipulate emotions. You must realize now how foolish it was to believe you could defeat me."

Shouting broke out across the clearing. Some shouted in agony after being wounded. Others shouted in anger after having a supposed ally turn on them. All across the clearing, High Queen Alessandra had gained control again.

She snarled at her guards. "Find me Prince Brannick. If you cannot find him, get *Elora*." She spat out the name like a curse.

Something tugged at Elora's hem. Once she turned her gaze toward it, she found Blaz biting her hem and trying to pull her toward a nearby tree. She wanted to ignore Brannick's advice about staying away from the clearing, but her gut told her to follow Blaz anyway.

The wolf led her to a tree. Behind it, Brannick, Quintus, Chloe, Severin, and Tindra all crouched close together.

Elora's hackles raised at the sight of them. She could barely take in a deep enough breath to speak. She looked at each of them, her gaze lingering on her middle sister the longest, and then she gripped her sword. "Where is Grace?"

Chloe sucked in a breath and clapped both her hands to her lips. She shook her head, which sent strands of blonde hair flying all over the place. "She is on the other side of the clearing with Lyren and Vesper. She was safe when I saw her last."

That did little to ease the tension in Elora's belly. Her middle sister looked far too frightened for her to stop worrying about her youngest sister. She knew Chloe only acted so frightened because she hated battles and not necessarily because Grace was in any great danger. Still, Elora would have been more at ease if her youngest sister had been there too.

"We need another plan." Even crouched down, Brannick still managed to take hold of the conversation. Maybe he just wanted to distract Elora, but then again, they did have bigger problems at the moment. "High Queen Alessandra is too powerful with all those crowns. We need a way to trick her, or we might never have a chance of beating her."

Everyone nodded at his words, but no one had any suggestions to offer up.

Tindra pressed her lips together and lowered her head. "I lost the second vial of formula."

"Oh." Elora patted the outside of her pocket. "I have it. I picked it up when—"

"Look who I have." High Queen Alessandra spoke with a graceful lilt that somehow still came out loud enough to shake the leaves on the trees.

The hair on the back of Elora's neck raised as she slowly turned her head toward the clearing. She already knew she didn't want to see *who* the high queen had, but she couldn't stop herself from looking either. When she finally looked, a part of her wished she hadn't.

Lyren and Vesper sat in shimmery golden chains right next to the still chained Soren and King Jackory. But someone else sat between them. With them sitting down, Elora couldn't quite see the other person.

High Queen Alessandra tapped the flat side of her axe against one palm. She spoke loud enough for all to hear. "I need Prince Brannick, or," her face twisted, "I need Elora." Again, the name came out like a curse. "If one of those two does not enter the clearing soon, I will kill your friends."

Throughout the speech, Elora stood taller, desperate to see the third person who had been captured. And then she saw it. A feathery wisp of rich, red hair.

Grace.

Her gut coiled into a knot.

A part of her had known it from the moment she saw Lyren and Vesper, but the sight of her youngest sister still set her on edge. She gripped her sword, ready to charge into the clearing at once.

The only thing that held her back was the knowledge that such an action would likely get her sister killed. And the high queen would probably find a way to capture Elora, use her as a vessel, and take over Faerie as well.

An ache stung Elora's throat, crawling all the way down to squeeze her heart tight.

346

"I have an idea." Quintus jumped up, grabbing Chloe by the hand to help her up too. "Chloe, come with me."

They darted deeper into the forest, which couldn't possibly help at all because Grace still sat in chains right at High Queen Alessandra's feet. The high queen eyed her axe with a little too much pleasure before glancing at her prisoners again.

Sucking in a breath, Elora grabbed Brannick's coat and shook him a little harder than she intended. "We have to do something. She has my sister."

Horror etched across Brannick's face. He gripped Elora's wrists, as if eager to help. But comfort wasn't enough.

Blaz came close to her side, trying to nuzzle close.

She gripped Brannick's coat tighter, only just keeping herself from screaming. "We have to do something now."

"Here she is." Quintus's voice rang out across the clearing. He stood tall, right across from High Queen Alessandra. In his arms, he held... Elora.

CHAPTER

42

Every sound in the clearing sucked away in that one moment. Elora stood behind the tree with Brannick's coat still tight in her fists. Except, she sat in Quintus's arms standing across the clearing from the high queen.

Shaking her head, Elora tried to make sense of it. She glanced at Brannick, hoping he might have some kind of explanation. He seemed even more confused than her. He even poked her in the forehead.

She glared at him and dropped her hands to her sides.

The only person who didn't look frightened or confused or distressed was High Queen Alessandra. She grinned like she had just gotten Faerie itself to be her vessel.

With a nod, Quintus took a step forward. The Elora in his arms started squirming, trying to free herself.

Quintus immediately lifted her off the ground and stepped toward the high queen. "I will bring her over, just do not hurt those others."

When her squirming did nothing to deter Quintus, the Elora in his arms let out a scream. "Let me go." She wriggled even harder. "Let me go, Quintus. I didn't agree to this. You can't make me do it."

Elora gasped and took a fistful of Brannick's coat once again. "He has Chloe." A breath shuddered through her as she locked eyes with the prince. "He glamoured her to look like me. He has Chloe!"

Brannick shook his head, leaned around the tree to get a better view. "Has Quintus gone insane?"

"I will kill him." Elora formed a fist so tight her nails dug into her palms. If Brannick hadn't grabbed onto her waist, she would have marched right into the clearing and killed Quintus on the spot.

Quintus continue to step forward. Chloe wriggled and shrieked with each step he took. It might have seemed like Chloe's plan too, except sheer terror laced each of her shrieks.

Quintus gestured to the three new prisoners in chains. "Let those three go, and I will give you Elora."

Still struggling against Quintus's grip, Chloe whimpered.

Chuckling, High Queen Alessandra lifted her axe into the air. "You are in no position to negotiate."

Quintus shrugged. "Fine. I guess you do not really want Elora then." He turned to go back into the forest without a second thought.

"Wait!" The high queen nearly screamed the word. She had to take a breath to compose herself again. "Fine. I will let them go."

Turning slowly, Quintus started moving toward the high queen again. With each step, Chloe's agitation deepened.

Even with Brannick's arm around her waist, Elora was determined to get into the clearing and save her sisters.

Of course, the high queen released Lyren, Vesper, and thankfully Grace at exactly that moment. But even once she freed them, Quintus continued to step toward the high queen with Chloe thrown over his shoulder.

"He is trying to trick her." Brannick whispered into Elora's ear, probably attempting to calm her.

"What are you talking about?" She flashed her teeth at him, pushing against his grip.

He released her immediately but gestured toward the clearing. "Your sister is mortal. She has no magic to lose. Without magic, she cannot be used as a vessel. Nothing will happen when she touches the creation magic."

Clenching her jaw tight, Elora raised her chin and stepped closer to Brannick. "And what happens when the high queen realizes Chloe is mortal? Do you think she will just toss her aside? Or will she kill her?"

At least his eyes flashed with an appropriate amount of panic. Even Blaz whimpered and put his paws over his nose.

She grabbed his coat, gentler this time. "You have to kill her, Brannick. Do not let the high queen hurt my sister."

He nodded and started moving toward the clearing right away. "Get your sword. We need to move close enough to use our weapons."

His feet moved silently over the soil and moss. He pulled the iron-tipped spear from his pocket, gripping it hard. Elora drew her sword and popped out her wings. She'd fly right in front of the high queen if she had to, but she wouldn't let anything happen to her sister.

350

By the time they reached the edge of the clearing, Chloe fainted.

She still wore Elora's face when her body draped over Quintus's shoulder like a rag doll. He set her down gently, careful to set her head on a soft patch of moss.

As soon as he stepped away from her unconscious form, the high queen yanked Chloe by the wrist and dragged her toward the creation magic.

Elora didn't dare use her sword while the high queen moved. Brannick clearly felt the same. They only had one chance to aim, and they had to make it count. Now they just had to wait until the high queen stood still.

With a heaving pull, High Queen Alessandra shoved Chloe right next to the creation magic. Careful to avoid touching the creation magic herself, the high queen lifted Chloe's arm and threw it into the pulsing light.

When High Queen Alessandra stood up straight to wait, two weapons shot toward her. Elora threw her sword and then sent an enchantment behind it to make it fly even faster and with greater accuracy.

Brannick threw his spear at the same moment. No enchantment moved behind his weapon. After spending so long teaching Brannick how to use a sword, she had forgotten he grew up in a court that used spears. He clearly had as much training with his spear as she had with her sword. The iron tip of the spear would surely pierce the high queen's heart.

But it didn't.

Both weapons stopped in midair. They hovered for a brief moment and then clattered to the ground. They landed several arm's lengths away from the high queen.

She had one hand lifted in front of her body with the palm facing the weapons. Even though she had just demonstrated great power by stopping the weapons before they could reach her, her face simply twisted in confusion.

She kicked Chloe's foot and glanced toward the creation magic.

When nothing happened, the high queen bent and gripped Chloe by the shoulder. All at once, the glamour hiding Chloe's appearance fell away. She no longer looked like Elora. She no longer even looked fae. She just looked like Chloe.

The high queen's face twisted at the sight. "A mortal?"

At least Chloe hadn't regained consciousness because High Queen Alessandra slammed her foot into Chloe's side. "You thought you could trick me?"

Once the high queen's axe raised into the air, all semblance of logic vanished from Elora's mind. With a war scream, she flew into the clearing. Enchantments burst from her fingertips, many of them slamming into the high queen.

Brannick sprinted into the clearing right behind Elora. He shot just as many enchantments from his fingertips. His had much more power behind them.

Blaz came next, growling and flashing his fangs for all to see. The three of them charged the high queen so fast, she could barely gather herself. When she aimed her weapon again, the other fae had joined in the fight.

Maybe hiding would have been a better option, but Elora refused to do it while her sister lay unconscious at the high queen's feet.

A tide had turned in the fight once again. The fae attacked more viciously than they had before. Elora managed to snatch her sword off the ground and use it against any Fairfrost guard who dared step near her.

Quintus crept closer and tried to get near Chloe. Elora's sword convinced him to back away slowly instead. When Lyren and Grace came toward Chloe next, Elora nodded and allowed them to carry her unconscious form deeper into the woods.

Brannick plucked his spear off the ground and positioned himself at Elora's back. Together, they fought off anyone who tried to attack them, all the while trying to knock the high queen onto the ground. If they could pin her down just for a moment, Brannick would be able to deliver a killing blow.

Fairfrost guards dotted the clearing, but none of them seemed sure of what to do. When High Queen Alessandra threatened their lives, they helped her without question. But now she was too busy fighting off her own attackers to worry about any of them.

One by one, the Fairfrost guards dropped their weapons and stepped out of the way of anyone trying to reach the high queen.

More curls came loose from High Queen Alessandra's bun. Her cheeks turned an even deeper shade of crimson each time she had to block an enchantment or a weapon. When she backed into a tree, the first flicker of fear danced in her eyes.

A shower of weapons flew toward her. She darted away from them just before they hit and waved a hand while she did it. A glittery white door appeared next to her.

For a moment, Elora expected the high queen to jump into the door and escape the fight. Then again, the high queen had never been the type to run. Jerking her head toward the door, she shouted through it. "You better be healed now. I brought you in on my plans for a reason. Make yourself useful, or I will step through this door and kill you myself."

It took a moment before anything changed, but then a figure appeared in her door. He stepped onto the soil with yellow eyes gleaming. He hobbled and clutched his chest with every step, but he was moving.

353

Ansel was alive.

Elora had to bend at the waist to keep herself from vomiting right there. Blaz came to her side, already spitting and flashing his fangs. At some point, the fight had moved Brannick away from her. He fought against one of the last Fairfrost guards who still fought on the high queen's side. If he had noticed Ansel's presence, he gave no indication of it.

Elora's stomach churned like a sea monster eyeing a boat before preparing to strike. She wrapped her arms around her stomach, but it did nothing because Ansel had found her in the crowd. He drew a dagger from his pocket, keeping his eyes on her the entire time.

Without breaking eye contact, he stepped up to the nearest Fairfrost guard and sliced his dagger across the guard's hand. Then, Ansel moved toward the creation magic. His steps and breathing came labored, but it didn't affect his focus.

When he reached the creation magic, he held the blood-covered dagger over the twisting swirls of the creation magic.

"What are you doing?" Elora's voice came out breathless. It didn't make any sense to speak to Ansel. He had no reason to listen to her.

But for some reason, he chose to answer her question. He smirked and glanced at his dagger while a drop of the guard's blood fell off the blade and into the pulsing magic below it. "Only the high queen needs a vessel. With blood, I can use the creation magic in a different way."

Once he finished speaking, the blood had made contact with the magic. It burst in a flash of pearly white light. Then the guard whose blood had been used stood up straight. His eyes widened with terror when he pulled an axe from his pocket and slammed it into the chest of the fae nearest to him.

Ansel turned to Elora once again. "My greatest magic is in blood. The creation magic allows me complete control over any fae whose blood I collect. I can even give orders with my mind."

Her stomach still twisted and writhed, but she fought toward him now. He sliced the hands of more guards and dripped their blood into the creation magic.

No matter how hard Elora tried to fight toward him, he just took control of another guard and used the guard to stop Elora in her path.

Brannick had finally noticed Ansel's presence. He pushed past fae and guards and even enchantments. He sent lethal magic wherever he could, but too many fae stood between him and Ansel to do much damage. And the high queen was trying capture Brannick again.

With his focus on Ansel, she slowly gained the upper hand.

Elora continued to fight, but the Fairfrost guards under Ansel's control closed in on her. She had been fighting the guards before, multiple guards at once even. But now they all focused on her specifically, refusing to let the attacks of other fae distract them.

The guards formed a circle around her, pointing weapons toward her as if they delighted in seeing her squirm. Ansel kept his gaze locked on hers, a sickly smile growing on his face each time he added another guard to the circle surrounding her.

"Ansel." The high queen shrieked from across the clearing. "Quit toying with her. I need my vessel. If you want to keep her for yourself, then I need to use Prince Brannick."

Rolling his eyes, Ansel sighed. "Fine."

He pulled another dagger from his coat, one that looked achingly familiar. Elora slapped a hand over her arm as she eyed the blood on the dagger. Her blood. Ansel had used that same dagger during her fight with him in his house. He had cut her arm. And now he had her blood.

But the blood had dried.

What could he possibly do with dried blood?

When he tossed the entire dagger into the creation magic, she understood at once. Her muscles seized and ached. Horrible scraping sensations flooded her chest and legs. Her spine shot up straight without her permission.

Ansel spoke again. Even though he stood a short distance away from her, his voice seemed to tickle right at her ear.

"Come over to me, my pet."

She hated her foot that immediately took a step toward him. She hated her hand that pushed her sword back into her belt. Most of all, she hated her heart that beat at exactly the same pulse as Ansel's.

No matter how she tried to fight it, Ansel had complete control of her.

CHAPTER

43

Soil and moss dragged underneath Elora's boots. She tried to dig her feet deeper into the ground. Anything to keep herself from moving forward. But her boots would not listen.

She just stepped and stepped and stepped. Closer to Ansel. Closer to whatever he chose to do with her.

He had used her before—but not like this. Now he could do whatever he wanted with her. She couldn't even fight back.

Brannick shouted over the noise of the battle. He shoved and fought, but he couldn't get to her with a wall of Fairfrost guards blocking the way.

Ansel's smile grew with every step.

She scowled at him. "I will dig your heart out with my bare hands if I have to. You will pay for doing this to me."

He chuckled, running a hand through her hair once she had moved close enough. "You know I like it when you are feisty, but we have to capture Prince Brannick at the moment."

"Capture him?" A genuine laughed tumbled from her lips. "You think my magic is strong enough to capture *him?*"

"It will be if you use a gemstone."

Her chest tightened. Her heart roared. She hated it, but Ansel was right. If she used a gemstone, she might be strong enough to capture Brannick. And then High Queen Alessandra would use him to take over Faerie.

Ansel spoke to her like a small child might speak to a kitten. "I know you have some of my gemstones hidden in your pocket. Go on then. Pull one out."

Her body continued to rebel against her, doing everything that Ansel wished. Desperate beyond reason, she glanced around for anyone, *anything* that might help her.

The sprites.

They floated up above, glowing even brighter than ever.

She had the small vial of Tindra's formula in her pocket, but it still wasn't strong enough to destroy the enchantments keeping the sprites in place. Unless...

Her fingers had found one of the gemstones in her pocket now. If she used the formula at the same moment she crushed a gemstone, would the gemstone make the formula strong enough to save the sprites?

Even as her hand began lifting out of her pocket, her head whipped around to look at Brannick. She had to save him too. Ansel would force her to capture him, but surely, she could do *something* to keep him safe.

A yellow-green gemstone winked between her thumb and forefinger. The sight of it made Ansel smirk. Luckily, he focused too much on the gemstone to notice Elora had the small vial of pearlescent blue formula hidden in her palm.

"Why are you helping her?" Elora did her best to distract Ansel. She needed to think. If she kept him talking, hopefully she could figure out a way out of this. "How does helping the high queen benefit you?"

He stepped close enough to whisper in her ear. The scent of sour milk licked her cheek. "Once the high queen has control of Faerie, she has promised to let me force as many fae as I like to touch the creation magic." He gave a wide grin. "Then their blood will have the power of a fae with none of the magic to fight back. Just like yours." He leaned in closer and trailed a finger down her neck all the way to her collar bone. "I will have an endless supply of the most powerful blood that exists."

She refused to shiver under his touch, even though he clearly wanted her to. Instead, she forced her mind to consider every possible thing besides him. Her head cocked the side when a spark ignited in her gut. Intuition. "What happens if I touch the creation magic now? Will the hold you have over me release once my magic is taken away?"

"What?" He sputtered and took a step back. But then he laughed. It came out forced. "Where did you get an idea like that?"

Intuition had given her the idea, and his refusal to answer provided plenty. He used his blood magic to squeeze her fingers together. The yellow-green gem crushed under her fingertips. At exactly the same moment, she dropped the vial with the blue formula onto the ground. When it hit a patch of moss, she crushed it with her boot until the blue formula spread into the forest floor.

A burst of yellow-green light shot out from the gemstone. The formula also released swirls of ice-blue smoke. The colors twisted together, floating on the air.

Just as Ansel forced her to do, she used the power from the gemstone to create a barrier that surrounded Brannick, capturing him. A yellow-green wall circled around him and even his wolf.

Her body collapsed to the ground in a heap. The gemstone had weakened her even more than she expected.

Brannick slammed his fists against the barrier, but it wouldn't budge. He drove his fingers deep inside it, already attempting to break it down with his magic. Blaz slammed his body against the barrier. He swiped his paws at it, but even that did nothing.

While Brannick worked, he glared at Ansel. "How dare you." His voice turned gravelly. Dangerous. "How dare you use her against me."

High Queen Alessandra took a deep breath, which relaxed her shoulders. "Guards." She barely even raised her voice when she glanced at the guards Ansel controlled. "Seize the prince and bring him to me."

They marched forward, which only made Brannick work harder to free himself. He glared and flashed his teeth and looked ready to rip Ansel's head right off his shoulders.

But when the guards got to the barrier surrounding the prince, they could not get through. Ansel, the high queen, and even the guards themselves expected the barrier to keep Brannick captured while others could still reach in and grab him.

But Ansel had never thought to specify that. Elora had been forced to create a barrier to capture the prince, yet she found a way to protect him too.

Brannick chuckled, which grew into a hearty laugh. "You should have known better than to underestimate my beloved."

Though she was on the ground and not capable of making eye contact with Brannick, Elora still smiled. Brannick had taught her well how to find loopholes in Faerie's rules. At least now she had done it to protect him.

With a hard swallow, Elora forced herself up onto her elbows. Almost all her energy had drained away when she crushed the gemstone, but she still had a little bit left.

The moment she started moving, Ansel lunged toward her. He didn't get far. Glowing green lights from above darted down and slammed into his chest. A particularly feisty sprite with a sparkle of pink in its glow pulled small fistfuls of hair out of his head.

Tansy.

Elora smiled again. The sprites had come to her rescue. Using the formula along with the gemstone must have freed them. And just like Tansy promised, they had come to her aid. Elora's arms shook when she crawled herself forward.

Ansel's arms waved around his head, swatting the glowing creatures. He shouted and cursed, but the sprites wouldn't leave him alone. While distracted, he couldn't stop Elora from what she planned to do.

Her arms shook harder every creep and crawl forward. She panted. She tried to draw strength from within, but it was difficult when her insides felt as crushed as that gemstone. Even moving as fast as she could, she still moved too slow.

Without the sprites, she never would have made it.

High Queen Alessandra and her guards all attempted to break through the barrier around Brannick. It wouldn't be long before they succeeded. The sprites had helped, but they couldn't hold Ansel off forever. Soon he would command her again. He would control her. She couldn't take any chances.

She would not do anything to hurt Brannick. Not again.

Before anyone had even noticed her crawling across the ground, she reached her destination. The creation magic swirled and twisted, giving off energy in random bursts. It felt wrong to lose her magic so soon after finding it, but deep down, she knew it didn't matter.

She could be great anyway.

Taking a deep breath, Elora thrust her hand deep into creation magic. It began stealing magic from her in the same breath.

The creation magic let off sizzles and pops and crackles that cut through the air. Its colors swirled and twisted, turning from colorful and colorless to a bright purple hue.

Brannick reacted first. His eyes widened like someone had just stabbed him in the chest. He slammed his hands against the barrier surrounding him and let out a strangled cry. Blaz howled in a tone nearly identical to the prince's scream.

Everyone else in the clearing froze. Gasped. Only the Fairfrost guards looked at Elora with something other than pity. Their looks held longing. Horror etched across the faces of nearly every other fae in the clearing. They could not fathom what she had done. But maybe none of them understood how it felt to be controlled. Only the Fairfrost guards did.

Brannick slammed his fists against the barrier again. His face had fallen even more than before. He uttered a single word. "No."

High Queen Alessandra's nose twitched for a moment, but then she strode toward Elora and the creation magic. She sighed as she came near. "Fine. I will use you as a vessel instead if I must."

Elora ripped her hand away from the creation magic and used it to draw her sword. Courage sparked from somewhere deep in her gut. It took hold of her even though she had no right to be courageous considering her situation. With a smirk on her lips, Elora eyed the high queen closely. "I would like to see you try."

It felt good to say the words. It did not feel good to be sliced by High Queen Alessandra's axe. In her weakened state, Elora couldn't move fast enough to avoid the axe completely. It sliced down the side of one leg, sending heat and pain through her calf.

"Do not touch her." Brannick screamed the words, breaking free of his barrier in the same moment. He hurtled forward with murder in his eyes. He drew his iron-tipped spear, and the fight raged again.

Enchantments and weapons flung across the clearing. Guards and other fae slammed into each other and shoved others to the ground.

With Ansel in the clearing, Elora's sisters must have been hidden by glamours that made them invisible, but Elora couldn't spot any of the other fae she sought either. It probably wouldn't have done any good any way. The gemstone had weakened her greatly. Just breathing felt laborious.

She vaguely noticed the sprites had stopped fighting and returned to their place above the fight. She never expected them to fight long, but it did beg another question she wanted to avoid.

Where was Ansel?

Using the last of her energy, she propped herself up against a tree. Her fingers gripped her sword hilt but only because it brought her comfort. Lifting her sword would have drained away the little energy she had left.

The scent of sour milk drifted into her nose. She winced and sensed the exact moment Ansel crawled to her side. Sharp, red marks broke out across his skin, probably from the sprites. Despite the damage he had incurred, he still managed a sickly grin.

"You are without magic again. Just how I like you."

He reached out to brush a finger across her cheek. She flinched, but she was too weak to pull away. That only curled his grin up more.

"You should have died in your house." She spoke through clenched teeth. "How did you live?"

He chuckled. "I might ask you the same question. I recall plunging a dagger into your chest. You should not have been able to move after what I did to you."

"I had help."

His nose wrinkled. "Your prince found you?"

"Yes." She gripped her sword hilt again. "But I took your brownie away when I helped the mermaid, Waverly, escape your house. And I took all your mortals. You had no one. Did the high queen help you?"

The first crack in his demeanor appeared when he flashed his teeth. "I do not need help from her. I do not need help from anyone." The moment passed quickly and soon he smiled at her again. Reaching for his lapel, he gave a meaningful twist to the red gemstone pinned to it. "I have the power to do anything."

She frowned. "You used a gemstone to heal yourself?"

"Yes." He drew the word out as he leaned in nearer to her. Though she wanted to spit in his face, she sat completely still. Waiting. She just needed him a little bit closer.

His fingers reached out to touch her hair, and finally he came in close enough.

Gripping her sword tight, she drew from the very last dregs of her strength and plunged her sword right through his heart. At least half the sword came out through his back. She twisted the sword with a great turn. He fell backward onto the soil.

When she yanked the sword out of him, she angled it so that his heart came right out of his chest, still stuck to her sword.

It pumped a few times with blood shooting out its sides. Digging the tip of the sword deep into the soil at her side, the heart pulsed once more. She clenched her jaw tight. "Try healing now."

He opened his mouth, but no words left his lips. She stared at him with an unwavering gaze until his eyes turned lifeless. No matter what, he wouldn't survive again.

He was truly dead.

A deep breath tumbled from her lips when she leaned back against the tree.

Enchantments flew across the clearing. They sparked and flashed with speed like Elora had never seen. With Ansel dead, the Fairfrost guards backed away from the fight. The other fae backed away too.

Every now and then a fae would jump forward and try to help in the fight, but Brannick and High Queen Alessandra moved too fast. They fought with too much intensity. No other fae could match their speed or accuracy.

Only the two of them fought now. Brannick had never looked so ferocious. High Queen Alessandra had never looked so determined.

The high queen must have felt Elora's eyes on her because she suddenly shot her eyes Elora's way. A tiny flicker danced across her eyes. It was the only indication that something was coming. Not that Elora could have done anything to stop it anyway. Every last bit of her energy had been drained when she killed Ansel.

High Queen Alessandra must have been eager to exploit that. With a wave of one hand, she lifted a rock from the ground. The high queen had never been able to lift rocks before, but maybe the crown of Bitter Thorn had given her that power.

With a shove of her hand, the rock flew toward Elora. It didn't aim for her chest or even her head. Instead, it slammed into her hand. Her *sword* hand.

Elora gasped as her bones crushed. Pain sent white streaks into her vision, temporarily blinding her. But all she could think about was her sword and how she might never lift it again.

Mortals who received such devastating injuries to their hands never recovered. At least not enough to regain their previous sword skill.

Tears welled in her eyes. She grabbed her stomach and gagged. Even before she could access her magic directly, she'd still had fae healing abilities. Surely, those had not vanished just because she touched the creation magic.

But deep down she knew.

The creation magic had taken away her healing abilities too. If it hadn't, she would have felt herself healing by now.

"I told you..." Brannick formed fists at his sides. His voice came out deep. Feral. He glared hard enough that the forest itself seemed to wilt. Except he didn't stare at the forest. He stared at High Queen Alessandra. His voice rose now, thick with anger. "Not to touch her."

When he lunged forward, his magic took on a power he had never used before. He blocked every one of the high queen's enchantments with a mere flick of his wrist. Where they had seemed equal only moments before, he now fought with twice as much power.

He rounded on her, his wolf snarling with each step. She tried to fight him off, but it did nothing now. He grabbed her by the neck and lifted her off the ground. His free hand dug deep into his pocket. Pulling out the iron-tipped spear, he aimed it carefully.

But she had one last card to play. From her own pocket, she pulled out a purple gemstone. Her last gemstone made with Elora's fae blood. The most powerful gemstone left in Faerie.

She crushed it before Brannick could even take a breath. He fell backward off his feet. *Everyone* fell onto their backs. Even High Queen Alessandra. Her breath shuddered as she tried to lift herself off the ground. Her arms shook just like Elora's had.

With a grunt, Brannick sat up. His glare returned.

But then they felt it. She had used her final gemstone. She had saved her most powerful enchantment for last.

Warmth bloomed in Elora's chest. It grew and tingled down her arms in a pleasant dance. Her mind knew the sensation came as a result of the gemstone, but it felt so nice. So warm.

Her heart thumped hard, basking in the feeling that overtook it.

Love.

All High Queen Alessandra wanted was love. How could Elora refuse such a reasonable request?

It wasn't until Elora glanced across the clearing that her mind could finally break free of the gemstone's power. Brannick wore the same awe-struck expression as every other fae in the clearing.

High Queen Alessandra smiled at him, and he... he smiled back.

The high queen moved to her knees, still too weakened to get to her feet. She stared up at him through her eyelashes.

He reached out and stroked her cheek.

Elora sucked in a breath, which turned into more of a sob. The love channeled out of her in a rush. The pain from her crushed bones sliced away the last of it that remained. She curled her uninjured fist over her chest, as if that would help. It didn't.

But her sob had captured Brannick's attention. He turned to her slowly and stared. He blinked twice while the rest of his body stayed still. Then his hand fell away from the high queen's face. He continued to stare at Elora, at her sword, at her hand.

His eyes pulsed and shifted just like the creation magic behind him. When he finally turned back to High Queen Alessandra, he lifted his spear. A glare began to creep back into his eyes.

The high queen grabbed his free hand and held it tight. She spoke in her most dulcet tone. "Please, do not hurt me. I owe you a debt now. *Please.*" Her eyelashes fluttered. Her voice lowered to a whisper. "Prince Brannick."

He yanked his hand away.

Her gaze grew more intense when she lifted her chin higher. "You loved me once. Can you not find it in your heart to let me go free?"

A puff of air escaped his nose, not quite a chuckle but close to it. "Maybe I could have, but then you hurt my beloved. And all of Faerie too."

Without ceremony, he shot his spear forward and slit her throat. While blood poured from the wound, he shoved the spear deep into her heart.

He'd done it.

Even with the most powerful gemstone at her disposal, he'd still fought its effects and defeated her.

High Queen Alessandra was dead.

CHAPTER 44

A collective sigh released from the fae still standing in the clearing. Elora let out her own sigh, but it came out a bit strangled. The crushed bones in her hand sent needles of pain up and down her arm. Her gossamer gown had rips and tears and blood splattered all over it.

Brannick had already rushed to her side. He ran a hand across her brow and winced when he looked down at her injured hand. Blood and bruises turned her skin purple and squishy. He pulled a tiny clay pot from his pocket and dropped a liquid of some sort onto the injury.

Her hand burned under the liquid, but then the burning turned to a tingle. After another few breaths, her pain dulled to a faint ache.

But she knew what healing felt like now, and the liquid did nothing like that. It simply dulled the pain. Nothing more. Her bones were still crushed, her ability to sword fight along with it.

After helping her to her feet, Brannick pulled her into his arms. She breathed in the scent of him, basking in his mere presence. He had survived. *She* had survived. Maybe it wasn't exactly like they had imagined, but at least they were alive.

And what did she need magic for anyway? Losing her sword skill hurt worse than losing the magic, but that didn't matter either. She could be great anyway.

Brannick continued to hold her tight. He kissed her hair and then her jaw. When he pulled away, his brilliant eyes softened with a pulsing light. "I know your hand is still injured, but you will be able to heal it soon."

He stepped away from her before she could correct his misspoken sentence. Of course *she* would not be able to heal her own hand. He must have meant that Kaia would heal it. But even with the dryad's help, she knew deep down that her hand would never be the same again.

Brannick moved to the center of the clearing now. He freed Soren and King Jackory from the chains that had held them throughout the battle. King Jackory's eyes looked bloodshot and frenzied, but at least he was alive.

Beckoning with one hand, Brannick looked out at the fae around him. "I need Lyren, Severin, Nerissa, and Deegan to come over here with King Jackory. All of you form a circle."

As the fae shifted around the clearing, Elora finally saw the others she had been searching for earlier. Chloe and Grace had dirt smudging their faces and arms, but they didn't have any injuries that Elora could see. Quintus and Vesper stood next to each other, watching as Lyren stepped toward Brannick. Even Fifer had come to join the fight. His floppy ears stood tall.

The fae Brannick had called all glanced at each other, wearing identical expressions of confusion while they moved to the center of the clearing. Only Jackory's face was void of the confusion, but maybe he was just too tired to show his expression.

With a deep breath, Brannick bent over the body of Alessandra. His nose wrinkled as he bent and stuffed one hand into her pocket. His body shivered as he reached in deeper. But soon, he pulled a crown from her pocket and then another.

While he worked, Blaz padded across the clearing to stand at Elora's side. She ran her good hand through his fur.

Beads and embroidery threads had snapped off her gossamer gown. She brushed a hand over them, wishing her dress had survived the fight even if her hand couldn't.

Brannick eventually found the crowns from every court. He even plucked the Fairfrost crown from the ground near Alessandra's head.

Blaz started nudging the back of Elora's leg, pushing her closer to the center of the clearing. She might have resisted, except she wanted to be closer to Brannick anyway. By the time he finished gathering the crowns, Blaz had nudged her all the way over to the rest of them.

Brannick smiled at the sight of her and tilted his head, inviting her to stand even closer. Now he turned to face the fae who had formed a circle in front of him. Understanding dawned all across the clearing as everyone realized what Brannick planned to do.

He lifted the braided gold and silver crown of Mistmount first. "King Jackory, I assume Alessandra never actually bonded to your crown since you are still alive."

"Correct." King Jackory responded with a tight nod.

"Then this is already yours." Brannick held the crown out, waiting until King Jackory placed it onto his head.

Brannick held out the turban crown of Dustdune next. "Nerissa, I know you gave up rule of your court to Alessandra, but now that she is dead, you should be able to bond with your crown once again."

She took the crown and magic immediately flashed out from it.

With a nod, Brannick turned to Severin and held out the Fairfrost crown. "Severin, your sister took the crown before you could ever bond to it, but you were meant to be King of Fairfrost at one point. I allow you now to take what is yours."

When the crown touched his head, it started shifting at once. The tall tines lowered to much shorter lengths. The white beads at the front that had hung over Alessandra's forehead vanished completely. The Fairfrost crown looked simpler. More like Severin. He straightened his spine once it finished changing.

A beat of silence landed on the clearing. Brannick took a deep breath. He gestured toward Lyren and Deegan. "I have chosen new rulers for the last courts. I believe them to be strong and willing to fight for the fae of their courts. If anyone objects to the rulers I have chosen, please step forward now."

But no one did. In fact, every fae in the crowd stood a little taller, clearly excited about the appointments. Except Lyren. She looked a bit like she was going to throw up. Deegan's eyes had gone wide. But neither of them said anything either.

When Brannick presented them with the crowns from their courts, they took them with the utmost solemnity. Light burst from the crowns as they took on new shapes and bonded to the heads of their new rulers.

Every court had a new ruler now. Every court except Bitter Thorn.

For another moment, Brannick stood still. He lifted the crown of Bitter Thorn and looked at it carefully. Blaz gave a short yip and settled down at Brannick's feet. Nodding to himself, Brannick lifted the crown closer to his face. He plucked away the imposter turquoise stone that sat at the front of the crown. Then his gaze flicked to Elora's. "I need the green crystal, the one that holds my essence."

Her heart had been beating excitedly until he spoke those words. She had thought he would use the purple crystal filled with *her* essence. It didn't matter if he had her essence inside of his crown, but she had wanted to keep his crystal for herself.

With everyone staring at her and Brannick waiting patiently, she couldn't very well refuse him. But her heart still squeezed when she dropped the sage green crystal into his hand. Magic sparked at his fingertips when he attached the crystal into the crown's setting.

The crown of obsidian and branches sat in Brannick's palms. He stared down at it, breathing slowly. With one last deep breath, he looked up. His posture had turned regal. "Any fae can place the crown of Bitter Thorn onto their head, but only someone who is chosen can access the full power of the crown."

His gaze slipped away from the crowd and focused in on one person.

Fifer.

The small brownie nodded at Brannick, his face solemn.

But why?

Turning to face forward once again. Brannick lifted his crown into the air. "I know with certainty that this crown has chosen its next ruler well."

She smiled at the words. Peace fluttered in her limbs as he lifted the crown higher. The feeling lasted right up until his arm moved out to the side instead of down.

Before she even realized his intention, he had placed the crown on *her* head. Her eyes opened wide. Light and magic sparked out from the crown, showering the air in front of her.

But the crown did more than that too. Sparks danced inside of her. They burst in her gut, down her limbs, at the tips of her fingers.

Her magic.

The crown was bringing her magic back.

Brannick had said there was one way to get magic back after touching the creation magic, but Faerie itself had to help.

But she didn't want Faerie itself to help. The crown belonged to Brannick.

The lights and sparks finally stopped. She tore the crown from her head and held it out to him. Her jaw clenched tight with insistence. "*You* are supposed to be High King. You cannot give me your crown. It is rightfully yours."

"It changed." Lyren let out a gasp as she pressed her fingers to her lips.

The other fae in the circle noticed as well.

"Look at all the purple stones." Deegan pointed at the crown as he spoke.

At least a dozen new purple stones had appeared on the crown. The green crystal containing Brannick's essence still sat at the front as bright as ever. The obsidian and branches still formed tines, but they curved more gently than before.

Brannick didn't quite smile, but he did look pleased. "The crown never changed its appearance for me."

Glaring, she held the crown out to him with more insistence.

He shrugged. "It has bonded to you. Even if I take the crown, it will do nothing for me. You are Queen of Bitter Thorn."

Anger lit like a fire inside her gut. How could he? He deserved more than this. Even as she clenched her jaw, deep down in her gut she had already known. When she first touched the crown after turning fae, it sent off a shower of sparks. Fifer had seen it. He said the crown had chosen her.

Even back then, a part of her knew it would end like this. Still, she didn't like it. Brannick was meant to be High King.

But then her anger wafted away in a single breath. Of course. *Of course* it had to happen this way, but that didn't mean it was over yet.

She placed the crown of Bitter Thorn back onto her head. She vaguely noted that her hand had already healed. Even her gossamer gown had repaired itself, the blood splatters vanished. Faerie itself must have helped with those things too. And now it would help with one more thing.

Holding her palm out, Elora waved her other hand over her palm. First a circle formed. It was made of thick brown branches and tiny green vines. The tines began to form next. More branches, tiny patches of moss, and even a few minuscule thorns twisted into the shape of a regal crown. Her hand continued to spin in a circle, magic sparking at every turn.

Every eye in the clearing had turned to her. Something told her conjuring crowns was not something fae could usually do. But she wasn't doing it alone. Faerie itself guided her, throwing magic into her movements.

When she finished, her mouth quirked into a smile. She stood as tall as she could and held the crown high. "I am Queen of Bitter Thorn, and I will do my best to rule my court." She turned and looked Brannick right in the eyes. "But Faerie still needs a High King."

Right at the center of the crown, an open setting waited for a stone.

She held her hand out. "Brannick, I need the purple crystal."

At last, *he* was too stunned to argue. He reached into his pocket and grabbed the crystal containing her essence without ever taking his eyes off the crown she had just formed.

With another wave of her hand, the purple crystal sparked with magic and slid into place. Standing on her tiptoes, she placed the crown on Brannick's head.

Though everyone had just watched the other crowns bond to the other rulers, it was nothing like the bonding that took place now. Sparks showered from above. Black and white lights danced and burst in the air. Music seemed to float on the wind, heralding in Faerie's new High King.

Standing tall, Elora turned to the others. Her voice came out sure. "Faerie itself has chosen its High King. Will the other rulers swear fealty to him?"

One by one, the rulers of each court nodded to Brannick and swore fealty to him. Elora's turn came last. She placed her hand on his arm and rolled her shoulders back. "I, Queen Elora of Bitter Thorn, swear fealty to you, Brannick, High King of Faerie."

Showers of sparks fell on them once again. Cheers broke out from around the entire clearing. Their victory had finally come.

Faerie was finally right once again.

And whatever troubles came, she and Brannick would face them together.

EPILOGUE

With her sword hanging on her hip, Elora stepped through a door into the mortal realm. Leaves crunched under her boots. Dry, cracked dirt covered the landscape. A chilly wind worked to yank any remaining leaves off the trees that scattered the ground.

Small wooden homes lined a twisty road. An ash tree with only a handful of red leaves clinging to it grew at the end of the street. She had never been to this place in the mortal realm. She hadn't even been to this *time*.

Everything looked different, and yet, everything looked the same.

Only a small group had come. She and Brannick, Chloe, Grace, Lyren, and Quintus. Most notably of all, Vesper accompanied them too.

The curse on Bitter Thorn had fully lifted. Brannick had been made High King. He finally had the power to lift Vesper's banishment and allow him to return to the mortal realm.

Vesper practically danced on the balls of his feet with each step. He gestured around the back side of the homes and trudged past piles of leaves and broken branches. Soon they neared the back of a home that was larger than the rest. The voices of small children drifted out from its open windows.

Near a small tree behind the large house, a woman sat bundled in thick wool and soft fleece. Fiery red hair cascaded down her back. She held a book in one hand and a bundled baby in the other. The chilly wind had turned her cheeks pink, but it didn't seem to bother her in the slightest.

At the sight of her, Vesper broke out into a run. The rest of them continued forward at a slower pace.

When Vesper grew nearer, the woman set the book in her lap and looked up with a pretty smile. "Back so soon, my love?"

He tugged her to her feet and wrapped his arms around both her and the baby she held. For a long time, he did nothing but hold her. Even when the baby squirmed, he didn't stop.

When he finally relaxed his hold, she pulled back and searched his eyes. "It wasn't soon for you, was it?" Her gaze turned mischievous. "Faerie did something funny with time again, hmm?"

He chuckled and placed his palm against her cheek. "It has been too long for me, Cosette. Much too long."

By then, the rest of them approached. Cosette pulled her baby close to her chest and looked toward Vesper.

"Ah, yes." He gestured toward them. "These are my friends."

Her eyes narrowed and then she cocked up one eyebrow. "Faeries?"

"Yes, but they will not hurt you." His spine straightened. "Oh, and these two, Chloe and Grace, are mortals like you." He swallowed hard, gesturing now to Elora as well. "And these three are…"

The longer he waited to finish his sentence, the more harried Cosette's expression became.

He offered a wide smile, which was probably meant to ease his own worries more than anything. "These three are my sisters."

Cosette's harried expression fell away as her mouth dropped. "Sisters? You never told me you had sisters."

"It is complicated." He winced and tapped his forehead with one finger. "They are technically related to you as well. Chloe, will you explain in mortal terms?"

With graceful posture and a gentle smile, Chloe stepped forward. "We are your great-great-great-great-granddaughters."

"My what?" Cosette's eyebrows had flown up to her hairline.

Slanting his mouth down, Vesper shrugged. "Faerie did something funny with time."

She let out an exasperated sigh and touched the back of her hand to her forehead.

Vesper stepped closer to her. He placed his hands on her shoulders and looked deep into her eyes. "Their parents died in a fire. Their home was destroyed. They have nothing in the village they left. They should live with family, right? Can they live with us? Not Elora. She is fae now and will stay in Faerie. But can Chloe and Grace?"

Such a question probably should have been met with more exasperation. Instead, Cosette laughed. "You certainly keep me on my toes, don't you, Vesper?"

He responded with a grin.

Laughing again, she turned to Chloe and Grace. "Of course you can live with us. You are family, after all." Her head tilted. "Although, I think we better tell everyone you're Vesper's sisters. No one but my children and I know what Vesper truly is."

Readjusting her baby's blanket, she addressed Vesper and started walking toward the home. "We will need some new rooms."

He threw her a mischievous grin. "I can conjure an entire new wing during the night. When the neighbors ask about the new rooms, we will claim they have always been there. No one will question such a bold lie." Vesper spoke over his shoulder to Chloe and Grace. "Come inside once you are done with your goodbyes. We will introduce you to the rest of the children."

Wrapping an arm around his beloved's shoulders, they entered the home.

Together.

The sight of it warmed Elora's heart.

Her two younger sisters turned to face the others. Chloe stepped toward Lyren and nodded. "*Queen* Lyren." Chloe grinned. "I'm so glad we got to meet you."

Grace's head bounced in a nod, surprising Lyren into a hug.

"Do you still have that bag of Swiftsea salt?" Lyren asked. "You never know when you might need it."

Chloe patted the pocket in her apron. "Yes, and I have the seashell you gave to Elora and all the other Faerie trinkets. I will treasure them always."

She turned to the next fae and wrinkled her nose when she realized it was Quintus.

He reached a hand out to her. "Are you sure you want to live in the mortal realm? I think…" He continued to stare without finishing.

She tapped her toe on the cracked dirt and raised an eyebrow. "I'll never forgive you, Quintus. And I'll *never* return to Faerie. If you have something to say, get it over with."

Maybe he was mulling words over in his mind, but he simply stood there as still as stone. Chloe rolled her eyes and stepped past him. Grace glanced at him through the side of her eye but only offered a small nod.

Chloe had moved in front of Brannick now. She pointed a finger at him with her mouth twisted in a knot. "You better take care of my sister."

After everything he had done during the battle with Alessandra, everyone knew just how fiercely he would protect Elora. Still, he gave a solemn nod. "I will."

Grace threw her arms around his waist in a quick hug. "We know you will," she said brightly.

The two sisters stopped in front of Elora now. She pulled them both into a tight embrace, holding on even when they first tried to pull away. "I love you two so much. I promise I will visit as often as I can."

Their replies got muffled by a mixture of tears and tight hugs.

When they stepped away from her, Elora placed a hand on each of her sisters' shoulders. "It will be better for you two to live in the mortal realm. You will be safer, and you will be with family."

They nodded, but it didn't stop them from jumping in for one last hug. They had discussed this decision at length before they ever came to the mortal realm. They knew this would be best for all of them.

Still, Elora's heart squeezed when she said her final goodbye and stepped into a door to return to Faerie.

Once they returned, Blaz reappeared at Brannick's side. He had used his glamour in the mortal realm, but it lifted now. Lyren and Quintus waved and disappeared down the castle hallways.

Brannick and Elora took a familiar route through the castle. Moss and vines crawled up the stone walls and floor. Black thorns still twisted among them, but they continued to shine. Their glossy surfaces sparkled in the light.

Trailing a hand under a vine of thorns, Elora glanced to her side. "The thorns of our court are not Bitter anymore."

"Indeed." He eyed the thorns carefully while stepping forward. "Our court needs a new name. Something that represents what we learned, how we grew."

She clasped her hands behind her back, letting a small smile tug at her lips. "What about Crystal Thorn?"

Right at the end of the hallway, he stopped. His body turned toward her slowly. Delight sparked in his eyes. "That is perfect."

As he said it, the thorns all along the wall sparkled even brighter with a glossy black shine.

She and Brannick turned the familiar corner, entering the hallway that led to his room. Just outside of his bedroom door, he leaned against the wall and pinned her with a stare full of an entirely different kind of delight.

Blaz bounded back the way they had just come, disappearing around the corner. Elora watched him go before turning back to the prince. "Where is he going?"

"Hunting." He raised an eyebrow, reaching for her waist and pulling her close.

Tucking herself deeper into his arms, she glanced up. "You seem eager to take advantage of his absence."

"Will you marry me, Elora?" He said the words so suddenly. So simply. His hands lowered onto her hips as he stared into her eyes.

She swallowed, heat flashing under her skin.

His gaze never wavered. "Fae customs are simple compared to the fanfare you knew in the mortal realm, but I still want to do it." He leaned in closer. "For you."

Wriggling out of his arms, she looked at the ground. "I do not want you to feel entrapped by me."

He set a finger under her chin and gently tilted it up. "And I want to marry you. We will simply not create bargains that entrap."

That sounded easier said than done.

Standing up straighter, Brannick took a deep breath. "I propose a bargain. You will..." His eyes narrowed as he stared blankly at the wall across from them. But then he nodded while the ghost of a smile played on his lips. "You will kiss me whenever you feel like it." Once the words left his lips, his eyebrows pinched together. "But only if it is an appropriate moment and if you are physically capable," he thought for another beat, "and if you want to do it."

Pride shimmered in his eyes as he gave a quick nod.

She smirked. "*That* is our marriage bargain?"

He donned a serious expression, but it didn't hide the smirk he couldn't quite hold back. "That is only *your* bargain. You still have to create one for me."

She shook her head at him, nearly chuckling too.

All at once, his face grew serious. "Do you accept?"

Her lips quirked upward. "Yes."

His eyes swirled and burst as he reached for her waist again. He leaned closer, clearly about to kiss her. After a quick shake of the head, he stood back. "You must create a bargain for me now."

"I propose a bargain." She took a deep breath. "You will live your life free. As free as you can be."

"I accept." He took her hand, placing a delicate kiss on her knuckles. "Now for the vows. To bind this marriage, I make this vow." When he said the words, a buzz filled the air. The leaves and vines on the wall fluttered like a strong wind blew through them. Sparkles appeared around them in shimmering bursts. "I vow to love and honor you, to remind you of your greatness if you ever forget, and to keep my heart tied to yours."

Warmth filled her chest, her cheeks, her heart. Tears welled in her eyes while she stared back at him. Her beloved. She hadn't been expecting anything at all, but then he'd gone and said the most beautiful words she had ever heard.

"I…" Her voice wavered while she tried to express how full to bursting her heart had become.

Before she could say any more, Brannick dipped his head down toward her. "You must say the words just like I did. To bind this marriage, I make this vow. Then say any vow you like. It can be the same as mine if you wish."

She nodded and swiped away the tears that had dropped from her eyelashes. "To bind this marriage, I make this vow."

Just like when Brannick said the words, buzzing filled the air. Leaves fluttered and sparkles burst. Deep inside her heart, intuition guided her until she knew exactly what to say. "I vow to love and honor you, to help you feel when you forget how, and to keep my heart tied to yours."

He kissed her then. Her feet seemed to float into the air while her cheeks grew even warmer. He ran his fingers through her hair, pulling her close with his other arm. It felt special. More important than any other kiss they had shared.

And it ended far too quickly.

But they were married now. And she had promised to kiss him whenever she felt like it.

That kiss was far from their last.

He brushed his thumb across her cheek, letting it linger along her jaw. "Well, my queen, we have many adventures ahead of us, I think."

"Indeed, we do." She stepped closer to him, resting her head on his shoulder. "And even more importantly, our lives will never be boring again."

THE STORY CONTINUES

Despite her promise to Quintus, Chloe does return to Faerie.
Read her story in *Flame and Crystal Thorns* (Fae and Crystal
Thorns Book 1) by Kay L. Moody.

*She vowed she'd never return to Faerie, but that was before a group of
mortals tried to take over.*

Read on for chapter one of Chloe's story.

ACKNOWLEDGEMENTS

Thank you for reading my book. It means so much to me that you stuck with me through the entire series. When I first decided I wanted to write a series with fae, I truly had no idea how it would go. Of course, I had all the usual doubts that writers struggle with. I wondered if people would like it. I wondered if my interpretation of fae and Faerie would work.

In the end, I loved writing fae. This world and these characters have become as dear to me as old friends. I hope that you enjoyed the journey as much as I did.

If you enjoyed the book, I would be incredibly grateful if you left a review for it on goodreads or on the retailer where you bought it. Your review could help a fellow reader discover this series!

My cover designer, Angel Leya deserves my utmost thanks. This series has found countless people just because they were entranced by the covers for it. Thank you so much for working with me and for making my vision even better than I ever could have imagined. You are the best to work with. I am constantly amazed by your skills as well. Thank you so much for everything.

Justin Greer, thank you so much for editing this book. Your insight has always been valuable, and that didn't change this time. I learned a lot while going through your edits. You truly helped this book become everything it was meant to be. Thank you so much for your editing skill and your willingness to answer my questions.

I can't write a book without taking some time to thank my amazing Queens of the Quill. You ladies are the absolute best! Thank you for being there for me when I needed to brainstorm and for commiserating with me when I needed to vent. I am so grateful to have you in my life. Thank you to Abby J. Reed, Alison Ingleby, Charlie N. Holmberg, Clarissa Gosling, Hanna Sandvig, Joanna Reeder, Kristin J. Dawson, Rose Garcia, Stacey Trombley, Tessonja Odette, and Valia Lind!

My bookstagram team and my ARC team are both so incredible. I can never thank you enough for all the time and help you give me during my release months. You help so much more than you know. Thank you for everything!

The biggest thanks of all goes to my wonderful husband. Meeting you was the best and most important thing that has ever happened to me. I never feel like words are adequate enough to explain how much you mean to me, but you truly are my everything. Thank you for being a constant in my life. This book never would have been created without your support.

ABOUT THE AUTHOR

Kay L Moody is proud to be a young adult fantasy author. Her books feature exciting plots with a few magical elements. They have lots of adventure, compelling characters, and sweet romantic sub-plots.

Kay lives in the western United States with her husband and four sons. She enjoys summertime, learning new things, and doing her nails with fancy nail art.

MORE FROM KAY L. MOODY

Your Next Fantasy Binge Read!

She wasn't supposed to become so powerful.
She wasn't even supposed to survive.

Royalty, intrigue, and magic. This epic fantasy series will have you on the edge of your seat with all its twists and turns.

THE ELEMENTS OF KAMDARIA

CHAPTER ONE

FOR SOMEONE who had once visited Faerie, Chloe found strange comfort in the simplicity of the mortal realm.

The cracking fire at her side warmed her small sitting room. She sat in a plush chair with a leather-bound notebook sitting open in her lap. The feather quill she used to take notes, often left smudges of ink on her fingers, but today they were especially dark.

Across from her, a neighbor woman with graying strands of dark hair sniffled. She dabbed the corners of her eyes every few breaths, but a few tears still escaped the embroidered handkerchief she held.

Chloe tapped her quill against the notebook page as her mouth screwed into a knot. "And did you say your husband developed a fever along with his rash?"

"Yes, but…" The woman sniffed while she tried keep her chin from trembling. After another moment, several sobs wracked from her throat. She squeezed her handkerchief as if it might save her from pain. "It's not a normal fever. I know it is not. Everyone says it's winter sickness and that the rash will soon be gone, but I am certain it is something much worse."

Before the woman could turn her entire lap into a puddle of tears, Chloe reached across and touched her hand. "Mrs. Nash, I agree with you. This does not sound like winter sickness."

The woman's chin trembled again, but at least her tears had slowed.

Sitting deeper in her plush chair, Chloe scanned the notes she had taken. "I will need to do a bit of research, but I am certain I can find a remedy for your husband."

"Truly?" Mrs. Nash sat forward in her seat with eyes as wide as clocks.

Chloe snapped her notebook closed before standing up. "There is a reason I have a reputation as the best apothecary in the city. I am certain I can help."

An expectant look lit inside the woman's eyes.

Chloe met it with a smile. "Return to your home. I will do a bit of research and fix up something for him. I'll be by later tonight."

More tears spilled from Mrs. Nash's eyes as she got to her feet. She walked toward the door and spoke between whimpers. "I am terribly sorry about your parents' deaths, but we are ever so grateful that you and your sister moved here to live with your brother afterward." She sniffed again. "I don't know what would happen to my husband without you."

The words put a lightness in Chloe's step. She even stood a little taller. Of course, losing her parents to a fire set by a vindictive fae queen had not been a great moment in Chloe's life, but she did appreciate how she'd been able to find a good life despite it.

It had been nearly three years since her parents had died. Well, the timing was complicated after her travels in Faerie, but Chloe had almost aged three years since their deaths.

She and her younger sister Grace had moved in with their brother, who was actually a fae hiding in the mortal realm. His wife and their older children knew the truth about his nature, but no one else did. By mortal standards, he wasn't even her brother. But they *were* related. It made things much easier to just refer to him by fae relational terms instead of mortal ones.

Wooden floorboards creaked under foot as she made her way to her work room. Her brother had been kind enough to add an entire wing onto his house for Chloe and her sister. Doing such a thing was much easier since her brother could conjure gold and jewels with his fae magic.

When she opened the door to her workroom, a wave of smells collided against her. Dried lavender and rosemary hung from the ceiling with thin strings. A worktable at one end of the room was littered with notebooks, papers, books, and empty pots of ink. On the other worktable, herbs and crystals sat next to a stone mortar and pestle.

Ignoring both tables, she knelt down and unlatched the trunk in one corner of the room.

She never set out to be the city's greatest apothecary, but it did help her accomplish many of the things she wanted out of life. With such a skill, she was finally seen as more than just a beautiful young woman. Her *knowledge* was finally valued by others. As an added bonus, she got to meet all the handsome men whenever they got injured. In a city surrounded by farms, minor injuries were frequent.

No matter how many times she opened the trunk, she still held her breath while lifting the lid. The air ignited with an unseen energy. Tingles spread over her skin as she reached into its depths. The tingles only multiplied when she touched the book sitting at the bottom.

She pulled the suede and leather book cover tight to her chest as she breathed in its mossy scent. Deep breaths moved in and out of her nose, but they never captured the energy the book continued to ignite into the air.

She kept trying anyway. Over and over again, the magic proved to be too difficult to ignore. After several more moments, she finally accepted the inevitable. She would never possess the magic of Faerie.

Sighing, she set the book onto her worktable. After getting comfortably situated, she thumbed through the pages. Mr. Nash's sickness seemed eerily similar to scurpus. It probably had a different name in the mortal realm, but the book from Faerie called it by its fae name.

Fae had power to heal almost any sickness without help, but they did have a host of remedies that helped speed the process up. Luckily, the remedies worked on mortals too.

Her finger tapped on the book once she found the page for scurpus. She set her notebook right next to it and compared the symptoms. As she expected, they were exactly the same. A simple poultice could heal him, as long as his symptoms hadn't progressed too much.

Wiping her hands on the homespun apron protecting her silk dress, Chloe began gathering herbs to crush and cut. A wisp of blonde hair fell into her face while she worked, but she just tucked it back into her messy bun.

Soon, she only had one ingredient left. Her finger trailed down the page of her Faerie book until it found the last ingredient. That's when her heart decided to stop.

Salt from the Faerie court of Swiftsea.

Chloe gulped. Swiftsea salt had magical properties that not even the other Faerie courts possessed. Shaking away her worry, she held the page open and flipped to the very back of the book. She had encountered this problem a few times before. Thanks to a very intelligent mortal who was long since dead, an appendix had been added which gave mortal ingredient substitutions for all the ingredients that were specific to Faerie.

A breath of relief dropped from her lips when she found that Swiftsea salt did indeed have substitute ingredients that existed in the mortal realm. The relief only lasted a moment. She needed juniper, goldenrod, and mullein. Juniper she had a few bundles of, but the other two she did not.

She had used the last of her goldenrod just the week before. The mullein she hadn't bothered to collect and dry during the summer since she had never used it before. Without all three of the herbs, she couldn't make a proper substitution for Swiftsea salt.

Her mouth went dry as she stared at the page. A part of her hoped staring would change the words in front of her. The book *was* magic, wasn't it? It came from a magical realm at least.

Her hope was fruitless. The words never changed. If she wanted to save Mr. Nash, she knew what she would have to do. Biting her lip, she reached under her apron and opened the small bag she always hid there.

It contained a seashell that would make any liquid taste like honey, but even more important, the shell could cleanse the liquid of any impurities or even poison. A light purple ribbon cut from a skirt that once belonged to her mother also sat inside her bag. There were a few other trinkets including a loose harp string that she probably should have gotten rid of long ago. And of course, there sat a small bag of Swiftsea salt.

Most of the Faerie items had come from Chloe's older sister, Elora. A lump formed in her throat as she stared at the bag. Her sister lived in Faerie now. Though she occasionally came to the mortal realm to visit her younger sisters, Chloe still missed her terribly.

Seeing the items did the same thing it always did. It made her miss *Faerie* too. She let out a wistful sigh as she plopped onto the nearest chair. Chloe hadn't spent long in Faerie, but her time had been filled with adventure. Even years later, she still pined for it sometimes.

But Faerie was dangerous. It had all sorts of rules and consequences, many of which could be deadly for a mortal. She had never been the type who loved adventure anyway. Reading epic poems provided as much adventure as she ever wanted to experience.

Still, the land had been enchanting. Beautiful. It had a whole host of magical books just begging to be read.

Her eyes slammed shut as she folded her arms over her chest. Not this again. She had already decided. She would never return to Faerie. She was mortal. She belonged in the mortal realm.

Letting out a long breath, she admitted to herself something she had only confessed to her younger sister. More than having her knowledge valued or being seen as important, more than anything in the world, Chloe just wanted to fall in love. But she wanted to fall in love with someone she could share a life with. Someone she could grow old with.

Fae were immortal.

If she stayed in Faerie and fell in love with a fae, there would be no growing old together. She knew this more intimately than anyone. Her brother was an immortal fae, but his wife was a mortal. They had been together for years without trouble, but now his wife was starting to age... and he was not.

Trouble brewed whether they wanted to admit it or not. Pretty soon, her fae brother would be forced to leave the mortal realm or else everyone would learn his secret. His wife would be forced to grow old alone.

Gritting her teeth together, Chloe grabbed the bag of Swiftsea salt. She could use it for Mr. Nash's poultice. Yes, it had properties that would keep fae from enchanting her food, but what did that matter when she never intended to return to Faerie?

Despite her surety, it still hurt to see the last sprinkles of the Swiftsea salt drop into the mixture of herbs. One of her last reminders of Faerie was gone forever.

The wisp of hair fell into her face again, but she was too busy wiping away a tear to bother with it. She forced the tears to stop. If they fell into the herbs, they could change the poultice completely, which would ruin the recipe.

Taking a deep breath, she moved past her moment of weakness. Now, she focused only on the remedy. It didn't take long to finish after that.

With the poultice secured in cloth binding inside a small basket, Chloe grabbed her fur-lined cloak and pulled it over her shoulders. Getting to the Nash's house wouldn't take long.

She barely noticed the ice crunching under her boots. The moon shone bright in the sky, lighting the path ahead of her. When she arrived at the house next to the large ash tree, she gave several determined knocks on the front door.

Mrs. Nash answered it, her face even more swollen with tears than before. The woman ushered Chloe into a dark room lit only by the fire in the fireplace. "Here he is." She whispered the words, as if speaking out loud would upset her ill husband.

The man's eyes snapped open. They darted around the room while fear seized his features. But once his gaze met his wife's, the fear vanished in a sigh of relief. "Mirielle."

He lifted his hand ever so slightly from the bed he was on, but his weakness must have stopped him from lifting it any more. It felt back to the blankets at once.

Mrs. Nash rushed to his bedside and took his hand in both of hers. She squeezed it and then brushed the hair off his forehead. Her whisper came out even gentler than before. "Don't you worry. Chloe is here to make you feel better."

She continued to speak soothing words to her husband while Chloe opened the poultice and spread the herbs over his chest. The woman's actions brought a smile to Chloe's lips.

Maybe growing old with someone wouldn't always be perfect, but Chloe knew it would be worth it.

Once finished, she offered a short nod to the Nashes and promised to return the next evening to check on Mr. Nash's progress. By the time Chloe returned to the wintery air outside, her heart was full.

It lasted three full steps before a tall figure just ahead forced her to jerk to a stop. She gulped as she glanced up, but then her entire body went rigid. She gasped.

The man before her stood taller than the average mortal, but that wasn't too out of place. His pointed fae ears, on the other hand, would make anyone stare. Not to mention, his gloriously perfect features made him look impossibly attractive, especially for a mortal.

"Quintus." She spoke his name like a warning. If he weren't so beautiful, she would have glared. He never should have entered the mortal realm without putting on a glamour that made him appear more like an imperfect mortal.

His eyes locked onto hers with a fervor she hadn't known since leaving Faerie. His expression commanded the utmost attention. Surely, his voice would too.

"You have to return to Faerie."

Visit kaylmoody.com to join Kay L. Moody's email list and get news on the release of Flame and Crystal Thorns.